DUNNES *of* BRITTAS

An Irish Family's Saga of Endurance

Kevin Lee Akers

Bassett Street Press

Designed by www.kevinakers.com
Cover and map illustrations by Kevin Akers
Gaby Michaelis, editor

The Dunnes of Brittas is a work of fiction. All incidents and dialogue, and all the characters with the exception of some well-known historical figures, are products of the author's imagination and are not to be construed as real. Where historical figures appear, the situations, incidents, and dialogues attributed to those persons are entirely fictional and are not intended to depict actual events or to change the fictional nature of this story.

In all other respects, any resemblance to actual persons, living or dead, events, or locales is entirely coincidental.

Printed in the United States of America
First Printing, 2021
ISBN 978-1-7923-5261-4

Bassett Street Publishing
Petaluma, CA 94952

www.dunnesofbrittas.com

For Judee & Gracie:

*Of all the family members I've had in the past
and those I will have in the future,
it is with joyful gratitude that I get to
share my timeline with you.*

GENERAL EDWARD DUNNE

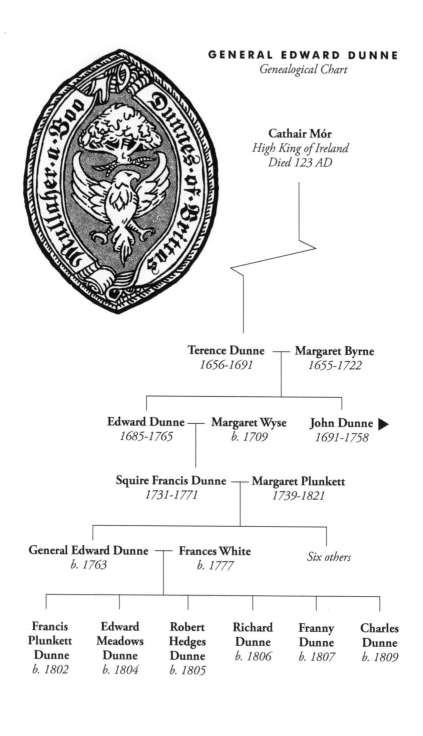

GENERAL EDWARD DUNNE
Genealogical Chart

Cathair Mór
High King of Ireland
Died 123 AD

Terence Dunne —— **Margaret Byrne**
1656-1691　　　*1655-1722*

Edward Dunne —— **Margaret Wyse**　　**John Dunne** ▶
1685-1765　　　*b. 1709*　　　*1691-1758*

Squire Francis Dunne —— **Margaret Plunkett**
1731-1771　　　*1739-1821*

General Edward Dunne —— **Frances White**　　*Six others*
b. 1763　　　*b. 1777*

Francis Plunkett Dunne	Edward Meadows Dunne	Robert Hedges Dunne	Richard Dunne	Franny Dunne	Charles Dunne
b. 1802	*b. 1804*	*b. 1805*	*b. 1806*	*b. 1807*	*b. 1809*

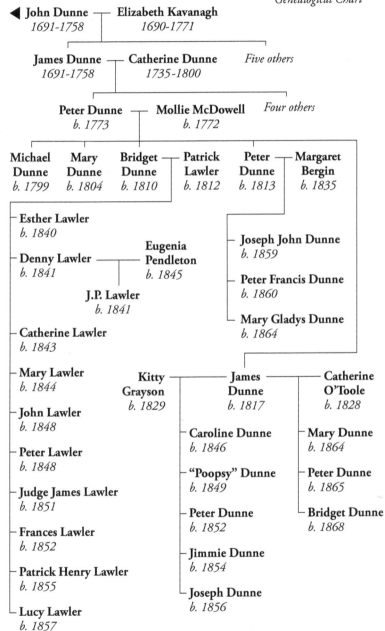

◀ John Dunne — Elizabeth Kavanagh
  1691-1758   *1690-1771*

James Dunne — Catherine Dunne   *Five others*
1691-1758   *1735-1800*

Peter Dunne — Mollie McDowell   *Four others*
b. 1773   *b. 1772*

Michael | Mary | Bridget — Patrick | Peter — Margaret
Dunne | Dunne | Dunne | Lawler | Dunne | Bergin
b. 1799 | *b. 1804* | *b. 1810* | *b. 1812* | *b. 1813* | *b. 1835*

─ Esther Lawler
  b. 1840

                    Eugenia
─ Denny Lawler ── Pendleton   ─ Joseph John Dunne
  b. 1841   *b. 1845*   *b. 1859*

         J.P. Lawler   ─ Peter Francis Dunne
           b. 1841   *b. 1860*

─ Catherine Lawler   ─ Mary Gladys Dunne
  b. 1843   *b. 1864*

─ Mary Lawler   Kitty — James — Catherine
  b. 1844   Grayson Dunne   O'Toole
                    b. 1829 *b. 1817* *b. 1828*
─ John Lawler
  b. 1848   ─ Caroline Dunne   ─ Mary Dunne
                      b. 1846   *b. 1864*
─ Peter Lawler
  b. 1848   ─ "Poopsy" Dunne   ─ Peter Dunne
                      b. 1849   *b. 1865*
─ Judge James Lawler
  b. 1851   ─ Peter Dunne   ─ Bridget Dunne
                      b. 1852   *b. 1868*
─ Frances Lawler
  b. 1852   ─ Jimmie Dunne
                      b. 1854
─ Patrick Henry Lawler
  b. 1855   ─ Joseph Dunne
                      b. 1856
─ Lucy Lawler
  b. 1857

PART I

CHAPTER 1

Fragment of letter from Lucy Rogers to Henrietta Welch

September 1, 1930

My Dearest Niece,

It was such a delight to see you all at the ranch party last weekend. So many new babies to meet and cuddle. I am glad it wasn't too hot.

After I returned home I was feeling very wistful and nostalgic. All the grandchildren were so lively—carefree and happy. I sat down at their table for supper. Of course I'm so old and craggy now they didn't even notice me, I just faded into the barnwood.

But I WAS there.

I marveled at how young and beautiful they were and how proud my parents would be if they could look down on them from heaven. I accidentally found myself eavesdropping on all their little conversations—and it wasn't so easy with these ancient ears I can tell you! I overheard your Sarafrances say she was praying for "a MIRACLE" that she'd get all her college classes.

It struck a chord with me.

I had to stop myself from telling her that the miracle she seeks now fails in comparison to the bushels of miracles that HAVE ALREADY HAPPENED to this family!

Of course you can't put an old head on young shoulders. Nevertheless, I have been stewing over this in my mind and I had an idea. When we were all out by the barbecue talking about the olden days, Sarafrances showed much interest in our family's history. My memory is long and I remember many of the things my parents told me. I think it's high time I jot down what I know before I start losing my marbles.

My hope is that just maybe Sarafrances will appreciate how many careful plans, impulsive decisions and MIRACLES of the past it took for her to have the kind of life she now enjoys.

Whenever I think about our ancestors I always start with my mother. She was very proud of her noble roots and would conveniently bring it up when she was doing some particularly disgusting chore around the ranch. Her home was in Queen's County, Ireland. All the fine houses back then had names and hers was called Brittas, the home of the Dunne family since time immemorial. She was raised in wealth and splendor with other members of her extended family living in and about the estate. She often spoke of all the servants and the high style in which they lived. I remember sitting with her at the kitchen table peeling potatoes and she would tell me over and over how much she cherished her childhood....

Spring always seemed to rescue Ireland just in the nick of time. In 1821, the bluebells that covered Brittas Woods were the first to herald the season followed closely by a rambunctious set of children who lived in the nearby manor house. For generations the forest had been their magical playground and now young Bridget Dunne was in charge of her own building brigade. She had dreamt of her little village for days and was now supervising its construction on the forest floor. Tiny faerie forts were fabricated out of oak leaves and twigs which had to conform to the strict building standards of her mythical society. Her older cousin Fanny was a willing apprentice but her younger brother Peter was proving to be a complete insubordinate with conflicting ideas accented by a superior attitude. Bridget was becoming exasperated as he scrutinized her every decision from behind the analytical gaze of his dark blue eyes.

"Bridget, if you have the mossy meeting hall in the middle of the village green all the faeries will be much closer and it will be easier for them to attend events," he said standing over her with arms crossed.

"Peter, don't be silly. They can fly. The mossy meeting hall should be hidden so evil forces will not find it!" pronounced Bridget. Round of face and fair of skin, her cherubic looks made her orders that much harder to take seriously.

The other children were exploring around the small lake that lay deeper into the demesne beside the bog. Bridget's oldest brother Michael was teaching the art of skipping stones to the youngest in the family James, the last serving in the pot. After some brotherly advice, James hurled a marbled gray stone out onto the lake. "Woah! Wee man with the big arm!" Michael hollered out. James lifted up his chin and puffed-out his chest. They skipped off the rest of their rocks and went out to search for more ammunition.

James was tearing away at a grassy patch trying to retrieve a thin piece of slate when he saw a shimmer under the dirt. He used a chunk of bark to dig out the crusty object. He scrapped around all sides as it began to take form. Suddenly the boy's imagination was on fire. "What the devil is this thing?" he said out loud. He brushed off the sludge with his pudgy thumb. The grime was wearing off to reveal red and green and silver. This was something special and he knew just what to do with it.

Bridget and Peter were in negotiations to determine what insects would make the best pet for the wee townsfolk. "Only bugs that can fly will make fitting companions," said Peter.

"Well, that is all fine and good but they must be beautiful, not hideous. They mustn't be dragonflies 'cause they look like they could be related." Just then a red ladybird landed onto the tip of Bridget's finger. She whispered, "This is the perfect companion." As she examined her new friend she drifted off into the many chambers of her mind, as she was apt to do. She wondered, where had those little wings taken the ladybird on this fine day? Where will it land next? And most importantly, where are my own little wings going to take me someday? Knowing the answer to this last question was far too maddening to ponder at the moment.

Crunching his way through the leaves, James ran to his sister who was putting acorn pillars in front of the mossy meeting hall. "Bridget, Bridget, look what I found." In his hand was a large silvery ring with a twisted, woven pattern dancing around the circumference. Four raised bevels encased one red and two glistening green gems.

She pointed to the empty bevel, "Oh, one of them is missing." James loved his sister with his whole heart and longed to please her.

"It's probably back in the bog. What is it?" asked James.

"I'm not sure but it is very auld I think."

"You can have it."

She kissed his dirty cheek, slipped the gift into the pocket of her tweedy jacket and went back to her project.

After working steadily since Friday last, the little community beneath the trees laid spread out onto the dabbled colours of dried leaves. It was looking just as Bridget had envisioned. Cheerful nasturtium blossoms were distributed equally to the houses which were connected to each other by neat pathways of dry straw Fanny had brought over from the barn.

Peter continued to point out that the paths were quite unnecessary since, as his sister had rudely observed, the faeries flew everywhere they went.

Michael and his cousin Richard had left the lake searching for James when they came upon the little settlement like marauding Vikings. "What do we have here? Isn't that just delightful," Michael said as he made a sweeping gesture with his fingers dragging through the air.

Sensing trouble Fanny called out, "Why don't you boys shove off!"

Michael went on, "Is this the little faerie land you have been droning on and on about Biddy?

Bridget didn't answer. Richard made mention of the various sexual practices of the faeries and had probing questions like where are they going to drop their turds? James instinctively scooted towards his sister's side, ready to defend her against these foreign invaders. He blinked nervously as if to summon his inner strength. Peter flanked her other side and began to logically argue the salient reasons for the gang to return to the lake and enjoy the warm day with a swim or perhaps a footrace to Drady's cabin. Bridget's daily battles with these people made her immune to their insults. She was prepared to lower her eyelids to half-mast, act bored and wait for them to have their quota of giggles so she could put the finishing touches on the town's bent wood entry gate.

Michael persisted, "Where are all the fairies Bridget? Maybe they think your town is just too ugly to visit?"

"No need to repeat yourself Michael, I ignored you just fine the first time."

Behind a majestic oak came a soft clicking sound. Richard ignited a small firebomb he placed in the back courtyard of the Queen Faerie's twiggy palace. As the royal residence erupted in flames the arsonist was pleased to see the children were oblivious to the fate of his high-handed cousin's playground. The dry straw pathways acted like a gunpowder trail as it set fire to the next building and the next, working its way through the dead leaves that lay beneath the town. Bridget's stoic veneer was beginning to crack as Michael was elaborating on some convoluted detail about the pixie prostitutes when she smelled smoke. She whipped around to see her miniature village being consumed by flames.

The older boys quickly wrestled the building brigade into headlocks and arm holds to prevent any rescue of the faerie forts. Fanny hid behind a spruce tree. James put up a fight kicking and biting but was driven downward on top of Peter with overwhelming force. They picked up their heads to witness the entire village slipping away and the fire getting disturbingly large. "Oh, look Biddy, your little faeries have a bonfire," Richard said as the surface of his face reflected the glow of the fire. James and Peter began crying under Michael's weight. "Pity you idjits didn't make all your huts out of stone," the older brother joked.

Fire was building to such an extent that smoke drifted out through the canopy of trees. Richard felt the heat and loosened his grip on Bridget. She put her pretty little hand over her mouth and started to cry, tears rolled over her dirty fingernails.

James looked up at her and said, "I'm sorry Bridget, your little city is ruined," just as a giant splash of water came through the air, right in the middle of the village green, followed by a second and third splash. From his vantage point at the bottom of the dirt, through thick haze, James saw the gleaming black jackboots of his saviour. The forced perspective only served to exaggerate the towering figure that stood before him. His white pants transitioned to the brilliant scarlet coat of a British Army officer. Medals of all shapes and sizes were clinking around his barrel chest. In his hand was an empty wooden bucket. His epaulets were still quivering from the run while his ruddy complexion, fuming with anger, made his bright eyes even greener than usual.

The General was not pleased.

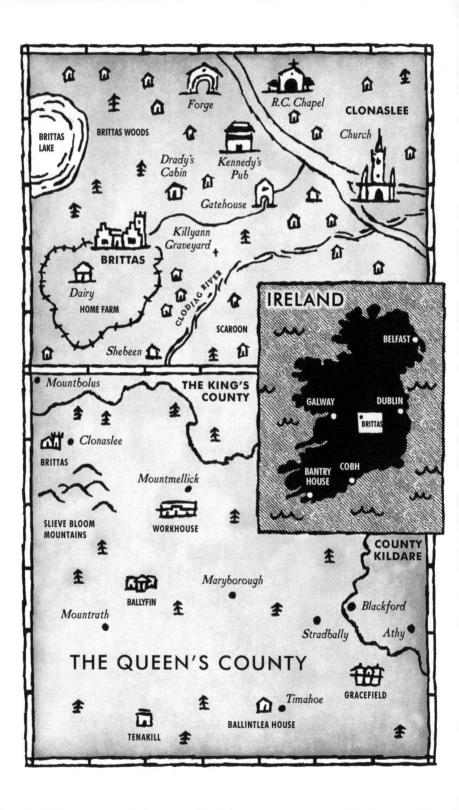

CHAPTER 2

Fragment of letter from Lucy Rogers to Henrietta Welch

[September 1, 1930]

General Edward Dunne was a General in the British Army, one-time aide-de-camp to the Viceroy of Ireland, Lord of the Manor Court, Deputy Governor, Magistrate and High Sheriff of Queen's County, Irish Member of Parliament for Maryborough, hereditary Chieftain over the Dunne Clan and direct descendant of second century Monarch of Éire. His seat was Brittas in the Queen's County.

I found all of this information at the library under "Dunne" in Burke's Peerage if you care to look it up for yourself.

As the smoke was clearing the children tried to explain themselves to the General.

"We were just helping Bridget build her little town and they came up and burned the place down," cried Peter.

"I didn't light the fire, it was him!" pleaded Michael as he pointed out his cousin to the enemy.

Seething, General Dunne quickly surveyed the situation. He fired off an empty bucket, hitting his son Richard directly in the forehead knocking him backward into the ruins of the Faerie Queen's Palace. "Take these buckets and make sure the fire is completely out. Then, you two, meet me in the library where you will account for your actions. Girls, are you all right?"

"We are not hurt sir," Bridget and Fanny answered with deliberately brittle voices.

Richard grabbed the wooden bucket from the ground as the General's assistant, Major Rowland, crammed his bucket into Michael's midsection so hard that the boy nearly lost his footing. Michael squinted out a look of teenage contempt from his angry eyes and wondered, Who was this big, fat oaf and what gave him the right to discipline me?

Most of the group made their way out of the woods and headed up towards the house. When Michael and Richard reached the horse trough, they dipped their buckets deep into the water and turned back toward the trees to douse out any remaining embers. Sitting alone on a rock, a devastated Bridget watched and mourned the loss of her miniature fantasyland. Although her village existed only for a moment in time it was a dream come true. The loss would stay with her always, never again believing anything could last.

Peter felt somewhat ennobled that the General called upon him, above all the other children, to report on the calamitous events of the day. Not wishing to squander a minute's worth of goodwill he asked for a favour, "General, may James and I go up to the top of the tower?"

He approved with a nod and headed back to his library with the Major groveling behind.

The younger boys outran the General to the three-storey tower that also served as the main entrance for Brittas House, a rambling Gothic pile of a mansion that became the Dunne family seat after their previous residence, Tinnahinch Castle, was blown to bits by Cromwell's army. A hodgepodge of wings connected to the tower on both sides. To the east of the tower was the handsome main house with its crow-stepped gables and punched sandstone dressings impressing onlookers with the desired effect of a forbidding fortress. To the west was the original hunting lodge of Brittas, a half-timber structure with an ancient swayback thatched roof. Its rustic construction contrasted awkwardly with the formal stone mansion it adjoined like an old ragged peasant hugging a duke.

The lodge housed the senior Peter Dunne, (known as Mr. Dunne throughout the Brittas Estates and beyond) his wife and their brood of five children. Mr. Dunne acted as estate agent for his second cousin, General Edward Dunne. When not on active service for his freshly minted king, George IV, the General lived in the main house with his wife, five sons and daughter Fanny.

An excited Peter opened the heavily studded oak door that lead to the top of the tower. James twirled up the three storeys of worn-down stair treads and uneven risers, easily beating his brother to the top door. The latch was set too high for James to reach. Peter sauntered behind, pushed his brother aside and clicked the rusted peg over as the weather-beaten door popped open to flood the interior of the keep with light. The illuminated cobwebs framed a bird carcass decaying on the windowsill of the musket loop. Peter strutted out onto the top of the tower as if he were an actor on Globe Theatre's stage then reminded James, "See, the first shall be last and the last shall be first."

How the boys loved this spot. James loved it because he could pretend to be a bold Black Knight defending his castle while avoiding farm chores at the same time. Peter's appreciation for the tower and what it symbolized went far beyond a normal child's understanding. He felt a profound reverence for the history and legacy of his proud Dunne family. Nowhere on earth could he breathe in the sheer power of privilege better than atop Brittas Tower looking out onto the rich fields of the Irish Midlands.

Peter peered through the ramparts as James hopped up and down to get a better look. The old Union Jack waved proudly from the rounded little turret at the corner of the tower. Peter delicately moved an empty cage used for homing pigeons closer to the wall and told James to get on top, handing him the General's spyglass he nabbed from the not-so-secret compartment notched in the stone.

Brittas clung to gentle slopes of the Slieve Bloom Mountains that separated King's from Queen's County, 70 miles to the southwest of Dublin. The plateau where the manor sat rose just above the handsome Georgian town of Clonaslee, the communal heart of General Dunne's 9,500-acre fiefdom. "Do you see it; do you see it?" asked Peter.

"No, it's all smudgy," said James

"Here give it, you have to focus the glass by twisting this piece… there, how about now?"

"I see it!"

Andy Brennan, the town's blacksmith, was one of a handful of villagers who did not rent from the General. He owned his little plot of land and his building. The entryway to his forge was shaped like a gigantic silver horseshoe and was James' favourite landmark to locate from the tower. However, the General saw Brennan's horseshoe as a subtle kick in the shins to the uniformity (and loyalty) of Clonaslee. The children's admiration only added to the General's disgust.

Next, the spyglass revealed Jim Kennedy's pub that lay equidistant from the two places of worship presiding at either end of Main Street. It was the one sanctuary where the Papist and the Protestant could come together in communion—over a whiskey.

James moved that old spyglass from side to side and saw a fine coach with a quad of matching dappled grays trotting by the Protestant church. "Give heed Sir Peter, a carriage approaches", said James in a medieval accent.

"Make way Sir Greenpus," Peter said with his slightly more convincing accent. He grabbed the glass and pushed James off the birdcage.

"Where?"

"By the Prod church."

"Now I say, that is clearly not one of the hoi polloi from around here, no sir," he said with his fake accent trailing off.

The horses' white manes were perfectly plaited and their heads were topped with bright green feathers. Two coachmen in top hats were riding in front with a uniformed footman at the rear watching over several trunks belted to the roof. The jet-black coach was stripped with green as were the cream coloured wheels. A conspicuous display, townspeople gawked as the retinue went down the cobblestoned street.

Peter's attention switched over to a girl he recognized rolling a hoop with a stick past Kennedy's pub and disappearing down an alley. He then turned his sights to the back of the house and noticed Bridget walking straight from the woods into the lodge followed by two very downcast young men heading toward the tower to meet their fate in the General's library. "Off to the gallows with ye," he said, resuming his Olde English.

Everyone was to gather for Sunday dinner, which was the only night of the week the two Dunne families of Brittas ate together. Earlier, Peter had noticed through the leaded windows the long dining room table had been set, signaling a much larger gathering than usual.

Jangling noises from the drive announced the evening's first visitor, filling the boys with giddy excitement. The fancy coach with the plumed horses pulled up directly below the tower and the coachmen set out a footstool covered in chartreuse needlepoint. All the boys could see from above was a gigantic white bonnet resembling a goose's hindquarters emerging from the carriage. The bonnet stepped out onto the gravel and drifted toward the entry doors of the house. Peter cried out "Hello down there!" The bonnet turned upwards and revealed a familiar face.

"Well, hello there dear boy!"

Mrs. Kavanaugh could make a visit to the dressmaker's shop seem like a Grand Tour of the continent and a Grand Tour of the continent like walking into a dressmaker's shop. Born Alicia Grace, she was heir to ancestral Irish fortunes from three different bloodlines. She was intimately related to both Dunne families as well as their wives'. She had made the 30-mile coach journey to Brittas from the picturesque estate of Gracefield, where the celebrated English architect John Nash had just conjured up a new lodge for her in the Cottage Orné style. Mrs. Kavanaugh knew Nash's next assignment was to spruce-up Buckingham House but she would keep that titbit, as it were, under her bonnet.

James and Peter bounded down from the tower and fell into the embrace of their favourite relative, her recently applied musk offsetting onto their clothes. She would always pretend not to recognize them claiming, "these imposters have replaced the little cousins I used to know."

Peter played along and tried to convince her they were indeed genuine only taller. As they joked with her their eyes averted up to the stack of trunks on the carriage roof, wondering what exotic gifts she had brought from her travels. The staff of Brittas had made ready the most hospitable guestroom in the manor and appeared in the doorway. Mrs. Kavanaugh couldn't help but compare her well-attired, handsome coachmen with the General's frowsy porters, although she did note while her men were adjusting their waistcoats and smoothing their hair, all of her belongings had been silently swept away. The young Dunne boys escorted the fine lady into the house but just before entering she turned to her servant, still on the coach, and softly said "Pretty is as pretty does."

The receiving hall housed an awkward menagerie of small tables littered with newspapers, novels, gloves, sporting mallets and the General's cocked hat. A rickety cabinet displayed a collection of Oriental china and Mrs. Kavanaugh spotted a small chair with a broken leg sitting in a lonely corner. By design or by default, the confusion of the entry made the grand staircase a majestic sight for the discerning dowager. It had all the baronial splendour of the Middle Ages. Finely carved balustrades elegantly marched up the steps. Family portraits painted by second-rate traveling artists mixed with finer works of Irish landscape and Biblical drivel all haphazardly mounted on large panels of burled walnut. The boys took Mrs. Kavanaugh by the hand to her bedchamber all the while she smiled and imagined how she would redecorate the old place.

Back down through the receiving hall the boys ran the length of a narrow corridor leading to the old hunting lodge section of Brittas where their eldest sister Mary waited in the wings. "Mother wants you two for the rosary," her radiant face of sixteen wearing the pinched expression of an aged spinster. Wobbly oak plank floors, wavy crown glass windowpanes and whitewashed half-timbered walls not only quartered Mr. Dunne's family but also most of the household staff. A butler, a scullery maid, a cook, and twelve others had the upstairs rooms. In truth, the General's family referred to it as the Servant's Wing and although the two families were intertwined in daily life there was much that segregated them from each other.

Mr. Dunne's family always said the rosary together at their dinner table except on Sundays when they would dine in front of the General's family who derided Catholicism. Mary, James and Peter patiently waited for the rest of the family with their rosaries by the fireplace in the comfortable yet spartan front room.

In the kitchen, Bridget was discussing events in the woods with her mother. She brushed her daughter's long, wavy red hair and said with frustration, "Oh child, you have pine needles poking out all over." Mrs. Dunne, formerly Mollie McDowell, descended from Colonel Luke McDowell of Mantua House in County Roscommon. She had an impeccable Irish pedigree and would often wonder how it came to be that she was living in servant's quarters.

After plucking out the last of the needles, Mollie took a mouldy chunk of bacon from the damp kitchen cupboard and rubbed it on Bridget's scrapes.

"There you are, that should heal you right up." She spoke in the soft whispering tones of an Irish gentlewoman, a voice never raised in anger but strictly obeyed.

She turned Bridget around by the shoulders and said, "Ahm, let me have a look at you. Ah, that's more like the little pink rose I know."

"Thank you, mother."

"Go change into your dress and we will pray that God gives us strength to get through dinner."

"Oh mother, I nearly forgot, James found this in the woods today." She took out the strange object from her pocket and handed it to Mollie. "Do you have any earthly idea what this is?"

"Why, I think it's an auld brooch of some kind."

"Like a cameo? How does it pin on?"

"No dear, this is a man's brooch. It would have had a straight pick that went through here and you held your cloak on with it, up here by your shoulder. It's quite extraordinary. If I didn't know better, I would say it's from the times of the auld Celts or even Vikings! Did any of the General's lot see it?" she asked making sure to look her daughter dead in the eye.

"No mother, James gave it directly to me and I put it right in my pocket."

"Would you like to keep it then?"

"That I would, please."

"Very well, but don't mention a word to anyone. Hide it away in your little treasure box."

"Why would I not tell anyone?"

"Because the General owns everyone and everything on these lands and by rights we should turn it over to him. We are little more than squatters here, don't you know."

"Oh, I see."

"Should we hand it over to the General right now, ahm, or keep it and ask for forgiveness when we pray the rosary?"

"Let's keep it."

"Let us pray."

In the main dining room, Frances, the General's wife was conferring with Sneed the butler on seating arrangements. She knew how important the evening was to her husband.

The room was light and bright with delicate plasterwork and an exemplary dining set crafted by Thomas Chippendale's London shop specifically for Brittas. A Waterford crystal chandelier hung from a high ceiling and on the east wall was a fan-shaped display of legendary swords and rapiers so dear to the family.

Sneed was moving place cards around the table as the lady of the house played-out various scenarios between dinner guests in her mind. She kept shuffling her mother-in-law further and further down the table teetering between her own safety and a snub. Other relatives needed to be separated as well.

These ill-behaved descendants of Gaelic chiefs gave Her Ladyship indigestion well before the first course was even served. She was the only true Ascendancy aristocrat of pure English stock in the family and often felt like a foreign body in their midst. Slight and subtle undertones of contempt hid just below the surface of their Irish warmth and charm. She believed, deep down, even her own husband was taunting her when he called her France rather than Frances. Her brother Richard White was made the Earl of Bantry after he mustered an inadequate army of British soldiers and local gentry to fight off an incompetent Irish revolutionary aboard a French ship that never landed due to bad weather. His adversary, Wolfe Tone, was eventually captured in his French admiral's uniform and became an Irish folk hero while Richard White settled for the coronet, an ermine robe and a seat in the House of Lords.

"France, how is everything shaping up?" the General said as he left the library with a trail of castigated faerie killers sneaking off into hiding.

"I am not sure where to put your mother. We have nine women and eleven men. Should I put her next to you?"

"No, put her next to my brother." He looked askance over the seating plan as he would review a prospective battlefield. "I say, who is this Captain Lichtenberg?"

"Mrs. Kavanaugh's companion."

"That fellow on the back of her coach? I thought he was her manservant."

"She told Sneed to seat him with us.

"Captain? Of what army?"

"Prussian, I think."

"Is he still in service?"

"I don't believe so."

"Have Sneed rewrite this then to say 'Mr. Lichtenberg,' he can't keep that lowly rank if he's not in service…of all things….copper captain."

"Oh Edward, let it be, there will be enough excitement without getting Mrs. K. all upset."

"He can be a captain if he wishes to sit downstairs with the servants but if he is to be at my table, he shall be a mister," said the General with such resolve that Her Ladyship surrendered the card over to Sneed for reworking. The Dunnes of Brittas were not just friends of the army; they were of the army and it of them.

Before dinner all the guests were milling about in the corridor waiting for the General and his wife to come take their seats at the table. The host graciously greeted everyone and was genuinely touched to have so much of his family surround him on this special Sunday. A lifetime of achievement was going to be acknowledged by the highest echelons of power. He had gathered his clan together for a glorious announcement and was still calculating the timing.

His heir and oldest child Francis Plunkett Dunne whispered in his ear "Father, am I to sit with the children? I think I should sit in here with the adults." He was home from his first year at Trinity College in Dublin and feeling quite important.

"Off you go Frank, it will be a jollier time in there than in here I can tell you that...."

Everyone was moving about to find their seats when Mrs. Kavanaugh brought up Captain Lichtenberg to meet the host, dressed in the dazzling dark blue uniform of a Prussian officer. Mrs. K. made the introduction in the same coquettish way she always addressed the General.

"How do you do Captain?" said the General. "I recognize that medal there, you were after Napoleon then. So, am I to believe you are still in service?"

"I do like the Prussian uniform and believe it is the grandest I have yet to see," said Mrs. Kavanaugh as she pulled Lichtenberg away before he could answer. Her fortune and class were like wings that allowed her to fly above the General's judgement.

In the adjoining drawing room all the Dunne offspring were amassed together at a makeshift table. The General's children on one side, (Frank, Eddie, Robert, Richard, Charles and Fanny) and Mr. Dunne's lot on the other (Mary, Michael, Bridget, Peter and James). Things were still tense from the faerie fort incident.

Seeing Fanny slouching, Bridget thought a slight reprimand was in order. "Cousin dear, we mustn't let our backs touch the chair. Straighten up."

"Oh, you're quite right. Thank you." Fanny righted herself and feeling a little more ladylike asked Bridget, " Do you like my dress? Father just brought it back from London."

"Oh, it is very becoming," said Bridget as she noticed it was already starting to bind at her middle. She had always thought dear Fanny must have been locked in the pantry when the looks were handed out and tried to help her when she could. She was indeed a kind cousin who gifted Bridget practically all her outgrown clothes. Rumour had it that chocolate cake was to be dessert tonight so she must remember to offer her piece to Fanny. Afterall, she figured, there is only so much one can do.

Sneed came into the drawing room and kindly requested the children join the adults for an announcement from the Lord of the Manor. Everyone was beyond curious as they crowded into the room.

General Dunne pronounced with much solemnity of manner a short grace and then performed the rituals of the table. Standing up from his spot at the head he addressed the room.

"I'm jolly pleased you all made the journey out to Brittas today. Not the most convenient spot on earth I concede but your efforts are to be commended. Now, it is no secret that this family is the nearest and dearest thing to my heart so I wanted you to hear it from me first. On Wednesday I received an invitation from my brother-in-law, The Earl of Bantry, along with this portrait of our new King George."

The General's wife held up the gift from her brother high so everyone could see.

"It seems that King George is to make a Royal Progress of sorts to Ireland at the end of the summer and he is going to visit Bantry House. The Earl has invited me, as a representative of the Dunne family, to attend the banquet held in the King's honour."

The family and servants all joined in a thunderous round of applause.

"Here, here!" said Colonel Dunne.

"Congratulations Father!" said Frank.

"What a horrible painting," Mrs. Kavanaugh muttered under her breath as she offered her congratulations with a wide smile and polite applause.

After centuries of toggling between defiance and capitulation, the Chieftain of the Dunne clan would soon come face-to-face with an English Monarch. A feat of historical significance for the native Irish of Queen's County and a great personal triumph for the General.

CHAPTER 3

Fragment of letter from Lucy Rogers to Henrietta Welch

[September 1, 1930]

There was always a hustle and bustle to Brittas according to my mother. In those days local squabbles were not decided in a formal courthouse like we do but at a Manor Court held in the big houses of the county. Apparently General Dunne, being Lord of the Manor, would officiate at these doings and Uncle Peter as a young boy was quite interested in the mechanics of it all. Mother always called Peter "the brightest of the bunch."

General Dunne expected much from his family, his troops and his tenants but the world expected even more from General Dunne.

Squire Francis Dunne died when his son and heir was only seven years old. Edward was quietly whisked away to a boarding school in the English countryside by his Protestant guardian, Lord Nugent, Privy Counsellor at Dublin Castle. Under severe protest from his mother, the former Margaret Plunkett, the boy was taken from his home and family for decades. Her influence as a member of one of the country's historic families was no match for the forces of the Ascendency which sought to bind Ireland to England with chains of steel.

Ancient Irish civilization had divided the soil amongst tribes and each tribe collectively owned its own district. Edward was heir of the Dunne Chieftains, which had legitimacy among his own people but he had to learn the ways of the English if he were to be recast as a useful tool of the Empire. So, his Irish brogue was beaten out of him by age ten, replaced without a trace by a clipped aristocratic accent. Lord Nugent configured a specialized, well-rounded curriculum of study suitable for a boy of the ruling class. Tutors truthfully laid out all the facts pertaining to Oliver Cromwell's total conquest of Ireland leaving out brutal details that would only serve to enflame his dormant native passions.

He was taught how once Ireland was conquered, she was divided up into plantations and given as gifts to the British nobility who funded the war or as back pay to the soldiers who worked on credit. England then planted its people and its crops deep into the Irish soil to insure a peaceful and prosperous future for both nations. His guardians systematically rebuilt this child of the Celts into a proper Anglican who could spread the good news of submission and cooperation.

At the tender age of seventeen he joined the British army as an Ensign in the 26th Regiment of the Foot, establishing his path of loyalty to the crown. Edward set sail for the Carolinas hoping to help crush the colonists in America's War of Independence. Before his ship could reach shore, a retreating frigate approached with news that Lord Cornwallis had just surrendered in Yorktown. Upon his return he proceeded through the ranks commanding larger and larger companies with postings from Holland to Spain, but was offered neither fame nor prize money.

There was always a certain amount of darting between military and estate duties, but after eighteen years of defending The Empire's interests all over Europe, he came back home to Ireland and was appointed Brigadier-General on the Staff. Absentee landlord no longer, at five-and-thirty he returned to his rightful place as Lord of the Manor and head of the Dunnes of Brittas. His life would be dedicated to keeping Ireland safe for her people and from her people.

After hosting the family banquet he was inundated with requests from every facet of Queen's County society. He had planned on discussing estate affairs with his agent, local militia needs with Sir Charles Coote; the Bishop of Kildare wanted to bend his ear and his wife wanted to bend the other. But on this day, he was to set all other roles aside for his duties as Lord of the Manor and preside over the Manor Court with his seneschal, Mr. William Drew.

Court days siphoned every ounce of patience from Edward and he usually declined all polite invitations. "The Great Unwashed" as the Lady of the Manor called them, came into their home, sat upon their finely upholstered chairs and quarrelled with other tenants over petty amounts of coin or they tried to plead their way out of paying what they owed to the Lord.

Townspeople and farmers from the jurisdiction of the Manor Court started to gather on the house lawn, looking forward to an entertaining day of neighbourhood gossip and scandal. The three large public rooms of

Brittas were separated by massive oak doors. Sneed and his staff arranged for the day's events and opened the doors to create an expansive space perfectly suited to a courtroom. Blue porcelain jardinières were filled with crushed lavender to battle the earthy aromas emanating from the spectators.

The court calendar was full but Mr. Drew, pale, tall and inelegant with a retreating chin, was experienced at keeping the proceedings moving along. Since young Peter was so fascinated with the Manor Court's last session, the General told Mr. Drew Peter would attend. The young lad looked smart in Richard's old blue. The General was required to put on the powdered wig of a court judge, which further aggravated him. Proceedings began with ceremonial rituals and legal-sounding language passed down from feudal, Medieval times. Young Peter stood at attention when the seneschal began the spectacle:

"The court leet, or view of frankpledge, and the general court baron of Edward Dunne, Lord of this manor, held in and for the same on Monday, five weeks before the Feast of the Pentecost, that is to say, the 7th day of May, in the first year of the reign our Sovereign Lord George the 4th by the Grace of God of the United Kingdom of Great Britain and Ireland, King, defender of the faith, and in the year of our Lord 1821."

Charges were read for the first case:

"At this court comes Owen Conroy, a customary tenant of this manor, in his proper person, and prays the lord thereof to consider his defence for the crime of stealing and selling property heretofore afforded to the Lord of the Manor."

The Lord of the Manor asked a question, "What did Mr. Conroy steal?"

Drew looked down for a moment at his black britches that displayed shiny patches here and there which bespoke long service to the General then answered: "My Lord, the tenant is by law not allowed to cut timber from the forest nor fish from the streams running through lands owned by my Lord— "

"Understood."

"My Lord, summarising the law, manure made by tenant's livestock upon a leased farm in the ordinary course of husbandry is the property of the landlord, and belongs to the land as an incident necessary for its improvement and cultivation; and the tenant has no right to remove it from the premises or apply it to any other use."

"Are you trying to say Mr. Conroy sold my cow dung?"

"Exactly, m'Lord."

Mr. Drew feared at this point the General might begin to make a mockery of the court and sped up the proceedings. "Mr. Owen Conroy, is this true?" An elderly man dressed in a worn brown jacket with stained green knee breeches rose from Lady Dunne's silk damask covered chair, twisted his farming hat in his hands. The village priest, Father Thady Dunne, a distant connection to the old blood served as translator for the tenant who was thought to speak only Irish and barely understand English. The question was repeated in Irish for Owen's sake.

"No, yer honour, I brought it to me son's plot to help with his potato crop," he said in English, circumventing the priest, as his hollow cheeks made a slight whistling sound.

"Were you aware it was not yours to sell or give?" said the seneschal.

Father Dunne gazed upon Owen Conroy with a quizzical look.

"My Sally made it and she's me cow."

"So you were not aware of such a law?"

"Who could make a law as silly as that?"

Drew spoke, "Mr. Conroy has just admitted guilt, the jury need not deliberate. We request that a fine be levied of £10 due and payable by year-end."

The General asked, "Mr. Drew, the cow itself is hardly worth £5. What basis do you value the manure at £10?"

"The court is under the assumption that Mr. Conroy has been committing these criminal acts over the course of his 23-year lease, sire."

"Mr. Drew, a word?" The General called his seneschal to his side and whispered out of range of the court.

"This man cannot afford a fine of £10, it would devastate him."

"Your Lordship, we must set an example and condemn this sort of activity for the entire estate to see. I am sure he was well aware of the statue."

"Reduce his fine to 10 shillings and let's get on with it for God's sake."

Mr. Drew stood in front of poor, old Owen Conroy, looked down upon him with all the scorn he could muster and fiendishly proclaimed: "To whom the Lord of this manor, by hands of his said steward, seisin thereof by the rod, according to the custom of said manor, do levy a fine on Copyholder, one Mr. Owen Conroy, of…" his voice lowered and he quickly muttered, "ten shillings. That is all."

Mr. Conroy collected himself and made his way out through the east entrance. Out in the rain. Out to his cottage. Out to face his wife. Out of ten shillings he didn't have.

Most boys of Peter's age would find it quite impossible to suppress their snickers at the mere mention of pinched pooh at such a pretentious gathering. Peter was different. He loved the artful language of the court and the dignity in which it could cloak something as crass as cow crap. He pictured the entire proceedings as a giant chess match. And most perceptive of all, he realized that the Lord of the Manor was moving both the black and the white pieces around the board. It was a game General Dunne couldn't loose and one his tenants couldn't win, Peter thought to himself.

Case after case, justice was meted out by the court. Disputes between merchant and customer were quickly resolved. Freeholder, leaseholder or copyholder were terms Peter had heard his father throw about his whole life but after just a day in Manor Court he had grasped the subtle nuances.

After the court was adjourned for the day, General Dunne's fingertips were clinging to the door moulding as his seneschal had a few last thoughts. Peter quietly approached the two men when the General grabbed him by the lapel and pulled his slight frame into the fray. William Drew was interrupted mid-sentence. "Well lad, what did you make of that carnival of delights?" asked the General.

"Sir, thank you for allowing me to be here today, I think I knew what was happening at least half the time—"

Mr. Drew cut in, "General, as I was saying, I found it most detrimental to the cause—"

The General clearly unwilling to be chastised by this stale prune of a man said, "Now see here, William, these Manor Courts are a relic of a bygone era, most Lords never turn up even when they're held at the pub! I shall be more than happy to follow that example but I won't have an auld man be fined £10 pounds for stealing shite. I won't."

"It's in the best interest of the manor—"

"Peter can sit in my place next time, here's the wig."

A lurking question had been on Peter's mind all day but he wasn't sure if he had the cheek to bring it up. But now with the General's thoughts in the open, he persevered.

"May I ask one thing?"

Happy to steer the conversation off-course the General nodded.

"If the cow is owned by the tenant and the tenant buys the food that feeds the cow, how could the droppings, made in the guts of the cow, not be considered property of the tenant?"

"There you are Mr. Drew, plain as a pipe-stem. Peter dear boy, that is some sound reasoning." The General scooped his wee cousin under his arm and marched off to his awaiting decanter leaving Mr. Drew wincing. Occasionally at Brittas, the Lord's explicit lack of courtesy was a gentle reminder of his omnipotence.

Upstairs in his small private study Edward Dunne sat with a glass of brandy brooding over the day's trials. With the exception of the blacksmith, a few shopkeepers, and the doctor, an entire population from this little part of the world was in one way or another his responsibility. Of course, his life had been designed with that simple fact in mind but at times he caught himself wishing for a lower rank. Duty had a trick of appearing like a majestic lion from afar but upon closer inspection was just a needy, injured kitten.

If only he had been able see how his father did it.

Staring out the window as the sun set over the west lawn, he poured his second glass of brandy. The lush green hills of Queen's County suddenly made him feel quite sentimental, an emotion General Dunne did not find productive yet was becoming more pronounced as he neared his third score.

Every inch of Brittas held special meaning for him and his family. Beyond the lawn was a stand of cypress trees planted in the pattern of troop formations from the Siege of Fort Louis du Rhein. He designed the memorial himself in honour of his younger brother Nicholas who gallantly lost his life in the battle fighting the French. Dynastic ghosts and the hobgoblins of obligation had always been his invisible companions but today their hauntings had put him in a mood most foul. Clearly, finishing the brandy would only take him further down a hole. He reasoned that, as long he was already in such a state, why not check on Mother?

It was said that mother and son were truly strangers. Most of General Dunne's childhood had been spent in the care of his English overlords and the British army took over from there. Margaret, a highly-refined person, understood how the Irish landed gentry needed to play the game but she drew the line at faith.

For generations, the Dunne family had been the proudest of Catholics, retaining their ancestral lands through a variety of ruses played on their English conquerors. It came to an end in 1771 when Squire Dunne, Margaret's husband, faced the tricky proposition of either losing his religion or his estate. He kept the latter. Through his apostasy he reckoned it would be easier to reclaim one's religion than one's land. He converted his faith to the deceptively named Church of Ireland. His wife did not. Blasting her husband as a coward to his face, she was determined to raise their children as Catholics. The Squire's untimely death meant the oldest child would inherit the estate and the religion; the boy became a mandated Protestant.

A shaky status quo existed between Margaret and her son up until 1814 when a rift developed that shook the very foundations of their spindly relationship.

Edward planned a Protestant church as the centrepiece to his revitalized village of Clonaslee. Margaret suggested a cross be placed atop the steeple of the new church since neither a steeple nor a bell was permitted on R.C. houses of worship. Edward explained that the cross was most objectionable to followers of the "new religion" at which point Margaret presented an ultimatum to the zealous new builder of towns and propagator of English churches. Either the steeple gets a cross or she would never speak to her son again. So be it. In retaliation his mother quickly funded the rebuilding of a Catholic chapel down the street and took refuge in the family's Dublin residence at 37 Harcourt Street. It would serve as her Dower House, a day's journey away from Brittas and her black-hearted Protestant son.

Margaret Plunkett Dunne kept her distance from Edward, purposely talking around him at the few occasions when they were together. She peppered her speech with anti-Protestant rhetoric. But she was at war with a military expert and he went about his business undeterred, waiting for the perfect moment for reconciliation. After six years of this pantomime, word had reached Margaret that Edward, in his role as magistrate of Queen's County, had decided not to press charges against a group of agitators touting Catholic emancipation in the county town of Maryborough. He was widely condemned in the newspapers but the patient tactician had found a way to end the silence and bring unity back to his family. His mother relented.

Margaret was feeling unwell since the family banquet the night before. Though rarely used, she maintained her suite of rooms in the south wing of Brittas. Most of her time was spent enjoying the capital life in Dublin. More than eighty years old, she had a full social calendar of lunches, flower shows and theatre, which she attended regularly with her remaining aged friends. France and the servants had been attending to her throughout the day, the General thought they might be able to cheer each other up. After walking down a long dim passage with steps in the middle he reached her door, lightly rapping.

"Are you still awake?"

"Of course, I am it's only half-eight!" came the robust reply.

The General opened the door to find his mother fully dressed in a lavender gown reading on the chaise. Sunset made the butter-coloured Chinoiserie wallpaper cast a warm glow over the room that stood out as a gilded highlight in an otherwise drab old country manor. The four best paintings in the estate's meagre collection were perfectly spaced on her walls while a prized turquoise and gold Sèvres washstand sat on the dresser behind her. She had retired her swirling rococo sedan chair that had once carted her through the bustling streets of Dublin and there it stood in the corner.

"How are you feeling, Mother?"

"Still alive by all reports. Your wife has been taking very good care of me and Sneed just brought up tea. Sit with me and share a cup."

"Right then. I had the most trying day in the Manor Court today." The General pulled up a gilt side chair.

"I do hope Sneed rolled up the carpets before they all came trouncing in?" asked his mother.

"Yes, Mother he always does. I have been meaning to ask, what can you tell me of the Manor Courts back in Father's day?

"I don't think he bothered turning up, really. Lots of petty nonsense."

"I'm sure Father was better at it than me."

"Well, you've got to do your own growing no matter how tall he was Edward."

"You've said that a thousand times," said the General who dashed all hope of hearing any new, sage advice. "That whole Manor Court charade is quite dreary but I do get some idea of what is happening out there," he said as his wrist rotated twice towards the window, "and I think the tenants need to see me as a guiding light of sorts."

"My dear son, you had better cherish your exalted position for I have a terrible feeling the whole thing is about to be turned on its head." Margaret nervously readjusted her pearls.

"Oh, please Mother."

"No, no, I am certain there will be some kind of appalling upheaval like they had in France. It may be a year or a hundred but it's coming. Mark my words. You know, the tenants used to look down at the ground or curtsey when I happen to come upon them and just yesterday one of your young tenants looked me right in the eye as I passed. She was as cold as ice. She could have pulled a dagger out from her shawl and it wouldn't have surprised me in the least."

"How theatrical," derided the son.

"Don't you mock me. I have lived a long time and I have seen stranger things happen. Just do the arithmetic, add in some…some gunpowder and things will all go up in smoke. I just pray I die before they come wheeling in the guillotine."

"Mother, the people of Brittas are happy and the country itself has never been so unified."

"So you think? Eight-thousand of us and six-million of them."

"Well, I think they will always respect the true Irish. Since the most remote period this territory has been in our family's possession. They would never dream of harming us. After all, heaven knows, I am a Chieftain. The *Ó Duinn!*"

"And what would they call an Irish Chieftain who prays in Cromwell's church?" she said, picking at all the open sores.

"They would call him a wise and prosperous one. Now Mother, let's not dive back into those deep waters again."

"All of this talk has made me quite exhausted."

"Confound it! I came in here to make you feel better and look what's happened. Can I have anything sent up for you?"

"No, no," she said and after a long pause continued, "but can I tell you just one more thing?"

The General looked at her with a reluctant tilt of the head and waited for the earful that usually followed such questions.

"Last night at dinner when you made your little announcement about the King's visit, well, I was…I am quite proud of you, Edward."

"Thank you Mother, I am glad."

CHAPTER 4

Fragment of letter from Lucy Rogers to Henrietta Welch

[November 22, 1936]

Mother never talked much about her father or what he did at Brittas. Don't really know. She did tell me though that he was supposedly quite handsome —all the women in the village talked about my mother's mother behind her back. Jealous I suppose. Oh, and that he was a true Irishman in the sense that he thought land was the only thing worth warring over—worth dying over. A precious resource on that tiny island.

General Dunne had entrusted his cousin, Mr. Peter Dunne, with the arduous job of estate agent to a sizable patch of Ireland's best farmland in Queen's County. The Big Lords of the Midlands, who lived in England most of the year, held the majority of the province but as the General often reminded his fellow landlords, the area was still known as Dunne Country. The Dunnes had resided there, as the family would say, "ever and always."

Mr. Dunne was still ruggedly handsome yet weather-beaten beyond his years. He had a well-proportioned face and twinkling eyes with his most marked feature being a broken nose that gave him a youthful, elfin-like appearance. He imagined it added to his appeal amongst the women of the area. The men naturally assumed he had won the trophy at fisticuffs. The humiliating fact was that an ill-tempered bull, not willing to have his testicles removed, was to blame for Mr. Dunne's nose.

He was undeniably intelligent, but not exactly a man of letters, he learned his basic three R's at a hedge school taught by a wandering teacher/poet out in the fields. There were a few haphazard lessons in the classics and history thrown in from Timahoe's parish priest but that was the full extent of his formal lessons. He was going to learn from the land and become a keen scholar of its animals.

The brilliance of Mr. Dunne was that he used his tenuous links to the grand old family as it suited the task at hand. When negotiating rents with the tenant farmers he was the fellow landless papist, just following orders from the gentry that likewise bubbled him out of Ireland's riches. He spoke to them in Irish with all the intonations and inflections of a cottager.

While conducting business with merchants or solicitors he acted as a half-sir descendant of Irish kings, willing to bestow his brand of royal warrant and access to the aristocracy for the right price. In reverse, he could feign weakness to better a deal or breathe a mighty judgement down upon a tenant if necessary. He mixed strong language with humour in ratios necessary to make an Irishman obey. He was striding along society's dividing walls, observing the subtle and not-so-subtle class distinctions that were lost on other professional and aristocratic men.

The duties of an estate agent as large as Brittas would be shared by three or four people if it were located in England but in a uniquely Irish tradition, Mr. Dunne would be part farmer, part attorney, part landlord and part enforcer.

As for compensation, he was paid a suitable salary in guineas like a gentleman not in pounds like a tradesman (the General's act of courtesy), in addition to three-percent of the estate's annual revenue. Then there was Ballintlea House. He had been given a 31-year extension to the lease of his own family's middling farm bordering the Cashel Bog, a mile from Timahoe. Consisting of a barn, a stone dwelling and 100 acres of productive fields, Ballintlea House had been a source of pride for his father and grandfather. The old place was sub-leased out upon the family's move to Brittas. On those lands Mr. Dunne became an expert farmer and celebrated stockman.

When Mr. Dunne was first recruited, an ambitious Edward had sold a large portion of his inherited lands to scrape together the £6,000 needed to purchase his commission as lieutenant colonel in the 7th Dragoon Guards. Cow by cow, tenant by tenant, lease by lease and harvest after harvest, Mr. Dunne took the diminished estate and made it more profitable than ever before. Since that miraculous turnaround, the General placed unprecedented confidence in his steward to run the estate without interference. The General's only instructions, in ascending order, were to treat the tenants with kindness, have respect for the animals and keep the land alive.

Mr. Dunne had growing concerns he wanted to share with his cousin. The population on the estates had nearly doubled since 1803 and it was getting harder and harder for the land to support the people.

Able-bodied male tenants had duty work of at least eighty days of the year on the landlord's home farm. A considerable portion of bog land lay north of Brittas Lake, which the peasants harvested for twenty-percent of the turf. After their work for the General was complete, they had to plant their own crops and raise livestock, mostly a few pigs or a cow, all the while living on the potatoes they harvested in autumn.

The cottages were bursting at the beams with families. Mr. Dunne kept foraging for more plots to accommodate the peasantry's demands even convincing the General to abandon his racetrack for more rentable acreage. To the south lay the Slieve Bloom Mountains where land got rockier and less productive. It had been deemed as wasteland in previous generations but times being what they were, it might be his only hope for more space. What about the squatters that lay at the dark fringes of the estate? Mr. Dunne knew they were there but never felt the need to roust them out.

In the summer of 1821 the rain that fell on Brittas was warmer than usual. The General was back in Dublin and the Dunne children were all home from their various grades of schools. The children that lived in the main house slept well into the morning but those that lived in the servant's wing had work to do. Mr. Dunne rousted James from bed and the two meandered over in the downpour to the rent room, a rustic two storey out-building a few paces from the lodge wing yet a world apart.

Mr. Dunne looked down at the old boot scraper outside his doorstep. Most of the brass had worn off the cherubs holding up the scraping bar. He slid his boot across the edge and witnessed the little figures slowly suffocate in a bulging gob of mud.

About a quarter of Brittas was leased to Catholic middlemen who in turn spliced up the land and subleased parcels out at a profit. Mr. Dunne classified the other tenants by size: The *Mór* (large farmers with at least thirty acres and a fine house), The *Lár* (middling farms of ten-twenty acres with a cottage) and The *Beag* (small farms of two-ten acres with housing that left much to be desired). Left out of the equation all together were those wretched cabinholders and their half acres who gave Mr. Dunne more grief than all the other holders combined. He preferred to lease out to middlemen or consolidate the smaller farms into bigger ones but in truth that had only happened once. On the wall of peeling paint behind his desk was an oversized map of Brittas drawn up by a

Dublin cartographer for Margaret in 1779. A red line delineated the tenant holdings. Over time, Mr. Dunne and his predecessor had divided and subdivided the map so many times that the sharpest pencil could not write small enough.

Today the agent had precisely forty-two things on his mind, which he had counted the night before during a restless sleep.

First thing on the Mr. Dunne's list; find a few salvageable perches in the wastelands or in the mountains that could be leased to the ever-expanding populace. It was also his habit to make surprise visits upon the tenantry. During a full bright moon he would brag about making evening calls on tenants who had made themselves scarce in daylight.

Father and son rode off in a two-wheeled cart to which was harnessed their favourite crop-tailed pony horse, Thor. The primitive cart was a rough mode of transportation to be sure but it manoeuvred well over the rocky, muddy terrain and lent a kindred, folksy feel to his often-contentious dealings with the tenancy. The agent's first visit was always to John Pigott, the General's largest tenant holding nearly 1,000 acres. Pigott, like other middlemen of Brittas, subleased the land to others in a tangled legal web that only the solicitors truly understood. Most of his time was spent in England but he always spent July in the stately farmhouse of Glanbarrow. They exchanged pleasantries, village gossip and an early morning nip. Pleased Piggot had neither a complaint nor a request, he and James rambled onwards to visit a few middling farms before reaching the foot of the Slieve Blooms.

Outside of the tiny townland of Scaroon, dusty cabins with green and brown straw rooves were interspersed between the potato patches and dung heaps. A facade of serenity masked the families on the edge of peril within the cabin walls. Silvery nasturtiums with their cheerful blossoms crawled along the shady sides. Picturesque poverty. The Dunnes passed an aged peasant by one of the estate bogs. He was sheepishly wheeling a cart full of newly cut turf along the road back to his shanty. Mr. Dunne considered stopping and confronting the poor old rascal but instead he made a mental note to investigate the matter at a later date. The business at hand was to find the isolated valley of his memory that lay west of the booley house, a scant sod outbuilding local shepherds used in summer while they watched over their flocks.

A few miles or so up from the pastures of Scaroon they reached the booley and quickly rode past it. Turning his head, James could see shadows of squatters move away from the windows. The agent noticed too. Annoyed more than surprised, Mr. Dunne brought the cart to an abrupt stop.

He grumbled to James, "Infernal beasts. Damn! They are worse than the rabbits that tear up your mother's garden. Here," the father handed the reins to his son, "Don't move. I'll be right back." He bounded from his seat and like a specter, suddenly appeared in the doorway. Panicky occupants scurried into the corner like wild beasts afraid of getting too close to a human being. At the back wall stood an emaciated middle-aged woman, dressed in ragged cloth with wild kinky hair sprouting from the top of her head. The flesh had fallen from her face caving in on her mouth as if decomposition had already begun its claim. Her hands nervously clutched her filthy scrap of an apron. Two half-naked children seemingly held together only by their rags were at her feet and other children cowered behind her willowy frame. Hollow faces accentuated their large terrified eyes.

In Gaelic, the agent asked, "How long have you been in here?"

"Not long sire, we were just getting a little shelter from the rain and we be moving on," the woman said in a frail, raspy voice.

"You had better, the sheep men are coming up here and you don't want to be in their booley when they do! Now, are you hungry?"

The Gaelic language has no word for yes so the question was answered by an assertion, "We are."

He reached in his satchel and took out two loaves of soda bread Mollie had packed for their journey. "Make this last and be on your way." The woman took the bread then made a slight bow that wiggled her unruly hair. Her involuntary gesture added a certain dignity to her ghastly situation.

Mr. Dunne watched the vagrant family disappear into the trees. When they were out of sight a confounded James asked his father, "What will happen to them now? Where are they going to go?"

"By the looks of it, the mother's on her last leg. She'll probably croak out in a few days and the nippers…." Mr. Dunne stopped mid-sentence when he noticed his son starting to cry. "The wee ones will probably get adopted by some kind farmer's family and have nice little lives. Now let's get on with it."

Mr. Dunne jumped back into the rig and glanced over at James to see that he had stopped snivelling but was lost in thought. The agent wondered how much his son knew of the ways of the world. Was he a weak sort?

They passed the numerous tiny farms of Glenkeen and into the woods. They drove onto sandstone hills where the graves of the ancient race lay deep under its slopes, over buried bones of fathers who had once questioned their son's fortitude and ashes of sons who had unquestioned reverence for their fathers.

Pulling over, Mr. Dunne said, "I remember rightly that little valley can't be far away. Wait here."

He went off on foot to find a route through the trees while James stayed on the cart bench. He reassured himself by putting the Brown Bess musket squarely on his lap. His head turned and twisted with the jerkiness of a red squirrel. Switching his posture from a bold sentry into a scared little child and back again. James found the forest to be a strange and beautiful place.

Emerging from the trees Mr. Dunne hollered, "Son, we have to go down towards the stream." Back in the cart he found a narrow path in hopes it would lead directly to the grassy patch of his memory. With remarkable skill he directed the rig through the dense trees and out through the passage. As if drawn by some magnetic force, he pulled up to the edge of a weeping cliff, soggy and ragged, covered in purple iris.

Looking down on the hidden valley below, the agent was shocked to find the pristine green field he had pictured in his mind were now a bustling shantytown of lean-to shacks and twig huts, rabbits on spits and shoeless children, cultivated gardens and a steaming moonshine still percolating poitín, the preferred drink of the peasantry. His overwhelming urge was to charge down and expel the outlanders with his whip and a few shots fired off from his gun. He looked over at his mesmerized son and put a finger up to his mouth. Slowly he backed Thor away from the cliff's edge and quietly turned the cart around. They drove back to Brittas again in silence.

Mr. Dunne returned in six days' time with the Tullamore Militia. Usually it was the sheriff's office that assisted in evictions but General Dunne was also commander of the Centre Militia District. The yeomen did a fine job of restoring the valley. Mr. Dunne hired a surveying team and netted the estate four new plots. Satisfied at the outcome, he felt he had gained some equilibrium over the delicate balance that was land management at Brittas. However, there was only so much control a rent room could have over kinetic things like people.

CHAPTER 5

Fragment of letter from Lucy Rogers to Henrietta Welch

[October 16, 1935]

In your last letter you asked about my mother's education. She was sent away to a convent school run by the Presentation Sisters in Stradbally at age eleven. Throughout her life she never lost her thirst for knowledge, she kept up on the world until her dying day. I gather there was some resentment from her older sister Mary who had only attended the local school in town. Mother said the family had become more prosperous by the time she came of age and that my Aunt Mary was not a serious student. I suppose she lived in her parents' blind spot. I must tell you, whenever she mentioned Mary she would always remark "Not to be mean…" and then follow it up with the most unflattering things.

"Father said to hurry and get out there or he is leaving without you," Mary screeched as Bridget was packing the last of her meagre belongings into her mother's old leather portmanteau. "And you had better not be taking any of my things!"

"Oh, I can assure you, there is nothing of yours worth taking," Bridget snapped as she made an exception for the tiny bronze dog that used to sit on their dresser.

Mother's last words of advice were "Obey the nuns" and James begged her not to become one. Mrs. Miguel, the General's cook, brought out some Spanish biscuits as Mr. Dunne loaded his daughter into the gig. A curious and intelligent girl, Bridget was excited to leave for school where she hoped to become a refined gentlewoman able to hold her own with any aristocrat she would meet in her sure-to-be exciting life.

She was feeling grown up and positively buoyant about taking the hired Bianconi car from Clonaslee to Stradbally all by herself. Mr. Charles Bianconi was the toast of Ireland for buying leftover Waterloo warhorses, strapping them to coaches and transporting people all around the island for a small fee. General Dunne said it was the best example of beating swords into ploughshares the world had ever witnessed.

"Father, do you think it will rain on us today?"

"No Biddy, I told God to keep it clear all day for your trip and for the four fields of rye I'll be harvesting." He loved his daughter and often told her things she wanted to hear.

Bridget gazed out from the carriage at Brittas Woods with faint sadness as the memories of her summer frolicked through her mind. They trotted through one of her favourite wooded sections where the trees bowed over the road covering the sky. A tunnel of leaves and branches allowed a few shafts of sunlight to poke through now and then. She imagined she was being reborn. Her sadness flipped back to jubilation.

On her lap was a volume of poetry that she hoped would pass the time on her journey. She had never been to the convent before and pictured the student dormitory in her head. She wondered if there would be marigolds, she loved marigolds, orange not yellow.

They made their way past the pond and down through the gatehouse. The old gatekeeper stuck his head out and exuberantly waved his worn tricorne hat to them hollering, "Ta-ta. Ta-ta, Miss Bridget. We'll miss you!" She waved back enthusiastically.

Pulling into town, Mr. Dunne brought the rig to a stop across from Kennedy's pub where a Bianconi car was scheduled to leave at nine o'clock sharp. He brought down Bridget's case then they crossed the street together. As he stood next to his daughter he wondered if the threshing crew was working at half-speed.

"Father, do you think Mother can manage without me? I help her quite a bit with the cooking you know." Bridget asked.

"She'll be sad to be sure but she is proud of you. You'll receive a first-rate education. If she needs help in the kitchen, Mrs. Miquel is always at hand."

"But who will bring you tea by the fire, that has always been my job?"

"Aye, I shall miss that. You are destined for much grander things than bringing a kettle to the boil. I have high hopes for you Bridget Dunne."

From behind the R.C. chapel, the sound of the cab approached. Suddenly Bridget broke out into a dramatic and audible cry surprising them both. Dear Lord, I'm not going to live here anymore! she thought. Mr. Dunne tenderly got down on his knee and wiped away her flowing tears with a fresh handkerchief. "Come now Bridget, you must buckle to. You said this was your wish and it comes at great cost to the family. I expect a glowing report from Mother Superior."

Composing herself she noticed Mr. Kennedy moving back the green cambric curtains of his pub to see that the she was the only fare to board from Clonaslee this morning. Since his tavern had become a coach stop he had not benefited from any additional patronage as promised; departure and arrival times did not coordinate with convenient drinking times.

The petite schoolgirl climbed up and picked an open spot on one of the long benches that ran along both sides of the coach. Mr. Dunne handed her luggage to the coachman who had just pulled a heavy canvas sheet over the legs of his passengers to shield them from road muck. Bridget, who toggled back from sadness, had one dainty hand on her book and held out the other for her father to kiss. She gave her father one of her bright smiles, forged in silent payment. "Be a good girl. Remember my high expectations for you lass. Bye, bye now."

The coach pulled away and Mr. Dunne allowed himself a moment of fatherly pride before rushing back to the threshers.

A curmudgeonly-looking gentleman sat on Bridget's right and an older girl sat on her left. Bridget guessed that she was two, maybe three castes down from herself by the looks of those frayed shirtsleeves and grimy gloves. Bridget was dressed in a handsome blue brocade dress that she had inherited from Fanny.

The girl asked, "Where are you headed off to then?"

"I am to attend school at the convent in Stradbally," Bridget answered feeling her superiority.

"Oh, poor you. My name is Annie and I am on my way to Athy to live with me grandmother."

"Oh, poor you," Bridget quipped.

"She's got one foot in the grave and me Da says I can help her flip it back out again. He says I'm like a little ray of sunshine. I'm quite the nurse you see."

"That is very kind of you. How long do you think it will take to get to Stradbally?"

"Three hours for you. Have you not never taken this ride before?"

"No, I never. And this will be my first year at the school."

"Ew, it sounds dreadful. All those long-faced nuns telling you what to do and how to think…and no boys about."

"Are you expecting a gaggle of boys on the horizon there at your gran's?"

Annie looked over at Bridget's crooked smirk and they both burst into fits of laughter, drawing scowls from their fellow passengers. Little Miss Dunne, who believed she was as good as anyone and better than most, made one new friend today and it had been effortless. She was confident by the end of the week the whole of the convent would be converted.

Earlier that summer in London, old King George was replaced by new King George in a spectacular coronation ceremony at Westminster Abbey. The English were the world's masters at creating such spectacles and this one brought the former prince Regent's lifelong spending habits to dizzying heights. It was decided that the King would sprinkle some of the leftover glitter on Ireland in the form of a Royal Progress.

The Earl of Bantry, General Dunne's brother-in-law, had been busy making Bantry House absolutely pristine in anticipation of the King's visit. The whole storybook village of Bantry was given a fresh coat of paint. Gold embossed invitations to the Earl's banquet had been sent out to a select group of Irish aristocrats and nabobs. All around Southern Ireland elaborate court dresses were being embroidered and family jewels were extricated from their velvet cases. Although they appeared quite nonchalant around the other inhabitants of Brittas, the General and his wife were euphoric behind closed doors. Over the centuries, English monarchs were used to seizing Dunne family property without so much as meeting a Dunne in person. But now General Dunne was going to be acknowledged by the King himself. It was a triumph for all those who inhabit the fiefdom of Brittas.

The General's children were invited to stay at Bantry House too but they had all gone back to their schools. He was most disappointed that Frank had chosen Trinity College over the King of England. His family had been tempted and tormented for generations by their English taskmasters and now, when they were about to be recognized with a royal nod, the heir to Brittas was not playing along.

Circumstances being what they were, the General shifted his outlook. A momentous occasion with such historic significance must be witnessed by a young member of the clan, one with the greatest chance of passing down the memory onto future generations.

General Dunne had not come down to his agent's rent room all summer despite Mr. Dunne's numerous appeals. Working out the details of a grain shipment from behind a mountain of leases and stacks of assorted paperwork, Mr. Dunne felt the commanding presence of the General. Although a man of considerable size, he moved elegantly and quietly as if he was on a continuous reconnaissance mission. "Good of you to come sir." Mr. Dunne rose from his chair and started to shuffle through the stacks, "I have all of the documents ready for your signature somewhere around here...."

"Yes, yes, just give it to Major Rowland, he will bring it to Bantry. Now, I had an idea this morning and I want to see what you think."

"Is it about the lease renewals?"

"No, it's about young Peter."

"Good grief, what's he bothering you about now? Does he want to go with you and meet the King?"

"Well, funny you should remark that, cousin, because I think he should!"

"What?"

"Meet the King! Frank doesn't want to go; the others could care less and Peter is the only child in this family who seems to give a tinker's damn about our heritage."

"Oh, Your Honour, the boy's head is just going to catapult clear off his shoulders."

"So then, we better not let him bow to the King."

"Perhaps maybe just a curtsey."

The Mrs. had shipped off her soldier-husband many times over the course of their marriage and she was used to his blowing in and out of Brittas with the breeze. This time however, duty called for both husband and wife. Preparations for the trip down to Bantry's royal banquet filled her with nervous trepidation. France had not been back to County Cork since her brother walked her down the aisle of St. Colman's in 1801. Of course she was honoured with her brother's invitation but was agitated beyond words over the prospect of all those grand people clumped in an undulating wave of gilded showmanship. In Queen's County, she always felt like the most elegant swan upon the lake but now, the prospect of mingling with the highest order of British royalty put her tail feathers in a ruffle.

Aside from family connections, the Earl and the General had formed a warm friendship over financial and governmental dealings. Both were members of Dublin's Kildare Street Club, an exclusive Anglo-Irish institution where the gentry lounged in leather wingback chairs and made wagers over whist or billiards. The Club, as rumour had it, was the only place in all of Ireland where one could enjoy decent caviar while covertly running the affairs of the country, like Parliament without the accountability.

A tiresome habit of noble Irish families like the Dunnes was to feign Englishness when it suited their purpose. As a rule, they cared little for family crests, heraldry and the like, preferring substance over symbols. However, it was a fact that throughout the Kingdom, a Coat of Arms with the right components opened doors that seemed locked shut. The Dunnes of Brittas possessed a cobalt blue crest comprised of a golden eagle with outstretched wings below a mighty oak tree. Although it bore no traces of English heritage it retained a certain eminence amongst the Ascendancy and was a familiar feature around Brittas. A finely sculpted version in stone sat above the tower entrance to the manor. Years ago, the Savile Row tailor who created all the General's uniforms had minted silver buttons stamped with the Dunne crest. Every male servant of Brittas had them sewn onto his livery and stray buttons seemed to lie at the bottom of every drawer of the house. Bridget had one in her pocket as a memento when she left for school. The newest display of their Coat of Arms was waiting in the coach house.

John Dunne, one of Mr. Dunne's brothers, was a master wainwright at the nearby Tullamore Carriage Company. The General had taken delivery of an opulent five-glass Landau just in time for his seven-day journey to Bantry Bay. It was arguably the finest vehicle ever built by local craftsmen. A sturdy coach with a boxy yet regal silhouette, it had a retractable roof feature at the back allowing in occasional spotty sunshine. Luxurious cobalt blue velvet stretched over the interior walls and tufted seats. Nestled right above the front window was a small gold clock that John Dunne had imported from Switzerland. Shiny brass oil lanterns were affixed to the midnight blue exterior, harmonizing perfectly with the stunning Dunne family Coat of Arms painstakingly painted on the doors.

It was the type of misty morning when summer and autumn walked hand-in-hand. General Dunne's little troop was ready to set off on their pilgrimage in a convoy of three coaches that would carry the family, the servants and the soldiers. Major Rowland insisted on a military escort as they would be traveling through territories of notorious highwaymen, Whiteboys and Rockities, a loose affiliation of radicals intent on land reform. Major Rowland didn't dare say so but he wasn't enamoured with that fancy crest the General had on his new carriage. He worried it would attract the same bandits he wanted to avoid. Rowland's entire persona revolved around his closeness to the General.

Departure day drew everyone outside the double doors of the tower to bid adieu. Young Peter, in his brand-new traveling suit, was mesmerized by the eagle on the Dunne crest. It was rendered with such conviction that he could not stop his fingers from stroking its feathers over and over. He was so proud to represent the young members of the Dunne clan and travel to Bantry House with the General himself. He dared not allow himself the vision of actually meeting the King; it was too fantastic.

His mother Mollie was excited for her son but had concerns that he would miss the first few weeks of school. Her husband pointed out that Peter was already reading years ahead of his schoolmates and was probably more capable than the teacher. In matters such as these Mollie would not get her way. Not ever.

Rowland had planned the route to Bantry and decided it was best to take the old military road out of Brittas over Wolftrap Mountain to Castle Bernard in King's County. The General's army had cut the road through large swathes of trees after the 1798 Tullamore rebellion. He hoped to deny future generations of rebels the cover of high forest and provide a quick retreat to the friendly Bernard estates if necessary. Each leg of the journey had been planned like a foreign campaign, which had been a strong suit of Major Rowland before he became an aide-de-camp to General Dunne. Fortunately, a smattering of relatives and associates had fine houses along the route necessitating only one night's stay at a common coaching inn.

The remaining Dunnes waved to the departing ones as coachmen prepared the caravan. Rowland and the General were discussing a dispatch that had just arrived by courier. The General kept adjusting his square-rimmed glasses that needed no adjusting. He folded up the paper, put it into his breast pocket and joined his wife in the middle coach. Michael noticed Major Rowland was having difficulty wedging his ample belly into the head coach. After the faerie fort episode when the Major manhandled Michael, he'd coined a nickname that quickly made its way through the back halls of Brittas: Major Rotund. Standing next to his mother he said in a slow, hushed voice "Goodbye Peter, goodbye General…farewell Major Rotund."

Never having been out of Queen's County it was clear to Peter as they made their way through King's County that he lived in the superior of the two. The lands he saw from his coach window were filled with bogs and empty fields, cottages looked smaller, people looked sadder. He wondered how the powers that be could have mixed up the names. Weren't kings always better than queens? Maybe not, Queen Elizabeth was a much better ruler than most of the kings he had read about. He started to concentrate very hard about the wider concept. He batted around the idea in his head arguing both sides of the question for nearly an hour. Branches scrapped at the roof and his body swayed with the rhythm of the carriage as it cut through wooded boreens. The last comparison that came to mind was how his brother Michael was going out into the fields today to help with the harvest and Bridget was at school learning Latin. After careful deliberation young Peter's decision had been made; henceforth, kings were not always better than queens.

The General had kings and queens on his mind as well. It had been all over the Irish newspapers that Queen Caroline had passed away just two weeks after King George's coronation. What wasn't in the papers was the fact that Royal Guards had barred her from entering Westminster Abbey, and she was unable to witness her husband being crowned King. His tumultuous marriage to Caroline and his boorish behaviour had kept the chattering classes busy for twenty-five years. Now there were whispers of poison and murder. A dispatch had arrived earlier at Brittas with Talbot's address tucked into the corner like it was ashamed of itself:

To General Edward Dunne, Brittas, Queen's County

August 25, 1821

My Dear General,

The King received a wonderful reception here in Dublin, arriving in high spirits on his birthday. To fulfill his commitments, he had to leave London before the Queen's funeral cortège left for Brunswick where there has been an unfortunate incident. Much intrigue surrounds the King at the moment and we must not surrender to rumour. He needs the support

and loyalty of his Irish subjects to make his Royal Visit a success. He looks
forward with great avidity to the banquet at Bantry House, County Cork.
Believe me, & c.
Talbot, Lord Lieutenant of Ireland, Dublin Castle

Viceroy Talbot had a way of sending quizzical pronouncements. Was he trying to head off a rumour or start one? Is this a call for celebration or a warning of danger? The General had made up his mind about bureaucrats long ago, they were either licking someone's arse or somehow trying to save their own. He much preferred the directness of a military man who would either beat your arse or he would not. For the moment, the only thing he was compelled to do was to put his hand upon his wife's and enjoy the beauty of the Irish countryside.

CHAPTER 6

A letter from Lucy Rogers to Sarafrances Welch

February 5, 1932

Dearest Sara:

Just received your latest letter and will be happy to answer some of your questions as best I can. Henrietta says you are thriving in college and by your insightful probing I can tell you are a fine scholar. Your thesis on "Cromwell's Conquest of Ireland" sounds like something I would very much like to read.

I am sure I cannot add anything to your research that would be worthy of a college paper but I can only tell you what my parents told me. When my father would talk about Oliver Cromwell he would become quite agitated and I often feared his blood pressure would knock him right off his feet. He described the terrors as if they had happened the day before yesterday rather than 200 years ago. My dear sister had the brightest red hair you ever saw and Mother would always tell her how Cromwell's army used red-haired Irish babies for target practice! If he could kill an English king what were a few thousand Irish worth?

Our English roots go back on my grandmother's side to a man named Thomas White who was Lord Mayor of London sometime in the 1550's under Queen Mary I. Our relative remained Catholic and was forced to flee. The family eventually made it to Southern Ireland where they started from scratch and built another empire on Irish soil. I believe they were lawyers. This is the where the Earl of Bantry (Richard White) derives his descent and our female line connects with the McDowell clan. One of the McDowell sisters married Grace of Gracefield (family of William Russell Grace, mayor of New York and founder of the great shipping line) and the other married Peter Dunne of Brittas.

My grandmother McDowell/Dunne (her Christian name was Mary but they called her Mollie) spent her last years with my parents in Mountmellick when she gave the White family crest silver to my mother. I vaguely remember we had a long silver candlestick with a bird crest that used to sit on the fireplace mantle but don't what happened to it.

I apologize if my ramblings are a little disjointed but that is all I can add to the family's dealings with Mr. Cromwell. Funny, how little artifacts of history have such an adventurous story to tell...if they only could. Maybe there is an old bent candlestick sitting on the shelf of a curiosity shop somewhere just waiting for a chance to chat.

    Your Loving Aunt,
    Lucy Rogers

The coach spun towards Bantry Bay past hedges, gates and trees, past churches, cottages and barns, past broken down castles, paddocks and rickyards dotted with haystacks, until finally the back of the Landau opened up for the last leg of the journey to the seaside.

The Dunne party had spent the last six days traveling from Ireland's Midlands down to the finger-shaped bays that lay at her south-western edges. Eight-year old Peter Dunne was on his way to see the King and experiencing the most remarkable chapter of his young life. He rode in a luxurious carriage, stayed in great country houses and wandered through lush landscapes all in the month of August when Ireland was in her best mood. As the coaches rode through the clearing, Bantry Bay greeted them with crystal blue waters and undulating green hills. The pink sun was just starting to set behind the handsome ships that were evenly spaced throughout the inlet. Although the General's wife Frances was born and raised on the shores of County Cork, its beauty still had the ability to bring out in her a sense of wonder.

"Oh, I'd forgotten how absolutely enchanting it all is Edward."

Peter had propped up on his knees, denting the plush velvet seats and stuck his head through the carriage's open roof. The salt tang of the sea smacked him in the face as he wondered what happened to all the white-caps and jumping fish. He had trouble believing the calm glass surface before him was actually the infinite ocean of his imagination, gateway to the world. A neat little hamlet was built right up to the water's edge and lay at the foot of the commanding estate that ruled over this idyllic place, Bantry House.

The Earl had expected his sister's family to arrive earlier but he was at the mercy of a busy day of preparations and distracted by all the details. France anticipated making a dramatic entry into the forecourt but was irked to find it filled with tradesmen's wagons and their unsightly paraphernalia. A thuggish-looking man covered in plaster dust glared at them as the coachmen battered through to find a suitable spot to let off his passengers. Major Rotund had decided to enter the house in search of the welcoming party and came back wheezing with a slew of the Earl's uniformed staff. They promptly emptied the cars and the guests were ushered into a reception room while General Dunne went to find their host.

It was just three days before Bantry House would be swarming with royalty, grandees and the small rackety peers and parasites that clung to the crowd. The jilted local gentry had left in protest and rented out their grand houses to banquet guests. Villagers in the tidy town had engraved portraits of King George in their shop windows and displayed the new Irish Union Jack, with its centre harp, all along the coastal road. Dublin Castle heaped tedious and expensive requests upon the Earl but Bantry House had never looked more regal. The excitement had manifested itself in visible displays and invisible anxiety.

General Dunne scampered up to the Earl's study with the agility of a new recruit and burst through the door, "Well Richard, it's the first time the King of England is coming to Ireland without an army at his side, aye?"

"It appears the army is already here, my dear General."

The two old lions then began to pour over minutia from the Lord Lieutenant's latest dispatches while defining their own objectives. General Dunne hoped Dublin Castle would allow him an audience with a few Irish MPs so he could voice his opinion on Catholic suppression and report on the unrest experienced by some neighbouring Queen's County estates. Dublin Castle had the variegated history of being founded by ancient, sea-faring Norsemen, a seat of power for colonial Englishman as well as the site of imprisonment and torture for many an Irishman. It currently housed a powerless Viceroy in the midst of a crisis deaf to General Dunne's agenda.

Before the King arrived on Ireland's shores, Lord Talbot had endured long days with sleepless nights where he worried that the sudden death of Queen Charlotte would prevent the Royal Progress from happening at all. Not only was he relieved that His Majesty arrived as scheduled but was overwhelmed with the earnest outpouring of goodwill from every facet of society. King George was at the head of a 200-carriage parade through the streets of Dublin, had taken in County Kildare's Curragh horse races and visited the lush grounds of Powerscourt in County Wicklow. It was scheduled that from Wicklow the King's entourage would head to Bantry and circle back to Dublin. But the latest dispatch was not oblique in any way announcing a sudden change of plans:

To Talbot, Lord Lieutenant of Ireland, Dublin Castle

August 29, 1821

Dear Lord Talbot,
*   It is with profound regret that I must inform you of the King's decision to abandon plans for the continuation of his tour through County Cork. Please notify all parties affected by this action. I will be accompanying His Majesty to Slane Castle in County Meath for the remainder of his stay.*
*   I have the honour to be, & c.*
*   Lord Forbes at Powerscourt House*

Lord Talbot knew what Slane Castle meant. The Marchioness of Conyngham had accompanied the King throughout his time in Dublin. They had been conducting an indiscreet affair since she wedged out all other courtesans in George's circle of mistresses. She was the one who had his confidence and the one he winked at before he received the crown in Westminster Abbey; a lofty position for a hefty 52-year-old mother of five. Slane Castle was the family seat of her husband Henry Conyngham, who was kept busy with an inflated list of responsibilities back in England.

Decisions made in haste are always difficult for a monarch who has legions of people awaiting his every move but this did not deter King George. He did not care or did not care to understand that loyalty garnered over centuries could be destroyed over one broken dinner engagement.

Lord Talbot was thoroughly ashamed but could not get word to the Earl fast enough and Bantry House was kept oblivious to the King's latest folly. The banquet limped forward as planned.

"Lady Anne allow me to introduce my wee relation here, Master Peter Dunne," said the General.

"Well, how do you do Peter, you are a handsome young man," replied Lady Anne Fitzgerald. He was one of only three other children to be at the banquet yet felt completely at ease among Ireland's elite. Too young to be intimidated and too old to be ignored, it was a fine age to meet a king. And the setting itself had cast a spell over the lad. Perched above the bay with commanding views, the majestic brick mansion put Brittas to shame at every turn. Where the doors of Brittas had cast iron hinges, at Bantry House they were brass. Everything that was made out of tin at Brittas was copper at Bantry House. Silver plate that was so impressive to visitors at Brittas was outshined by the gold plate used by the Earl of Bantry. Why Brittas even smelled old compared to the sweet fragrance of freshly planed oak floors.

Looking about the gathering, Peter worked out the pecking order rather quickly. The ones who received the most deferential treatment were only civil in return. It was like a staged opera to the youngster. He was fully engrossed and took nibbles from passing silver trays. Adults were closing in and at his vantage point he observed at close range detailed embroidery on the pale silk dresses swishing by and gilded details of passing sword handles. All around him, the noisy rustling of taffeta.

Perhaps it was the waiting, or the heat, or the bright blue paint in the dining room that made the great house seem so small that afternoon. Egos and uniforms can shrink a grand space as well. The women had had their fill of tea and the gentlemen were monitoring their intake of punch with their conversations chained up by etiquette. After dispensing with all the niceties they could muster, guests began to wonder out loud if the King was ever invited.

"Should be here momentarily." Peter heard the General make excuse after excuse and he didn't believe any of them. What was going on? Fear welled up inside the beleaguered General just as it had done when his troops were facing danger. Serving as proxy host for his vanished brother-in-law, he declined two conversations in route to search for the Earl. And there he was, Lord Bantry himself appearing at the dining room's far wall flanked by enormous portraits of George III and Queen Charlotte peering out from the cobalt walls. The room fell silent. The music stopped. Voices hushed.

"Her ladyship and I sincerely apologize for keeping you waiting but are in turn thankful and humbled by your presence today. We had confirmation earlier in the week that the King would indeed be here with us but now it seems he has been detained and I have received no word on the reason for his absence. We can only hope and pray that he is out of harm's way and that there has been urgent state business that has kept him away from Bantry. So, please, please be seated and let us carry on...."

The Earl was respectfully solemn but the General's face became as red as his tunic, incandescent with rage. They had both sensed the trepidation from all of Talbot's dispatches, the King obviously had other plans. A lifetime of service to the crown and this was the General's reward? Ireland's reward? The Ascendency that filled the room went back to the party taking no umbrage in the King's rudeness. Though for General Edward Dunne, it would become a pivotal event where he would cast off his blind loyalty to the British Empire and see himself for what he truly was, an Irish Chieftain, one accountable only to his clan. His family had been wronged by the English for the very last time.

Young Peter Dunne reacted with tears, of course, feeling embarrassed for the General. But he took a demented pleasure in seeing such elevated people, aristocrats in their own right, at the mercy of one man's whimsy. Social structure clearly fascinated the boy and he had every intention to climb as high as he could go.

CHAPTER 7

A printed handbill posted on the door of Jim Kennedy's pub in Clonaslee:

Notice to Tenants upon GENERAL DUNNE'S Brittas Estate

The tenants on the estate of General Dunne in the Queen's County are requested to take notice that the rent room at Brittas House will open for the receipt of rents due when it is hoped the following arrangements will be observed between the hours of 10 a.m. and 3 p.m.—

Wednesday, October 29, 1828 – Mór Division:
    (Above 20 statute acres of arable land)
Thursday, October 30 – Lár Division:
    (Above 10 acres & not exceeding 20)
Friday, October 31 – Beag Division:
    (Cabinholders & tenants not exceeding 10 acres)

Mr. P.F. DUNNE, Agent

The soaked streets of Clonaslee were strewn with wayward branches and autumn leaves as the town began to dry out from a fierce four-day storm. Jim Kennedy, a convivial man with sparkling eyes, spectacles and an abundance of red curly hair around the perimeter of his head, was looking forward to his pub once again being filled with patrons. His operation served as a dovetail joint of sorts for the village's various cliques. Its main room featured a handsome counter carved from a single giant oak tree. A scant selection of provisions sold from behind the bar provided rationale for husbands and fathers to step in before heading home, several hours later.

Staggering amounts of whiskey and porter flowed from Kennedy's place every day. On the short wall was the focal point of the room, a chiselled fireplace of Kilkenny marble that had once been in the main hall of Tinnahinch Castle. An inglenook had been built around it with two wooden benches on either side where gossip could be transferred at close range. Next to the inglenook, a rippling green velvet curtain cordoned-off the second room. Affectionately known as The General's Office, it was reserved for the exclusive use of The Landlord and his business. An ancient reach-me-down table from Brittas was at the centre while the Dunne's impressive collection of hunting trophies gazed down from the forest green papered walls.

On this particular afternoon, the General was commingling the cream of Queen's County society with his tenant and houseguest, John Piggot, ahead of the gale days scheduled for the end of the week. The topic of conversation revolved around a former barrister from County Kerry, Daniel O'Connell. He was the Papist's new hero hailed as "The Liberator."

General Dunne had become a silent proponent of Catholic emancipation, giving them back all the rights that had been systematically taken from them since penal times. His heart had been turned against British rule over Ireland since his snub at the Earl of Bantry's disastrous banquet seven years earlier.

Sir Charles Coote of Ballyfin sat next to O'Connell in Parliament and currently sat next to the General interrupting his every word on the matter. A familiar balancing act beset the Lord of Brittas as he tempered his support of O'Connell with his role as a British army officer. Discussions got heated and the Tullamore whiskey Kennedy kept bringing 'round wasn't helping. The publican whispered something in the General's ear, prompting a gruff response:

"Send him in."

"Apologies sir, but he thinks it'd be wiser to meet out by the fire."

"Does he now?"

"Aye sir, he said it could be a sensitive matter."

General Dunne grunted as his belly glided against the edge of the table on its way to the next room where Finlay, the old sexton of the nearby Protestant church was perched on the inglenook bench next to another man. His lips were pursed. The General had been on friendly terms with the caretaker of "his little church" since it was built in 1814 and guessed the sexton must just be too timid to speak in front of the local gentry.

"What is it man?"

"General, as you know, the vicar is away in Dublin during gale days and these winds have just wreaked havoc on our church. Many panes from the coloured windows have blown out, the cellar is flooded and the tin cap has been ripped from the steeple."

"Well, get it repaired as soon as you can and send the bill to the rent room."

"That's not all sir, Larkin here went up to put the topper back on the steeple and found this hidden inside…show him!"

Larkin pulled from his frayed pocket a familiar relic and dangled it before the General's nose. It was a gold chain of eleven black marble beads with a ring at one end and a handsome pewter crucifix on the other; a penal rosary. When the English forbid the use of the rosary in Ireland, Roman Catholics secretly hid this condensed version in their palms and moved the ring down their five fingers to keep track of the decades. Most Irish papists still had one in their family and this one was known to the General as The Plunkett Rosary. It once belonged to his Anglican recusant mother who had been dead these seven years.

As Finlay frowned and Larkin grinned the rosary plot quickly assembled in the General's mind and made perfect sense. After he had refused his mother's request to place a cross above the new church she had found her own way to do it, without him. Finlay too had immediately suspected the doctrinaire dowager of Brittas because the family squabble was quite public at the time. "General, could this jewelry belong to your family?"

Equal amounts of embarrassment and pride swelled up in the old warrior as he imagined his devious little mother conceiving of such a caper and the satisfaction it must have given her to know that the Plunkett Rosary presided at the top of the English church. "It was my mother's" he said without remorse and quickly snatched up the beads from Larkin.

"I must inform the vicar upon his return; he will be quite mortified I can assure you."

"Well now, I don't see any reason for that, 'Where ignorance is bliss, 'tis folly to be wise' they say…"

"I have never been involved in any skilamalink I would keep from Reverend Baldwin and I shall not start now."

"Dear Finlay, it would only upset the man and he would look the fool to his flock, which I can assure you was my mother's intention all along. Add up the repairs, send me the bill and I'll put in a little extra for the damage," the General added with a wink.

Finlay sat stone-faced, waited a moment and said, "I suppose that is the correct thing to do as long as we all swear here and now not to tell a soul."

The men agreed and Finlay hurriedly made his way out of the dark pub bumping a table where the men were playing chess, knocking a pawn and bishop to the floor. Larkin took the opportunity to drift over to the counter and get a little whack before heading back to work. The General followed and tapped Larkin on the shoulder, handing him back the rosary coupled with two gold sovereigns whispering, "Put it back where you found it."

"Nothing would give me greater happiness yer honour."

"That's a good man."

In point of fact, General Dunne and Reverend Baldwin both had their hands in the pockets of the tenants. The General took his rent and the good Reverend took his money in the form of tithes, a compulsory contribution of ten per cent of the annual produce from the farmer. A formidable industry was built around the practice of tithe collecting. At least the rent paid for a plot of land but the tithes went directly into the coffers of the Anglican Church, which provoked the Quakers and Methodists but made the Catholic farmers' blood boil. They were forced to pay for a church that for generations had clinched its heel to their very throats. Throughout Ireland a war was brewing over the collection of tithes and the General's tranquil demesne was about to become a flashpoint.

Gale days at Brittas amounted to a ritualistic trade-off. Once a year the estate's tenantry came up to the big house to pay the rent and were given a meal in return, commensurate with their holdings. Supper was served on Wedgewood china in the dining room to the three most important tenants on the first day with any left-over food reconstituted for consumption by the lesser tenants down the line. Large tenants got a fine claret, middling farmers got whiskey and cottagers got ale.

Mr. Dunne had staged the tradition to make gale days less acrimonious and more celebratory but he knew it was always a struggle to pay the rent. With so much commotion crammed into a few days, something could always go wrong.

He would need help from all of his children. James was only eleven but a hard worker. Bridget had completed her years of school at the Presentation Convent and Peter had exhausted all the local educational opportunities available to him. Having made up his mind he was to be a lawyer, he was looking beyond Queen's County for his next step. Papists were rarely accepted into Ireland's best colleges let alone her law schools.

The antiquated kitchen at Brittas was brimming with commotion on the third morning of gale days. Giant copper kettles simmered over the open fire while cooks cleaned mutton off the bones of yesterday's uneaten scraps and tossed in assorted vegetables to fortify the stew. Mr. Dunne told the staff to prepare for 150 hungry tenants. Mary was chopping carrots at a furious pace as Bridget started washing up dishes in a large metal tub on the stone floor. The General's heir, Frank, was now a Captain in the 7th Dragoon Guards and was summoned back to Brittas to witness how the estate steward orchestrated rent exactions. He was eating a quick bite in the kitchen and on his way out plopped his plate into Bridget's washing tub without a word or salutation. She brushed the suds off her cheek hoping the others hadn't noticed the humiliation.

When she was at school she longed to be home and with the slightest irritation she wished to be right back at school. This loop had repeated itself throughout her convent years but was now bringing her to a crossroads. Girls of the convent not yet engaged looked to a religious life. Although Bridget had become an earnest and devout Catholic she had no such inclinations. The beautiful, confident girl that once ruled over Brittas woods bore little resemblance to the young washerwoman on the floor doing dishes. She had become a downcast, gangly and hollow-looking creature; taller than necessary with greasy skin and unruly hair. She hadn't told her family but fellow students would relentlessly ask her if she had been beaten by the ugly stick.

James was growing into a young bruiser and preferred being outside with the animals. His father wanted to breed the ideal sons and would often pit Peter's intellect against James's hardiness, hoping the boys' traits would rub off on each other. It usually just created rancor and today called for efficiency of the highest order. Peter would assist with the books and James would help the farmhands sort out livestock tenants would bring in lieu of ready cash.

At ten o'clock sharp the first group of tenants appeared with money, pigs, excuses and their wooden plates. Mr. Dunne sat at a wobbly table just outside his rent room door. The General would never go amongst the tenants himself but would observe the spectacle for a little while from his vantage point atop Brittas Tower. His oldest son, Frank, was sitting next to the agent. His upright and haughty military posture telegraphed his supremacy to the others. To the agent's left sat the General's second son, Edward Meadows Dunne. Anglo-Irish aristocrats, if they were lucky, would father an heir, a spare, a barrister and a clergyman. Eddie was to be the spare as well as the barrister and had recently been called up to study law in London at Gray's Inn, one of the four Inns of Court. On this day however, he would be buried in Mr. Dunne's paperwork.

Kitchen helpers brought out kettles of stew to the large gravel forecourt that ran the length of Brittas house and makeshift tables had been set up around the perimeter. It was all a wonderfully arcadian scene except for the red-coated troops of militiamen standing guard as tenants began to cough up their rents. Renters rarely paid in coin but if they did, the money would be shuttled away to the safe under heavy guard. Livestock went right out into the pens of the home farm and arrangements were made for grains or other in-kind payments. It would matter not if they showed up with remittance or a long-winded story, they all got to eat.

Every lower-class tenant had been issued a double-sided, flat wooden plate with slightly curved edges. On one side was a crudely carved oak leaf, on the other side a "D" for Dunne had been burned into the middle with a number. The first side would hold a hardy helping of stew and when finished turned over to receive the pudding.

Throughout the morning and into the afternoon the people came with their offerings and appetites. Rumours had begun to circulate amongst the tenants as they ate their stew. The tithe collector had been seen confiscating the Doolin widow's goats before she could bring them up to Brittas as rent. By law, tithe debt took precedence over any other debt but no one could remember a time when tithes were collected right before a gale day. Reverend Baldwin had attempted to find somewhat honourable men to collect his tithes but the only ones who wanted the vile job were vile people. Tactics such as this signaled a new low.

Bridget was helping serve the tenants' meal when she saw Peter come out of their father's rent room balancing a large stack of leases. A sudden gust of wind blew the papers in all directions. She laughed and made a wry face. Peter yelled, "Bridget, help me get these…." She put her ladle down and went to retrieve the papers that had reached all the way to the edge of the trees. As Peter gathered them back up, he put them in proper order all facing the same direction, Bridget's stack was topsy-turvy.

The children were both on their knees when they were startled by a man rushing out of the woods. His momentum slowed, he stumbled then collapsed face-down right between them. Bridget recoiled and shrieked. Peter instinctively stood up. James came running over followed by a crowd of tenants.

"It's him, that collector!" said one.

"What's gotten into him?" asked another.

Bridget could see the back of the man's head was a bloody mix of brains, shattered skull and clumps of hair, the most horrific sight of her young life.

She froze.

"What's going on here?" said Mr. Dunne as he shoved the onlookers out of the way. He knelt down to get a closer look. Blood was oozing out all over the raked gravel. Reacting as if it were a routine foaling in the barn, he grabbed the white apron off a delirious Bridget and squished it into the cavernous hole, holding it tightly as it instantly turned red.

"Bridget go inside! Peter, run down to the village and get Dr. Ashley, hurry!" Without moving the man, he put his head down closer to the ground revealing to him a face. He knew that face. It was Tim McEvoy and he was surely as dead as a doorknob. Mr. Dunne wondered what kind of an insurrection he was facing as he tried to calm the frenzied tenants.

Soldiers abandoned their posts at the rent table and dashed off, retracing McEvoy's steps. They trampled down the well-worn footpath of soft, bog mould that traversed through the demesne looking for witnesses. Spalpeens and peasants were usually walking the trail but were strangely absent. The sergeant decided to split up the group, rapidly firing off orders: "You two go to town. You two that way. You two come with me." In years past he remembered the tenants would sip their sorrows away on gale days at a little shack by the river known as a shebeen-house. There, they would sell each other homemade poitín and drink until dawn.

Fading sunlight filtered through the dense trees along the sorrel-lined path that lead to the shebeen. Wedged between the trees and shrubs, men in their gray frieze coats loitered outside with tin cups. With a deliberate nonchalance they bobbed their heads slightly as the troops approached then parted like the Red Sea before Moses.

"There's been trouble over at Brittas. What do you know of it?" asked the sergeant.

"Well, we've all had trouble coming up with the General's rent, haven't we?" said the man who looked to be the drunkest.

"I'm not talkin' about the General, I'm talkin' about the tithe collector whose lyin' face-down with a piece of his head gone missing."

"Well, I don't have it. Tom, you got a piece o' head in your pocket there?"

At once the drunk was thrust up against the side of the shack and a bayonet pressed to his throat. His friends moved towards the soldiers but a subtle click from the sergeant's pistol encouraged a second thought. The noise against the rickety wall startled the people inside and they began to pour out into the cramped clearing. Continuing with his questioning, the sergeant wondered how this wretched little hut could hold all those ruffians that suddenly surrounded him.

"Now see here, we don't want no trouble with youse but we need to know what happent to McEvoy. I'm guessin' he came after one a your animals and he got clocked. They'll find out sooner or later so explain now and they'll be reasonable about it." The crowd wedged in closer. "Back off now" commanded the sergeant as he lifted his pistol in the air and fired off a warning shot into the wilderness. From behind he was grabbed around the neck, disarmed of his weapon and pulled to the ground.

As the other soldiers attempted to raise and aim their rifles they were blocked on all sides like rising flood waters engulfing Pharaoh's men. Lacking the training of a proper British soldier, the militiamen were quickly sucked down into the melee and met with the brute force only centuries of pent-up rage and intoxicating courage could provide. Rocks and knives, fists and clubs made Tim McEvoy's injury look superficial.

It was not an unusual sight to see various bodies strewn about the Clodiagh River shebeen on a peaceful Saturday morning but the ones that laid out on All Saints Day, 1828 would not be waking from their stupors.

CHAPTER 8

Letter from the General's second son, Edward Meadows Dunne, to his mother, Frances Dunne

December 10, 1828
Gray's Inn, London

My Dear Mother,

 I arrived back in London and delved headlong into a stack of law books. I hope things have settled down at Brittas since my dreadful visit. Met with Frank last night before he departs with his regiment to the Greek Islands. After all of his military training at Sandhurst it seems they want him to draw up little maps rather than command any troops. He suspects it has something to do with father's handling of the militia in Q.C. and the murders on our grounds. Why haven't they found the culprits? Please don't mention it to anyone, I think Frank was only grousing because he has been mocked quite relentlessly by his chums. They were talking against father using that "Shun-battle Ned" insult again.

 My studies have become terribly difficult and I am simply being run ragged. All the law students from the good families have valets or have hired-boys to fetch things for them and do simple research. I need a gossoon of my own or I think I'll go mad. London is no place to be trapped inside a dreary room washing out one's socks in a basin.

 Please let's talk about this when I come home for Christmas. There are a few festivities here at Gray's that I have been told I should attend but do have Eades pick me up with the landau from Harcourt St. on the morning of the 23th.

 Yours in Haste,
 E.M.D.

Repercussions from the gale day's massacre had been mounting for weeks. A tithe taker, two instigators and three soldiers were murdered with no arrests despite harsh interrogations. Dublin Castle had in their pay a honeycomb of spies throughout the Midlands yet no information

came forth. Increased numbers of troops had fortified the nearest garrison at Tullamore and thrust the sleepy village onto a warlike footing. The streets echoed with military drums and the ear-piecing shrill of fifes put town and county residents on notice; The Midlands would not be allowed to erupt in rebellion.

Armed guards now patrolled the estates of the Big Lords and Brittas was exceptionally secured on direct orders from General Dunne. Every facet of his purview as Protector of Ireland (soldier, tenant, church official) fell victim to violence that day on his own lands. Insurrection had been a top concern for him since 1798 when the island was on the brink of revolution. Services rendered to the Crown in dispatching rebels gained for him considerable merit and distinction in high places. He spent years gaining trust back from the lower ones.

The General was practically barricaded in his gothic library fending off a litany of indictments over his handling of the murders. He was expected to keep his little part of the island subjugated and peaceful. That's what the Empire had groomed him for his entire life and it still held sway over his future as well as his family's.

Reverend Mr. Baldwin, who so gallantly escaped to Dublin during gale days, was leading the charge and wrote a scathing open letter in *The Leinster Journal*. He blamed General Dunne personally for the lack of security in the district and for not supplying his tithe collector with an armed escort as he made his rounds. Baldwin's team of tithe evaluators who went out into the fields to access crops and determine produce values was also insufficiently protected, he claimed. Furthermore, the meddlesome pastor proposed a solution that would alleviate any danger to his tithe collection; have the country's landlords collect the tithes themselves from their tenants and then distribute to the Church. A proposal that would send the General's fellow landlords into a frothy frenzy.

In the meantime, the county's tenants were living in fear knowing murderers lay dormant in their midst. But no one had been held accountable yet. And what would accountability look like? A trial? Transportations? Hangings? Public savagery? Just how could the landlord, who was also the head of the militia and a local magistrate avoid making the final accounting?

General Dunne loved Ireland with his whole heart and soul. At this stage of his life, the only love he had left for England was for her army.

Forty-five years of devoted service to the empire and his single black mark was an absence from Waterloo's battlefield, a point which had been oddly referenced in the latest army dispatch from his Field Marshal. In between the words of concern he sensed a prelude to censure or maybe even a subliminal request to retire and sell his commission. He'd let rumours of his cowardice and the outrageous moniker of "Shun-Battle Ned" go unanswered for years, preferring to ignore such obscenities as an officer and a gentleman. Now at this critical juncture he took pen in hand, ready to set the record straight and righteously defend.

The foundation of the damage began with the election of 1818 when his neighbour and rival for Irish Parliament, Sir Charles Coote, with all the bitterness of an old friend, circulated gossip that the General had refused to fight at Waterloo. Knowing every worthy political opponent needed a scandal and a suitably wicked nickname, he coined the phrase "Shun-Battle Ned" and peddled the myth of Dunne's refusal to fight. The slander would become legendary. They both lost the election to the Duke of Wellington's brother, William Wellesley-Pole. Unfortunately Sir Charles Coote's defamation lived on, reaching beyond Ireland's thirty-two counties to the Palace of Westminster in London. Making matters worse, Margaret Plunkett Dunne, knowing how much the Irish peasantry idolized the hopeful invader Napoleon Bonaparte, thought she could modify the rumour to benefit her son. She concocted a story that when orders came to Brittas for her son to report for battle they were intercepted and ripped to smithereens by his wife Frances. This suited Margaret's cross-purposes of fence-mending to the tenant population while the slur upon her daughter-in-law in the eyes of the gentry was bonus jab. These competing fables swirled and metastasized to the point that the General was heard to have been court-martialled before a military tribunal, only narrowly escaping a guilty verdict.

The plain and simple truth was that the Duke of Wellington had a trail of grand personages trying in vain to make their way onto his staff. He needed generals that were old Peninsular hands to take on the final battle with Napoleon after the Emperor's escape from Elba. General Dunne had esteemed himself senior to the Duke but not nearly as glamorous. He always believed he could have prevented the Irish troops from being used as Waterloo cannon fodder. But alas, someone needed to remain in Ireland to put down the thrashers and Liberty Rangers.

On the parquet floor, next to his souvenir display of cannon balls, scattered wads of stationery lay in ironic silence. His attempts to chronicle the whole affair into a dignified rebuttal became an exasperating study in self-pity. He scrawled out the same beginning words over again then loudly shouted, "Damn it all to hell!" Forcefully shoving himself away from the desk, he quit writing altogether, resigned to whatever fate God or the army or Ireland had in store.

A thin fall of snow had dusted the grounds and buildings of Brittas that December. White against gray accentuated all the contours of the old manor house. It also worked its way into the cracks and damage created by time, revealing an aged noblewoman still stunning but well past her prime.

In a curious twist, the rustic pre-Cromwellian servant's wing with its lovely thatched roof and timber-frames was the picture of light-hearted youth. Inside, the agent's family prepared for the holiday. In the kitchen, Mrs. Miquel, the cook, was asking James a question:

"Como se dice en Español?"

"Wouldn't it be Conteno Navida?"

"No, vuelve a intentarlo."

"Navidad Contento?"

"James dear, we just went through this, *Feliz Navidad!*"

Peter was listening to the lesson and thought he'd add some encouragement, "James, you are dumber than a milk cow." Mrs. Dunne snapped her towel right at the tip of Peter's ear and yelled, "Nobody asked for your opinion El Pro-fessario, now get out!"

"Aye, go away!" said Bridget as she cut up dried plums for the barmbracks.

Peter had learned everything the local teachers could teach, read nearly every book in the General's library and had been routinely annoying his family for lack of more rewarding intellectual pursuits. He was jealous that Mrs. Miquel was teaching James Spanish even though he had all but mastered French. "What need would anyone in Ireland have for a moth-infested old language like Spanish anyhow?" asked Peter as he went back to the main house in search of someone else to ridicule.

James had asked Mrs. Miquel to teach him Spanish not only because he liked the sound of the words but he liked the way she said them. And the way she smelled. And the way she looked. Actually, James had been sweet on Mrs. Miquel ever since he could remember. She was kind and thoughtful, saving him special treats from the fancy dinners she prepared for the General's table.

Delores Miquel arrived at Brittas from a war-torn Spain in 1794 with her young baby boy. There in her tiny Pyrenees village she had met Edward, a dashing, amorous British officer who was assisting the Spanish Army in a clandestine operation against the French. Her patron installed Delores as a kitchen assistant in his Queen's County household. Over time she advanced to head cook with her recipes adding a Continental flair to a culinary wasteland that was the Irish midlands. In her home village of La Jonquera it was common peasant food but for dinner guests at Brittas it was an exotic taste of distant lands. An invitation was rarely declined.

The General's wife did not care for Spanish food, nor the Spanish cook. Since Mrs. Miquel had been a fixture of the place before her own arrival, they had developed a certain détente. When her ladyship entered a room in which the cook was present, the cook must vacate, backing out with head down. Eye contact must be avoided. To Frances, a thoroughly Protestant woman, that crucifix the cook wore around her neck symbolized all the sorceries of Popery and must be hidden out of sight under her apron. The cook must not speak to her ladyship. Notes exchanged via Sneed the butler would be the only form of communication between the two. It was a tortured and awkward procedure that everyone believed was a traditional quirk of all Irish gentry. Making matters worse, Delores at four and fifty seemed to be immune to the effects of age. Her seductive black eyes had not lost their lustre, her olive skin had barely a crease and her svelte figure proved she could sidestep the perils of her own profession.

"Debemos detener la lección por ahora," Mrs. Miquel notified James the lesson was over.

"Gracias, Señora Miquel," James answered back in perfect Spanish.

A knock at the kitchen door usually signalled a tradesman or wandering beggar searching for food scraps so Mrs. Miquel was quite surprised to see the Grand Dame of Gracefield making such a humble entrance. *"Buenos días Señora Miquel!"* bellowed Mrs. Kavanaugh hugging the cook as if she had just been rescued from a deserted island. The two embraced long enough for Mrs. Dunne to be a bit perturbed by the camaraderie displayed between classes.

"Cousin Mollie! And Bridget, my darling, come here!" Mrs. Dunne's frosty bearing melted away with the warm embrace. "I saw Bridget through the window and just had to duck in, I hope you don't mind."

"Not at all, Happy Christmas to you Alicia," said Mrs. Dunne, "Come through to the front room. Ahm, Bridget can you bring in some tea?" The relatives settled into a worn blue settee before the fireplace which was adorned with vases of holly. Bridget placed the tea on a side table and joined Mrs. Miquel in the kitchen to continue with holiday preparations.

As she poured, Mrs. Dunne began, "Tell me all about your latest travels. You've been to the continent again?"

"It's true. I spent the last six months in Spain and travelled to Portugal. It is simply charming." Mrs. Kavanaugh had enough swash-buckling stories to fill a set of novellas but conscientiously spared such elaborations to her cousin, who mostly travelled the distance between the kitchen and its walled garden. Widowed by her mid-thirties, Mrs. K. had been denied the blessings of her own children but closely monitored the progress among the generations of her extended family. "So, I understand Bridget is finished with the Sisters of Stradbally. What are we going to do with her now?"

Mrs. Dunne never really felt like the mistress of her own household and acted very guarded living in General Dunne's Brittas. She had a superficial relationship with the General's wife compelling her to spend her days amongst the servants. She would never gossip or divulge much about her personal life to anyone.

Mrs. K. was different.

She was a devoted listener who would not only hang on every word but would often nudge the conversation along with prompting words and hints. She did not listen out of duty but with a genuine interest. And so Mrs. Dunne explained that her husband had rooted-out a possible match for Bridget in the personage of Fintan Lalor, oldest son of Patt Lalor, a Catholic middleman and "strong farmer." Mr. Dunne had conducted business with Lalor at Queen's County fairs and thought him to be an upright chap with a successful enterprise. From his family residence at Tenakill, south of Brittas, he had acquired leases on hundreds of acres of rich farmland. Patt's lad was 22, had attended Carlow College and supposedly possessed a keen intellect compatible with Bridget's. He was to make a call that afternoon at the lodge and meet Bridget for the first time.

Prosperous Catholic families were few and far between in the backwoods of Ireland. In hushed tones the ladies spoke.

"Since she's been away at the convent she's become quite introverted, ahm, doesn't seem to give a fig about her friends or her family or," her voice lowered an octave, "…her appearance."

"Oh dear lord, but she is a raving beauty!"

"She certainly can be but her life is now spent stuck between the pages of a book. She always saw life in such vivid colours but now I fear all she sees is drab. Ahm, I think she has lost her joie de vivre, as you would remark. Those nuns have taken my strong carroty girl and made her into a dour little religious waif. Now, that Lalor boy is coming here today and she cares more 'bout the amount of fruit in her barmbracks than what her hair looks like."

"We must bring her back from the brink! I have brought lots of pretty things to wear and I've a few secrets up my sleeve. Bring the girl up to my room and we shall see what we can do." With a wink Mrs. Dunne lifted-up her tea cup and took a measured sip.

Mrs. Kavanaugh was given Margaret Plunkett Dunne's former suite for the Christmas holiday. She noticed the fine paintings which used to hang from silk cords were replaced with simple line-engravings. The sun had stolen nearly all pattern from the Dowager's beloved yellow wallpaper. Visible water stains from a leaky roof above the windows got the house guest to wondering.

Mrs. K. was rifling through her wardrobe trunks with wild enthusiasm when Bridget and her mother appeared. Light filled the room as always making it a perfect place for the doyenne of taste to evaluate her young specimen.

"Stand here, Biddy."

Mrs K. encircled Bridget a few times who stood slumped-shouldered in the harsh light. "Make a proud posture, pretend the Mother Superior is coming to inspect your bed." Bridget grinned and straightened up. "You are quite thin dear but what elegant proportions you have. Show your teeth girl!" Bridget complied. "Just so, just so. Those things could light a harbour." She then got uncomfortably close to the girl's face. Bridget had never been fawned over or scrutinized like this before. She quite enjoyed the attention. The way in which Bridget's face had interpreted the Dunne traits of pinkish skin, green eyes and red hair was nearly lyrical and caused Mrs. K. to stare with concentration.

"Lovely, lovely," Mrs. K. slowly repeated.

Undeniably pretty yet there was something preventing Bridget's true beauty from shining through she thought. Something in the eyes. Bridget suddenly decided she felt more comfortable being judged by her intellect rather than her looks. Now she was nervous and a bit irritated. She unknowingly made a scowling expression.

"Do that again." Mrs. K. requested.

"Do what?"

"Make that squint with your eyes."

As she exaggerated her winks, Mrs. K. felt like an absolute imbecile for not noticing a conspicuous problem that she herself shared. Bridget's colouring, as majestic as it was, left her long eyelashes with just a whisper of colour, which blended into her pale skin tone, her pearly teeth and the whites of her eyes. Those gorgeous green eyes had no outline to draw them out. Mrs. K. flashed on a vivid memory of a flamboyant Parisian dresser comparing her own young face to that of a pig. He had created a compound in his studio on the Rue du Bac and applied it to young Alicia's eyelashes on her first visit to France before the Revolution. This heated mixture of lampblack and elderberry juice had a transformational, magical power to bring her face to life. The trio raced back down to the kitchen in search of elderberry preserves.

Normally, visitors to the lodge entered through the front room off the gravel forecourt but Mrs. Kavanaugh thought it best that young Mr. Lalor should arrive through the tower entrance for the full, Dunnes-of-Brittas treatment. Sneed agreed to play along but insisted that he would only open one of the double entry doors as a sign of respect for Her Ladyship's strict societal regimen. He escorted Lalor through the hall and presented him to Mr. & Mrs. Dunne who met him at the doorway to the servant's wing.

Mrs. K.'s new creation was poised on a low chaise in a cream-coloured muslin gown with transparent puffy sleeves and a low neck. A pink satin sash accentuated the tiny circumference of her waist. Regal, yet unaffectedly casual. Her abundance of wavy hair had been swept from her face and collected in an elegantly-shaped heap at the back of her head, tied with a pink grosgrain ribbon. The long, formally-pale eyelashes were now lush and dark framing Bridget's green Irish eyes like the work of art they were. She was lit in a seductive glow from the red rods of turf in the fireplace.

"Bridget, I give you Mr. Fintan Lalor," said Mr. Dunne with the formal voice he used to conduct business.

"How do you do?" Bridget held out her hand just like Mrs. Kavanaugh had suggested and it dangled there in the air for a while before she quickly lurched it back in.

"Hello, apparently our parents want us to meet," said Fintan.

Annoyed that he did not take her hand and bolstered by her new eyelashes she snapped back to her bold self. "Well, we just did!"

Mrs. Dunne who was eavesdropping from the kitchen covered her face in horror.

"Do be seated," instructed Bridget.

"I better not. A little muddy from the ride," said Fintan.

"Suit yourself."

"They tell me you are well-read and a smart student of the world," Fintan continued.

"Yes, so? Would you like me to recite Socrates or something?"

"Would you?"

"Pst," she paused for a moment as if thinking mightily. She already had the quote in her mind but stalled for effect, "I know that I am intelligent because I know that I know nothing."

"You know enough to know you know nothing?" asked Fintan.

"I'm not saying I know nothing, I'm just quoting Socrates."

"Is that to say you're not intelligent?"

Bridget was repulsed and intrigued. He seemed quite sure of himself, which put him at odds with his strange appearance. Although young, he was balding. In addition, he had a crooked nose, patchy long sideburns, huge ears and no neck. On second thought, it wasn't so much the lack of a neck, it might be a hunched back. As Fintan repositioned his stance she got a better look and it was indeed a hunch back which helped distract her, only for a second, from his abnormally long arms.

"Touché, Mr. Lalor." Sympathy had prevented Bridget from continuing with her defiant behaviour. She felt as though a wounded little starling had flown into the house by accident. But now all she wanted was to shoo it back out. "I think we have done our duty by our parents and I bid you a good day." Oh, too harsh, she immediately thought to herself.

"Miss Dunne, perhaps we should start over. As you can see, I am a bumbling sort of bloke and I don't mean to be rude I just wasn't expecting…." he quietly rattled off some phrase in Irish unknown to her. Perhaps she deciphered the word *áilleacht*, Irish for beauty. That is what she decided to believe and did not have the courage to ask him to repeat it.

"I suppose I won't be troubling you any further so I'll just wish you a Happy Christmas then."

Relieved that the encounter was over Bridget got up from her seat to usher Mr. Lalor out the lodge door only to discover she was noticeably taller, adding insult to injury.

A complete mismatch, she thought.

"And Christmas Blessings to you and your family as well," she said with all earnestness. Bridget then watched as he made his way outside, unhitched his horse, clumsily mounted and rode off through the woods. She slowly closed the door and quickly ran up to her room slamming another.

Christmas at Brittas in 1828 followed the usual rituals. The Catholic side of the family bundled up and rode down to midnight mass at St. Manman's. The next morning the General and his family attended Protestant services at his little church which was overcrowded with soldiers from the peace-keeping force. With the older children off on their own, Bridget, Peter, James and a few of the General's children were the only ones left to carry on Christmas traditions. Brought together in the grand room, various conversations could be heard, adults lamenting the passage of time and children grumbling that lunch was late. Plans were being discussed for the new year and Peter was delighted to be informed that he would accompany Eddie back to London. It was explained to Peter that he would assist Eddie in researching case law while getting a taste for the legal profession. Eddie was told Peter would be his errand boy and valet. At first apprehensive, Mr. & Mrs. Dunne were grateful their son had the opportunity to see England and that his future was beginning to take shape away from the place he found so restrictive.

Mrs. Kavanaugh, always excited by new adventures, had travel advice for the boys. Tucked off in a quiet little corner she asked Eddie, who had grown monstrously tall with the build of an ox, "Now, will Peter stay with you at Gray's Inn?"

"Well ma'am, the English students actually board within the school but most of the Irish stay at this ancient building right outside the gates. The skips live on the top floor."

"How lovely," said Mrs. K. as she cast an eye on Peter looking for any reaction to the word skip. A waifish and delicate-looking Peter knew Eddie had a skip when he studied at Trinity College but had always thought the word described a scholarly assistant rather than a servant.

"Oh, but I will be spending most of my time in the law library, aye Eddie?"

"Yes, yes, lots of books to be had," said Eddie.

"Now boys," continued Mrs. K., "When you get off the ship at Holyhead you must stay the night in Llangollen, Wales on your way to London. You can lodge at my late husband's aunt's home. You'll find her most interesting."

"Oh, I think we'll be anxious to get back to school ma'am," said Eddie revolting in the idea of visiting some musty relative.

"No, no, I checked with your mother, there is plenty of time. Anyone who is anyone drops in on the Lady of Llangollen on his way from Ireland. It's a must." Appealing to Eddie's rebellious nature she added, "But you cannot tell your parents." As predicted Eddie's curiosity was sufficiently piqued.

"Is visiting some auld lady now considered bad behaviour?"

"You see she is quite notorious. Her name is Lady Eleanor Butler and she eloped with her lover right out the window of Kilkenny castle then ran off to Wales to live in seclusion. Her father was the Earl of Ormonde and he was mortified."

"I recall meeting the Earl of Ormonde at Bantry House," Peter said in a tone so haughty that Mrs. K. noticeably recoiled.

"How the devil could you remember that, Peter, you were barely auld enough to talk?" said Eddie.

"Indeed, I was nearly nine and I could tell you the exact shade of his tunic."

"Utterly fascinating," said a recovered Mrs. Kavanaugh, "lots of shades of blue bloods there I imagine. So, the two of them were disowned by their families, set up house in this Welsh village and have lived happily ever after. So romantic! Over the years their peaceful little oasis has become a waypoint, so to say, for the libertines, you know… First

Society people coming and going to Ireland. The Duke of Wellington is often there," she interjected in the hopes of tempting young Peter into adding another noble to his collection.

"It sounds entertaining." Peter was willing.

"Is it really on the way to London?" asked a skeptical Eddie.

"Nearly a straight line," insisted Mrs. K.

"For me I don't see the fascination of calling on an elderly couple in exile. And what exactly makes The Lady of Llangollen so interesting after all these years?"

"Well you see it's actually the Ladies of Llangollen."

Eddie thought for a tick and burst out in hysterics.

"Sssh now, be quiet!" said Mrs. K. nervously looking around as if she were planning a bank heist.

"But that is the most ridiculous story I have ever heard! A couple of auld frumps? Really Mrs. K." said Eddie while Peter sat quietly digesting the whole scenario.

"It's all very true and very endearing. They have so many visitors that even people of the highest order are turned away." Trying a different tactic of exclusivity on Eddie.

"What makes you think they will accept us? Asked Peter.

"Not to be vulgar, but the ladies have been living off donations from their flush relatives for years. I've always sent my stipend over—even after my husband passed and I've never been to see them. I want you to go and tell me what it's like. You can be my little snoops. Besides, it will broaden your mind. Maybe you'll meet someone who can set you up in a law office or introduce you to the right people."

"Just the one night then." Eddie relented.

"Glorious! I'll write off a letter of introduction and send it with a little consideration for good measure!"

After lunch was served, Mr. Dunne and Frances were standing in the doorway of the library discussing their special Christmas present to the General. Years earlier Frances' brother, the Earl of Bantry, had sent a small portrait of King George IV to her husband. Ever since, the painting languished on a cellar shelf which personally offended Frances. Unpatriotic and ungrateful was how she viewed her husband's reaction to a thoughtful gift. So, she commissioned a portrait of the General's illustrious ancestor, Cathair Mór, legendary High King of ancient Ireland, to accompany the

King George portrait. A Dublin artist who was restoring the murals at St. Patrick's Cathedral painted it in a naïve style. She had the artist use her husband's likeness as a reference for Cathair who lived in the first century. Power vibrated from the savage depiction of a red-bearded warrior, his shield and sword prepared for battle. The artist not only produced a beautiful painting but he aged it in such a way that it looked like an authentic archaeological treasure. In turn, Mr. Dunne had the talented estate carpenter, Mr. Drady, create an elaborate frame to display both the King of Ireland and the King of Albion together. Sneed and Drady were quietly hanging the double portraits over the mantle in the library.

"Are they finished yet?" Frances asked Mr. Dunne.

"Aye, they are just straightening up."

"I'll fetch him."

An anxious family stood behind General Dunne as he was placed before his Christmas gift hidden behind a drape of blue velvet. France pulled the drape off the portraits eliciting claps and whistles from the assembled crowd. The General was silent but was clearly drawn to the paintings and the intricate custom frame that Mr. Drady had fashioned out of black oak from the Brittas demesne. Mrs. Kavanaugh, standing next to the Irish chieftain, marvelled at the skill of his tenant/wood-worker. She ran her graceful fingers around the Celtic-inspired carvings, "Simply marvellous. Oh, the detail is just scrumptious and look here, it says 'Cathair Mór', he looks like you Edward!"

"The family resemblance is striking, what-what," the General mocked.

"Do you like it?" asked Frances.

"By Jove I do! And I see you finally found a way to get No-Show George to show up." Frances understood that for her husband, a kindness would never be forgotten and a wrong would never be forgiven, it was just how the man was built.

Family members filtered out of the room leaving the General still admiring the stunning creation. Mr. Dunne shut the door behind them and touchingly put his arm on his cousin's shoulder, "And here you are dear friend, stuck in the middle between these two monarchs."

"So it seems," pointing to the warrior King "but a man can only serve one."

"This is true. Though what a perfect thing to hang up here when you are dealing with army business or with sycophants like that Coote."

"Manoeuvring but clever, Mr. Land Agent, I'll give you that."

"Consider it a tool of the trade." He got in close to the General, "Now, when you are all alone in here with your thoughts and your brandy you can press this little shamrock here..." as Mr. Dunne pushed the sculpted button on the frame, concealed gears magically slide the Irish king over the English one revealing a third, hidden portrait. Depicted atop his horse moments before his death at the Battle of Aughrim, was their favourite and common forefather, the legendary Jacobian outlaw Terence Dunne. England's last Catholic King, James II had 800 soldiers stationed at Brittas in 1691 to fight against his rival and nephew William of Orange. Terence and a handful of other Dunnes fought to the finish for their religion and sovereign. When it was all over the Williamites seized the Brittas estates and Terence Dunne was denounced as a traitor of the highest order.

"You scoundrel!" screeched the General as he pressed the shamrock to move the painting back and forward again. And again. And again.

CHAPTER 9

Letter from Alicia Grace Kavanaugh to her late husband's aunt, Lady Eleanor Butler

January 1, 1829
Gracefield, Queen's County

My Dearest Aunt,

It is with great pleasure that I introduce two fine relations of mine, Mr. Edward Meadows Dunne of Brittas and his cousin, Master Peter Dunne. They are descended from and connected to some of the First Families of Ireland. Both are making their way to London where Edward will study law at Gray's Inn. You would do me a great kindness if you should take them in for a night at Plas Newydd. Tho' the lads are young in years they are ancients in understanding and would benefit greatly from getting to know you and Miss Sarah.

Your Loving Niece,
Alicia

P.S. Your legacy is lodged at Mr. LeTouche's and you can draw on it when you chuse.

—A

The Irish Sea had juggled Peter and Eddie around for countless hours before depositing them on the shores of Wales. At 15 it was Peter's first voyage on a real ship and he only felt sick half the time. None of the Dunnes ever did well on the sea. Presently, they were at The Hand Inn awaiting an invitation from the Ladies of Llangollen. The innkeeper, a doddering, snaggle-tooth with a frayed yellow bonnet had been regaling the boys with tales of the gossip house and its famous visitors the ladies had entertained over the years.

"Of course Miss Sarah really rules the roost over there now that Lady Eleanor's blind as a bat. She'd like the looks of you bonny lads if she could see you. Dunno why fair maidens like them two always had an eye for the beautiful boys but they did. I thought hating men was the whole point? They just fawned all over the Duke of Wellington, his gran was their neighbour don't you know. Oh yes, and Lord Byron was there quite a bit before he was carried off by the fever."

"How long do visitors typically wait here before they are allowed to see them?" asked a weary Eddie.

"Well, that's why they have you wait here at The Hand whilst they read your letter of in-tro-duction innit? 'Cause if you gets rejected you can always pay to stay 'ere," the old innkeeper said with a telling grin as the gardener came back with an answer.

"My ladies will see them now."

The gardener grabbed the boys' luggage and carelessly stacked it on a rusty iron hand cart, leading the way out the door into the village. Chimney smoke was spinning up in thick columns from tidy little houses as they made their way through the town. They cut into the woods onto a footpath meticulously lined with blooming white cyclamen plants, no doubt the handiwork of the gardener.

During the walk Peter imagined all the famous poets and statesman that would be hanging on every tantalising word he uttered. Maybe they'd sponsor his education at Oxford once they got a taste of his brilliance? He nervously chatted away to his cousin.

"Eddie, if the Duke of Wellington is there, what would we say to him?"

"I'd ask him about my father and what really happened at Waterloo."

"Oh, wouldn't that be monumental?"

"If it did happen, no one would believe you back home anyway Peter. You aggrandize everything." And with that the boys continued on in silence.

There in the clearing with a backdrop of craggy golden-purple mountains stood the quaint timber and plaster cottage of Plas Newydd, fabled home of the bluestocking sapphists. A broad-shouldered and dour-looking servant woman, hands folded across her chest, met the travellers at the ornately carved entrance door and began shouting orders: "Put their belongings up in the blue room. You boys go in that room there." She pointed straight with a bent finger.

The gardener unloaded the cart and brought the boys' luggage up the dark, narrow staircase made all the more suffocating by intricately carved black wooden walls closing in as far as the eye could see. Peter and Eddie exchanged looks of regret then proceeding to a cramped, low-ceilinged sitting room surrounded by more carved black walls, stacks of newspapers and cabinets crammed full of books, china and whirligigs of every shape and hue. A strange smell of camphor permeated throughout the house. They heard the struggling gardener go up and down the stairs several times bumping the walls along the way.

Two Dunne boys sat fixated on one of the ticking clocks in the corner. Tick. Tick. Tick. Evidently this was not going to be the champagne-soaked Bacchanalia of Britain's brightest lights that had fuelled Peter's imagination. After an excruciating wait, the boys saw two curious figures outside wending up to the house through the murky leaded-glass window.

A tall person with a sportsman's gait was lovingly holding the arm of a slump-shouldered round person, both dressed in dark blue riding habits. On their heads were matching black top hats and on their feet were enormous shoes with brass buckles.

"That's them!" Peter said to Eddie as he lightly tapped at the window.

"Good grief, they look like a couple of fossilized parsons."

The boys heard the clomping of the shoes coming closer and stood up at attention. Then the sound went bashing up the stairs and the visitors got back to the noisy clocks. They wouldn't get another look at the women until they came back down at suppertime.

All were seated at a cramped oak table, the lamplight slicing up the room into faint yellow and brown shadows with the sickening odour of bad food about. Eddie was cursing that daft old Mrs. Kavanaugh in his head and Peter wondered what was to be gained from their visit. Two fine young men and two elderly woman ate and searched for common ground.

"Now, which one of you is the law student?" Lady Eleanor asked not bothering to wait for a response. "Sir Walter Scott once gave me a wonderful book on the foundations of English law I thought you'd find useful. I had Sarah search for it in the library but it must be one of those volumes never to return after being lent out to some ungrateful soul. Makes me so cross," she fumed. Lady Eleanor had a perennial perturbance for lost books she was too blind to read. Peter, trying to never-mind the soup that had spilled on her white silk cravat, interjected:

"I have read through every book in The General's library at Brittas and am very familiar with Sir Walter's own writings."

"I don't know which I like better his poems or his novels. Such talent," said Lady Eleanor.

Every name that Lady Eleanor dropped Peter picked up and polished much to the amusement of the ladies. He had all the makings of a first class suck-up, just what a fading flower of the Georgian-era smart set craved. However, both ladies found the teenager quite engaging and well-bred much to the detriment of Eddie who came off as lack-luster, bored and boring.

Sarah Ponsonby descended from a respected yet non-titled Irish family and was sixteen years younger than her companion. She had always been the quiet, pretty one of the union with her headstrong and prickly senior. Throughout the salon years of famous visitors and worldly conversations her support never wavered as Lady Eleanor spouted off divisive opinions to superior people and condescending demands to subordinate ones. In her evolved role as caretaker to her incapacitated friend and mistress of the manor, Sarah felt obliged to bring in a little tenderness where she could and tonight repeatedly tried to draw Eddie into the erudite banter between Eleanor and Peter.

"Eddie, how was your Christmas?" "Eddie, how do like London?" "Eddie, have you met any pretty girls you fancy?" One-word responses from Eddie made uphill work for Sarah while Eleanor completely forgot he was at the table. Over a meal of roasted goose and hog's pudding, topics ranged from Ireland's Catholic Emancipation, Shakespeare, the Clubs at St. James's, farming and Wellington to the amazing new gas lights at the local cotton factory. Sarah marvelled at Peter's breadth of knowledge and his adept handling of Eleanor's pontificating although she sensed he might trying a bit too hard. He was far too polite to be an actual patrician. Eddie, who did not suffer from the same courteous affliction, took the first opportunity to excuse himself and scamper up to bed leaving the ladies chatting with Peter until eleven o'clock.

To avoid being pressed into another night's stay at Plas Newydd, Eddie roused his cousin at daybreak.

"Get going, we're sneaking out," ordered Eddie as they quickly dressed. "Let's GO!"

"Hang on, how am I supposed to carry everything?" Peter said.

"You're too loud, you're going to wake them, I'll be outside." Eddie made his way out the door undetected leaving most of the luggage with the younger boy to wrangle.

Peter finally balanced everything and tried to be as quiet as one could be when faced with a creaky staircase. Silently he crept down the narrow descent but was startled when he was met at the bottom by Sarah holding a book.

"Well, you young men are getting an early start."

"Good Morning ma'am. Aye, we need to get back to Gray's Inn. Session starts on Monday," Peter whispered.

"I mustn't keep you but wanted you to have one my favourite books. It's a selection of Prose and Verse from Shakespeare. Lord Thurles gave it to us." Facing the approaching twilight of their years together, Sarah had been systematically distributing the ladies' possessions to special visitors. Deserted by their own kin, they had bred a new family of friends from all over the world and Peter was their newest member.

"Oh my lady, this is so precious. Thank you kindly, and for the chance to stay with you and Lady Eleanor. Please give her our thanks as well," said an effusive Peter.

"To Thine Own Self Be True Peter. We must always remember that quote. And I can tell you for one it will not be easy. No, not in the very least." And she placed the gilded book in Peter's hands and gave him an old-fashioned trinity kiss on the top of his head.

"I understand," said Peter with a crimp of the lip and a nod. Her kindness reverberated deeply inside him. Running outside he caught up with Eddie making the turn back into the woods.

"Look what Sarah gave me!" he flashed the book, its gold binding caught a glint of morning sun. Eddie grabbed the book and hurled it far into the woods then thrust Peter to the ground, getting on top of him. He punched his face over and over, spewing red blood out onto the white flowers lining the path. Then Eddie wrapped his gigantic hands around Peter's neck.

"You little maggot pie. Who the hell do you think you are? You're not a noble, you're not a damned law student. You're the son of a servant SPALPEEN. You're NOBODY! I am the son of a chieftain, not you!" And to emphasize the point he slapped the boy as hard as he could on his bloody cheek with the back of his hand. A dumbfounded Peter grimaced in pain. Sarah's kindness had been beaten straight out of him within seconds.

"When we get to London YOU are going to be MY servant. You will wipe my ass, you will fetch me whiskey and find me whores! You will call me Sir and you will tell NO ONE that we are in any way related! Don't use the family name. You're Peter son of a dirt farmer, that's all. Get that through your deluded skull. And the way you bowed and scrapped to those disgusting old perverts sickens me! You're as worthless and revolting as they are." Eddie got up and dusted himself off. Peter tried to get up and was kicked back to the ground three times.

The Honourable Society of Gray's Inn was a small, self-contained sphere set at a deliberate angle to the rest of London with a sterling reputation for producing the finest barristers of the land, back in 1629. By 1829 it was the lowliest among the Four Inns of Court with most of its shabby buildings appearing more like workhouses than exalted palaces of learning. An empty treasury and diminished enrollment forced the institution to take in the least celebrated students; even foreigners; even Irish. Situated a distance away from the other inns, it was well within reach of all the dangers the capital city offered to young men of means. Eddie had kept his behaviour in check while a Trinity student in Dublin, knowing the General had eyes and ears reporting back any damaging news. London was different.

The first three months at Gray's Inn were a blend of drudgery and misery for the young skip Peter. His expectations were bashed out of him on the ground in Wales and he wondered how he would ever extract himself from the situation. He thought about writing about his captivity to the General a thousand times. But after all he was in London. Being a servant wasn't all that bad. He was in fact so good at the domestic chores of housecleaning, laundry and manual labour that Eddie hired him out to do work for other students. Physically demanding indeed but it was the constant harassment and degradation the spindly teenager felt from Eddie and his gang that brought him to a state of wretchedness. Peter thought maybe he could escape but knew he would be just another penniless urchin on the dark streets of London.

After sending his first son to study in England, General Dunne learned that extending credit to such callow creatures was a risky move. This time he set up a system with the family banker, Jeremiah Dunne, giving Eddie a monthly stipend of £13 through the Hibernian Bank out of which he would pay for everything including books, clothes, clubs, food, drink and Peter.

At the beginning of each month Eddie could be found in the gambling and pleasure palaces of the West End riding in open carriages with expensive strumpets. His favourite haunt was a beau monde brothel in St. James known among those who knew as Cousin Tom's. By the end of the month he would send Peter out to the dangerous unlit alleys of the East End to procure cheap whores. Shuffling them in and out of their lodgings was demeaning enough but if the women fell below the standards of Eddie and his mates another sound Irish trouncing would be in store. On a few humiliating evenings they would make a discarded prostitute work over Peter while they all watched and wagered on various aspects and outcomes of the event.

Peter would lay on his bed in the cramped and freezing attic where ghoulish light filtered through the green glass windows of the dormers waiting for the broom handle to thump on the floor as his master beckoned. True to his word, Eddie kept Peter as far away from the study of law as possible going to great lengths; forbidding his entry onto the grounds of Gray's Inn or talking with his classmates, even locking up books and legal papers in his leather trunk when he went out.

The demands of life at law school began to wear on Eddie as the term progressed. The sheer volume of reading necessary for exams was exhausting. Learning to write persuasive and accurate legal briefs was tedious. And in order for a student barrister to be called to the Bar by an Inn of Court one needed to participate in dinners held in Gray's splendid Elizabethan panelled hall. It was expected that Eddie would return to Brittas when elevated to the bar and help his extended family with land issues, wills and the provincial law needs of Queen's County. So bowing over and over to English legal elites at dinners seemed like squandered time.

As winter turned into an early spring things began to change. It started with a thundering noise at 3 o'clock in the morning from Peter's floorboards. Eddie had just gotten in from a boozy night and remembered he had an exam in six hours but he was too cross-eyed to read. Peter was instructed to make coffee and they both sat in ladder back chairs at a small table.

"You need to read to me." Eddie plopped down a book with the invigorating title of *Cases in Crown Law Determined by the Judges from the Fourth Year of George II 1730 to the Present Time, Volume 2* and instructed Peter to read from page 862, Deakin's Case.

"The King against Deakin and Smith. At the Old Bailey in April Session, 1800…." Peter read into the night and would poke at Eddie when he dozed off, quizzing him on salient points. When the time came, the valet dressed the student in his robes and they walked together through the garden of the inn to the examination room.

"Best of luck sir."

"Ta," that word gave Peter all the satisfaction of a fully-executed sneeze.

Eddie attributed his passing grade to his servant's dutiful assistance but would not give Peter the satisfaction of another word of thanks or praise.

As the months wore on at Gray's Inn an uneasy partnership was forged, things weren't perfect, yet there was not to be another beating.

"James where in God's name are you?" shouted Mr. Dunne as he sat eating his stirabout and thick milk before a great turf fire in the kitchen of Brittas lodge. The agent had a long list of chores he needed accomplished by the only two children left at home, Bridget, 19 and the elusive James, now a sturdy 13-year old.

"Father wait just a moment, I think I can find him," Bridget said in a sweet voice. Running upstairs to the boys' room she quietly lifted the covers of the bed skirt to reveal James on the floor reading under the straw-stuffed mattress.

"How long do you plan on avoiding work hiding under here, James?"

"Just until I finish this chapter. Five minutes more."

Mr. Dunne's brood received most of their early education by drafting off tutors the General sent to Brittas to teach his own children. After a time the tutors stopped coming and some of the children went on to local schools with the exception of Bridget who received her education at the Strandbally Convent. Missing out on a lot of higher learning, James' formal education had stopped when the work on the estate took priority. His mother held out hope that he might resume his studies and fulfill her dream of having a priest as a son. James had no interest in saving souls and came to accept what he overheard his father say, "the lad is thick as a brick, he's best suited for farm work." Notwithstanding his perceived lack of intellect, he was a voracious reader like his brother Peter, granted his tastes ran more to adventure novels like James Fenimore Cooper's latest tales of the American wilderness.

"Out you come my little laggard." Bridget grabbed her brother by the foot and tried to pull him out from his hiding place. James clung to the bed as it began to scrap along the pine floor prompting his sister and his hobnailed boot to fly across the room, landing with a crash.

"Oh no, are you hurt?" James asked as he scooting out to her rescue.

"I am terribly damaged."

"Father's auld boots are still a little too big for me I'm afraid."

Muffled hollering came from below. "He is in an aggravated state this morning as you can hear. You'd better get down there."

The General's estate agent had been under increasing pressure to generate more income. He was organizing wagons for a 15-mile caravan to the nearby market town of Maryborough, where he hoped to sell 75 hogs. Rumours were rife in the county about gentlemen from Liverpool buying every hoof and horn in sight, paying heaps more than Irish buyers at local livestock fairs. James and the farmhands would transport the pigs and Bridget was going to be dropped off at Donnelly's Hotel & Tavern. Her sister Mary needed help with the three babies she produced in quick succession after her marriage to a much older Hugh Donnelly. The family lived in cramped quarters above the pub. Hugh and Mary were busy on weekly market days but positively frantic by the time fair days came around, six times a year. Donnelly had erected his handsome new establishment right in the centre of town with a modest inheritance, impressing Mary's father and worrying her mother. She had never met a tavern keeper that couldn't keep his hands off the bottle.

The narrow streets of Maryborough were teaming with livestock, carts, hansoms and people of every description. Leathery shepherds spinning crooks were keeping their sheep in formation with amazing acumen, poets and bards were reciting Ireland's history at street corners. A fair lass set up a booth selling pigeon pies and jugs of porter. Bridget was having difficulty making her way between the makeshift stalls of barkers trying to hock goods and farmers meeting up with old friends. Fetid urine wafted through the air and she skipped over piles of dung that littered the normally tidy town. Hugh Donnelly was outside his hotel leaning against a fancy-looking pilaster, puffing away on a clay pipe. He had been using a broom to swat away wayward cattle and clean the walkway in front of his establishment when he spotted Bridget, ushering her inside. He was a rough and tumble sort of fellow, a bit portly, a bit puffy, but pleasant enough to welcome travellers and oblige drinkers.

Mary, looking ten years older than the last time they'd met, handed Bridget a screaming baby and asked, "By Garra, what took you so long?" She was wearing her dark hair in a long pleat that ran down her back ending at her substantially enlarged derrière. Bridget took notice of her sister's shape as she followed her upstairs to the family quarters where the other two children were crying. A quick run through of the routine and Mrs. Donnelly was back at work tending to lodgers. It wasn't until late in the evening that the two sisters had a chance to sit down and visit over tea.

They raced through all the family gossip. Their brother Michael had married a disagreeable woman and was managing the family farm at Timahoe. Peter and Eddie were still in London, Robert Hedges Dunne was on his way to becoming a Protestant vicar and the other three of the General's sons were in the army. Poor Fanny, his little girl, was frittering away her time at Brittas. "As nice as pie but no one seems to be interested in dessert," Bridget said in an uncharacteristically hurtful tone, accidentally emulating her sister's malicious style. She immediately felt guilty and un-Christian for being so spiteful to a girl who had showed her great kindness throughout her life. So she believed it was her penance when the conversation turned directly to her own marriage prospects.

"I've seen those Lalor boys around town, seems like there's a hundred of 'em," said Mary, "but out of all those strapping young steeds it was the crippled one that was sweet on you wasn't it Biddy?" Bridget blushed with embarrassment.

"Oh, Mary I swear you are so nasty you could eat vinegar with a fork."

"But still…"

"I put him right off. Father was pushing on me but, no, honestly." Fintan Lalor had been writing to Bridget and she had answered one or two of his letters though not sincere nor hearty but he was a relentless suitor. As impassive as she purported to be, she'd kept every single letter in a special box on top of her wardrobe closet. Since college, Fintan had become a downright radical and was associating with O'Connellities who called for sweeping changes to Irish society. Most of his letters droned on and on about political philosophies and reform but woven in between his hysterics and platitudes were poetic verses about her beauty and intellect, claiming she could help him find the answers. She had drifted into romantic little daydreams of her own about being the wife of a professor or famous politician in Dublin or maybe even London then quickly yanked herself back from the brink when she pictured the two of them together. Didn't she deserve someone as attractive as she was? Isn't that her God-given right? Wouldn't a handsome young couple lead a charmed life?

Mary patiently listened to Bridget's prolonged protestations and was confident that her designs for tomorrow's clandestine rendezvous would not be completely ill-favoured.

At fair time the Midlands overflowed with quality cattle, sheep and hogs, so it was difficult for sellers to differentiate their animals above a commodity. Negotiating top price was usually a mixture of bravado and chicanery. However, Mr. Peter Dunne of Brittas and Mr. Patt Lalor of Tenakill had just signed a private treaty with the Liverpool buyers that also the included shipping to England. A network of canals had been engineered following the flood plains of the Barrow River that snaked its way around Queen's County. A waterway dubbed the Grand Canal had just opened through the manufacturing town of Mountmellick and it was quickly becoming the port of choice to get passengers and goods flowing to Dublin and out to the Irish Sea through a rigging of horse-drawn boats.

Taking advantage of General Dunne's connection to the Grand Canal Company, his agent was able to secure a favourable fee for livestock shipping on company barges. At the fair's conclusion, their pigs sold at a reasonable price but it was the supplemental fee Dunne and Lalor added to the drayage that produced for them an astronomical profit. The celebration that followed at Donnelly's Hotel and Tavern was colossal.

"Let's have 'nother round for me boys, man. And you can add that to yer father-in-law's tab," said the notoriously tight-fisted blow hard, Patt Lalor.

"Aye sir, I'm working the barrel as fast as I can," replied a frazzled Hugh from behind his bar. There had never been so many revellers packed into his place and in the middle of it all, Lalor was holding court surrounded by his sons and relations with a smattering of men from Brittas thrown in.

"To be sure it's quite a haul. Now the sadness for you Dunne is you've got to bring all that money back to the General's coffers. What a shame.

An industrious man such as yerself, spent his whole life working for the damned people that have brought this country to rack and ruin."

"Now Patt wait just a minute…" an irritated and inebriated Mr. Dunne had no intention of being lectured to by a man who had just made a pile of money from his enterprising manoeuvres. But it wasn't going to matter what he said, he could not be heard over the din of the crowd cheering Lalor's castigations.

"In this country, the rights of the people are sacrificed and trampled on by a base and sordid aristocracy. And we're expected to support their so-called church with bloody tithes on our animals and grain? We Catholics are getting nailed to the cross all over again just like the Almighty. Times are changing, lads, and we've got to be the ones to say no more. No more I say!"

At this point it sounded like a political rally with a room full of fervent and fermented supporters to cheer him on. Tithes and repeal of the union with England being exclusive topics, in between, songs were sung and glasses were smashed to the floor. Despite the deafening babble, Patt Lalor's roar could be heard above it all. In a dark corner table, all alone, sat his son Fintan saluting, fist thrust high in the air. His own ideas on government were even more radical than his father's. Mary, who had been serving the tables and wiping up spills noticed the poor soul and slunk upstairs.

"I don't know how they can do it but the babies are sleeping through all the hubbub," a relieved Bridget told Mary.

"Right then, come and help. It's pandemonium down there and Hugh is about to burst a blood vessel."

Bridget descended half a flight of stairs before she was immediately taken back to the streets of Clonaslee where she would catch this same peculiar aroma wafting out of Mr. Kennedy's pub. A comforting amalgamation of peat and pipe smoke, beer and sweat rose up from the ground floor. She was escorted by the hand directly to Fintan Lalor's table. "Oh lookie what I found upstairs," Mary said as she practically threw her sister in a chair opposite Fintan. As if on cue, Hugh swung by with two frothy pints and set them in front of the couple.

"Why good evening Miss Dunne, what are you doing in here?" a surprised and delighted Fintan chirped.

"I'm sure you know. Mrs. Donnelly is my sister and I was requisitioned to come here on what looks to be a ruse to help with her nippers. This is quite a stunt."

"Now see here, I had nothing to do with any ruse. I might have known she was your sister but I am with my own kinsfolk celebrating the end of the fair. But I must say you are a sight to behold."

"I bet I'm a sight, being pummelled by kids who dabbled in raspberry jam and custard all day." Bridget nervously tucked some flyaway hair back into her house bonnet. Her dress was sprinkled with assorted stains and she had forgotten to put on her daily eye paint that she discovered right before their first meeting. "So, well, good to see you again Mr. Lalor. I should be getting back to my duties upstairs."

"Oh no, please, uh please. I dreamed of seeing you again and here you are, pretty as a picture. Please sit with me a bit."

"Well, I think it's all a bit too convenient." She looked over at her brother James who appeared to be three sheets to the wind and her father who was surrounded by Lalor boys. Mr. Dunne turned his head with bleary eyes, tried to focus on his daughter, then lifted up a half empty glass in mock salute. He was in on the fix and Bridget was furious. Taking a breath, she took a stand of her own and decided to stay, drink and avoid any further work upstairs.

"We're all getting wound up in here about the tithes and the aristos."

"It seems you spend a lot of time getting wound up about things you can't control Mr. Lalor."

"Aye, we aim to control it soon enough. We are growing in numbers and in power. We are ready to take on the gentry, half of which are just greedy pigs."

"Take that back! You don't know what you're talking about."

"I apologize. Half the gentry are not greedy pigs."

"Pst."

"We might see things a tad differently Miss Dunne. Take our two stouts here." Fintan picked up a spoon and scooped out all the foam from Bridget's drink. "You may see your dear aristocracy as the cream of the crop so to speak, sitting on top of everything like this." He put the spoon in his mouth and smacked his lips. "But to me it has no taste, no substance at all, full of air, doesn't really do anything but sit here and look tasty. The real heart of the drink is this brown mucky bit down here. This is the sweet sustenance that fills you up, makes you warm and sing like the people in this room. To me, the top is not the cream of the crop at all, it's surface scum." At which point he blew off the head of his beer narrowly missing Bridget's already stained frock. She put her dainty fingers up to her mouth and giggled at such roguish behaviour coming from such a solemn soul. They continued with their back-and-forth jibes to the point Bridget was actually enjoying their conversations. She liked him.

Donnelly's place was now so crammed with drinkers that the couple got lightly jostled in their chairs and it was getting harder to hear each other above the din. Fintan kept asking Bridget to repeat every little thing she said until she was practically yelling. Of course it was loud but she wondered if he, in addition to all of his physical abnormalities, was deaf too. A pack of burly young men dressed in similar frieze coats and corduroy started gathering behind Fintan. Bridget bristled. They were trying to listen in and soon began taunting him.

"Ain't this a pretty picture?"

"What the hell is going on here?"

"Aye Billy, look at your brother with the comely lady. What a sight!"

Catcalls and jeers from the rest of the gang added to the tension. Fintan tried to warn his brothers and cousins to sod off when three of them picked up the feeble suitor and pushed his face close into Bridget's.

"Why don't you give her a little kissy-kiss like a real man?" his brother Joseph needled. Fintan struggled to break loose before Bridget, disgusted and upset, bolted upstairs.

A game of Ireland's Troubles and Drunkard's Solutions then played out between the revellers. Brash intentions and outright sedition plans carried on far into the night until the next morning when the streets of Maryborough sprung to life again. The air was crisp and light with a slight overnight fall of snow on the ground. Tents and booths were being disassembled, livestock was crowding the lanes and alleys with horse-drawn carts bringing fairgoers back to their towns and villages. At the courthouse, an early meeting had been called by Sheriff Kelly to discuss the repeal of the union and parliamentary reform.

The hell raisers from Donnelly's place had a thing or two to say En masse they poured out of the tavern into the streets and headed off to the courthouse around a corner. The meeting was already in session. Formal speeches, elegant soliloquies and gentlemanly manners all within the dignity of a beautiful courtroom helped to take the edge off the revolutionary zeal exhibited by the Lalor gang hours before. Each speaker was allowed to be heard and politely applauded. It was only when the sheriff called on Mr. Patrick Lalor of Tenakill that the gathering took a dramatic turn.

He walked over to the lectern looking a bit rumbled from the night's celebrating but stone cold sober. He removed his hat and adjusted his neckerchief. He began by praising his friend Daniel O'Connell and the work he was currently doing in Parliament to give voice to the majority of Ireland's people. And then he defiantly fired the opening salvo:

> "I declare before you good people of Queen's County that I will never again pay a penny in tithes to some foreign faith. Understand what I say – I never will again pay tithe! I will obstruct no law. I will put up no fight. The tithe men can come and seize my property and offer it for sale if they like. But I am proud to say my countrymen respect me and they will not find a bidder or a buyer in all the land. We shall be a society of friends leagued against oppression and unjust exaction."

Silence befell the courtroom. A prominent, intrepid citizen of the County had declared, before witnesses, his act of defiance against the Church of Ireland and the government that backed it. Murmurs and whispers began in the gallery gradually transforming into "huzzahs" and "hear, hears" in the back. As the crowd began to realize the significance of the moment it erupted into euphoric excitement and thunderous applause. The Tithe Wars of the Midlands had officially begun and a fissure was forming that would eventually break apart the Dunne family of Brittas.

CHAPTER 10

Excerpt from an article titled "Happenings in Europe," *The Evening Post*, New York

April 16, 1831

We've been excitedly following the story of Patrick Lalor of Queen's County, Ireland who, after declaring his refusal to pay his fair share of Church tithes, had 25 of his sheep confiscated as payment. Before the animals were seized, the clever Irishman branded the entire side of his sheep with large block letters spelling out T-I-T-H-E. His relations and countrymen procured and distributed a large quantity of tin horns and spread word throughout the county to boycott any sale of the TITHE sheep. Whenever the sheep were discovered moving about, the tin horns sounded. Even the bargain hunters at Smithfield Market in Dublin refused to bid on the tainted flock. Apparently the animals all died out after they were sent to Mother Albion by their frustrated sellers. We're guessing the Irish are learning something from their American cousins and want a little separation from their Church and their State.

After 50 years of service to the crown, General Edward Dunne retired from the British army. He was feted with a banquet at Horse's Guard in London, a resplendent reception at Dublin's Kildare Street Club and a homecoming through the streets of Clonsalee where townspeople had erected an impressive laurel arch under which the General passed in his hansom up to the family seat at Brittas.

Nearing 70 years of age, he was still robust and vital, loathing the whole idea of retirement. He felt it was a compulsion thrust on him by an army that disapproved of his anemic response to the tithe murders on his estate three years earlier. He might have pursued the case with more voracity but the suicide of a troublesome tenant involved in the incident provided an opportune excuse to close down the investigation. The General had no desire to see any local people drawn and quartered. He would need every vote for his next run at politics.

Jeremiah Dunne, the Dublin banker and family member was seated in the General's library discussing options for unearthing the electioneering funds needed to win a seat in parliament representing Queen's County.

"Now the way I see it sir, you are going to have to come up with at least £5,000 to attract decent influence from the top down. You know money is tossed to and fro like hayseed in these elections. Surely Sir Charles Coote will run again especially with the size of his war chest. Don't you agree?" asked Jeremiah.

The General had a slight delay in answering. He hadn't seen the man in years and was busy scrutinizing the dandy he had become. Darker than any of the other Dunnes, he had large brown eyes with striking aquiline features. He wore the perfectly tied cravat, groomed side-whiskers that came to a sharp point at his cleft chin and he had an odd cut to his coat that the General assumed must be the latest fashion. He was especially annoyed with the moiré silk waistcoat that slightly creased onto his flat, concave abdomen. He himself was feeling a bit constricted by his own tweed hunting vest and decided to unbutton it.

"Yes, I think Coote will stand again. Most of the snobs will be with him."

"And he has twice your fortune with half your merit," added the banker.

"The devil doubt you, but I don't. I'd like to concentrate on getting all those Catholic votes Coote won't. There are tactics in these matters. I'm a law and order man but I'm not some English transplant, I am an Irish chieftain. I've been governing these people in my own way for a very long time. I think they respect me. For weal or woe I've been through it with them like a father. Besides, half the county's got the last name Dunne."

"It's a different game than it used to be. You can't just go by auld alliances or buy a borough. The Catholic priests are influencing the rank and smell from the pulpit and they want a candidate that will get rid of tithes, support a new, purely Irish parliament and…frankly, loosen the grip of…forgive me sir, the landlords. They feel the English have no understanding of them."

"There's plenty of poor people in England…."

"Between the poorest of English peasants and the Irish ones there's ample room for ten or twelve degrees of poverty, sir."

"I suppose I must thank you for your candour Jeremiah; a bit of straight talk, yes. If I'm going to win I'll need to be up on all the latest thinking from young minds such as yours. I imagine I have much to learn and at the same time, much to forget. But you must remember I once had a seat in the auld Irish parliament and voted for the union in 1800. I believed then, as I do now, that we get better representation in the English commons— paid us no heed whatever 'till we faced them down directly in Westminster."

"People don't remember it like that these days. They think you were all paid your £8,000 and herded into our Parliament for the last time to vote for its demise."

"Hogwash!"

"Well, you must agree that Ireland should have received at least a 30% representation based on our population but we were given a paltry 15% minority."

The General reluctantly agreed with a slight nod.

"Some people feel it was just a ploy to pawn off surplus goods onto the Irish market. Mr. O'Connell believes the union cost Ireland 90 million pounds of revenue and caused our industries to collapse. They want autonomy back."

"Damn it lad, your phrasing comes straight out of some penny pamphlet! These blasted renegades who want to repeal the union with England are taking on a lion they aren't equipped to fight. They need to work through the appropriate channels and stop trying to intimidate everyone with their thuggish behaviour, their, their sinister attacks!"

"General, I know you've the good of the people in your heart but—"

"I am just a sound voice of reason. They ought to slow down and realize if they're going to demand some kind of revolution it could lead to the ruin of all the classes; instability, invasion, starvation…death. For my part, I'm just hoping to keep them all alive and fed while keeping myself solvent."

"I think you've worked out your first campaign speech, sir." Jeremiah said, thinking the General now had more than enough rope. The two of them talked financing and forecasting until mid-afternoon when Jeremiah said he must be on his way. They walked out the tower entrance and the General waved him off into an awaiting phaeton feeling ennobled and inept in equal proportions. As it rolled over mounds of fallen leaves past Brittas gate the banker yelled out from the cab to the driver, "On to Tenakill."

O'Connell "The Liberator" had vast plans for Ireland across her financial, religious and political divides. He needed compatriots in Parliament that believed in his vision and would follow his legislative agenda. Patrick Lalor was the man of the moment and had made a name for himself in his tithe battle, an issue at the very top of the agenda. Lalor knew where the shoe pinched his unfortunate fellow countrymen. He seemed to have the gift of Blarney about him and a true Irishman to the bone. But would Queen's County have the fortitude to return another Catholic to parliament? For safety's measure, O'Connell and his electioneering committee were also eyeing a liberal magistrate and Protestant country gentleman named Peter Gale of Ashfield Hall if the choice of Lalor proved too radical.

Upon Bridget's return from her time with the Donnellys she had kept up a steady correspondence with Patt Lalor's son Fintan, although she was far from smitten. In a few short months, she had been transformed from a gangly and awkward product of Stradbally nuns to a captivating beauty. Although she spent much of her time wearing an apron or work boots around Brittas, she had a regal bearing about her that was undeniable.

Mr. & Mrs. Dunne now raised their expectations for Bridget's future as all of her womanly charms came into full fruition. Her intelligence was profound, obvious and practical. She fully comprehended the complicated, intellectual manifestos Fintan wrote from Tenakill's attic but preferred application over theory. At the moment she was ruminating, analysing and perfecting her recipe for butter, a product much desired by every class of Irishmen. She had learned the process of butter making from her mother and now had surpassed her in talent and skill. Her father had allowed her to keep all the money she was making from her efforts and it was becoming an enterprise unto itself.

A traditional necessity of the Celtic diet, butter added richness to the diets of those who couldn't afford much meat. Bridget had invented specific techniques of churning her butter and continually scrutinized the quality of her only ingredients; butter cream and salt. Laborious experimentation led her to believe cream from Guernsey cow's milk was more flavourful than that of the Friesian. Salt mined from the Atlantic Ocean at Cork City was plentiful and cheap but she preferred the salt from the Irish Sea. A shop in Mountmellick sold a variety from County

Wexford that she found to be powerful and perfect. It was a little gray and coarse but she liked the way the crystals burst onto her tongue. So many young men were clambering up to the kitchen door to buy butter from Bridget that her mother and Mrs. Miquel were getting interrupted throughout the day.

"I've never seen such a thing, why don't their mothers come to buy the butter?" asked a perplexed Mrs. Miquel.

"Ahm, they would if you and I were handing it to them," observed Mrs. Dunne.

"Ay! What an auld fool I've become."

Yet another knock came at the kitchen door and Mrs. Miquel could see through the lace curtain it was James.

"*¿Por qué esta puerta siempre está cerrada?*"

"*Los extraños siguen subiendo y piden la mantequilla.*"

Mrs. Miquel had refused to listen or answer to James in English after she had given him rudimentary Spanish lessons. She took great pride in his fluency.

"Father wants to see Bridget in the rent room," he said in English for the benefit of Mrs. Dunne.

In the cold office, Bridget could not find a clear place on her father's desk to rest her hands so she kept them folded in her lap. He had that serious look on his face as he peered over his reading glasses. "Seems your butter is more popular than whiskey around here," Mr. Dunne said with a smile.

"Aye, the word is spreading."

"Clever. So, I've seen a few letters going back and forward between you and that Fintan Lalor of Tenakill. What is the nature of these letters?"

"He is very interesting. He writes a lot about the changes he'd like to see. He wants to improve the country."

"What else does he want? Does he want you? More importantly, do you want him?"

"Oh, please no, nothing of the kind. He is a strange little man."

"I am glad to hear it. He's a radical and sure to be hung anyhow. You know his father is taking a run for parliament and he is going up against the General."

"Of course, the whole county is talking about it."

"Nothing could be worse for all the gossips than having a Dunne girl being courted by a Lalor boy. Couldn't have it."

"I never thought of that."

"Better start thinking of that. You need to stop writing to him and have all his letters sent back. He needs to bugger off and bugger off quick," Mr. Dunne said with a considerable amount of heat.

Back in the dairy behind her father's rent room Bridget thought about their exchange. Churning away at her butter she started to make herself annoyed, then agitated, then angry, working herself up into a full-blown fury. Her slender figure, wrapped in a dark gray woolen coat, hovered over the churn in a curious posture. Her frantic churning motions made the bright red plume of hair bunched up on top of her head flicker like a flame, giving the impression of a blasting artillery cannon.

For some time now she had unsuccessfully tried to convince herself of Fintan's appeal. She couldn't quite envision their coupling, it was a bruise to her vanity. But now, she imagined strong forces conspiring against her happiness. She thought about all the books she had read about destiny, providence, forbidden love. What could be more romantic? Forget about her heart, her mind was made up, she was in love with Fintan. No longer a child, she was at that curious stage of womanhood where she remained untested by experience and believed anything was possible. Only maturity would prove to her it was not.

In the general election of 1832, many Irish MPs faced no contest in their districts and could plan on being returned to Parliament unopposed. Others had weak opponents. But in Queen's County, four very different individuals and ideologies would compete for voters. Peter Gale concentrated on campaigning at Anglican churches. Since the tithe wars began, it was nearly impossible for any Church of Ireland clergymen to collect his salary derived from tithes. The church now faced arrears of nearly £2 million and Gale was proposing pathways to placate Catholics without giving too much away.

Sir Charles Coote held elegant soirees at his luxurious Ballyfin showhouse, twelve miles from Brittas. He entertained local aristocracy with unionist promises of a greater role for the Monarch and the Anglican Church, increased military security and lower taxes in exchange for large sums of cash he could use to buy votes. He would provide transportation for tenants to get to the polls and ply them with drink and food, squeezing as many votes as possible from each man.

General Dunne opted for the pageantry of a parade through Clonaslee where he would ride on horseback followed by his 400 tenants. His pledge to maintain the status quo held quite a bit of appeal for those who weren't paying attention.

Although O'Connell advocated and Lalor demonstrated a Quaker-inspired, non-violent protest in his anti-tithe pledge, violence was erupting throughout the country. Tithe-proctors were visited nightly by men in blackened faces threatening death if they carried out their duties. Villagers had banned together hooting and pelting tithe men out of their parishes. Threats were now being levelled at persons paying their tithes. Sporadic murders were followed by an all-out massacre in nearby County Kilkenny. And yet, a campaigning Patt Lalor defiantly called for an open-air rally in the market square of Maryborough, welcoming the chance to dance a jig on a lit powder keg.

Bridget had come back to Donnelly's Hotel and witnessed from the second-floor window a processional ushering candidate Lalor to the centre of town. Cottiers and shopkeepers, widows and woodworkers, gentlemen farmers and agitators were among the throngs of people passing by the hotel, ready to hear what the chief tithe protester had to say. Bridget called her sister over to the window.

"Mary, look. They can hardly move through the street. Is no one working today? Why the devil are they carrying those bushes and branches? That one there has a whole tree! It looks like a walking forest."

"I have no earthly idea, they look like fools, the lot of 'em," replied a weary Mary.

It was unlawful for anyone at a public demonstration to bear or wear any flag or emblem that might provoke sectarian animosity; especially the green flag of sedition carried in past rebellions. Crafty tithe protesters and repealers substituted actual greenery for the green flag with the symbolism being lost on but a few.

"Biddy, I know what you're doing. Get away from that window now and help me," Mary said as she grabbed her by the arm.

"Your tavern could soon be packed with these rabble-rousers. I'm thinking you might want to board up your windows rather than open up your doors!"

"Hugh already set up a tent down there hoping he could keep the drinking at bay but we better get ready for 'em just in case. I can't see your delicate little Fintan fairing too well with that mob, maybe we could at least let him in...."

"Do you think he's here?"

"Ah ha! I knew it. You're still in touch with him!"

"I am not. Father won't allow it."

"If I know you, Bridget Dunne, that won't stop you much."

In Market Square a makeshift stage had been set up with pine boughs forming a backdrop upon which a huge banner was displayed reading "Elect Honest Patt Lalor." At the front stood a podium surrounded by large crocks of shamrocks. People crowded around the stage holding up their own T-I-T-H-E branding irons. Tree branches and bushes were waved in the air as local dignitaries who wanted the public's attention took turns issuing vehement statements and resolutions in the run up to the candidate's introduction. Hidden from the public behind the backdrop, men of industry dressed in broad cloth and top hats paid their respect and their dues. Farmers weren't the only constituents in the county, for all factions knew a local voice at Westminster would better their chances of pulling from the public purse.

Before the crowd got too drunk or listless, Honest Patt Lalor took his place behind the podium. For a newcomer to politics it was quite remarkable how he mastered the sport. He covered all the outstanding issues facing the county, placing heavy emphasis on his own tithe protest which sent the audience into a bout of hysterics. Promises and platitudes were spewed out into an adoring sea of support. He put into words what they yearned for in their hearts. They wanted the future he was describing. He concluded his campaign speech with a humorous lampooning of his opponents, dredging up a scorching castigation for "his honour," General Edward Dunne:

"I was never more surprised in me life than to hear of an aged ol' British general what thinks he can represent the good people of this county. To be sure, he served his master well, he did. He waged war on us for years! Any man that called for change was locked up, sliced up or hung up! He relished it, oh, the power. Seems he'd rather put a boot to the throat of his tenants than to go fight like a real soldier against a real enemy. They don't call him Shun Battle Ned for nothing!"

It was an everlasting credit to Patt Lalor that he quit his speech while he was ahead, leaving the mob in a state of euphoria rather than seething anger. Peaceably disassembling, they happily made their way home or into Donnelly's tavern much to the relief of the constabulary headquartered across the street.

The next morning Mary woke up Bridget squishing a crying baby into her face, "Can you make them some breakfast, I'm still cleaning downstairs?" With one eye still shut she calmly took the baby and said "Well, mornin' to you, bright eyes."

"I've got to get everything back in order. Hugh has to leave. There is nearly a hogshead worth of ale the Lalor people bought for the rally that wasn't drunk. That chap Honest Pat is so mean he won't even tip his hat. He wants all the ale back so Hugh's got to drive it out to Tenakill this morning. If you get the children settled maybe you could go out with him…" Mary said.

"You mean just turn up?"

"Why not? You'd be helping your brother-in-law. No harm in that."

"Bedad, no one is going to believe I can lift a keg."

"No, you could steady the horse while the men unload. Makes perfect sense."

Tenakill was a three-story stone farmhouse that sat on a beautiful western bluff of Queen's County. Its marked characteristic was a side of bricked-up windows, a result of a window tax imposed by the Crown on Ireland to fund the war with Napoleon. By blocking off unnecessary windows the previous generation had poked a finger in the eye of the King but left the house dark and gloomy. A landmark of protest itself, the house currently served as Patt Lalor's election headquarters and was a bustling place after the rally. Handsome carriages not usually seen in this part of the county brought important personages to meet with the candidate. Hugh's donkey cart had to pull off the road several times to make way before finally driving through the front gate into a farmyard of loose chickens and burly workmen. One of them took Hugh's horse by the bridle and led him to a dilapidated outbuilding where he was tied.

"Hugh Donnelly here, delivering some leftover ale from the refreshment tent at the rally."

"Very good, I'll get some help to unload it," said a farm hand.

"Tell me, do you know if Fintan Lalor is here?" Bridget coyly asked.

"Most likely, he's always up in his room. Doesn't really help out down here."

"Would you mind collecting him for me too?" said Hugh.

"I'll go see if I can find him."

Hugh helped Bridget down from the cart and she nervously strolled about the yard waiting to see if the scribe of Tenakill would appear. Her eyes kept darting around at the various men passing by as they worked the farm. Some of them were familiar to her from her time at Donnelly's, the night of the big fair celebration; the faces that so mercilessly teased Fintan were etched into her memory. Their brutality had repulsed her when contrasted with Fintan's helplessness but had also aroused her in a wanton, primal way. Remembering every second of that night, she was thrust back to reality as Fintan himself stood in front of her. In the cold light of day he was everything she never wanted in a man.

"I am beyond words to see you here at Tenakill, in the flesh," a mawkish yet excited Fintan exclaimed.

"Hugh is bringing me onto Mountrath for some provisions so it was convenient," Bridget lied right through her perfect teeth.

"Let me show you the house, you can meet father."

"Oh no, that would not be a good idea. I just thought I would say hello to you and be on my way. But, uh, what does your father know of me?"

"When I am not talking about Ireland I am talking of you."

Bridget got a deep pang in the bottom of her stomach. What was she thinking coming to this place? It was all wrong. A passing whim. She had stolen the affections of a man she didn't and couldn't love.

"Hugh, let us be off, have they unloaded the cart yet?" she yelled.

"Oh no, please don't leave, you just arrived."

She continued walking back to the donkey cart while Fintan followed after her like a lost puppy dog. Hugh had reins in hand ready to shove off as the last barrel was pulled from the back.

"Won't you stay, I can have some tea brought out to the garden. You won't have to meet anyone."

"No thank you Fintan, we really must be going but thank you ever so much for your hospitality," said a mortified and embarrassed young fool.

Fintan did his best to gallantly help Bridget to her seat next to Hugh but she pulled herself up and he was indeed no help whatsoever. He kept his gaze upon her as she stared straight ahead with shoulders back waiting to be extricated. Pulling away the donkey brayed and swished her tail. A forlorn Fintan moved his fingers back and forward at the knuckles in a sad little wave as the cart moved out of his sight.

The front gate was closed and an alert young man who had been cutting twine came running up to help. Before he opened the gate he brazenly bounced onto the wheel hub and offered Bridget his hand, "Hello, I am Patrick." Taken aback by his interception she was momentarily speechless.

"Hello Patrick, are you going to open that gate?" blurted a disgruntled Hugh.

"Absolutely sir, but I couldn't let such a beautiful bird fly by my face without introducing myself."

"Well done, now open that gate."

Bridget composed herself enough to put out a delicate gloved hand, which was quickly engulfed by Patrick's powerful grip.

"How do you do, I am Bridget, Bridget Dunne."

"Pleased to meet you miss. I've seen you at Donnelly's."

"Aye, Hugh here is my brother-in-law."

"I see. Patt Lalor's my father's cousin." Pointing over to the stone house, "This used to be my grandfather's place but my family lives in County Kildare now."

"A bit far from here." Bridget said as she sized up the man.

"No not really, just over the border near Athy. I had to come for the big rally yesterday, what a show."

"So I heard," said Bridget in a tone not of a congratulatory nature.

"The gate, sir," repeated Donnelly.

"Apologies, right away."

Patrick jumped down from the cart then hopped up on the gate's bottom rail clinching a buck knife in his teeth. With a mighty push he rode the slowly swinging gate, tipping his hat and flashing a smile in her direction with all the mannerisms of a corsair on the high seas. She nodded and met his eyes directly as the rickety old donkey cart passed out of Tenakill.

It would be remembered as a rather magical twinkle in time.

In the final weeks of the campaign the newspapers were writing of nothing else but the huge crowds attending the glorious speeches of Honest Patt Lalor, provoking an ecclesiastical emergency among the Anglican ministers. General Dunne was summoned to the Glebe House in Clonaslee for a meeting which he countered with an alternate invitation to join him at his back room in Kennedy's pub. At this stage of the race he could not be seen waltzing into a house built on tithes, besides, he would enjoy the little poke of having the holy men walk through the "Devil's Den."

When Rev. Baldwin pulled back the green velvet curtain of the General's unofficial office a steady stream of sour-faced men entered and filled their places around the table. The curtain was snapped back together with such force the brass rings clanked and chimed. General Dunne knew all of these men and was much impressed by their presence in his backwoods town. There was the Reverend John LaTouche and his brother, private banker to the aristocracy, Robert LaTouche. A few attorneys he recognized from the Kildare Street Club and the Anglican Bishop, Robert Fowler. He suspected they had abandoned their support for Sir Charles Coote and were ready to endorse his candidacy.

"Good afternoon gentlemen, and to what do I owe this auspicious gathering of such luminaries?"

"We've come to you with disturbing news that could affect the outcome of the election," said Rev. Baldwin. "I am sure you have heard the defamatory language Lalor is using against you at these idiotic rallies of his."

"What of it? I've called him, let us see, a blockhead, a blow hard, the village idiot, oh, and a rural agitator of the lowest order. I've been having a go at all of them and quite enjoying it."

"He's a little man that can cause big troubles," Bishop Fowler retorted. "At this rate, Lalor will be elected over any of you!"

"Have you seen the outpouring of support I have among my tenantry?"

One of the LaTouche's attorneys began to school the General in a most patronizing screed, "I'm not sure if you are aware of the recent changes to the election by-laws sir. These so-called 40-shilling leaseholders you trumpet cannot vote, the new law requires holdings of at least £10, rendering most of your tenants useless to you." The General's blank stare revealed his ignorance.

Hoping to save the General from prolonged embarrassment Rev. Baldwin proposed a solution.

"Now this might be able to change things. I hold in my hand a document proving this Honest Patt Lalor is nothing but a fantastic fraud."

"What's it say?"

"This was given to me by the Sequestrator of Mountrath declaring that a good deal of the uproar Lalor is stirring up comes from the fact that he applied for the position of Tithe Commissioner himself and was turned down by Rev. Harper."

Digesting the news for a moment the General said, "This all sounds like a bloody rumour. You know the three things that run the swiftest are a stream of fire, a stream of water and a stream of lies—believe me I know."

"It's all true. That post paid £1 a day and Lalor wanted the money."

One could hear Rev. Baldwins's axe grind as Rev. La Touche explained the situation to the General. After all, it was tithes Lalor owed him that started this ghastly movement in the first place. He urged the General, "You must bring this to the public's attention at once."

"I say now, does this righteous little committee think it is far too sordid for Sir Charles to offer this evidence to the newspapers?"

"We think you can act as the conscience of Queen's County, no one is more august than yourself," said Baldwin. The General sat quietly for a moment, unconsciously holding his hand over his mouth.

"May I have a look?" Baldwin handed him the document. The General put on his square-rimmed reading glasses and read through the charges. It appeared legitimate but he was leery of Greeks bearing gifts. "I'll have to take this under advisement and deliver my decision to you tomorrow."

The attorneys quickly offered their expert opinions, "We need not remind you that time is of the essence sir."

"Tomorrow. Now, will there be anything else?" The meeting adjourned and the General rode back to Brittas on horseback to plan his next move.

His faithful wife Frances was there to meet him the moment he came through the door. Her excitement about the meeting quietly eroded after looking into his face. She tightly wrapped her arms around him. He remained unresponsive, dropping his riding whip to the floor. The entwined couple stayed locked in their embrace until Frances broke the silence, "Are you going to go have a talk with yourself?"

"I'll talk but whether I'll listen is another story."

The General handed Sneed his riding gear then shuffled down the corridor to his library sanctuary. Pouring himself a brandy, he looked up at the portrait paintings Frances had given him and pushed the shamrock button. King George was slowly eclipsed by a pair of Dunne chieftains that stared back at him through the centuries.

Since early nonage it had been his practice that when a momentous decision presented itself, his intentions were to be clearly spoken out loud to himself. If his actions sounded entirely idiotic or especially evil, the spoken words themselves would be enough to shock him to his senses. Moving over to the desk, he placed the Lalor letter in front of him and read it through one more time.

Swirling issues pulsated through his brain: Catholics, tithes, truth, landlords, justice, England, Ireland, peasants, elections, duty, enemies, honour, triumph. Formulating one sentence that he could pronounce, precisely encapsulating his actions was the goal of the exercise. It must not be tainted with prejudice, malice or flowery rhetoric. After all, the crafting of an accurate statement was the most difficult part. Shifting his eyes around as he thought, he patched it together. He coughed up some phlegm, swallowed and began:

"I am going to take this accusation, being unclear of its accuracy, given to me by proven cowards and try to ruin a fellow Irishman's reputation," simple and to the point. The words hung in the air for a moment then General Dunne took the parchment, held it up to the lit taper and watched it burn.

Violence marred the election returns in one of the severest elections in Queen's County history. Sir Charles Coote had to be rescued by the Calvary when he was attacked by an unruly mob, resulting in the death of two Lalor supporters. Nevertheless, Honest Patt Lalor easily took the first seat with 772 votes. Peter Gale was winning the second slot by the time the Dublin Evening Post prematurely declared him duly elected. In the morning, Coote "brought up" 50 additional votes and narrowly maintained his seat with 694 votes.

Retired general of the British army, clan chieftain and squire of Brittas, Edward Dunne walked away with 23 votes to his name.

Patt Lalor, M.P. Queen's County, faithfully served his constituents in London's House of Commons despite being distinctly rural and distinctly Irish. Fellow members esteemed him a lowly O'Connell operative, unpossessed of a proper coat to wear into Parliament. He navigated his way through the strange and inhospitable institution with suspicion. Eventually finding his voice, he spoke out in a brogue thicker than Irish cream on land reform issues and the need to repeal the union. He became a champion of the kingdom's agriculturalists when farmer's nicknamed him, "the poor man's magistrate." His famous opposition to tithes eventually lead to a symbolic repeal of the "odious impost" Irish tenant farmers were forced to pay Anglican churches. Going forward, landlords like General Dunne would pay the tithes themselves, which calmed tenant protests for a time until their rent was summarily increased. A scheming shell game disguised as victory.

Lalor's talent for forming friendships back home was admirable but in England he was an absolute genius at making enemies.

Distracting him from his legislative duties, Lalor faced a court case challenging his own election victory where once again the ecclesiastical bullies brought out the claim that he had sought a position as a tithe commissioner. Although he won the court battle in the end, it cost him £5,000 and a tarnished reputation. By the time the 1835 election rolled around the full might of the Ascendancy came bearing down upon him with a vengeance. Sir Charles Coote had colluded with the other big lord of the county, Viscount deVesci to defeat Honest Patt Lalor. The Viscount's vast Abbeyleix estates held the key to winning in the form of its one thousand tenants. They would be compelled to vote against their conscience or face eviction.

Battered and bruised beyond any military battle he had ever faced, General Edward Dunne retired to his family seat questioning everything he knew about leadership, loyalty and Ireland. One thing he knew for certain however, the name Lalor would forever be akin to a curse word to his ears and its use would be banished from Brittas, the last vestige of his realm.

CHAPTER 11

Letter from Michael Dunne to his sister Bridget Dunne

May 15, 1835
Ballintlea House, Timahoe

Dear Sister,
 I am proud you got father & the General to build that dairy for yourself & the tenants of Brittas to use—I've heard your butter business is making a pretty penny. That is all fine & good—tho I harbour not one hard feeling towards you, I know many other angry people (high & low) who think father has set a dangerous precidint. Sevral tenants here at Ballintlea showd up at my doorstep tonight & said they saw a dairy being built up the road at Gracefield & now they be wanting a dairy for their use here—which they know I could never afford. I wd have them drive their blasted cows up to Brittas if it wrn't so far. They all owe me back rent and yt they demand a dairy? Tell father what is going on here—he needs to know.
 Also, a man stopped me in town last week asking all sorts of questions abt. you. He said you met a while back at Tenakill. His name is Patrick Lawler. We jist made a deal over hay he grew on his Blackford farm. He said he's going to make his way up to Brittas and call on you. I said he best be careful that he doesn't get shot as soon as he sets a foot on the General's land.
 Fair Warning.
 —Michael

Radiant sunshine filled the home farm at Brittas, revealing the bright colours of rooster feathers, wildflowers and the green hills beyond. Deep shadows caused by the harsh light made outbuildings and fences appear more dilapidated than usual while barnyard animals seemed more alive with their quick movements being duplicated by the black outlines below their forms.

James felt more alive too in the rarefied luminosity that now fell onto the Midlands, usually rendered flat by a misty gray filter. Gobs of russet hair passed down from generations of Dunnes could barely be contained beneath his woollen flat cap, a darker shade of whiskers covered his angular face and parts of his apple cheeks. Tightly pursed lips cut through an opening in his beard. His eyes were deep set and light blue, emitting an electric intensity. Having the bulk of a sturdy farm hand he moved about the day performing his duties with a quiet dignity and marked precision, for in his mind's eye he was not a common peasant toiling in the fields, he was a powerful guardian of the earth and its creatures. Thankful to have the oats and barley planted, he could now oversee lambing season when abundant new supplies of wool would bounce about the meadows in bouts of pure joy. As a young boy he'd made a keen shepherd and now assumed more responsibility for the livestock, inheriting his father's abilities with animals.

But James was also in possession of a restless spirit coupled with an adroit understanding of the facts. No matter how many precious things he would inherit from his father, land would not be among them. He was too ambitious to settle for the life of a tenant farmer. He had a good head for figures, could spell and write commendably and had developed a solid understanding of his father's business. His intimate mingling with the important families of Queen's County exposed him to a gentile world of privilege and wealth that left him with a strange split nature, a have-not that had something. He hadn't spent much of his young life concerned for his future but today he was satisfied that the ambitions for his life, wished by others, would not take precedence over his own. It was like a change had occurred below the surface of a lake, appearing calm to the boats above.

Mrs. Dunne had gone to extraordinary lengths to procure a seat for her son at St. Patrick's College despite his protestations and complete lack of interest in theology. She understood that Bridget had far too many prospects to enter the convent but held out hope that her last child would want a religious life. Although James was raised within the strict confines of the Catholic religion, it was God's complex and glorious gift of nature that made the young man believe. Deep in his soul he felt the Creator's might as he planted a seed and watched it grow or witnessed a lamb being born or felt the gentle rain on his face. He didn't need an Irish school, a Roman church or his mother to convince him. Yes, he was a believer but as he repeatedly told his mother, he had no compulsion to baptize, consul, console or recruit and would make a pathetic excuse for a clergyman. Their final bout over the priesthood that morning had sent his mother running to her bedroom in a flood of tears as his proud father looked on. Mr. Dunne would rather see his son doing the physical work of a farmer than be some meddling parish priest, convincing people their happiness lay in a metaphysical afterlife. Besides, he had heard rumours his son had taken a liking to a girl in a nearby village, a randy Protestant girl.

Freshly milked udders wobbled back and forward as James herded the cows down to the lower field with a wand of hazelwood. On his way back to the dairy he stopped to quickly patch a hole in the fence when he noticed a lone rider galloping in fine form up the cart path from town. A rare bout of jealousy surged through James as he monitored the regal way the stranger stood in his saddle and how skilfully he directed his horse up the constricted road. The man seemed faintly familiar. As James and the stranger converged towards each other, he remembered the face. They had shared a celebratory night of drinking at Donnelly's pub after the Maryborough Faire and now they met again at the fence line.

"Beautiful morning," said the mounted trespasser in his friendliest voice.

"That it is," said James in a curt, flat tone. "What brings you this way?"

"I'm looking for a Miss Bridget Dunne. I was told she might be in the Brittas Dairy."

"Aye, and what is your name then?"

"Patrick. Patrick Lawler."

James had long gotten used to young suitors poking around the estate in search of butter but this was the first time someone actually admitted to seeking out Bridget and so, he admired the direct approach. Although he agreed to take Patrick to the dairy he would decline the offer of riding double, never one to grant friendship on such scant credentials.

James opened the bottom of the half door into the dairy barn with Patrick, a half foot taller, pushing in on him from behind. Bridget was sweeping up the stone floor of the milking parlour that was flanked by four stalls.

"Biddy, a Mister Patrick Lawler here to see you," said James in a mockingly formal tone.

Dressed unusually well for the hard work of a milkmaid, a look of total surprise came over her outlined eyes, a look James had caught her rehearsing in a mirror the day before. Bridget coyly delivered her line, "I don't believe we've met."

"Hello Miss Dunne," Patrick said as he held out his hand, "we met at Tenakill one lovely day."

"Oh wait, I think you let our carriage out," a moment that rested in a special fluffy corner of her mind. He was even more handsome and more magnetic than she remembered.

"That's right. Now miss, I was told that you may have given your heart away to my cousin Fintan, is that true?"

Taken back by his complete lack of tact or finesse she twitched and playfully replied, "Oh, I think I only let him borrow it for a couple of days."

"So that's over and done with, correct?"

"Mr. Lawler, you have quite overstepped your mark. What makes my heart such a concern to you?"

"That day at Tenakill you were so kind and dainty and beautiful and here today I see you working away so hard and rugged. You just might be the perfect woman."

"Far from perfect," Bridget said as James grimaced.

"I'd like to speak with your Da."

James knew his sister well enough to see she was smitten and offered to take Patrick to their father's rent room. With folded arms across her chest, shifting her weight to one leg, Bridget feigned indifference as the two men left to meet a third man who could completely change her life, forever.

"What!" came the voice after James knocked on the weathered door.

"Da, we got a visitor." James yelled back and walked into his father's musty room where brash sunshine illuminated the filth built up on the glazed windows. "This here is Patrick Lawler, he wants a word with you concerning Biddy?" Mr. Dunne did not rise from his chair when he shook Patrick's hand and took an agonizing amount of time for inspection before telling him to sit down.

The young suitor was dressed in bleached white shirtsleeves with no jacket, blue calico neckerchief and dark green corduroy dungarees. His long brown side scrapers framed a rugged and well-proportioned face featuring a small straight nose, square jaw and far-set light green eyes the colour of sliced cucumbers. His boots were well-worn but clean. Mr. Dunne did not smell money but he did smell sweat and he knew it was possible to turn sweat into money, with proper application. He thought this Lawler improved very much upon acquaintance. Usually, he would brow beat applicants back into the wilds from which they sprang but Bridget was getting older and, besides, this suitor reminded him of himself. He would go easy on the lad, at first.

"So what do you want with my sweet colleen?"

Patrick began his earnest plea, delivering himself with precision. "Sir, I met your daughter some time ago and I was dazzled by her. I knew I had a lot of work to do to be the kind of man that would deserve someone like her. But now I feel I'm ready, so with your permission I'd like to make her my wife?"

"Are you daft man?"

"A few days ago I saw her on horseback riding through an open field. I was done for."

"Does she even know who you are?"

"Aye sir, she does."

"They come in droves up here trying to whisk her away."

"I've been chatting with your son Michael at Timahoe, our family farm is right up the road at Blackford. I had a few words with Bridget just now. I believe she would be amenable."

"I know your family, so was Denis your father?"

"Aye."

"He was part of the Tenakill clan?"

"Aye."

"How auld are you Patrick?"

"Three and twenty. Oldest of three sons."

"I see, you're the Widow Lawler's oldest then. Tragic thing what happened to your father. So, you've been farming the land over there since then? How much land?"

"68 acres on our place but I am leasing another plot of 25 acres and aiming to get more."

"Oh, you are in high clover now Lawler," Mr. Dunne replied in that patronizing tone of his.

"Thank you sir, I am a hard worker, just like your daughter," he answered nonchalantly.

Mr. Dunne couldn't tell if Patrick was dim and did not know an insult when he heard one or if he was just being respectful. All the same, he took note of how the insult was turned into a compliment about his daughter as well as a boast about himself.

"Aye, she'll have to work hard because there will be no money coming from me. She doesn't have six of ev'rything. The men that come prowling after her think she's an heiress of Brittas you know. They got it twisted in their heads that somehow she's the General's daughter. They turn around when they find out it's just the land agent what's her father. That's not what you thought is it?"

"I think she comes from a good family and that is all. I will make my own fortune."

"Pretty hard to make a fortune from a few acres in this land I can tell you that."

"I'll have to agree with you, sir."

"Have you any sort of education then?"

"When my father died I had to quit school and work on the farm. I have gone to night classes and got a prize for reading though."

"Oh, big reader are you?"

"I only read to learn how the world works." If Patrick Lawler had ever cracked opened a novel there was no record of it.

"Me too," said Mr. Dunne noting the similarity. "My Bridget loves to read. All sorts of books and stories: history, astronomy, poetry. When she's not in the buttery she's with a book. The nuns instilled it in her, a love of learning."

"Aye, Michael told me she was taught by the sisters at Stradbally. I might have to live with the fact she has a better education than I do. She can correct me English," trying to reveal his self-deprecating, humorous side to Mr. Dunne.

Unfazed, Mr Dunne continued his line of questioning. "They also made her quite pious. Fond of the pew, she is. Are you a Godly man, Patrick?"

"Through and through Mr. Dunne."

"What about the drink?"

"Drinking gets in the way of a man's ambitions, sir. I'll have a drop now and then but it does not bedevil me."

"Bully for you. But I must warn you, Biddy is no mousy little wench that'll be going along with whatever you dictate. No sir, she has a will of iron and is seldom content with anything. Plus, she's rather fond of her own ideas."

"I gather she is a strong woman and that's what I will be needin' in life."

"She's older than you too. Are you sure you wouldn't rather have a girl?"

"I want Bridget."

"Girl's a lot easier to manage."

"I think we'll manage perfectly."

"What does the Widow Lawler think about you getting married? Do you plan on having her live with you and your new bride?"

"I haven't told her until I get your blessing. She'll stay at the farm with the rest of my brothers and sister. There is a small cottage on this new plot that would be our home."

"Good, good."

"My mother doesn't know anything about anything but Mae Coughlin thinks we'd make quite a formidable couple."

Mae Coughlin was a notorious and beloved character around Queen's County. She would visit country houses and make grand predictions, cast spells or conjure up curses from the shadowlands for a few pence and a meal. She could be persuaded to wail over your body after your death for a fee. The Catholics revered her as a mystic, a relic of old Ireland and its forgotten ways. The Protestants thought her a witch.

"What Mae Coughlin thinks is neither here nor there," he said softly as if speaking too loudly would conjure up some evil spell upon him. "I am more concerned with what General Dunne thinks."

"Do you think he would have difficulty with a hard-working farmer?"

"It's your name that's the difficulty. You must know that since he lost the local election to your kin Patt Lalor he's had it in for the Lalors."

"Well, I don't involve myself in politics, sir."

"Just the same."

"My grandfather built Tenakill, true, but that was generations ago. My people are now in Kildare and we spell it L-A-W-L-E-R."

"How did that happen?" asked Mr. Dunne.

"Me Da blamed the parish priest or an illiterate town clerk."

"Let's go with the parish priest, probably him."

"Ha!"

"Believe me son it doesn't matter, either way you spell it, it spells trouble for the General."

Mr. Dunne had given Patrick Lawler permission to court his daughter with the understanding that Bridget must be in compliance with any marriage contract the men might negotiate. He would not bind her to a husband without her consent. However, Mrs. Dunne, envisioning a more sophisticated sort for her daughter, would have no say in the matter. Her own mother's aspirational plans were crushed when she married Bridget's father and now she witnessed the children, one-by-one, descending further into the rustic classes. At this rate her grandchildren would be paupers. A family heirloom had once passed over her head when her mother declared, "…the farm is no place for a diamond necklace." An act that once seemed merely spiteful now appeared painfully prophetic.

A so-called "Cave of Natural Curiosity" had been discovered by a shepherd adjoining the demesne of Brittas and locals were flocking to the site. Patrick thought this would make a suitable excursion for Bridget and him to get to know each other a little better. Bridget's oldest brother Michael and his wife Elsie would act as chaperones and brought their buckboard over from Ballintlea House to collect her. Patrick rode alongside on horseback arriving at Brittas just before noon.

"Elsie scoot over and let Bridget up here. Patrick you can get in the back," said Michael.

"No, my dress will get wrinkled. Why don't they both get in the back?" pleaded Elsie.

Bridget looked at the wagon's bed with a thin covering of hay and other assorted farm residue then glanced up at Patrick with a helpless shrug.

"Are you sure she can't squeeze in up there with you ma'am?" wondered Patrick.

"No, you two can snuggle up in the back."

Bridget timidly shook her head. Patrick bent down and outstretched his arm, "Grab on with both hands," and as she did he flung her onto the back of his gray stallion in one clean jerk. "There now hold on. Michael lead the way," Patrick ordered. As the touring party made their way down from Brittas, Elsie peered over her shoulder at the two following on horseback and summoned up an audible "Humph."

A small crowd of people in a sea of gray and brown clothes were huddled around a wooded patch by the edge of the Clodiagh River, just upstream from the site of the shebeen killings several years past. The entrance to the cave was being guarded by a self-appointed group of guides who were charging a few coppers for a torch-lit journey through the cave. Patrick made his way past the crowd, quickly interviewed a few men then hired an aged history enthusiast named Dinty O'Hara to bring the group down. Mr. O'Hara introduced himself, handed out three lit torches and spun a yard about the mysteries he was about to reveal. Like a carnival barker he was quickly judged to be more salesman than historian but he did get them inside and paused before descended a few paces into the darkness.

Twisted vines cascaded down the sharp, rocky rim of the opening. When he finally found a small plateau to continue his discursive thoughts, they got a good look at his face, which resembled a wrinkled bag of burlap with tiny eyes peeking through folded slits. His large hook nose perched above his mouth where Bridget could make out two, maybe three teeth. Orange light emitting from the torch only added to the eerie manifestation. Before them were stone steps leading into a pitch-black oblivion as he dramatically recited:

"Imagine yerselves here one t'ousand years ago, you'd be dressed in animal skins and nothin' a'tall on yer feet. This is where you'd be escapin' from rampagin' Vikin's and wild beasts. You can see how the entrance was disguised in all them trees and shrubs and such...."

Bridget was clinging to Patrick's bicep, repulsed, fascinated and forgetting all about proper decorum on purpose. Elsie quickly inserted her hand between them and pushed her sister-in-law aside.

"It's not that dark, I can see what you're up to, Biddy!" whispered Elsie.

"It's frightening down here."

"Well, might be why Mr. Lawler brought you down here, out of sight."

"Oh hush up now, we're missing the story...." switching over to her brother's arm purely out of spite.

Mr. O'Hara continued, "Now I can tell you fer a fact that the people what lived down 'er were early, early Christian of the True Faith. See here, huddle 'round me as we go down deese steps they're mighty steep and frail. And make sure you're countin', dare's twentee."

All five of the adventure seekers slowly made their way into the cave. O'Hara's fire illuminated the calcite formations on the walls that looked to Bridget as if rock itself was dripping tears down the sides of the cave. Preparing herself for putrid and rotten smells, she was happily surprised at the freshness that filled the space. It smelled like a new place, not an ancient place. O'Hara beckoned them through a series of chambers into a corner where he revealed a large carved stone table.

"Dis is ware our people celebrated the holy Eucharist, I'm sure of it. Maybe St. Patrick himself stood right where you are now Missy," pointed to Elsie. "I'd like us to just envision, if youse can, the terror of peaceful Christians down 'ere gathering like we do only to be tracked down by the savage Vikin's who want to kill you and steal everyt'ing you have. Oh, once you got down here there was no hope for ye."

"I think we get the idea Mr. O'Hara. I'd like to go up now," said Elsie.

"Well, I want to give the man 'es money's worth."

"Thanks all the same but I think they'd like to be released." Patrick said with a smile.

"Suit yerselves, I have a lot of very good knowledge about the cave formations but if you don't want it, dats fine." Although Mr. O'Hara wanted to hear himself talk a bit more, he reluctantly delivered the group back to civilization. Beaming sunlight stung their eyes but they quickly reoriented themselves. Patrick rounded up the torches and passed them back to the guide. Michael pulled a wicker basket out of the wagon and they headed to the river's edge for a picnic.

"It's too cold now for a picnic," complained Elsie. Bridget ignored her and set out the food on an old horse blanket and said, "Thank you Patrick for taking us on such a fascinating little trip." She offered him a strawberry from its cabbage leaf wrapping.

"It was my pleasure indeed, Miss Bridget. Seems you and I both have an affinity for history," he replied trying hard to lift his manners up a notch. His barley field did not expect thanks and his cows never required smooth talk. Patrick was a bit out-of-practice conversing with humans.

"I would love to have heard more about the Vikings. They fascinate me. When we were little James gave me an auld brooch that he found in a field. I wonder if Mr. O'Hara would know anything about it."

Patrick glanced over at Bridget and took a juicy bite from the strawberry.

"He'd probably take it for evaluation and if it was worth anything you'd never see him again. What a buffoon," huffed Michael.

"I think he was just feeling important for once in his life. He's all right." Patrick wiped the corner of his mouth with a knuckle. "I wanted to ask him if there was a holy well down there, it smelled so clean."

"To be sure, if so it would be a new pilgrimage spot," added Bridget.

"Such a strange place and to think it's been right down the road from you all this time," said Patrick.

"Who knows what lurks under the earth. 'And still they gazed and still the wonder grew.'"

"Aye Bridget that's lovely," Patrick gushed, beaming over at her.

"That's not me, it's Goldsmith!"

"A poet and a goldsmith, there's a good man." Bridget rolled her eyes and looked at Elsie for a reaction. Elsie sat stone-faced and purse-lipped. Patrick continued, "Just the same, my mother would not approve of going into such a place for fear of disturbing the faeries."

"Is she the believing sort?" asked Bridget.

"She made us leave a tree smack in the middle of our ploughed field, does that tell you anything?"

"A Faerie Tree?"

"That's right. She says, O' Patrick, we mustn't disturb the faeries living in that tree, they'd never forgive us."

"How can people traipsing about this island believe in Jesus Christ and faeries at the same time? It's madness," asked Michael.

"I don't see the harm. It's actually quite prudent. Better to believe in everything than nothing at all," Patrick said as Bridget giggled.

"Our parish priest said if you believe in such nonsense you're damned to hell or Connaught," revealed Elsie causing Patrick to look down and stab at a chunk of cheese with his knife which proved inconvenient as he tried to dislodge it again. Silence. Awkward silence. Bridget had been admiring Patrick's tanned, rugged hands when she averted her eyes back to Patrick's. She was tempted to change the subject, heading off any confrontation but then she waited. Just how would he handle her disagreeable sister-in-law?

"Who am I to argue with a holy man, Elsie? I can only tell you my mother is a saintly woman who loves the Lord and she faithfully raised her children in the Catholic Church all by her lonesome, mind you. AND she believes in faeries. If hell is to be filled with such people, let me in." Just then, a random sunbeam poked through the cloud cover, gleaming right down onto their picnic spot.

Bridget Dunne had fallen madly and completely in love with Patrick Lawler.

CHAPTER 12

Letter from General Edward Dunne to his cousin and agent, Mr. Peter Dunne

December 10, 1836
Bantry House, County Cork

Sir,

> *I am in receipt of & returning your letter & papers with the various issues concerning Brittas. I have noted in the margins my reply to each case you outlined. I concur on all of your suggestions for the upcoming crops & you have my approval to sell the livestock you list. In personal matters, your decision to marry off your daughter to a Lawler boy I find most distressing – of course you knew what my feelings would be & your flowery & fawning prose does not persuade. Nevertheless, I am powerless over such things. My only request is that they marry & reside a good distance from Brittas & do it before I get back in late February. I can't bless such a union but I wish her luck all the same.*
> *—General E. Dunne*

In a cramped little room above a public house, a certain Shane Moore was trying to find his boots after an endless evening with a woman considerably older than himself. She made her living by taking in sewing and the occasional man but with these encounters no money had ever been exchanged, only passion, pleasantries, white lies and aliases.

Tiny Mountbolus village in King's County was a 6-mile horse ride through the woods from Brittas, it had become a haven of sorts for young James Dunne these past months. He was usually saddled-up and out of sight before sunrise. As destiny would have it, the current parish priest of Clonaslee had spent the night at the village's chapel rectory and was preparing a hansom to continue on with two other priests for their meeting with the Bishop of Ossory. Spanish in appearance, the chapel was unfortunately situated directly across the road from the public house. Father Graham first recognized the handsome Connemara pony belonging to the Dunne family and then he recognized James. Mrs. Dunne had convinced Father Graham to seek a dispensation of sorts from the administrators of St. Patrick's College Seminary so her son could attend, an opportunity readily squandered but not so easily forgotten.

A fortnight had passed since the priest had spotted James. With each visit to his seamstress he was getting more brazen and less guarded. This time he was returning home from a three-day cattle drive that took him through the Charleville Forest and a convenient overnight stay again in Mountbolus.

Entering Brittas lodge through the kitchen door he came upon an unusual sight, his mother and father sitting over tea, mid-afternoon on a Friday.

"Well, boy, you'll never guess who's just left here?" said Mr. Dunne, casually returning the dainty porcelain cup to its saucer with fingers resembling misshapen parsnips. James looked over at his red faced, teary-eyed mother and asked, "Who now?"

"Oh James, why must you torture me!" cried Mrs. Dunne, pressing her wet linen towel to her mouth before darting upstairs, an act that had multiplied in frequency over the years.

"Sit down, James." Mr. Dunne plucked his spoon from the tea and tapped it against the rim of his cup before ceremoniously resting it on the saucer.

"What's all this about Da?"

"Father Graham saw you where you shouldn't a' been."

"Saw me where?"

"Coming out a' some big-boned trollop's room above a tavern at daybreak."

"Oh, that, aye, I was sleeping one off…." James anxiously scratched at his scalp.

Mr. Dunne interrupted, "Son, spare me the excuses. Everyone knows about that woman."

"But no, it's not like that at all…."

"I knew about it a while ago but the priest comin' here telling your mother, so cruel. Broke her heart, it did."

"But he doesn't know…."

"Well, he saw enough to come over here and tell your Mother all about it."

"He's got no right…."

"I imagine Father's still in a heat that he stood up for ye at the college and ye turned 'em down."

" I never once told anyone I wanted to go to the seminary, not even a little did I…"

"All that aside, Bridget and Patrick are getting married at Timahoe and Father Graham won't be getting any offerings, so I suppose he's on a bit of a tirade about that too."

"Poor Mother. Should I go talk to her?"

"For God's sake no. There's nothing you can say."

"No, there surely isn't."

"So, this woman's a big woman, aye?"

"She is taller than me, an older than me."

"I heard tell, 'When we're head-ta-head me feet are in it and when we're feet-to-feet me head's in it!"

Caught off-guard, James let out a nervous giggle of relief. Sitting up a little straighter in his chair he puffed up his chest as if bragging to a chum. And yet Mr. Dunne persisted.

"I imagine she's been teaching you all she knows?"

"But I am telling you it's not like that."

"You must be at it all night long then?"

"Please, no. If I can be excused I have a lot of work waiting for me."

Mr. Dunne winked and took a sip of tea, "Go ahead, carry on my good man, carry on."

James went directly to the woodpile and began chopping away, relieving his embarrassment and distress.

Mrs. Dunne heard the splintering of wood outside her bedroom window and looked out momentarily controlling her conniption. Slumping back into her gray easy chair she had a far-away gaze in her eyes. Now, after months of nagging he decided to honour her request for cook wood? Surely her son was doing penance. For a brief moment she grinned at the absurdity of it all.

As the sun went down and supper was served Mr. Dunne announced that he and James were going out to visit a few tenants who had promised payment on delinquent rent. Daylight attempts to collect had failed and he proposed that the occupants would surely be home at night. He also claimed the bright full moon would provide some illumination. Bridget and Mrs. Dunne would busy themselves with wedding preparations.

Father and son headed out to the Scaroon neighbourhood on the estate. Although the land was as fertile and generous as any other part of the Midlands it simply had too many guests to feed. Dwelling within a checkerboard of dormant potato patches, sod houses and misery, any tenant could be chosen at random for rent extraction. Mr. Dunne rolled up on a shabby one-room dwelling known as a bothán with mud walls and a thatched roof. Scaroon was chock-a-block with the places like this. The potato patch before the front door had a sad looking winter cover crop of spindly peas and, as predicted, there was a light inside.

"Come with me boy," Mr. Dunne directed. They knocked on the wicket door, shaking loose a fragment of mud from above. Answering the door was a middle-aged farmer James faintly recognized. "Jasper, I'll be needin' the rent now," said the agent as he peered into the room where he saw the family pig by the fire with two young lads.

"I didn't know you'd be over so soon Mr. Dunne."

"Aye, you're coming up on a year back rent. I don't consider that soon a'tall."

"I just need a few more months until I can get some farm work, then you'll be paid in full."

"Looks like your wife is not here, did she leave you now?"

"No, she did not! At the moment she's helping her sister with a new babe."

A dubious Mr. Dunne inquired about Jasper's daughter only to find out that she had married without the landlord's consent and built a squatter's cottage down the road. More words and threats were exchanged and a deadline was agreed upon which, like other deadlines, would come and go. If the men of Scaroon hadn't been so helpful at harvest time on Brittas' home farm they would have been ousted long ago.

The pair got back into the wagon and meandered down to the spot where Jasper's daughter had set up house. Moonlight illuminated a rickety fence that kept the wagon a distance from the cabin. James was instructed to stay put as the agent approached, things might get acrimonious if negotiations fell apart. He could see a young man about his own age in the doorway, nervously running his fingers over his head in a futile attempt to tame his floppy hair while Mr. Dunne remained motionless, hands in his pockets. Discussions were out of James' earshot. Finally, they walked inside the tiny hovel and shut the door. After a while the young man reappeared in a slouchy brimmed hat and stormed out the door in the direction of Jasper's.

A considerable time elapsed before James got fidgety. What is taking so long? Curious rather than concerned, he decided he needed to check on his father. Leaping out of the rig he made his way to the cabin door just as his father was creeping out. Putting his hand on his son's shoulder he whispered, "I got her ready for you, she's all yours now lad." James peered in to see a naked young girl, no more than 16, on the dirt floor covered by a thin blanket. He could not speak. He stood motionless as if his body had transformed into a Biblical pillar of salt. His mind swirled up into a wretched, turbulent storm. His soul was pulverized, all within a single heartbeat.

"Go on," Mr. Dunne gave him a nudge into his shoulder blade, "don't be shy." A silent James bowed his head at the girl and went back to the wagon in a daze. Mr. Dunne tipped his hat, winked and followed after quietly shutting the door.

"What in the blazes is the matter with you, son? She's got to be better than that ol' Amazon woman of yours. You can try out all the tricks you've been learning about."

James had no response and turned his head, unable to look his father in the face. "I thought you're a man now, what with all the gallivanting. Now's the time to sew your wild oats boy. I don't understand ye." The horse lurched and they headed home.

Oblivious to his son's anguish, the agent told how the women of this meagre neighbourhood had paid rent with their bodies for generations. James' awakening had given his father a reason to boast. In a spirited mood, Mr. Dunne chatted away, likening himself to a wolf springing to life at the full moon. Stopping before a dilapidated barn he boasted, "See that place right there? Why I was in there once thrashing about on some girl and her mother walks straight in and says, 'What do you think you're doing?' I says, 'What does it look like I'm doing? Now get out!' And I just went back to pumping away." He bobbed his head and chuckled, amused with himself. James sat fuming and fretting on the springboard seat listening to his father's escapades all the way back to Brittas.

February first was a lucky day to wed. The newly constructed Roman Catholic Chapel proudly stood near the ancient round tower in the wee village of Timahoe. Gothic, gray and stern on the outside, it was filled with bright colours, white alabaster and handsome stained glass windows on the inside. Lawlers, Lawlors, Lalors and Dunnes from every corner of the Midlands filled the space to witness the marriage of Bridget and Patrick. A recently widowed Honest Patt and most of his sons ventured out from Tenakill, though Fintan busied himself in the attic to write another anti-government screed.

General Dunne had forbidden members of his family or the Brittas staff from attending the wedding, which only truly upset Mrs. Miquel, the cook, and his daughter Fanny. She and Bridget had become fast friends since the Dunnes had moved in with the Dunnes. She wondered if it might have been her only chance to get close to an altar as she was widely considered to be on the shelf. Sitting in the first pew, dressed in a sumptuous mauve silk gown with pleated, puffy sleeves and a white ostrich feather in her headdress sat dear Mrs. Kavanaugh. She took orders from no one, not even a General. Indeed, most of the community approved of the love match, uniting these two ancient local families.

The night before, Bridget was submerged in pre-nuptial superstitions and Irish invocations. She feared some traditions bordered on sorcery but it seemed to please the elders, which in turn pleased her. Earlier that morning, groomsmen accompanied by a troupe of fiddlers had been sent to Ballintlea House bearing a gift for Bridget. Patrick had secretly procured the ancient brooch James had found in the dirt years before and had it restored by a local jeweler who polished it up and refitted the missing stones. Touched beyond words, she nestled the gleaming treasure into the lace that surrounded the top of her blue wedding gown. Patrick noticed the glint bouncing off her brooch as Bridget entered St. Michael's on the arm of her father.

In a sublime Catholic ceremony the hopeful young couple entered into a marriage pact before an adoring crowd, who happily bestowed God's blessings upon their heads.

Drinking to excess occurred each day throughout Ireland but it was highly disrespectful and uncouth to get drunk at a wedding. It simply wasn't done, which made James Dunne's behaviour that day even more regrettable.

Zig-zagging its way across the entire length of the barn behind Ballintlea House, a makeshift table had been erected for the wedding banquet. At the head was the parish priest sitting next to the bride and groom. Mrs. Dunne's lady friends were all clad in white aprons serving boiled ham, fresh venison and assorted dishes of their own making. The women were quick to announce the popularity of their creations to whoever would listen. After the priest blessed the wedding cake Patrick gave Bridget a gentle kiss of peace on her cheek. Guests lined up to be served their slice and were obliged to lay down a donation in front of the priest as he noted their generosity.

Merrymakers began to clear out space for a dance floor and the fiddlers sawed away breathing life into the wooden crowd. Patrick's family seemed to be quick to dance a break-down with whoops and laughs. The Dunnes were more reserved but excelled at the quadrille. Michael, being the bride's oldest brother had the wearisome task of keeping peace among the drinkers. At the first sign of drunkenness men would be unceremoniously tossed out on their ears.

Occasional lulls in the music prompted heart-warming toasts and a few friendly jeers. Only a wake could provide a more colourful display of Irish traditions. Strawboys, local young lads who weren't formally invited to the celebration, invaded the barn requesting to dance with the new bride. Bridget did not refuse the revellers who were dressed in white robes and wore conical-shaped straw hats that attempted to hide their identities. They spun her around the dance floor and proceeded to pry every woman off her seat. It was a joyous scene. The proud father-of-the-bride was accepting congratulations from around the room. Alone on a side wall, a dissipated James Dunne had put his frieze coat on the back of a chair and sank lower and lower into his cups. He was repulsed by the thought of his father let alone the sight of him. James looked over to witness Mr. Dunne chatting up a group of Bridget's friends wondering what disgusting escapades his father was planning next.

He was experiencing an emotional crisis from within that threw his young mind into turmoil. He was certain he was the first man in civilization to experience such disappointment but of course it was only new to him.

An eagle-eyed Mrs. Kavanaugh, fresh from a romp with the strawboys, plopped herself next to James, caught her breath and attempted to engage in a little light conversation.

"Oh James, doesn't your sister look so beautiful?"

"That she does."

"I think she will be very happy with Patrick."

"I pray to God she will be," James said with a cruel edge to his words.

"What's the matter dear? Why so cross? Don't you like him?"

"I bet she could've done a lot better. I bet my mother could've done a lot better. I think maybe I can do a lot better too. I just want to leave this place."

Mrs. Kavanaugh promptly grabbed him by the chin and looked him in the eyes causing James to squirm.

"What on earth is eating you, James? I've never seen you be such a sour puss."

"I don't know, I just suddenly want to run. I hate everything. This island, this family."

"Oh no, you mustn't talk that way. You come from such a noble family. They've paved the way for you. Use that heritage to stand on their shoulders and pull yourself up...."

"That's what's wrong! I feel I'm in a 100-foot grave and all those noble dead Dunnes are standing on my shoulders pushing me down. The live ones too! I want to go where nobody knows my name. Where nobody wants me to be a priest or a farmer or this or that. Someplace where nobody knows I'm that estate agent's son! I could join the army and go off to India. I could sail away tomorrow and get my own town in Australia."

"James, I must tell you, no matter where you go, there you are."

"Any place but here."

"An upside down perspective in Australia would change everything? Come to your senses James. You'll think differently in the morning."

"Like hell I will!" he said as he clumsily staggered from his chair like a stag who'd taken an arrow to the chest. Mrs. Kavanaugh surveyed the room to see who might have overheard James' outburst. Believing him to be deadly serious about running away, she quietly emptied the contents of her small purse into the button pocket of his abandoned coat; £18 worth of gold coins.

Patrick had taken notice of a few tipsy guests stumbling about the barn earlier but raised no alarm. However, his spine stiffened when James stood wobbly in front of the musicians and shouted at people to quiet down for a toast. With a mug over-filled with brown stout James looked around the barn for a moment until he could lock eyes with his father. Thunder and lightning gathered in his head causing his cheeks to flush. He began the speech.

"I just want to remark, we all have our secrets, I mean all families have secrets don't they? All the gaps and spaces are hiding secrets. Some, I'm talking about the worst ones of all, are hidden in plain sight. Playynnn syyyyght! So Patrick, and for that matter Bridget, if you two have secrets never keep them from each other...."

As James continued his slurred ramblings Michael and his father moved in to shut him down before he stained the entire family for generations. Mr. Dunne put his arm around James and tried to hush him up, "Very nice lad, a fine toast, now let's get back to dancing." James threw up his hands nearly tossing his father to the floor.

"There is a scared trust now placed between the two a' yas that must never be destroyed..." Michael stepped in and wrapped his arm around his brother's waist quietly moving him to the open barn door.

"I'm not finished, brotherrr!" said James.

"Ah m'lord, you are quiet finished," Michael said in a playful voice that hid his disgust.

"Take your hands off me, BROTHER."

"Off you go," Michael whispered as he tightened his hold and nudged James across the dirt floor.

"Whoa, bust me!" James wound up and threw a mighty undercut to Michael's chin causing him to stumble backward. Both brothers sprang into a fighting stance. They circled around each other.

"James, now calm down. You're ruining everything." Michael reached out and his hand which was quickly batted away. Peter rushed to quell the disturbance before it drew in more men eager to be part of the scrimmage.

Bridget said, " Oh, Patrick what has gotten into him?"

"By God, he is loaded to the hilt. They need my help." Patrick drew himself up to his full height.

"No please," Bridget gripped her new husband's wrist, "let them sort it out. Just sit back down. We shall just ignore it."

Other men soon surrounded him. James looked like a caged animal, kicking and throwing wild punches into the air. His fist haphazardly connected with Peter's shoulder and he slammed Michael against the wooden plank walls sending dust puffing out into the air and a few hanging tools crashing to the ground. After several failed attempts they finally subdued the young hellion enough to wrestle him out of the barn and onto a drift of snow. Michael barred the door. James got up and hurled loud indecent insults, demanding to be let back inside. Mrs. Kavanaugh made her way through the frenzied onlookers to Peter, handing him James' coat. "It's freezing out there, at least give him back this." Michael took it and tossed the coat out to James through the crevice in the door. With a hearty laugh, he mocked, "Here's your coat, what's your hurry. Go to bed!"

Tired of drifting around the margins of the Dunne family's story, James left.

CHAPTER 13

Fragment of letter from Lucy Rogers to Henrietta Welch

[September 1, 1930]

After Mother and Father married in 1837 they settled in Blackford on the border of Kildare and Queen's Counties. In quick succession they had their first two children, Esther and Denny. Father worked the farm growing grain and rearing cattle. Mother told me they had a second farm of 27 acres rented from Alicia Kavanaugh in Mountmellick. I believe around this time he started accumulating land leases in Kildare, which he would sublease out at a profit. Lots of comings and goings between the farm and his Kildare holdings back in those days.

He was a kind and indulgent landlord.

Patrick Lawler was the worst kind of landlord.

His tenants considered him a meddlesome tyrant. He demanded rent quarterly rather than yearly. He would show up unexpectedly to count how many people were living on his lands. He told his tenants what crops to plant and what livestock to buy. He rousted them out of bed at dawn when he believed they should be working. He had only seven tenants but he treated them all like his children, lazy and misbehaving children. He was willing to do his duty to others but downright insistent that others do their duty to him.

Defaulting on his rent payments meant certain disaster. He had invested every inch of capital on lands that were entrusted to other men. Irish Catholic middlemen were gamblers and every day was a roll of the dice. He believed he could make the bountiful land productive if his tenants would only follow his strict instruction.

Lawler's tenant farmers were no different than the millions of others throughout Ireland. They had small cottages with patches of land where they grew their family's main food source, the potato. A man could eat ten-twelve pounds of them a day so a vast supply was required. It was a monotonous diet but amazingly nutritious. With a year's worth of food grown under the ground the tenants needed very little else. They would trade their labour or livestock or grains like cash money. Many tenant farmers had never even seen cash money let alone saved any. The hand-to-mouth existence was accepted commonplace for Ireland's poor but infuriated Patrick Lawler. He didn't approve of the precarious nature of the whole system based on a potato, a food he loathed. That's too much power to give a vegetable. In a constant state of agitation about rent payments, he was buying supplies on the tick for his farm. Bruce Duffy was one of Patrick's biggest worries.

The mist looming over the fields quickly burned off to reveal a dazzling March day. It hadn't rained for two weeks and Patrick knew the dry conditions provided the most opportune time to plant spring barley. He had purchased more than enough seed to plant his farm and copious amounts of ground limestone to fertilize the soil. Determined to beat the weather, his fields were sown in two days. With the zeal of a preacher man on a quest to reform the sinner, he went out surveying the fields of his tenants looking for fallow ground and lost opportunity. His newest tenant had a large empty plot that needed attention but he was nowhere to be found. A little investigating brought Patrick to the nearest village where three taverns sat bunched together on the main road. He was on the lookout for Bruce Duffy, currently seated alone at the long bar of O'Brien's Pub, a bit slightly-tightly. It was half-past ten in the morning.

"It's a fine morning now isn't it, Bruce?"

"Oh, Mr. Lawler, out making the rounds looking for truants are we?"

"I assume you can enjoy that whiskey there because your field is all planted?"

"Aye, maybe tomorrow. I always have luck on a Thursday." BAM! The gnarled head of Patrick's shillelagh came crashing down on the bar top sending glass splintering around the dingy saloon.

"We're not promised tomorrow, Bruce, only today." Patrick said in a calm, soft voice. He then picked up the flabbergasted little man by his collar and threw him outside to three awaiting farm hands.

"And you," pointing his stick in the publican's face, "he's married to your sister isn't he? Have you no sympathy for her? She's got five brats at home to look after!"

"Well, now it's not for me to say and it's not for you to say either."

"Listen to me you money-grubbing bastard, the next time I see any tenant of mine drinking here when he should be tending his farm I'll come back with a torch! Do you understand me?"

"You wouldn't."

"Do you understand me?" Patrick glowered at the man with an intense, wild-eyed stare that indicated he might just be crazy enough to burn the place down.

"Fine, I won't serve him in the mornings."

"Only after sundown…dear Uncle," he snarled.

Patrick's men had hoisted Bruce up into the wagon for a ride back to his field, all the way he was lectured, ridiculed and shamed. When they reached his plot he was brought down and delivered. "Now, let's show Farmer Bruce how to plant a field," Patrick said to his men as seed and lime, ploughs and shovels were quickly off-loaded from his wagon. There was much to do when half the daylight was burned-up in a dark pub.

Patrick oversaw the entire operation pointing out rudimentary and sophisticated subtleties of planting to his ornery tenant. He found fault in the way Bruce wielded a spade, grabbed seed or bent his knees. Despite the exasperation and browbeating, an entire field was ploughed, enriched and seeded by nightfall. Bruce Duffy gazed upon his newly planted barley patch with a hint of pride and fresh hatred for his overseer. A light rain began to fall just in time to play its part in the production. Patrick Lawler went off into the night with his crew and his tools and not a word of thanks. Hardness and tenderness lived side-by-side in his soul but he had no taste for penury that could be prevented. He knew his intentions and could live without the gratitude for the time being.

In the spring of 1840 Brittas had the look of a house in which important things had once happened. The lonely monstrosity contained only a General, fully into his chair years, his wife and his spinster daughter. His agent Mr. Dunne and his wife Mollie still shared space with a mix of employees in the servant's wing. The bunkhouse had become uninhabitable so the rough outside farmhands now slept down the hall from the smooth inside servants. Shrubbery was still meticulously trimmed and an army of red tulips fought for attention at the tower entrance but malaise hovered over every inch of the estate waiting for a change.

General Dunne had three sons in the military, all headed down the road to confirmed bachelorhood. Francis Plunkett Dunne or Frank, the heir, was now a major in the British Army while Charles and Richard stalled at lower ranks. The two spare heirs, Edward Meadows and Robert Hedges were married with families of their own, delighting the General, his wife Frances whom he called France and their only daughter Fanny, a nickname for Frances. Among the grandchildren there would be two boys named Francis and a girl named Frances who hated her name because it sounded like a boy's.

The agent's sons and daughters had all stayed close to home in the Midlands with the exception of their youngest, James. After his ejection from Bridget and Patrick's wedding he seemed to vanish from the face of the earth. Not a soul had heard from him and his reported sightings fizzled-out on closer examination. He had been seen at a boarding house in Dublin; buying eggs at Cork's English Market; working at a northern farm outside of Galway. But no one really knew. After speaking with Mrs. Kavanaugh, who confessed to giving James money to run away, his parents were convinced he had taken a ship to Australia. Mr. Dunne imagined he had procured a little sheep farm in some grassy romantic meadow with a waterfall. Mrs. Dunne pictured his scattered bones at the bottom of the sea, a victim of a treacherous voyage. What else could explain the agonizing three years they had spent without him, without a letter, without anything?

James' older brother Peter had been meandering through the narrow streets of Dublin with a woebegone expression on his young face. He carried his wiry frame with a slight awkwardness yet there was also some elegance to certain movements and those yellow kid gloves.

It was mid-day on a Wednesday. He had been excused from his seventh law office in three years with the departing words, "Peter, we have no room for popinjays here. Good luck sir." His unbridled intellect, vocabulary and blarney would get him in the door. His knowledge of the law, researching skills and stamina would, for a time, make him a valuable barrister's assistant. His smug, condescending and superior attitude could perhaps serve him well in open court with an opposing attorney but not with an employer paying him a wage. Peter also had a tendency to misrepresent his time spent at Gray's Inn and his connection to connected people. And when he got going they weren't just exaggerations, they were eighteen-carat lies.

The handle he continued to tack onto the end of his name was brazenly unmerited. He blamed stupid bosses with fragile egos for his continued sacking and blamed his religion when he did not get accepted into Ireland's colleges and law schools. It had become a pattern that he refused to recognize. His youthful appearance as a full-grown man made his arrogance that much harder to take. Dreams of becoming an eminent lawyer had dissolved into a puddle of vapid drudgery, toiling away for years as a common office clerk. Reliving his time spent as a servant to Eddie in London, he lashed out at every superior who made him feel inferior. He was contemplating a humiliating move back to Queen's County.

While Peter floundered, his cousin Eddie had become a respected barrister-at-law for the noblesse of Queen's County, taking an office in Mountrath before dutifully marrying the daughter of a prosperous Antrim Orangeman. Morose and pleading letters Peter had sent to his mother mysteriously made their way to Eddie. Did he know of any local positions that would suit the talents of his tedious cousin? Dublin's legal pool was quite small and floated on waves of rumours, several featuring the smug and unemployable young Peter Dunne. In a rueful effort at redemption from his antics at Gray's Inn, Eddie recommended Peter for an open position at the Grand Canal Office in Mountmellick. His legal background would be beneficial but not crucial to his duties as a canal agent. Working alone in a gatehouse by the water's edge, Peter could satisfy his unshakable need to be the smartest person in the room.

CHAPTER 14

What follows is the second longest letter James Dunne would ever write in his lifetime:

January 9, 1840
New Orleans, Louisiana
United States of America

Dearest Mother:

Please forgive me for not writing any sooner than now. I must have started a thousand letters to you and then decided not to send them. In Ireland I felt as if I had a noose around my neck just waiting for the floor to fall out beneath me. People were not who I thought they were. I imagine all of you wondered if I was dead or alive. I just couldn't write to anyone because I myself was not sure if I was dead or alive. But I now find that I am very much alive— alive & well praise God, & I am anxious to tell you my story at last.

When I left Ballintlea the night of Bridget's wedding I was quite out of my head & more than a little drunk—Please give my apologies to Biddy I would never want to hurt her. My mind was in a terrible state. I had every intention of going to Cobh harbour & catching a clipper ship to Australia but I didn't have enough money. The next ship that came into port was a cotton trade vessel that was returning from England on its way to New Orleans—America. Cheap enough but I had to work on the ship to supplement my fare. It was a long journey—I did pretty well for a "landlubber."

New Orleans is a big, busy place full of lots of gigantic buildings & interesting people. Americans are very different from us. They dress different, act different & most importantly think different. I had a feeling I could be different here as well.

When the ship came to shore I helped unload cargo & found day-work around the riverfront. I slept rough a few nights. I went from boat to boat loading & unloading goods. Many times I slept in the warehouses on bales of cotton, which was bad enough but all night long the sound of steamers & fighting river men kept me awake. I got used to the noises but will never get used to the smells.

I got a permanent job at a different warehouse full of Irishmen. At first I only associated with men from Queen's County or at least the Midlands *but then I decided nobody cares what county you're from, we're all just Irish. After several months I got a better paying job working as a digger on a new canal. Lots of Irish worked with me digging night & day there too. Many of them died from the summer Yellow Jack fever. Foreman said it was better to pay an Irisher than to risk the life of an expensive slave—they would cost more than $1000 to replace.*

I slept on the ground floor of a rooming house near the canal—it was so dank in the morning my shoes grew mildew. Walls were covered in bloods marks & splotches from all the squished insects. I thought I would never meet anyone nice again like you Mother. Worked canal-building for nearly a year & saved up a little bit of money. I couldn't wait to quit because it was hard & horrible & I hated it. Went back to the warehouse district & found a position loading freight & maintaining a large warehouse. Mr. Grayson who owns the warehouse took a liking to me & brought me into the upstairs office where I could learn the nature of things with accounting books & do something more meaningful than sweep floors & kill rats. I hope you think my copperplate has improved & that every word in this letter is clearly legible. (That's what Mr. Grayson wants).

My only day off work is Sunday. They have built a R.C. church for all the Irish people to worship—the sermon is in English & not French—I go every Sunday & pray for you. I walked around the city after Mass last week to a park in the back of town they call Place des Nègres. Slaves are allowed the day off work too & go there to practice their own rituals & sing & dance. My friend was trying to explain their religion to me. It's called Voodoo & I think they believe in Jesus but they also caste spells & curse people & conjure up the black magic—exactly like some Old Celts do back home! I wasn't scared. One of them was selling candied pecans she made herself. I bought some. Our hands touched & for a minute I thought her colour was going to rub off on me. (But it didn't.)

I suppose I am finally able to write home so I can tell you I am fine—do not twist your tail about me. America is good. Someday I will write again when there is something important to tell you but for now I must sign off & go to bed. I wake early. If anyone cares to write to me I would welcome such letters. & please forgive me for running off the way I did.

I remain your affectionate son.

James

c/o Grayson & Company
201 Julia Street
New Orleans, Louisiana, USA

James Dunne had arrived at the New Orleans levee wearing velveteen knee-breeches, a frieze coat and cape, coarse blue stockings and heavy leather brogans that reached to his ankles. He was the perfect picture of an Irish immigrant, confused and scared. Agents of madams and pimps quickly recruited comely young women for work in the brothels while gullible men were fleeced by swindlers or robbed outright. Goons loitered about itching for a fight.

A rough-looking man approached James on the dock where ships were moored on the levee three abreast. His long, greasy hair trailed under his large floppy felt hat that had lost all its shape to the rain. He wore a dirty buckskin tunic and trousers made of sturdy canvas jean. Traditionally, locals called all these feral men of the river Kaintocks, thinking they floated down from Kentucky. "Hey you there," he croaked out in a loud call, "come 'ere." James proceeded with caution, casually patting his shirt to make sure the concealed coin sack hanging around his neck was still there.

"What is it?" he asked.

"Name's Enoch Henderson. I need help unloading five boatloads of cotton. Interested?"

James had just met his first bona fide American and it wasn't a pretty sight. He was a tall sinewy mass of a man with red, watery eyes practically swollen shut. The effects of exposure had singed his eyelashes clear off. The stench surrounding him sent James staggering backward, never having confronted such an odor growing up in the sweet country air of Ireland. Enoch dashed the goo from his eyes with one hand and popped out the other, not in a token of friendship, but because every character on the levee baits his hook with a little kindness.

Confidently James took his hand and squeezed, hoping to impress Enoch with his manly ways.

"What are you paying?"

"Pays twenty-five cents."

"Those boats right there?" he pointed to the barges he saw through the mist behind Enoch.

"That's them."

"Where are the men that brought those boats down the river with you?"

"They went up to town to get screwed, boozed and bruised."

"They're piled pretty high. Might take a while. I'll do it for fifty cents."

"Oh, a hagglin' man are you? OK. Let's go."

"You can give me twenty-five cents to start with."

"It don't appears you trust me much?"

"You seem like a good fellow but I think that's only fair, we've just become acquainted."

"Well, as ya say ya God-damned bog-trotter, here ya are. Now let's get. Oh, and make sure them fancy velvet knickers don't get wet." Enoch laughed a hardy laugh and handed James his first American money, hoping he didn't run off before the job was done. James was hoping he wasn't helping Enoch steal five boatloads of cotton.

What emerged in the ensuing three years of steady work was a confident, capable man who could move upwardly from job to job with ease. In Ireland, once a stevedore, always a stevedore. In America, anything was possible and in New Orleans, her most alluring of her cities, possibilities seemed endless.

Located on a crescent-shaped piece of high ground between Lake Pontchartrain and the winding Mississippi River, New Orleans was a natural distribution centre for overseas imports and exports. The river itself was lifeblood for the growing United States, pumping provisions and raw materials from the plantations up and down the gargantuan waterway. Only the Amsterdam of the 1600s could rival its excitement and promise. Virginians dominated the commission business; the Scotch and Irish competed for the commerce of exportation and importation whereas the Spanish and French ran shops and restaurants. People of colour and free Negroes kept inferior shops or sold goods and fruit on the streets.

The port city also became a dumping ground of sorts for transported tenants from Ireland's poorhouses and jails. Ships would be loaded-up with American cotton at the Port of New Orleans, its cargo dropped at the doorsteps of Britain's Northern textile mills and then the ship would be filled with Ireland's surplus people for a return voyage through the Gulf of Mexico. These lowly immigrants, termed *Shanty Irish*, were housed in the city's worst sections and roughest neighborhoods below Canal Street.

Because New Orleans herself had traded nationalities from Spanish to French to American she actually didn't mind newcomers despite the backbiting and name-calling. The expanding metropolis once home to generations of old Creole families became filled with transient adventurers devoid of local feeling, bond or union. It was a city state.

Before his recent promotion, James lived in the heinous Connaught Yard, a block of brick boarding houses on Julia Street, chiefly inhabited by spiders and rancid smells. Violence, drunkenness and pestilence greeted him night after night. He kept his head down, only concerning himself with work while the other boarders drank and fought amongst themselves until the break of dawn. James esteemed them men without knowledge, nor principle, nor direction. They would never be happy until Connaught Yard ran red with blood. He had left that copy of himself prone to anger and rash behavior back in Ireland.

He felt a good deal safer and a good deal more productive when he was given his own small bunk room on the floor of the Grayson & Company warehouse. He was happy that he could now afford to get his daily meal at one of the many coffeehouses that were sprinkled throughout his neighborhood. The egalitarian coffeehouses of New Orleans served many purposes: tavern, restaurant, bakery, hotel, card room, grocery store, trading post, dance hall and political club, all in one place. A few even served a decent cup of coffee.

Upstairs at Grayson & Company, the tidy business office was jammed with men working at high slanted tables wedged between piles of sample goods from the downstairs warehouse. James, being the first to unlock the door in the mornings and the last to shut it in the evenings, was hunched over his table wrestling with numbers from a ledger. A group of businessmen in broadcloth suits and stovepipe hats congregated by the oversized windows that overlooked the masts and smokestacks sprouting from the river. Their glowing cigars quickly overpowered the smells of burlap and sugar that normally hung about the room. Each of them wore the tailored trappings of wealth but one man stood out amongst the others with a bright red carnation pinned to his label. He was the eponymous owner of Grayson & Company, one Elias P. Grayson.

Mr. Grayson was a native born Cajun of hazy heritage. His slight paunch was usually covered in a checked waistcoat hovering above skinny legs in tight-fitting breeches. His exceptionally small feet made him appear precariously off-balance. A long waxy moustache extended out in opposing directions from his face like the balancing bar of a man on a high-wire. He was a New Orleans commission merchant. He made his riches buying cheap and selling dear. Operating at a cautious remove from the production of supplies he preferred to exploit the differences in commodity values from place to place. He let the farmers take all the risk of lost crops, bad weather and price fluctuations. He would take the reward, for there was nothing he wouldn't buy or sell. Cotton, sugar, grain and produce became his staples but he could also trade in Mexican silver, Vermont ice or an entire Louisiana plantation. He served as the home agent to many inland planters. He was at once his merchant, his banker and sleeping-partner. Competitors admired his bold trading style and whined that Grayson could parade through Hades with his hat off. The company's expansive warehouse spanned a square city block.

"We should be going," Mr. Blackman said to Mr. Grayson.

"Oh yes, the time has gotten away from us," replied Mr. Grayson. He called over to his right-hand man, "Mr. Lambertus, pack up your books we mustn't be late."

"Sir?"

"I want you to go to the market with us and tabulate the transactions."

"I'm afraid I am due to get these receipts over to the custom house by three o'clock or we will be fined."

"Why didn't you get that done yesterday?"

"Dreadfully backed-up in here sir."

"Very well, I'll take the new boy."

"James?"

"Yes, James."

"But sir just look at him, he's dressed like a wharf rat."

"I see that. You're about the same size. Trade him your suit and books and tell him to meet us at the hack."

Perturbed beyond measure, Lambertus obeyed and reluctantly readied James for the market while the cadre of businessmen made their way downstairs. Waiting by the carriage they made small talk.

"Who is your new office boy up there, Elias?" asked Mr. Lacroix with his retreating chin nestled into a blue silk scarf.

"Another Patlander I hired off the dock," murmured Grayson as he relit his cigar.

"Don't we have enough of his type clogging up the streets—you have to go and bring them upstairs?"

"He's not like the others."

"Irish should only work outside at physical labor. They need fresh air and exercise," said Lacroix.

"Nonsense. He's a hardworking lad. Skilled with the numbers. Straight as they make 'em. Even speaks Spanish. Had him negotiate with an incoherent Cuban over a shipment of rum and Havana cigars. Don't know what he said to the dolt but we made $200 off the deal." His defense of the boy ran counter to his normal practice of ridicule and torment, artistry he imagined his audience found delightfully entertaining.

Lacroix disapproved, "Half of these Patlanders are dead drunk in our alleyways and the other half think they're descendants of Irish kings!"

James had arrived. Standing directly behind Mr. Lacroix he held his head down, ledger in hand with a slight grin on his face, resisting the urge to puff out his chest. The chartered clothes from Lambertus were up to scratch with the pants only being about an inch too short. "All assembled? Good. Everyone in. To the Saint Louis Exchange Hotel and make haste, boy!"

Grayson directed the driver down Tchoupitoulas. James Dunne was at this moment literally rubbing shoulders with the barons of the New Orleans merchant class. He could never have dreamed of such a thing when he appeared at the levee, a penniless castaway. Maybe he could learn the secrets of success in America from this lot.

Tchoupitoulas Street followed the river and was lined with brick warehouses and busy storefronts. After the rain it was ankle deep in mud. Whistling steamboats caused the men inside the carriage to shout at each other above the din. James was privy to their conversations and was surprised at how much cursing went on between men of such Southern charm. Language as filthy as this wasn't even used among the drunkest of low-class New Orleans gutter creatures.

Many of the ladies on the sidewalks wore caps or veils rather than bonnets. Conveyances of all kinds criss-crossed the street with sacks and barrels, crates and bales, blocking progress. Directly in front of the merchant's carriage a man stopped, his slave set down his dolly and attempted to unsuccessfully light his master's cigar. Grayson's driver furiously cracked his whip and called out for the oblivious duo to make way.

Trotting at a dangerous pace they arrived at the portico entrance of the gleaming white hotel. Hastily the group navigated through the majestic entrance parlor down the hallway laid with elaborate Persian runners to the Grand Rotunda at the centre of the building. Corinthian pilasters encircled the gilded plasterwork walls in between seashell-shaped alcoves of remarkable elegance and beauty. Beams of celestial light shot through the glass dome bulging above them, throngs of men covered the floor. Grayson's group was late.

"Damn it to hell!" a frustrated Mr. Grayson cursed, "Now we are stuck here at the back." The rest of the gentleman made their way through the crowd as James cleaved to his boss, not having a clue about his duties at this elusive, so-called market. All the men ignored him on the ride over and he was at a complete loss as to what was happening.

"Sir, what shall you have me do here?" James inquired.

"Well, I want a thorough written description of each lot auctioned off and the final sales figures. See if you can write down each incremental increase and we can tally up later."

"Yes, sir."

"I may bid myself but I want to know who I am going up against. Make sure you find out the names of all the winning bidders too. Try to stay by my side, it may get rowdy. I know most of these scoundrels and I'll tell you their names if they bid," he continued in a stern, avuncular manner.

"Yes, sir."

"Come along boy. Pardon me, excuse me." Grayson slithered to the front with James closely following. A stout, bespectacled auctioneer was at a podium yelling out the terms and conditions of the sale. From a side entrance a gruff- looking buffalo of a man led in a chained gang of Negroes stripped to the waist. Men, woman and children lined up behind a raised platform.

James Dunne was stationed in the front row of the New Orleans Slave Market.

Proceedings started quickly and James sprung to duty.

"First up is a fine young buck of five and twenty years. Goes by the name of Amos, he is Chattel Number 1 in the catalogue. Experienced field hand from a cotton plantation in Maryland. Well-behaved. Healthy as a horse. Good teamster. His owner passed away and the widow is selling out. I trust you all had a good look at him yesterday at the viewing. He got a wife and three childrens who are Chattels 2-5 in the catalogue. They beg to be purchased together but we are selling them all individually. Starting bid at seven-hundred and fifty dollars."

Bids flew around the room at a dizzying speed. James, keeping pace, scrawled down numbers in the journal trying hard to keep his writing legible and even. After two minutes of bids and counter bids, Amos was sold for $1275 to a gentleman from the Evergreen Plantation. He did not purchase the wife nor the children of Amos who were all sorrowfully auctioned off in different directions. James conscientiously wrote down slave descriptions and perceptive details with the attention of a trained numbers accountant. He was proud of his work, purposely ignoring the nature of it all.

Four and a half hours had elapsed when the last few lots were brought out. Chattel Number 61 came up on the auction block. Mr. Grayson poked his young assistant in the leg and said, "Take special notes on this one boy. Be suave, that's the ticket." James became jittery, his heart beat faster. The auctioneer began his sales pitch:

"Chattel 61 comes to us from the sugar plantation up yonder known as Oak Alley. Seems they need to swap some workers around and y'all get the benefit of this perfect specimen. Take note of his broad shoulders and massive wing-span. He knows his way around a sugar field and is capable of working several stations. Good sawyer. He could carry twice as much cane as an ordinary field hand with those arms of his. 2 and thirty years we have here a servant named Peter for your consideration. We'll start Peter off here at $800. $800. Do I hear $800?"

Fatigue was starting to set in amongst the buyers and many of the men had left the rotunda not wanting to miss any of the Friday evening festivities in town. Bidding had stalled.

"See here good people, Peter can turn your sugar fields into gold. He is a sound investment to be sure. He's a bone-black burner, he's a good cooper, he knows how to work the vacuum-pan, just a fine sugar maker. He's like a steam engine! Now, who will bid $800 for this dependable laborer?"

"I'll bid $500." Mr. Grayson had entered into the fray.

"$500, sir, couldn't buy you an ox that will work this hard."

"Just the same, $500."

"Very well, we'll start Peter here off at $500. Do I hear $600? Six-hundred dollars?" the auctioneer drew out the words hoping to draw out a competing buyer. "$600 say anyone? $600? Don't delay now, 600?" Time was evaporating and the auctioneer tried in vain to stimulate the bidding with more of Peter's super-human qualities but it was useless.

"$500. Sold to Mr. Elias P. Grayson of Fairview Plantation." James scribbled the details into his book, completely unaware that Mr. Grayson even owned a plantation. As Peter was led away in chains from the auction block a sparkling ray of twilight came down through the skylight upon his head, illuminating the dark, handsome face. Such a civilized, palatial setting for such an uncivilized, barbarous transaction.

James relaxed his body after the bidding was complete and it was only then that he took notice of the dichotomy. Did Mr. Grayson just purchase a person? The fact that this slave bore the same name as his own brother brought out a flush of mercy provoking a tear to trickle down his face and land on his neatly inscribed ledger paper. Ink pooled up around the tear and James worried his work had been tainted.

That day Grayson had bought 3 men.

It was late in the evening by the time financial arrangements and delivery instructions were settled. James was praised for his fine note taking and was offered a ride back to Julia Street with Mr. Grayson. His atrocious complicity was salved by the plush interior of a warm carriage.

"As far as I can tell we just bought $4,500 worth of slaves for $2275. I knew Friday night would be a horrible time to hold an auction in New Orleans. I could have made twice as much if I were brokering those slaves."

"Indeed. Are you going to move into the slave trade business as well sir?" asked a hesitant James.

"There is money to be made there for sure and I've brokered a few in my day but for now I need help on the sugar plantation I bought up Baton Rouge way."

"I was unaware you owned a sugar plantation. I thought you preferred to be a wholesaler."

"Still do, making things is for stupid people. I bought Fairview from a desperate seller at a bargain. It was almost robbery. It might take five years to get her turned into a first-class plantation but I'll do it. I like to always seek out new opportunities you see. Lots of irons in the fire. Spread my investment around and I can sell my own sugar for the next five years too. Make money on both ends."

"I see. And who's to say you can't be a plantation owner and a commission merchant?" asked James.

"Nobody."

"America."

"America."

When his head hit the pillow that night, James reflected on the eventful day and his time with the business tycoons of New Orleans. He imagined his own future as one of them, an untouchable commission merchant fueled by the prodigious power of wealth. The house he would have, the beautiful wife, the refined children. To get there he might need to overlook uncomfortable things that would block progress. He turned in his bed and flipped the pillow over to the cool side. Restless, he turned the pillow back again and he thought of the slave named Peter. Where was he sleeping tonight? James abruptly flipped himself over beneath the covers and fell asleep.

Even as a boy James Dunne saw the world in black and white terms. The nuances and circumspection required to see gray tones only blurred his vision and kept him from achieving his goals.

CHAPTER 15

Article titled "Special Notices," The Daily Picayune New Orleans

March 12, 1844

TAKE NOTICE

    Mister J. Dunne has been promoted to General Manager of Grayson & Co. Commission Merchants— Julia Street. Grateful for the confidence reposed in and favors extended to me I humbly solicit the continuance of patronage as I depart for an extended tour of South America. I know J. Dunne will continue to act with honor and integrity and strict attention to the interest of our correspondents in my absence. I shall return by year's end.

    E.P. Grayson

    President, Grayson & Company

Mr. Elias P. Grayson deputized James to run his commission merchant business while he explored a lucrative opportunity to sell discarded British military weaponry to the armies, revolutionaries and despots of various South American countries. Money was flowing into the Grayson firm from North, South, East and West. James handled the accounts, procured goods, arranged shipping, financed trading partners and supervised the company's numerous employees. The management of the Fairview plantation and sugar production was out of his purview but Mr. Grayson requested intelligence on its progress so a trip was planned that would oblige James to leave New Orleans for the first time since his arrival five years earlier.

    Seven miles outside Baton Rouge, Fairview had a Mississippi river frontage that allowed the sugar and molasses produced on the plantation a direct shipping route to Grayson & Company's New Orleans operation. The point at which the water ended and the land began was in question until the 900 acres of sugar cane appeared like a flat, green billiard table all the way up to the neglected, colonial-style farmhouse. Camouflaged by the tall stalks of cane, a network of wagon roads and drainage ditches pierced through the plants. James became disoriented in his search for the sugarhouse where he was to meet Pierre Calou, an aged man charged with turning Fairview into a profitable enterprise. A young Negro boy found him wandering in the field and brought him by the hand back to Mr. Calou waiting at the red brick structure.

"Dunne, I guess my directions left you a-wantin'?" said Calou, a careless dresser who despised James at first sight for the calculated effects of his city costume.

"How do you do Mr. Calou? Yes, I got a little discombobulated but I was rescued."

Calou pointed to the young lad, "That's my little scout Micky, I done sent him after you. He knows this place better than I do."

"Thank you, Micky," said James, quite unsure of slavery etiquette.

"He don't need no thanks," Calou reassured, sucking his teeth.

"Very well. Mr. Grayson sent me so that I can report back to him on all the headway you're making up here," James said in his quiet tone of cool refinement. Disguising his abilities with a frosty veneer of gentlemanly reserve was his way of disarming an opponent.

"Well, I tells the man ev'ry thing he needs to know. Why he need you say the same thing?"

"Oh no, rest assured you have Mr. Grayson's every confidence. I mainly have to report on the dollars and cents. But I would like to familiarize myself a little better with how the plantation works, if you don't mind."

"All righty. I come here a year and a half ago and the place was a dee-saster. I had to reconfigure everythin'. At first I hired a bunch of traveling Irishers, like yourself, to dig all new ditches and trenches. They hacked away and cleared out more land for planting. They even lost one of their lot in that far swamp over there." He pointed with his old hickory cane. "So, in terms a' dollars and cents, we didn't have to pay him. Owed him three weeks' pay too." Calou looked over to see if James had any noticeable reaction. No. He continued, "Could have risked a slave but I knows better. You can write that down and report back on all the cost savings here at Fairview." James had no intention of writing that down, but he quickly understood Calou was ready for combat and he would do his best to demur to the old man at every chance.

"Work around this place is brutal. It's hard to plant the cane, it's hard to harvest. It's hard to make into sugar. But Mista Dunne, I can make mo' money for your boss man with sugar than any cotton planter could ever dream of."

A brief tutorial of the process was followed by a tour on horseback of the plantation. Micky ran alongside the pair, whisking away flies from the horses with batons of leaves. James was impressed by the organization and efficiency he observed.

They passed a cart loaded with large casks of molasses followed by another with pails of hominy and dried fish. Tin pannikins hooked onto the sideboard swung and rattled as it slowly rambled over to the field hands; a slave chuck wagon. Up ahead was the overseer, a pudgy Creole on a spindly pony with a thonged whip draped over his shoulder. Calou and James waited at the edge of the cane field to witness white dots suddenly emerge from the bright green thickets, called by the clanging triangle. Dark men, woman and children gathered around the back of the wagon in an orderly fashion. They curtseyed and bowed to Mr. Calou, shy and silent. On their heads were coarse straw hats, the men wore white cambric shirts, the women wore skirts made from discarded white flour sacks. Heavy and poorly made shoes covered their feet.

"Hungry Mista Dunne?"

"I suppose I—"

Calou let out a loud and uproarious laugh. "Oh no, I'm just joshin' wit you. I wouldn't let you eat dat nig-nog chow. Supper's waiting at the house." More chuckles followed. James felt foolish. Calou liked making people feel foolish.

Trotting up to the big house they passed through an avenue of live oaks dripping with Spanish moss into the area of the slave's quarters. Woven cages constructed of twigs contained domestic birds of all types. They were stacked up haphazardly in the yards strewn with assorted rubble and rubbish. Eggs and poultry were allowed by the master to be sold and slaves could use the cash to buy tobacco or flour. Forbidden liquor was procured on the sly. James brought his horse to a halt outside one of the windowless wooden huts that housed the workers. He did not dismount but ducked his head to get a peek inside the doorway.

A strange maudlin feeling overwhelmed him and he was immediately transported back to the squalor of his own family's tenants upon Brittas. The dreariness of servitude was exactly the same but the penalties for escape were different. Just how many young slave girls had Calou and the like abused here over the years? How many seemingly descent men got away with atrocious behaviour in the dark shadows of slavery, poverty and misery. Men like his father. An analogy that was not lost on him for a second but a second's reflection was all that he would spare.

His advancement to General Manager of Grayson & Company had inadvertently frosted the sensitive, sympathetic heart of his youth making him hard and callous. He lived without the judgement or guidance of a mother hovering over his every move. He allowed his conscience to collapse in the vacuum. Injustice that appeared so crystal clear to him a few short years ago was now rationally assigned to an asset or a liability column of the balance sheet. He had come to believe in America all that really mattered was the bottom line.

Out on the expansive veranda, Mulatto house servants laid a bountiful spread before Calou and James. It was time to get down to brass tacks.

"I appreciate your hospitality Mr. Calou, very much."

"But...."

"But, as you know, Mr. Grayson does not particularly like to make things, his business is selling things. Much quicker. Cleaner. I was very impressed with the sugarhouse efficiency. The improvements in output is staggering but Mr. Grayson is concerned with the outlay of cash you have spent in doing so. We need to document Fairview's profitability so she can be sold and Grayson can move onto other ventures."

"We've had a good year but I cannot say we all that profitable yet."

"You're not." James shot back.

"I'm getting there but one good frost next year could kill off everything. My anxieties are great Mista Dunne."

"Such is the life of a planter."

Negotiations, excuses and head-pinching continued on through the meal with dates and financial goals agreed upon. Conversation turned in a more convivial direction.

"I know you people in New O'lens would like to economize but this here house were sittin' on could use a little sprucin' up if you're going ta get top dollar."

"Maybe just a few cans of paint," James suggested.

"Mista Grayson's kin have been here for three months and they have a list more extensive than a few cans a paint."

"How many people are here?"

"We got his sista, daughter and two ol' aunties. They got sent up here ta get outta New O'lens for the fever season. You know the fever took Grayson's wife a few years back."

"I was unaware of that or even that he had a daughter. I thought he was a carefree bachelor."

"That's what you get for building a city in a swamp I suppose."

"But at any rate, I imagine they'll soon be back in town and you can wait on any expenditures until next spring."

Walking out onto the veranda with perfect timing was Grayson's sister Amelia, her ruffles and flounces swishing on the corroded green porch planks causing flecks of paint to pop off into the air as she moved. "Mr. Calou, who have you brought with you? I don't believe we've been introduced," she declared while waving a palmetto leaf on her exposed neck.

"Mista Dunne, Miss Grayson," said with the all the fervor of a pent-up yawn.

James did the graceful and rose from his chair, taking Amelia's hand. "I work for your brother in New Orleans."

"Why yes, my brother speaks very highly of you. Will you be here long?"

"No ma'am, taking a steamer back tonight," James said to Amelia with the ambivalence he had shown to every woman he'd met since his arrival in America.

"Oh, yes I imagine you are a very busy man, Mr. Dunne."

A soft, infectious giggle could be heard drifting from behind the oleander hedges blooming in radiant fuchsia. "Look, look, look," whispered Kitty in her lilting Southern way as she slowly glided up the steps toward the group. On her elegant fingers perched a gigantic, complacent dragonfly with wings of dazzling opalescent beauty. "Isn't it marvellous?"

"Oh Kitty, this gentleman can't be bothered with your silly ol' bug," huffed Amelia.

James however was most intrigued.

"That's lovely, I've never seen anything like it."

"And your accent is lovely, I've never heard anything like it," said Kitty as she kept her attention on the dragonfly.

He wanted a better view of the face that complimented his Irish brogue, an affliction that had only brought mockery from other Americans. Captivated by the insect, Kitty kept her eyes down frustrating

James. "Kitty darling, I want you to meet Mr. Dunne." Amelia said, "He works for your father in the warehouse."

"Oh, hello." She did not reach out a hand or glance his way. Bits of grass clung to the tussled blonde hair that cascaded down to her shoulders. The alabaster skin on her face hosted an assortment of freckles and a slight flush from running around the yard. Her dress was simple in design but vibrant in color; a garish shade of pink that seemed to have been born from the very same oleander hedges from which she had emerged. James said, "Your friend seems right at home on your finger."

"He really does. He hasn't moved a muscle. I think he's just showing off." She flittered over to James on the tips of her toes to give him a closer look. Her head slowly tilted upwards and she bestowed the full presentation of her face upon a decidedly worthy guest. Unknowingly, she'd played this game with her eyes since she was a baby. She knew they had special persuasive powers. Large and blue and drooping in the corners they were her most marked characteristic and they were beguiling.

"All right now Kitty, you may go. The gentlemen here need to finish their business talk."

"That's all right ma'am. I think Miss Kitty would be fine to sit right here," James patted at the seat of the empty wicker chair.

"How kind. Bless your heart Mr. Dunne." Amelia said with a phrase all Southern women knew to be more of a curse.

James wrote his report to Mr. Grayson on the evening steamer, capturing all the interesting and pertinent issues facing Fairview. He included his predictions on the plantation's expected profitability. He did not include the probability that he was in love with the boss's daughter.

Plagued by old age and dementia, General Dunne had forgotten nearly everything about his storied life except the grudges. At his seat of Brittas, in his 82nd year, he passed over the great divide. The family gathered in his library where they stopped the clock the minute he died.

"I'm envisioning a large military service in Dublin where we can accommodate the maximum number of people," said the heir and new clan chieftain, Major Francis Plunkett Dunne.

"Frank, of course that would be lovely but nobody knows him there anymore," said the General's widow Frances. "Something small and dignified here would be better."

"Your ladyship, if I may interject, I've been going through his papers, preparing for the solicitors and I found a directive from your husband." Mr. Dunne timidly continued. "It does state that, aye, he would like the service at his little church in town."

"Sounds like him," the widow agreed.

"Aye, he was eminently clear." Mr. Dunne then produced the General's handwritten notes.

Frances grabbed at the papers, "Why have I never seen this? We've been married more than 40 years."

"My apologies ma'am, I should have been more organized."

"What else does it say?" wondered a curious Frank.

"It goes into who he wants to carry his casket, hymns, scripture, very specific…burial instructions at the Killyann graveyard and that he'd like to open the house up for a wake." Mr. Dunne knew this last request would be difficult to hear.

"You mean open it up to everyone?" asked Frances.

"Specifically he writes there, you can see it for yourself, '…low and high, far and near…' Which I would assume means everyone, ma'am."

"No. Absolutely no. It will be worse than a country fair."

"That is one fantastically horrible notion," added Frank.

"It was a very specific request, Frank. A wake brings the family together and we know he esteemed the whole county his family. As his land agent, and now your land agent, I suggest it's the perfect way to demonstrate a definitive changing of the guard, so to speak, at Brittas. Good way to show you will respect tradition, respect the tenants. Anglicans can attend the church service and Catholics can have their wake."

"So it would be to our advantage to have the house overrun with drunken stupidity and Papist witchcraft then? Is that what you're telling us Mr. Dunne?" Frank sneered.

"Or you can barricade yourselves in here without so much as a nod to the people's mourning. To me, that is the riskier proposition." The new heir considered his new counselor's advice and asked, "Mother, that does have a certain convoluted logic to it and Father sounded adamant. Would you be at all willing?"

"Very well. I'm tired. Hide the silver, lock-up the gun room and drape everything in black," Frances relented, worn down by the day's events and all the ones leading up to it.

Frank went into action discussing details with Mr. Dunne of how the vigil would be organized. He had attended a few dignified Irish wakes but they were for local upper crust Catholics and could hardly compare with the behaviour exhibited by the poorer, Papist classes. Sadness united with joy. Often raucous and raunchy, the drinking event could lead to card games or sex games, as if God Himself was too overwhelmed with grief to notice. Over the centuries, the Irish wake had shocked and fascinated foreign visitors who often attended such happenings as curious tourists would visit the ruins in Rome.

Central to the event was the keen, Gaelic for crying. Keeners were could wail in strange and savage tones over the dead. Mae Coughlin, famous local oracle, was also known as the best keener of the Midlands. Mr. Dunne was tasked with finding the wandering mystic and securing her services.

Word of the General's death spread like flocks of blackbirds over Queen's County. In droves people were making their way to Brittas so that by nightfall there were well-over 500 mourners on the grounds trying to make their way inside the house.

Patrick and Bridget Lawler had entered through the kitchen door, avoiding the mayhem taking place out on the front lawn. Tenants were carrying on, arguing, singing, flirting or praying. Couples disappeared into the bushes. Jars of contraband poitín passed among them right under the noses of British cavalry soldiers stationed throughout the estate.

Two very regal specimens from the 7th Dragoon Guards stood as sentries outside the main entrance doors. Polished golden helmets, black feathers, white cross shoulder belts and bright red tunics were presented for maximum intimidation. Mae Coughlin had arrived to begin the keening but stopped first on the stone steps to inspect them at such close range, they could smell liquor wafting up from her breath. Her prolonged and exaggerated scrutiny gnawed at their silent decorum, finally prompting one guard to ask;

"Does my gun scare you, woman?"

"I'm not afraid of your gun, it's your fleas I'm worried about." And with that she entered.

Once more the three grandest rooms of Brittas were opened up to each other creating the expansive space used for public events like the bygone Manor Court sessions. Some of the mourners reminisced about their long-forgotten court cases as they got a last look at the General laid out in his dress uniform. His oak casket had been made to his own specifications months earlier by the estate's carpenter. Austere in design, its only frill being a handsomely carved family crest and a few brass fittings. All the ancient accoutrements of an Irish wake surrounded him on his bier: candles, flowers, plates of tobacco and snuff.

Keening would normally follow the reading of the rosary at midnight but that custom was abandoned at the request of the General's widow and her sons. Mae Coughlin, well-aware of the religious restrictions placed on her, shuffled through the crowd of mourners to the head of the General's coffin, an oversized rosary in her hand.

In her flowing purple muslin she appeared as an apparition unto herself. On her face one could see a glimpse of her former beauty under crepey wrinkles and raised barnacles. Her hair was full and as black as treacle. It seemed to wave in a wind that wasn't there. She looked about the people before closing her eyes, seeming to go into another dimension, a trance. It was hauntingly quiet. Snaps of candle flames provided the only audible sound amongst the hush of anticipation.

Mae began to writhe as if she was summoning a snake from the depths of her bowels. Then, the strangest trickle of noise sprung from her throat getting louder as it left her body. It was a beastly cry like a wounded wolf in the forest yet it had a strange, humane melody. Primitive and savage, the wailings had no discernible words but through a consonance of tones produced a feeling of such bleak loneliness. It continued for several excruciating minutes.

Bridget looked up at Patrick, gripping his lapel, "Patrick, it's taking the heart right out of me." Women were wiping tears away with their apron corners and wringing their hands in agony. The mouths of stout men trembled with emotion. Mae began to mumble softly as if she was assuring herself of her next keen. Lamentations slowly transitioned into words. Irish words. A harpist improvised. Others softly moaned in the background. She was composing a poem about the deceased in song as the spirit moved her:

"Why did your Honour lead us and then decide to leave us? Oh, why I beg to know brave man? We are left to wage war without your command. We now must face the invaders on our own somehow. Your steady hand is missed. Man of the people, man of our soul, your family, your people forever ache. Misery. Destruction awaits us all without you."

Like some ancient banshee, Mae had conjured up a storm of unbridled proportions above the heads of the crowd. A dark pall fell over the rooms of Brittas and filled the people with anxiety, with dread. Was this keening at its finest or the incantations of Satan cursing the house, the county, the island itself?

Saturday was the day General Edward Dunne was to be buried. Black draperies adorning Brittas quivered in the wind as his body left feet first. The coffin was carried on the shoulders of men from families of the highest condition. Black ribbons adorned their hats and helmets. Teams of casket bearers lined the road down to the church at the centre of Clonaslee, shouldering the General down in shifts three times without once breaking step. Tenants and curious townspeople crowded the square in front of the church and graciously moved in waves to accommodate the procession. Mr. Dunne's family gathered close to the front of the Anglican church, their faith forbidding their entrance. Catholics waited outside. The General's family and chief mourners were already assembled in their pews.

At the appointed time the Gothic red door of the church opened. Reverend Baldwin awaited the body in the doorway along with the final set of pallbearers, among them Major Rotund, the General's loyal aide de camp. His medals twinkled in the morning sun, his belly protruded out from his dress-blue britches. Effortlessly the casket transitioned to the final set of men who walked a few paces and began to ascend the church steps.

Patrick Lawler was transfixed by the military precision and marvelled at the strength required to hold up such a heavy wooden coffin. Major Rotund had the brunt of being the end man shouldering the most weight as they all slowly climbed up the steps. He felt sure of his grip on the casket but began to imagine his dress-blue pants coming loose from the sash around his amble waist. He couldn't let go. His trousers promptly dropped to the ground exposing his white drawers to the assembled crowd. "WAIT!" he yelled as the procession came to a stop. Patrick quickly ran up the steps and held the end of the casket while Rotund pulled up his pants. Embarrassed and ungrateful, he pushed Patrick aside and waved him off. The cortege entered the church with the red door closing behind them.

Wild and wicked laughter erupted on the streets of Clonaslee the likes of which would become legendary.

CHAPTER 16

Letter from Anton Oster to Major Francis Plunkett Dunne

December 2, 1844
Junior United Service Club
Charles Street, Waterloo Place
London

Dear Major Dunne:
    It is with pleasure that I accept the terms and conditions put forth in the enclosed acceptance for the Agency of Brittas, The Queen's County, Ireland. I shall remove myself to Ireland forthwith and assume my duties on January 1, 1845. It is my understanding that the present agent and his family shall vacate their residence at Brittas House so that I may fully avail myself of their former quarters.

    I will endeavour to make the substantial changes we discussed at our meeting as immediately as is feasible. My former employer, Admiral Farnham, has returned from India and is quite satisfied with the work I have completed on his estate in his absence—so I may leave England with the satisfaction of a job well-done and well-received. I very much look forward to helping restore your estates to their former glory.

    I have the honour to be your humble servant and remain,
    Sincerely,
    Anton Oster

After General Dunne was laid to rest a complete accounting of his estate's ledgers were conducted by Frank and his attorney brother. The full fury of the brothers rained down upon the head of Brittas' estate agent when it was discovered that not only was the General flat broke but he was many thousands of pounds in debt as well. Jeremiah Dunne, Director of the Hibernia Bank, allowed nepotism to cloud his judgement when he granted mortgage loans on the Queen's County holdings that far exceeded their value. The Earl of Bantry had lent monies on securities from the estate's furnishings, paintings and stock certificates. Mrs. Kavanaugh and her purse intervened over the years. The only collateral she required was the answer to a question, "How much do you need and when do you need it?" No records existed of her generosity. She was spending the winter, as was her custom, at a resort on the Mediterranean Sea, Nice to be exact. When Edward Meadows Dunne sent enquiries asking the specific amount of his father's debts to her she replied, "…it was all a gift, isn't everything?"

Mr. Dunne knew as soon as the General passed his own day of reckoning would not be far behind. In addition to the oppressive debt, Brittas was burdened with rent arrears going back 10 years. He had stacks of papers documenting the decline in receipts. A full 88% of the tenants owed back rent of one kind or another. Compounding it all, now that the burden of tithes had been thrust upon Irish landlords, an ungodly sum of money was owed to the United Church of England and Ireland.

Tragically, the General who had been larger than life itself left debts even larger in death. These discoveries completely blindsided the General's widow so she was in full compliance with any remedy her sons had in mind. Mr. Dunne must be relieved of his position, post-haste. This meant his family was given 48 hours to remove their belongings out of the servant's wing and off the Brittas estate. As a way of recompense, he was deeded the Ballintlea House and farm that had been leased to his family for the past two generations. It carried with it a mortgage held by the Hibernia Bank for £373. Mr. Dunne's oldest son Michael collected his parents and brought them to live with his wife Elsie and their family back at Ballintlea House. Mrs. Miquel, the Spanish cook hired by the General decades earlier, was also given her walking papers along with her son and his family who lived on the grounds of Brittas. Scores were being settled.

Ballintlea House was a grand name for a farm by the side of a bog. Mr. Dunne was having difficulty returning to live in his childhood home now ruled over by his son and tiresome daughter-in-law. His thoughts toggled between memories of the life he had lived at Ballintlea and the failures that brought him back. It was Sunday and the rosary had been said before dinner but now as they sat around the table no one said anything at all.

Patrick and Bridget Lawler, with four little children in tow made the trip over from their nearby farm. Peter was living bache in Mountmellick and had no interest in family dinners. Mary Donnelly came alone, leaving her four with Hugh to run the hotel up in Maryborough. Over the course of their marriage he had contracted habits unbecoming a family man. After a ten-year reprieve, she was pregnant again.

"I'm having another baby," Mary decided she could bring a little gaiety to the sombre meal.

"Raising children above a pub must be difficult for you Mary," sympathized Elsie.

"It's no different, really, than raising them on a farm, they just clean up after drunks instead of cows."

"I never met a cow that could cuss up a storm or start a fight," Elsie said tersely.

"Is that right? I know a cow who is quite handy at starting fights."

"Well, it's a fine thing you having another baby Mary. Congratulations!" Trying to right the wrong footed conversation, Bridget stepped in and brought the table back to silence. Cutlery clicked about the plates.

Embolden by a sense of duty to his father, Michael chose to bring up a topic that was heavy on everyone's mind. "I heard there are wholesale evictions going on up at Brittas since you left, Father. Some of them went straight into that workhouse in Mountmellick."

"I know," said Mr. Dunne, "the General himself laid the cornerstone for that building. Prophesy. He could read the writing on the wall."

"It's not fair you've been blamed and banished when it was the General that drove the place into rack and ruin, not you!" Michael protested.

"Son, he did the best he could. I did the best I could. It's a marvel we kept up the trick as long as we did," Mr. Dunne muttered as he slowly spread butter throughout the corners and crevices of his bread, dragging the knife repeatedly over the same spots. Bridget fed a daughter with one hand and wiped her son's mouth with the other. She would take a bite for herself now and then but she wasn't feeling hungry. She was worried. The father she knew, the one who radiated energy, the one in constant motion, the one who lamented that there weren't enough hours to the day would never spend that much time buttering his bread.

Within a fortnight he would be motionless under the graveyard at Timahoe.

Anton Oster, an Austrian-born friend of Frank's had served alongside him in various skirmishes the British Army had gotten itself into on the

Ionian Peninsula. Oster was hailed as somewhat of a miracle worker in his return to civilian life, transforming encumbered estates into fruitful ones. However, his methods were ruthless and he did not take long to implement them.

Mr. Dunne's former rent room had been stripped clean. The teetering towers of paperwork that had once crowded the floor were now placed with Bavarian efficiency into neat filing cabinets following a numbering system of Oster's own design. Crusty wooden walls were painted a dazzling white, taking three coats to achieve the brilliance required by the new agent. Windows were cleared of the cobwebs Oster called Irish drapery and in his top drawer was a new American invention, a revolving pistol. Oster called that Versicherung, a German word for insurance.

The tattered old map of Brittas commissioned by the General's mother, a fixture above Mr. Dunne's desk for years, was replaced with two new maps drawn by Oster himself. It depicted how Brittas is and how it shall be. All the tiny plots assigned to this tenant or that and all the community rundale leases that clogged up the estate were shown in exacting detail on the map titled "Brittas 1845." The alternate map titled "Brittas 1850" showed an improved system of drainage, an extended home farm and planting fields with vast tracks of grazing ground replacing existing tiny plots.

Dunne lands would be transformed into an enlarged grain plantation and stockbreeding farm with a suitably expanded dairy. Any remaining sections would be partitioned into rentable plots of 20 acres or more. Working hand-and-glove with Edward Meadows Dunne, they'd break every current lease and rewrite them in terms more agreeable to the new owner. Gradually displacing the hundreds of excess people that the agent believed had spoiled the land was of paramount importance.

Oster was infatuated with the notion of planting large fields of wheat since overhearing conversations at a London military club of an impending shortage. The expansive Scaroon neighbourhood was identified as being conducive for producing nearly 50 acres of the cash crop he so badly needed. It was level ground and free of excessive rocks or trees but at the moment was chock-full of squalid mud huts where there was no health and no hope for the occupants.

Most of the Scaroon tenants left of their own accord once they received eviction notices admitting they could not stay rent-free in perpetuity. The special favours Mr. Dunne demanded of them would be no substitute for tangible payment. It seemed Oster had no use for pleasures of the flesh or any other kind. Four families had refused to leave. So, with the approval of a local magistrate, himself a member of the land-owning cabal, the new agent assembled an ejection party. The party of the first part was the law in the form of a sheriff and a bailiff. The party of the second part was law enforcement, represented by British constables from Tullamore and a wagon full of thugs who would serve as housewreckers.

Sheets of rain poured down on the men headed to Scaroon that morning when the bailiff suggested the eviction could wait for better weather. "No. Today's the day. These are shabby little shanties we're talking about. They'll come down like a-house-a-cards and we'll be done by dark," replied Oster with a guttural German accent. The forked veins in his temples throbbed as if cogs and springs were whirling around inside beneath a thin overlay of taut skin. He nervously whipped at the horses carrying his crew and pulled a soggy broad-brimmed hat further down on his shaved head. Cocks heralded their arrival in cries from different cottage yards.

Jasper and his wife were first on the list. Men assembled in a semi-circle around his sad little door and the bailiff yelled in that high-pitched squeal of his, "Jasper Flynn! You are hereby ordered to leave this dwelling place at once." He banged away so fiercely on the frail door that one of its brittle leather hinges broke loose. The new agent sat a safe distance away on the buckboard. When Flynn finally opened the door it came off in his hand. He carefully placed it against the house with great reverence and looked around at the eviction party stationed in the rain. Jasper grunted loudly, "Such a revolting sight on a revolting morning!" He spat on the ground narrowly missing the bailiff's boot.

"You've paid no mind to the notices nor requests, you've got to go, Jasper. It's the end of the road," demanded the bailiff.

Jasper's wife had bundled up their remaining belongings into sacks on the dirt floor, waiting weeks for this to happen. She pushed passed and brought them out to the yard. "There's room at the Mountmellick Workhouse so I suggest you be on your way and don't look back," Oster barked out to the couple. Doing as they were told, they picked up their sacks and loaded them onto a little wheelbarrow along with a stool and a lantern they had managed to salvage. Mrs. Flynn pulled her apron over her head guarding it from the rain and the shame. Jasper wheeled away.

Once the Flynns were at a safe distance from the cottage, the bailiff snatched a twig from the roof and ceremoniously handed it to Mr. Oster, signaling the transfer of property back to the estate. The wrecking crew got right to work with crowbars and axes. They used logs as battering rams to tear apart the pokey little house where the Flynns created their family. It was flattened in 15 minutes. On to the next, and the next. Raw building materials of mud and straw were ploughed back into the earth from which they sprang. Former inhabitants scattered to the four winds.

Great change had come for the Dunnes of Brittas in a matter of just a few months. A tribe had lost a chieftain and a family had lost a patriarch. Sadness and recovery followed. With the end of an era a new generation had emerged, successor to an Ireland still laden with the old burdens but hopeful and excited about new prospects.

Patrick Lawler continued to use every spare quid to buy up leases throughout Kildare and with each successive deal he became more obligated to the land. His rent rolls now numbered 16. It was a profitable business as long as everyone honoured the agreement. Patrick's latest find was a larger farm in Mountmellick owned by Alicia Kavanaugh. At 75 acres, it was just what was needed for his own expanding family. It had plenty of fields for growing crops or raising cattle, a fine stone house with six rooms and an apple orchard. Bridget dreamed of building a buttery where she could get back into the business of making butter. They were blissfully building a life together, complementing one another's very nature. He had vision and drive. She had intelligence and wisdom.

Amid the bird songs, the bleat of lambs and the rustle of leafy trees, warm September sun beat down on Patrick slashing away at the abundant wheat in his field. He was an amalgamation of tanned skin, muscle and skill. Trailing behind with a threshing crew, Bridget sang to herself as she bound the stalks together into sheaves and set them to dry in perfect conditions. A soothing breeze wafted under her bright red petticoat. She stopped for a brief moment to allow sunshine to kiss her creamy face before tucking back under a broad-brimmed bonnet. In the full-flower of her womanhood, she was more beautiful than she had ever been. Sheep dogs paced alongside the two oldest Lawler children, Denny and Esther, who were handing stray sprigs to their mother. She patiently worked them into her bundles. Bridget's own mother had moved in with the young couple after her husband's death and watched over the other two babies in the house. A reconstituted Dunne family was folded into a fresh thriving Lawler clan.

"Have a look at my wee helpers!" Bridget called out to Patrick who winked and smiled. The sky was never bluer and the land was never greener. Europe's most gifted artists could not have painted a lovelier, more bucolic scene.

The gentle pace of the day was disrupted by a black colt dashing through the field with a frazzled tenant on his back. Bruce Duffy from Kildare rode up on Patrick and yelled from his saddle, "It's here now. It's here!"

"Slow down Duffy. What are you all lathered up about?"

"Contaminated. They're all contaminated?"

"Who's contaminated?"

"The lumpers. They're all rotten."

"Your patch?"

"No, the whole bloody parish."

Patrick took off his hat, wiped the sweat from his brow and quietly said, "Christ have mercy." It was all about to go terribly wrong.

CHAPTER 17

Letter from James Dunne to his brother Peter

July 4, 1845
New Orleans, Louisiana
United States of America

Dr. Peter—
    I rec'd yours of the 5th May. I am busier than a prostitute on nickel
night. Grayson's business is a behemoth. I could use your help. Please come.
    James

Peter had spent years holed-up in a little room that served the Grand
Canal as a gatehouse. He would check shipments or help unload cargo
but mostly he just buried himself in a sea of paperwork. At 32 he had no
marriage prospects and very few friends. His younger brother James had
sent pleading letters from New Orleans begging him to come but Peter
had always dreamed of life as a London lawyer. Perhaps he could be a
lawyer in America instead? Surely the Americans would know brilliance
when they saw it? What was keeping him in Ireland anyway? Would
being a lone shipping clerk on a river flowing with provisions out to
England be the safest place for him?

    After inscribing his elaborately designed signature, the one with an
extra flourish, at the bottom of a shipping receipt for 10 barrels of hog
hooves he paused. The signature of such a refined gentleman looked
strangely out of place on such a lowly document. With his new found
perspective he decided to leave for New Orleans right then and there. He
would go without a word to anyone just like James had done. No one
really noticed.

Every night on his way back from the warehouse James would walk
along the Mississippi river, checking on her like a father would watch
his sleeping daughter. Without her, New Orleans would have been but a
dream and he would be nothing.

For all intents and purposes he was now more Grayson than Company of Grayson & Company. His business acumen was enviable; his bargaining powers were smooth and effective. The entire operation was in his hands with the owner continuing his South American shenanigans brokering weapons from Europe. A monthly dispatch of letters between the two would apprise Mr. Grayson on the progress of his New Orleans business and inform James where he could forward the next month's reports. Bank drafts came in from as far away as Brazil, Paraguay, Argentina and London forcing James to acquaint himself with international finance and banking regulations. Combined with the earnings from the commission business he was entrusted with a significant amount of capital and not a penny was out-of-place. This trust had fueled his every move and every decision while at the same time it gnawed at his conscience. Secretly he had been courting Grayson's only child, Kitty.

In her father's absence, Kitty was being raised by her Aunt Amelia at the Grayson's family home, deep in the French Quarter. A beautiful court-yard alive with fountains and flowers hid behind an unassuming little façade. Aunt Amelia was much older than James and although they had a flirty rapport it was understood that the dynamic was only constructed to make her feel young and alluring. Along with the compliments and flattery came an understanding that Kitty's courtship would not be disclosed to Mr. Grayson. After a lifetime of submitting to her domineering brother, Amelia smugly encouraged the pairing. On Kitty's sixteenth birthday she proudly accompanied her niece to St. Patrick's Church where James Dunne patiently waited for his bride. Their names were entered into the church registry along with pages of other Irish immigrants. The two set up housekeeping in a large flat above a brick warehouse on Tchoupitoulas Street.

During the day while James would buy and sell at the office, Kitty would draw and paint at home. She had taken lessons from a French painter of some renown who worked on Bourbon Street. A canvas she had produced of the Fairview Plantation won high praise from her teacher but she would create for the sake of creation, not needing approval or praise. She would draw little pictures for James that he would discover in his breast pocket at work. She knew it would make him smile which gave her joy. Kitty was an entirely different creature from her husband. He was sharp and focused; she was ethereal and quirky to the point of being silly, which occasionally brought a gentle rebuke from her husband. That's when the twelve extra years he had on her would show. Regardless, they coalesced in interesting ways. During his short stay at Fairview Plantation James noticed the slave women were dressed in skirts made from old white flour sacks. Kitty, with artistic eyes oblivious to oppression, gave James the notion to gather up all the company's empty sacks and dye them in a variety of gay colors before being stuffed with flour. He designed the product exclusively for the plantation markets they served. It wasn't long before all the sugar and cotton fields around the river delta were dotted with dark-colored slave women toiling away in brightly-colored skirts made from Grayson flour sacks. Kitty was inspired to paint numerous versions of the pastoral scene.

Inside the best innovations lies an outsider.

James and Kitty waited at the dock for the sailing ship christened Windsor Castle to deposit Peter Dunne on American soil. She was swathed in a bright lime green dress of frills and ruffles. He, dressed like a legitimate New Orleans businessman in a smart yet inexpensive, black woolen suit. He wore a flint-lock pistol at his side for show hoping to ward off evil rather than engage it.

When Peter had last seen his brother he was a willowy teen with spots and peach fuzz. James now sported a bushy red beard and a moustache tinged with tobacco smoke from his trusty companion, the Cuban cigar.

"Now you're saying he looks nothing like you? How ever will I spot him then?" Kitty said to James as she surveyed the usual crowds at the levee.

"I've told you nearly everything I know about him. Let's see if you can detect him."

"Is that him?" Kitty pointed at a broad shouldered blonde man wheeling a large trunk.

"No! That ogre is obviously German. Try again," said a bemused James.

But behind the German he spotted Peter at the far end of the dock only by his distinctive gait and the pompous way he held his head. Both men had changed in appearance so much that on any other day they would have passed each other unnoticed.

"There! That's him, I know it, that's him!" Kitty excitedly pointed.

"You are absolutely right! How did you know?

"He's walking like he has a stick up his ass just like you said!"

The pair erupted into giggles as they moved toward Peter.

"There you are brother!" James grabbed his brother by the shoulder.

"James."

Their greetings were those of strangers, stilted smiles and stiff handshakes. Kitty reacted as if she was the one who grew up with Peter—kisses, hugs, tears. Above the din of steam whistles, she told him he was quite handsome.

"This hustle and bustle reminds me of my time in London," said Peter sounding like the world traveler he wasn't.

"London? How fascinating. Is it as magical as I imagine?" Kitty wondered.

"Magical? No. You've been reading too many faerie stories. It's as common as any other town, just better."

The newlyweds heard all about his momentous voyage on the walk to the Grumwalt's coffeehouse. Kitty was a good listener, James was not. He was just very good about keeping quiet while Peter rambled at the table until their drinks came.

Hoping to put an end to the endless story James finally spoke, "Sorry dear brother, now your adventures are over and work begins."

"I do believe you have an American accent!" Peter noted.

Eavesdropping from the next table an inebriated Kaintock dressed in castoffs from a scarecrow yelled out, "Both-a yas sound like a couple–a bog-trotters to me," as tiny peanut shells became dislodged from his beard and sprinkled onto the table.

"A bog-trotter?"

"Peter, it's all right, it's what they call Irishmen down here," James said.

"Boatloads of you poor idiots coming here every day. Why can't you stay in your own damn country?" asked the galoot.

"Sir, I am not poor and I am not an idiot. We are the finest Ireland has to offer," Peter insisted.

"That's a shame."

"Our family is of noble heritage. We are the Dunnes of Brittas."

"The Dungs of Shit-ass?"

Incensed, Peter quickly popped-up from his chair to defend his family's honour and just as quickly was knocked-out cold by the Kaintock who sat back down to his bourbon. Kitty became hysterical and James hardly flinched.

After years in New Orleans, James had avoided the slightest brush with violence but within minutes of arrival his arrogant brother managed to receive a sound thumping.

Back at the flat Kitty tended to a shaken Peter. "Oh, you dear man, what a terrible welcome you've had here in America," she said with her consoling eyes, helping to ease the pain.

"Not gentlemanly at all. The degenerate didn't even wait for me to get a proper footing. And James you, dear brother, were useless."

"You were flat on your back with one punch. Talk about useless. You should have just ignored him." James had hidden his disgust far too long. "In this place they can spot a phony at twelve paces."

"Our heritage is too grand to let a remark like that go unanswered."

"Peter, you're going to have to shed those airs and graces of yours."

"This would never have happened in London."

"People don't like snobs anywhere," replied James.

"I'm not a snob, I'm just better than everyone else," Peter said as he winked at Kitty, only half kidding.

"Like hell you are!" James was irritated.

"But I am not some downtrodden runaway."

"No, but you're not royalty either. What some distant relative on some distant island did a hundred years ago doesn't amount to a hill of beans around here—and it's kept a lot of Dunnes from doing anything important with their own lives—for generations! What, just brag about the ones who did something?"

"James, Father would turn in his grave to hear you talking like this."

"Father. Now there's a noble gent."

"What do you mean?"

"Peter, what I mean is forget about using your Duke-this and Earl-that talk or you'll get punched in the head again. Americans hate it. Forget that. Money is all that matters here and you don't need to cozy up to some king to get it. All you have to do is earn it."

"By the looks of this wee place it doesn't look like you've earned much at all."

"I've earned a bit and spent even less. I cut my coat according to my cloth for now…but I'm not finished yet."

CHAPTER 18

Fragment of letter from Lucy Rogers to Henrietta Welch

[November 20, 1930]

When I would ask either one of my parents about those troubled years in Ireland I got nowhere. They simply wouldn't discuss it. The only thing I ever remember my mother saying was that children would eat grass and their faces were stained green. My father said nothing at all. I suppose it's like a few years ago when all the soldiers were returning from the Great War. They were just too ashamed of what God had done or too ashamed of what they had done. That's all I can say about that....

Ireland was on the brink of a cataclysm. In the fall of 1845 her people's main food source had rotted away beneath her soil. People were dying in waves of starvation. Gale days came and went without the slightest payment made to her landowners. Winter was coming. Most people only saw disaster ahead. Patrick Lawler only saw opportunity, ignoring the unexpected ways in which trouble comes.

Like a diamond broker selecting the best stones, he had carefully vetted every parcel of land he leased. Middlemen could pick and choose. Landowners with estates like Brittas had to inherit and cope.

Potatoes were ravaged but other crops were robust. Patrick sold his entire harvest for ready cash and was preparing to do some fancy finagling.

His expanding family was quite comfortable on the lands leased from Mrs. Kavanaugh in Mountmellick. Bridget's dairy operation thrived and the grain crops bountiful. There were a few cottiers at the lower end and Patrick needed those fields. His Kildare subtenants had stopped payments. He was concerned he would default on his. An expansion of the farm and livestock operations in Mountmellick could offset the Kildare losses and generate capital for the coming year but what to do with the tenants? He formulated a plan.

A meeting was called at the Lawler home. Bridget created a generous meal for the men with enough to take home to their families after the discussions. A red ale was served and over-served. Cheek-to-jowl the men gathered in the front room to hear what Patrick had to say.

"Gather 'round, gather 'round, I want you all to hear this, I'm not chewing my cabbage twice. Gentlemen, I've asked you here tonight to obtain a pledge. I know you've all hit a rough patch with the potato murrain. The whole bloody country has. You're worried. You're worried about the winter I know. Some of you are about to run out of food altogether. If you want food you'll have to buy it with money, money you've saved for rent. And if the rent's not paid, well, you know what happens then. Now I have an interesting proposal I'd like to offer you."

"Are you going to feed us like this every night then?" said a mangy soul in the corner causing the men to do something they hadn't done in weeks, laugh.

"No, I want to give you the chance to feed yourselves! My sister and her husband manage a very large hotel in Smithfield next to the Dublin auction houses. They need women to work at the place and they reckon there's room for plenty of you men to work in the stockyards. It's a chance to give up the fickle farming life for something better."

The gathering erupted into a melee of questions and heckles.

"We've been in that house for twenty years, we can't leave," said a man up front.

"You're just trying to clear us all out aren't you Mister?" said another.

"You couldn't pay me enough to live in that God-forsaken city!"

"I've heard some of the Big Lords are paying for passage to Canada, can you top that?"

"Aye, if we're being transported to Dublin might as well go all the way to Canada!"

Patrick patiently listened to their jeers and addressed their concerns. "I am not offering to ship you out of the country you love. Desert your homeland in a time of crisis? You're no traitors. I am offering you an open door in Dublin. You're Irishmen not Canadians for God's sake! When things settle down here next year you can come back."

Negotiations went on through the night and agreements were reached.

With a few pounds and a promise the cottiers dusted out, stripping Patrick's apple orchard bare on their way.

Other parts of Europe were suffering from potato blight as well; from Sweden and Russia in the north all the way down to Turkey and parts of

Egypt in the south. These governments wisely forbid any food shipments out of the country ensuring their populations would be fed. However, Parliament acted as if Ireland only existed to be Great Britain's grange and granary therefore the island's produce must continue to be sent to the home country. No alarm was raised in London. Quite the opposite. Prime Minister Robert Peel publicly said, "There is such a tendency to exaggeration and inaccuracy in Irish reports that delay in acting upon them is always desirable." In private, policymakers wondered if it was in fact a visitation from God to solve Ireland's over-population problem. A few less poor Catholics could be a blessing for the Empire.

A wretched winter passed in Queen's County, getting dark at 4 in the afternoon. Night time brought about a special dread on the Lawler farm. That was when the creepers would come in search of food or livestock. Patrick slept with his musket next to his bed and would wake throughout the night at the slightest sound. His spring cabbage patch was planted right beside his bedroom and the open window annoyed Bridget to no end.

"Can we please shut that window, I am freezing."

"No, I need to hear."

"Patrick, if you do hear someone are you going to shoot them over a head of cabbage?"

"Maybe."

"We can have the children scrape them up in the morning," Bridget said in disgust pulling the covers up over her head.

"Last week I caught one of them on the roof of the barn trying to poke at the turnip pile with this long rod and fish 'em through the thatch. They're coming at us from all sides."

"Surely we can spare a turnip."

"I'd have given him some if he'd have come to the door and asked politely like the others do."

"Still too proud to beg."

"Do you remember the kennels built for the hunting dogs at Brittas?"

"Aye, father had them built out in the demesne so we wouldn't hear them bark all night."

"There be no barking anymore."

Bridget popped her head back out looking at her husband with wary eyes.

"No, you're trying to scare me."

"It's getting bad. The workhouse at Mountmellick is overflowing and we are only a few miles away."

"Mrs. Phelan asked me to come there tomorrow. They need help."

"Don't go near that place, it could be dangerous."

"Oh Patrick, it's the Christian thing to do."

"I like it better when you are safe inside this house."

"The nuns taught me the strong do what they can and the weak suffer what they must. I need to do what I can."

"If you go, leave the children here with your mother. That place is disgusting."

"Of course, there would be no need to expose them to such a sight."

"You know I'm worried about marauders getting into the grain fields, they'll be sprouting up soon. I have in mind to dig a deep trench right after the gate. We can put spikes at the bottom and I can cover it over with brambles. They fall in there they'll be regretting it."

"If you're after revenge they say you'd better dig two graves," came a muffled reaction from Bridget who had retreated back under the bedcovers. Patrick mulled the diabolical plan over in his mind refining and revising it as he drifted off into a light sleep.

In the morning, he woke up before the sun and started digging his man-traps.

Mrs. Dunne looked after the children as Bridget strapped up the mule to a cart. With a mellow pace she set off into town where she'd meet with Mrs. Phelan. Bridget hadn't really ventured far from the farm for nearly six months at her husband's request. She was ill prepared for the misery that awaited her.

Mountmellick, once hailed as The Manchester of Ireland, had gone through a steep decline in less than a year. Its market square, a former hub for the Midlands, desolate. Her factories had been shuttered, her businesses closed and armed guards stood outside the few remaining shops that still sold food or comestibles. The former industrial giant now was infamous for hosting an overcrowded Union Workhouse. Window boxes usually filled with cascading pink geraniums were bare or filled with nettles.

This had to be another world, a murky dream.

On Market Street a pack of emaciated dogs confronted Bridget traveling in her cart. They barked and snarled. They began nipping at the mule's hooves causing the animal to back up and kick wildly. The wheels lifted off the road knocking Bridget about until she pulled back at the reins and screamed loudly. She cracked her whip at the dogs. Frightened, the pack moved back into the shadows to search for the evicted families that once had cherished them. Casually, Bridget tucked back the red curl that had been dislodged from her riding habit and ploughed ahead.

Up the street, shoeless wastrels in tattered clothes accosted a couple of scurrying townspeople pleading for a morsel or scrap of anything. Bridget took a moment to absorb the deteriorated conditions of the place. It seemed the world was on the edge of Armageddon to her. In the distance she noticed a strange little urchin in soiled baggy clothes, she wondered if he would ever grow old enough to fill them. She watched as he approached the cart and attached his filthy little hand to her footboard. In his wobbly voice he asked, "My lady, can you give me something to eat? Please! My parents are dead and I haven't had any food since forever."

He was no hallucination. He was very real. With sorrow and pity she said, "Oh, I am so very sorry dear boy. Get into my cart, maybe we can find you something."

He got up on the bench and proceeded to impress her with an eloquence of gratitude that belied his bedraggled appearance. Not only was every office of Jesus Christ and The Virgin Mary invoked but she got the blessings of six named saints for herself and her entire family. For eternity.

"Your word to God's ear. What's your name then *a stór*?" using a sweet Irish expression.

"Zacharias."

"How lovely. Did you know that is a name of a wandering saint?"

"No. So St. Zacharias blesses you too, ma'am."

Bridget laughed and smiled at the boy noticing he had a strange affliction below his mouth.

"Zacharias, what is that green colour on your chin? Are you sick?"

"Maybe. My stomach hurts. It might be the grass I've been eating."

"Now you know you can't eat grass, child."

"Why not, the cows do."

"They are beasts, we are not. We are children of God, made in His own likeness," Bridget said snapping at the reins, "Walk on."

They headed out of town a little where they passed a queue of desperate people at the gate of the workhouse. The gray stone edifice stood before them like a heartless prison designed only with utility and frugality in mind. There was no elaboration whatsoever on the building save the curious pointed arch above the entrance. Bridget caught a bone-chilling glance from a warden keeping the waiting hordes in line with a switch. She imagined she was entering a medieval torture chamber. A municipal guard in a smart uniform gave her permission to take the cart around the back of the complex telling her where to meet Mrs. Phelan.

"Oh, Mrs. Lawler, you came," said a delighted Mrs. Phelan dressed in various shades of miss-matched browns, "who is this you have here with you?"

"His name is Zacharias and he is a darling, hungry child. All he has had to eat is grass."

"That won't do, lad, you're just in time for soup. Come with me." Mrs. Phelan took them into an annex where soup was being ladled out to cadaverous inmates. She plopped Zacharias at the front of the line then whisked Bridget back to her adjacent office.

"Please have a seat, Mrs. Lawler." The freshly whitewashed walls smelled of lime and were a welcome relief from the rancid odour of the soup room.

"What can I do to help?"

"I apologize, I am a bit flustered." Mrs. Phelan adjusted her blouse and out of habit reached for the cameo that was normally pinned to her collar. She'd forgotten she'd decided to keep all of her jewelry in her armoire at home. How could she justify wearing something so extravagant?

"Must be simply overwhelming," said Bridget.

"It's terrible on a good day and today is a horrible day."

"To be sure, the line outside wraps around the block."

"They can't all be admitted but they're hoping we have soup left over after we are through with the inmates."

"And when you run out, you run out?"

"Indeed. They have to give up everything they own to live here so it is the last desperate step to stay alive. This morning we found three cold dead ones at the entrance gate."

"Christ's peace be upon them. What are you to do?" asked Bridget.

"The constables have a wagon they bring 'round. They load 'em up and bury 'em in an open pit just yonder," she pointed over her shoulder with her thumb in a casual gesture. Bridget could tell apathy had already overtaken the girl she once knew from their student years at the convent.

"So would you like me to find an apron and serve? Do you need help with the cooking?"

"Mrs. Lawler, I have enough hands today but I must ask you for a larger favour."

"Certainly. What can I do?"

"Do you still make that marvellous butter that made you so famous around here?" said Mrs. Phelan, knowing flattery was the best way to grease the skids of her patron's charity.

"I just make little batches now."

"Would you consider being my butter supplier? I can only pay you with God's good grace."

"How much do you need?"

"We have 800 poor souls here."

"Right then."

"We would use as much as you could make."

Bridget took the hand of her former classmate and clutched it to her own breast. "Dear woman, I will do my very best."

"I know you will."

As the spring of 1846 passed into summer the hunger did not wane but hope itself surged. Ridges upon ridges of glorious white blossoms appeared throughout the Midlands. The potato plants looked absolutely magnificent. Their appearance brought wide smiles to the farmers who predicted a bumper crop was on its way. Plans were once again being made for the future. In a collective sigh of relief it seemed the populace might just be saved from complete oblivion after all.

It wasn't until the last dog days of July that a strange mist drifted over Ireland, recounted by storytellers as a gray cloud of Biblical proportions. Echoing the deadly plagues that befell Egypt, the blight came again. Lush green leaves curled up overnight into brittle brown clots. Like gangrene it crept down the stems where it rotted the potato right in its underground refuge. People would remember it came in silence and silenced everything around it. Normal zephyrs did not blow. Rivers ran without a sound and birds withheld their songs.

What people would remember most of all was the smell, the stomach-churning, nauseating vapours of decay. The stench of certain destruction.

Trusting that they might find a few healthy lumpers that miraculously avoided the disease, farmers rushed out and dug away at the dirt only to find vile pools of mush lying in wait. For generations their pigs were considered the gentlemen what pays the rent. They survived on the peelings and scraps of the potato plant before it could one day be butchered to pay the landlord. Now, any animal that managed to survive the previous year would need to be sold or eaten before it too starved. The whole scheme for survival had been shaken off its flimsy foundation.

Patrick managed to protect his own livestock on the farm over the course of the year. His cows were producing milk for sale and for Bridget's butter contribution to Mrs. Phelan. His barn was large enough to keep the herd safe at night but he had been forced to hire amateur shepherds to watch over his sheep in the fields. He paid the help with produce he grew on the farm as his supply of cash money was running dangerously low. Rent was coming due on the Kildare property and his Mountmellick tract. This rock solid man of sound character and durable constitution, the one that had captured Bridget's heart, was now reduced to a composite ball of nerves and paranoia.

The famine was destroying lives all around them and now had its sights on their marriage.

A shepherd appeared at the barn early in the morning while Patrick was herding the cows in for Bridget to milk. He slapped the last milker on the rear and turned to herd the shepherd out.

"Mr. Lawler, I know you'll find out sooner or later but we lost one last night." He presented Patrick with a cut rope and a bell. Out of courtesy the thief had left it on the ground to inform the owner that the sheep had not strayed.

"What the devil do I pay you for?" Patrick was infuriated.

"I'm very sorry, sir."

"What, were you sleeping out there? You are one lazy lout." Patrick looked around the yard as if he'd find footprints leading directly to the animal and the thief. There was nothing. What's to stop the whole farm from being invaded? He continued berating his man when he noticed in the distant foothills a tiny ribbon of smoke spiralling out from the trees. Patrick pointed and said, "What is that now?" He ran inside to get his rifle, mounted his horse and took off like a hound in pursuit of a fox.

As he sped up to the hills his mind raced just as fast. What gives anyone the right to steal from him? He has worked too long, too hard… no this cannot stand! By the time he had reached the woods he had convinced himself of his righteous cause, imagining he was defending his entire way of life. Quietly dismounting, he left his horse tied up to a tree then followed on foot.

He stealthily traversed up the hill with all the care he would take to stalk a buck. The smell of smoke got stronger the deeper he went into the woods until finally he came upon a discarded sheep's head lying on the forest bed. Just beyond that, hazy figures moved about a bonfire. Crouching down Patrick took steady aim and fired off his gun. He clearly witnessed a flicker of redness and heard a low whimper. Quickly they all vanished into the hills.

Running to catch them Patrick stopped at the firepit. He seethed with anger staring into that half-eaten carcass. Thinking through his next move and the one that would follow that one, he decided to end the pursuit and return home.

"Did you find your little lost lamb?" Bridget sarcastically asked from the barn doorway.

"I found it all right. On a spit up in the woods."

"Sorry, love."

"I think I shot someone."

"WHAT?"

"I fired and think I hit someone."

"WHAT?"

"He ran off into the woods."

"Patrick Lawler, are you telling me you shot a man today?"

"I believe I did."

"Oh dear God. He might be lying up there dead?"

"Not sure, maybe I only hit his shoulder. Couldn't really tell. It all happened so fast."

Bridget dropped her pail to the ground and grabbed Patrick by his lapels. She looked up and shook him with all the strength her womanly body could muster. He seemed dazed.

"You've gone completely mad. I saw it happening right before my eyes and I've said nothing. How could you shoot someone? What has happened to you husband?"

"I'm protecting our family."

"Patrick, we were not in danger. We have four lovely, healthy children. We have enough food to eat. We are blessed. Can't you see that?"

"But I won't be stolen from. People need to follow the rules."

"There are no rules anymore. To the starving it's the end of the world."

"It's not right! Order must be maintained."

"You can't kill people who are only trying to stay alive!"

"I'm no murderer."

"If that one dies you are most certainly a murderer." Her biting words hit Patrick like a slap in the face. His body went limp and his eyes started to well up. He hugged his wife tightly and would not let go. Bridget's cheeks were squished to his chest and she could still smell the gunpowder. Softly she said, "You need to change your way of thinking and decide how you want to survive this, if we do. Honour might be the only thing we can keep. Use your abilities to try and help people instead of shooting them or piercing them in one of your traps."

"Oh Bridget, God is watching over us."

"To be sure. He's also just watching us."

CHAPTER 19

Letter written to James Dunne from Patrick Lawler

June 8, 1846
Mountmellick

Dear Irish Brother:

When Bridget wrote last she gave you an account of the predictable loss that would attend the failure of the potato crop. You must have seen in your American newspapers the number of deaths from starvation and disease here— so she was unfortunately completely correct in what she said was coming.

Her Majesty's government has lived up to the highest expectations of the people to be as useless as possible. They have put on all sorts of restrictions and confusing arrangements for foreign aid from countries like America. You, being in the shipping business, must know all about the rigamarole surrounding such things—so you are the perfect person to ask for help. Farmers like myself have been selling our harvest to the grain brokers who pay the best prices. Our reapings are eventually shipped to England. If we were to try and sell it here without the aid of the brokers no one would have any money to buy it. We farmers have to feed our families too and are walking a razor's edge.

A fellow farmer and acquaintance of mine is on a committee set up through the colony of Quakers here in Mountmellick. He's heard of your success in America and asked me to propose an interference on your part that might save some of your poor countrymen and women from starving to death.

Is it at all possible to hire a ship in New Orleans, fill it with as much Indian corn as you can give and send it to us directly? I will make sure it goes directly to the citizens you remember in this place. Time is not on our side so please start arranging this directly after you put down this letter. Your mother and your sisters are both holding up. Michael is keeping Ballintlea running—he told me to tell you he is paying the mortgage for now but would not refuse it if you sent him money.

God is watching over us and watching to see what you will do to help this country you left behind.

Truly Yours,
Patrick Lawler

James was lost in the avenues of inventory that lined the wide plank floor of Grayson & Company when Patrick's letter arrived. Stock had been piling up in the commission merchant's warehouse for several months waiting for prices to climb. James was also expecting bulk sugar from Fairview in the coming weeks and needed an empty warehouse.

With hands so full it was easy to extend one to charity.

James had been putting off a letter of his own to Mr. Grayson, now thought to be conducting business from Montevideo, Uruguay. Seems James had neglected to ask his boss for Kitty's hand in marriage, so he scribbled off a missive asking Grayson to give away both his food and his daughter. He reasoned he'd ask for forgiveness if the permissions never came. Since James came to the fore, revenues at the company had quadrupled. Who wouldn't want him as a son-in-law?

Peter was employed as an assistant to his brother, at times chaffing at him like a trouser full of thistles. With a little give on both sides they found a way forward and this goodwill undertaking tested their skills.

His time in the Grand Canal offices enabled Peter to move efficiently through the bureaucracy surrounding maritime law. To protect British interests, legislation was passed stipulating that no relief food could be shipped to Irish ports from any country except in British ships. James had cotton leaving monthly on a British ship and had procured an American vessel to take the foodstuffs to Dublin. After discovering the restriction, Peter simply convinced the Captains to switch cargos. Kitty read an account that Parliament had made an attempt to sell Indian meal at reduced prices to the Irish poor but firstly, they couldn't afford to buy it and secondly, if they could they wouldn't know how to eat it. She wanted to contribute an idea too.

Within six days of receiving Patrick's request the Dunne brothers had discretely set a British ship sailing to Ireland with American aid. On board were 1,923 bags of Indian meal, 925 sacks of wheat, 416 barrels of seed corn, 215 barrels of white beans, 73 barrels of dried peas and a stack of printed handbills with a recipe for New Orleans-style johnny-cakes. It was written in English and featured an illustrated woodcut of interlocking shamrocks and corncobs all designed by a proud Kitty with a little wordsmithing from Peter. James appreciated the sentiment but didn't have the heart to tell his new bride most of the recipients wouldn't be able to read it.

Now that Patrick's ship was out at sea, James could concentrate on a trade mission of his own. Mr. Grayson had asked him to study the superior techniques Cuba was using to harvest sugar cane and pilfer any practices that could be employed at the Fairview plantation. After years of doing business together, a communiqué from the island's largest rum producer came into the offices inviting James to tour their sugar operation. Kitty was having difficulty parting with her new husband, not knowing when she'd see him again.

In the sanctuary of their sweltering red bedroom overlooking a narrow alley, James was completely hers for the night. Behind the translucent mosquito netting they romped around the large bed, the mattress stuffed with soft and fluffy Spanish moss. Between sessions of an amorous congress she giggled and beamed. She studied him in the low light. When he would try to go off to the Land of Nod she would call another meeting to order. Her desire for him wasn't just the randy experiments of a teenager, it was a deep and passionate love. She saw him as her protector, companion and guide. As for James, Kitty was his enchanted docile muse, the sun and sum of all domestic happiness. She continually inspired him to be the man she thought he already was.

"Do you really have to go tomorrow and leave me in this sweltering little flat?"

"I thought maybe you could go to your auntie's house while I'm away.

"Don't trust me here alone with your brother?" Kitty flashed her eyes and gave him a come-hither look.

He chuckled a little and said, "I know he likes you very much. And you, quite the temptress! Aunt Amelia's place. That way I know you'll be looked after until I can come ravish you once again."

"Can't I just go with you? I can take notes and draw pictures of the expedition like some traveling artist going off to a foreign land. You can have a record of everything you see. I won't be a nuisance at all."

"Very interesting proposition but I don't know what to expect there. If you think it's hot in New Orleans you would think Cuba is hell itself."

"It sounds so exotic."

"What I don't need is some Latin lover trying to sweep you off your feet."

"Oh, so you are the jealous type?"

"I will go this time and make sure it's safe for you and the next time you can come and make your drawings." He brushed the tussled hair from her forehead.

She whispered, "But won't you miss me? Won't you miss this?" Kitty crawled around and initiated a final round of untamed lovemaking that caused James to fantasize about her the next day as waves slapped him about the ship's deck.

CHAPTER 20

Article titled "From the Queen's County," *King's County Chronicle,*
Tullamore

September 19, 1846

HELP FROM ABROAD
 *A shipment of foodstuffs has been sent down the Grand Canal to
M'mellick where the Quaker Committee is doling out as they see fit. It has
all been claimed by various sorts already. The committee wished to thank
P. Lawler and his generous American benefactor, J. Dunne—formally of Brittas
—for their efforts.*

X

Streams of Mountmellick's needy took the American food as calmly as
they received the Body of Christ from their parish priest. No shoving, no
grabbing, no rudeness. In any other part of a desperate world, a giveaway
of such magnitude would spark violent riots, stampedes even but the
Irish were either too polite or too weak to fight. They were preparing for
another winter of famine without potatoes, eking by on cornmeal, beans
and the turnips they grew to replace the diseased lumpers.

The Society of Friends, grateful to Patrick for organizing such an
abundant blessing, allowed him to take a wagon full of meal and seed
to his tenants in Kildare and neighbours in Mountmellick. This much
pleased the hungry and destitute while angering some of the big lords of
the district. Not at all comfortable with handouts from the colonies or
the accompanying little tribute in the local newspaper.

Francis Plunkett Dunne was one of the luminaries on the Famine
Relief Commission who was particularly peeved. He was running for a
seat in Parliament and that kind of recognition would better serve him
rather than a turncoat American Dunne or another Lawler show-off.

Over that excruciating Black Winter of '47 the weather was the
worst Ireland had faced in 100 years. Mountains of snow smothered
the island. Swarms of hungry people drifted from town and country
begging for food, searching for shelter. The Mountmellick workhouse
provided both but was overwhelmed with inmates. They were often too

feeble to perform at expected levels and they would be turned out again or buried. A quarantined block of rooms had been set aside as a fever hospital and the government had finally allowed the soup kitchen to run independently and serve non-inmates.

Mrs. Phelan also had a pittance to pay Bridget for her weekly butter deliveries, which she gladly accepted.

"Here you are, Mrs. Lawler. I know it's not much but it's something."

"Thank you Mrs. Phelan. I promised to bring the girls with me so we can buy something sweet in town."

"My, my they are just beautiful. What are your names then?"

"My name is Esther. I'm six."

"Oh I see, a very mature young lady," Mrs. Phelan joked. "And who might you be?"

"I'm Caty. I'm only four. I like cats."

"Caty and Esther. What a vision you are. You've brightened my day more than I can tell you."

"Come along girls, Mrs. Phelan has a lot of work to do today." Bridget exchanged a full basket of butter for an empty one and shuffled the girls out of the building. A line had formed at the locked gate causing the Lawlers to wait with the others to be let out. No one spoke. Caty and Esther's eyes were as wide as Spode saucers, they saw everything. Sickly skin, skeletal fingers, ragged clothes, filthy toenails, louse covered scalps, cracked lips. Nothing escaped the observations of the horrified girls as they waited.

The disheveled crowd closed in on Caty and she tucked herself into her mother's dark blue cape. Bridget held her head high giving her a haughty profile but she was only trying to keep her nose above the putrid potpourri of odor. Up ahead the guard finally opened the gate and the people squeezed through, wandering off in various directions seeking asylum where they could find it. The threesome, feeling rather queasy, rode back to their farm forgetting all about sweets at the bakery. Esther remembered but feared her mother's wrath if she attempted to mention it.

Seed potatoes were scarce in 1847, being nearly completely wiped out by the preceding two years of blight. Little had been sown and Patrick had encouraged both his Mountmellick and Kildare tenants to switch over to safer crops. He opened their eyes to the science of crop rotation. Since all their fields adjoined each other he convinced them to create a cooperative workforce where they all tilled the soil together. They were in debt to him for three year's back rent and he owned the big landlord two. This was the year the whole thing would turn around, they hoped. Winter and spring batches of turnips were excellent and brought in a little cash money. With summer coming to a close, 25 acres of luscious corn now reached for the sky in Kildare and just another few weeks to grow. Patrick and his tenants turned their attention to the 7 acres of wheat growing in their community field.

He shouted out orders as he directed the threshing crew in the field. Tenant farmer techniques hadn't evolved much in 10 generations and Bruce Duffy was swinging Patrick's prized scythe that had once belonged to his father. "What's the mat' with you? You're chopping at it not slicing it. Here, give it to me." Naturally imperious, he grabbed the tool and elegantly mowed down swath after swath, giving Bruce a smug look after handing it back.

Oh, how Bruce hated him.

Around the perimeter of the field a black coach approached followed by several men on horseback. Trying to stay three moves away from checkmate had been exacting and exciting but now Patrick feared what he saw on the horizon.

"What's all this about?"

"Are you Patrick Lawler?"

"Aye Mr. Benton, you know who I am."

"I must address you in a legal fashion. This is my bailiff, Mr. Wiggins."

As they talked, two wagons of additional emergencymen wearing uniforms came up from behind. Patrick recognized a few. He knew them as friends. Taking off his broad brimmed hat in an effort to show some form of respect he addressed the agent.

"If this is about rent, I thought we'd agreed I would have until the end of the year and then I will pay everything I owe. Everything. We had that conversation on this very spot."

Benton, talking right over Patrick, began reading a tossed salad of words that had enough understandable phrases to be damning. They were here to evict everyone, take the land back and worst of all, seize the entire crop of wheat and 25 acres of corn. The middleman had been outsmarted at his game.

Bruce Duffy and a few others joined in the questioning of Mr. Benton who continued his contractual ramblings unaffected by any interruptions, only answering "if necessary" when Duffy said they would take that wheat over his dead body. Benton's deputy keeper, who would be in charge of detaining and protecting the crops, addressed the threshing crew:

"Men, hear me now, I want you to continue your harvesting. Go right ahead. I don't know what arrangements Mr. Lawler had with you but we will pay each of you four shillings to complete your work here today. Carry on."

Happy to get a little coin in their pockets the crew got back to work. Devastated and humiliated, Patrick agreed and joined the men in gathering up the wheat but was in no mood for their abuse and curses.

"Just look at him, the great farmer himself losing it all and taking us down with him." Duffy knew that ridiculing his nemesis would be the only bright spot in his near future and piled on with gusto. "Not so high and mighty now, eh? You're nothing more than a simple spalpeen."

Simmering below his seemingly cool surface Patrick tried to remain dignified as he silently worked. Bridget would want it that way. But it was hard.

"That man squeezed us like lemons for years and now our families are going to be thrown out into the wilds. I hope you rot in hell Patrick Lawler."

Steady, steady. He moved to the other side of the gathering wagon to get away from Duffy's torments but he was followed by the persistent little horse fly.

"I envy all the people that never had the misfortune to meet you. What a stain you are on the Lawler name."

Having no cheeks left to turn Patrick fired back, "You blithering idiot. I could have thrown you out years ago. You lived here on my back. Free! I got nothing out of the deal but headaches trying to teach born-tired morons like you a thing or two."

"You didn't teach me how to do shite."

"Certainly didn't. You are a stupid little man who'll never learn anything from anyone."

"Maybe you could've taught me how to be a greedy bastard such as yourself. That's the only thing you filthy landgrabbers are good at."

"Kiss off, Duffy."

"Your wife must be a fool to have married such a failure."

Snap.

Pulled down to the ground like a roped calf, Duffy's eyes bulged as Patrick constricted his scrawny neck with superhuman strength. Blinded by fury he barely felt the lashes on his back. He soon detached and grabbed at the keeper's whip instead, pulling him off his horse. The keeper fell right beside Duffy. Patrick took the whip and held it up to both of their necks, pushing down with the entire weight of his body. They coughed and squirmed. He wanted to spout off something insulting and profound. He could be as biting as any man. He settled for, "I'm sorry." He released his captives, dusted himself off and replaced his hat to its jaunty angle. Patrick turned back to the wheat for solace.

Seven acres of wheat had been harvested and now in the hands of the agent's men. Knowing their houses would be tumbled the next day the tenants inquired about their pay.

"Yes, we agreed on a price and I'll not quibble," said the keeper.

Lawler, still acting as if he had any kind of authority said, "Do you have the cash with you now? We'd like to be paid."

"My dear sir, you are indebted to your landlord for more than two years' worth of rent on acreage that stretches from here to there." He made expansive gestures with the whip he had regained. "That does not simply get expunged. Oh, no, no, no. Your salaries for today as well as the money we get for the grains will be deducted from what you owe. Believe me, that will not even come close to covering it." Duffy starting blaming Patrick again when the keeper smiled and noted, "Come now, you're a couple of bald men arguing over a comb."

Patrick, realizing his own stupidity, formed an imaginary gun with his hand and pointed it at the keeper. He pulled the trigger. Click. He smirked and shook his head before saddling up and heading home to his family. He left his erstwhile tenants in Kildare to face the darkness without him.

Arriving home just after 1 o'clock in the morning Patrick was exhausted and ashamed. He needed some reassurance of his worth from his wife and was heartened to see the house aglow with candlelight. Bridget was waiting for him at the back door.

"Why were you gone so long?" She seemed to have aged in his eyes since he left for Kildare.

"They seized everything. It's gone." His voice cold.

"Caty's sick."

"Sick how, what's wrong?"

"She's got a terrible fever."

"Poor petunia." Patrick took off his hat and scratched at his scalp. "But I'm worried."

"I'm sure she'll be fine; she's had a fever before."

"But last week—" Bridget trailed off into inaudible tones.

"Last week, last week what?"

"She went with me on my delivery."

"To that workhouse?" Patrick's face was turning red.

"Uh huh."

"Why? I thought we agreed never—"

"It was just for a quick drop off but we got detained."

"Did she shake their hands or something? What? Bridget!"

"No, but when mother was bathing Caty she found lice in her hair so she must have gotten close enough."

"Lice isn't going to give her a fever. Just calm yourself. Did you send for the doctor?"

"I thought about it but can we even afford that now?"

"Let's see how she is in the morning." Patrick went to bed dreading what would happen to his old tenants at sunrise. Bridget worried about Caty.

In the morning the girl's condition had not improved, Patrick fetched the aged Dr. Ashley over from Clonaslee in his buggy. Caty had developed a pinkish discoloration on her tummy. After a thorough examination he called the couple into the front room.

"When I first looked at her I thought, maybe just a touch of the grippe. But. I must tell you, I do not like that rash."

"She sleeps on her stomach and maybe the wool blanket is causing some irritation," said Bridget.

"Maybe, but I don't think so," the old man said. Appearing in the doorway was a stark-naked Esther calling out, "It's hot in here!"

"What do you think you're doing; we have a guest!" Her mother quickly ran over and covered her plump little body with a linen shawl. "Remember your manners young lady!" Esther thought it was funny. Dr. Ashley thought she looked red. He didn't know if she was blushing from embarrassment or something more insidious.

"Come here once, wee one." Bridget brought her over to the doctor for a quick inspection.

"No wonder you feel hot, you're burning up." Peeking under her wrap he quietly pointed out the beginnings of a small rash developing above Esther's tiny rump. Her parents looked at each other with concern.

"Go get some clothes on now." Bridget shooed her out of the room.

"Let's see how things go with these two. Take this quinine and give it to them every two to three hours."

"Quinine?" Patrick was suspicious. "That's what they use for typhoid fever. They surely don't have that, Doctor?"

"I suspect they both do, Patrick. It's spreading around here like the plague."

Befuddled he started to stammer. "So, but, the, when—"

Bridget stepped in. "Well if it's what you think… they quarantine them at the workhouse. It's contagious. Isn't that right?"

Dr. Ashley gave her the cold look of agreement.

"But the other children?"

"It's concerning."

"Patrick!" shouted Bridget who could see her husband had gone catatonic.

He was muddled and staring right through her. Bridget twisted the skin of his arm tightly out of the doctor's sights. "Patrick are you listening? Take Denny and Mary to my sister's right now. Go! Pack them up. Hurry!"

"Don't they need, eh, things, coats and, ah—"

"They can use the Donnelly's clothes. Please just go. Take mother with you."

She did not quiver. Her voice was strong but her mind was frantic with worry.

Death had been hovering over every hill and dale of the island during the famine years. The rich and not-rich-enough thought the grim reaper would only call on the poor, the needy ones, the lowest of castes. Why should they worry? They would never be in want of something so basic as food. Perhaps some hoped to escape death's clutches with a good deed or a charitable act. Surely that would provide some cosmic shield, some protection for the privileged.

But after three weeks of shear torture death did come for Esther Lawler. The next night he took Caty.

Double obsequies were held at the Catholic chapel in Mountmellick and the tiny white coffins were placed in the graveyard with solemn ceremony. Down the road at the workhouse a single casket with a trap door would be used over and over again to lend a trace of dignity to the columns of dead right before they were dropped into a paupers' pit and covered with lye and more dead bodies.

Men, women and darling little children like the Lawler girls who once walked the green earth of Ireland were not celebrated for the life they once lived or the vital people they once were. There were just too many of them. Instead they were reduced only to statistics in Dublin Castle's ledger book.

CHAPTER 21

Letter to Kitty Dunne from James Dunne

October 3, 1847
Casa Guachinango
Valle de San Luis
Cuba

My Dear Kitty:
    *I have spent today in the company of gentlemen who know about
7 words of English between them. I believe they can understand my Spanish
but laugh when I talk—we are getting our points across. Don Hererra owns
the plantation & sugar refinery of which he is quite proud. I doubt if your
father wants to invest in the type of machinery they have here but it would
certainly make Fairview more profitable in the long run. My journal is filled
with things I've learned & things I want to do to improve the plantation as
well as other business notions that I think your father will appreciate. A little
time away has given me great perspective of what I need to do when I return.
And return I cannot wait to do! For now, I have a few more deals to make
before I can leave. I get the woefuls thinking of you every minute. I hope you
have been getting my letters as I have gotten none of yours. I miss you & love
you more than I have ever loved anyone.*
    I am Ever Yours,
    James

James gulped in the night air, as heavy and dank as a swamp, like it was
his last breath. He savored the aromas wafting up from the gutters and
down from the riverboats' smoke stacks. New Orleans, that jeweled city
of chaos, was once again at his feet. After his ship had docked, he was
happy just to be jouncing along the streets of the French Quarter, tipping
his hat at every sober wayfarer or stumbling drunk. He looked up and
admired the variety of metalwork patterns on the balconies above his
head. Streets illuminated with gas lighting, how civilized. He thought I
must look up more often, I've been missing so much. Always concerned
of where I am stepping. Who cares? Chilled by the December winds he

stopped and bought a hot stuffed crab from an old Creole vendor and devoured it as he walked onwards to retrieve Kitty. Cuban food and his innards had not agreed.

He approached the Grayson family home anxious to share his triumphant mood with his wife. He waited at the stoop appreciating the muted vermilion plasterwork and how well it was complimented by the shutters, painted the color of asparagus. His powers of observation had been sharpened by three months of surveillance on Cuba. Pushing through the door he entered the courtyard, its fountains dripped a soothing tone, its gardenias perfumed the space like a Pasha's sensual harem.

Bacchus was the Roman god of plenty and had been adopted by Mr. Grayson as a trademark of sorts, popping up in a variety of places throughout the firm. His menacing likeness on the knocker of the inner courtyard door looked more devilish than god-like; as soon as James dropped the brass ring on the strike plate he heard scurrying from within. Mulatto fingers pulled back a gold brocaded curtain then disappeared behind the billowing fabric. He knocked again, waiting. He tested the doorknob by slowly turning it but it quickly turned in the opposite direction. James assumed a dignified pose with his hand resting on his velvet lapel. Out from behind the door a grave-looking Aunt Amelia stepped into the courtyard all in black, a heavy opaque veil concealing her face. She closed the door behind her and led James to a lit corner.

"Oh, James you're back."

"Yes, I came to bring Kitty home. Why the dreary outfit Amelia, is something wrong?"

"I have painful news."

James expression changed instantly, his body tensed, his blue eyes turned fierce glaring at her.

"Amelia?"

"She's gone. I'm so very sorry."

"Gone? What are you talking about?" His eyes bulging and darted back and forth like he was following the flight of some microscopic organism.

"As soon as you left she came down with the fever. It's been like a scourge here, haven't you heard?"

He grabbed her by her shoulders squeezing the black taffeta until it made a crinkly whimper, "Hold on, she's dead? Amelia, she's dead?"

"I'm afraid so. I can't let you in the house, one of the servants is in the attic with the fever right now."

"That is impossible!"

"It's true James, I hate to be the one to tell you."

"There's been a funeral already? When? Where is she buried? Good God, Kitty!"

"No, she didn't. She died on the 29th of September. The authorities rounded up all the victims in a dead cart and either buried them or burned them. That's what they do."

"What about Mr. Grayson? Was he here?"

"Was he here? No, he wasn't here. He's not here now either. I had to inform him by letter."

"How could she get the fever, it doesn't make sense."

"James dear, it never makes sense. That Yellow Jack hops, skips and jumps around here all summer. They say this time it started in the French Market with all that filthy, rotting fruit and meat but I imagine it's those wide open sewers. No one really knows."

Aunt Amelia was very matter-of-fact when it came to the fever, it had struck so many of her relatives and friends she had built up an immunity over its power to shock. James, visually agitated, was not offered an embrace nor the slightest reassuring touch. Any sympathetic expression, if it existed at all, stayed concealed under crepe. Nothing remained of their easy friendship. Aunt Amelia had an answer for every question James asked except, "What will I do now?"

A forsaken figure walked the lonely sidewalks back to his flat not once looking up from the ground below his feet. He was followed overhead by an immense flock of bank swallows screeching loudly. He didn't hear a peep.

Peter erupted in tears when James told him the news. He had a special spot in his heart for Kitty. There had been no whisperings of her death at Grayson & Company. Peter had assumed she was safe in the hands of Aunt Amelia. Horrible guilt set in. Why didn't he check on her? He surely could have taken a moment to consider her well-being.

At Grumwalt's coffeehouse they sat down with a bottle of cheap whiskey and tried to piece together the whole story. A second bottle was ordered. Disbelief dissipated into a sea of emotions remembering Kitty.

The squeak of the bottle's cork broke the long, awkward silence. James got sloppy and began to slur, "I had so many plans for us. We were only starting. I will never believe it. I can't—"

"Brother, I can't, it's just—"

"She was young. She was beautiful. She was good," he said as he turned his face up to Peter but kept his eyes focused on his glass.

"Yes. So slight and exquisite. Earth was not worthy enough to keep her."

"She was dazz-ling."

"No doubt she was gorgeous."

"And a true, a true artist at heart."

"Maybe she was no mental colossus but she was one of the most creative people I've ever met."

James sobered up at the remark. "God dammit Peter, just when I start to think you've changed you say something insulting like that proving once and for all what a downright bastard you truly are."

"I apologize, I didn't mean it like that. I loved her as much as you did."

Grumwalt kicked them out at midnight and they would finish the whiskey by the river's edge.

At sunrise the levee awakened with activity like it always did. Boats and barges scurried above the people separated from destruction by the narrow mound of earth that kept the Mississippi in line. The Dunne brothers were splayed out on the wharf like vagrant drunkards. Barrels rolled by Peter's head one after another, squishing his hat. A dockworker kicked James in the thigh and brushed at him with a broom. They both got back on their feet and headed to the Tchoupitoulas Street flat, staggering like a Virginia fence. Entering the home they all shared brought a new dimension of grief to both men.

Peter pictured Kitty on the settee by the fireplace laughing. James saw her in bed sheets seducing him. They were moving about the place like two pollywogs suspended in a block of foggy gelatin. It was impossible to be there. Work could be James' only salvation today.

It had been months since James set foot in the warehouse and it was a feeling bit odd to be back. The way the light came shining through the transom windows and the familiar smells brought him a quiet sense of peace. Mr. Lambertus, who had been in charge during his sojourn to Cuba, met him at the top of the office stairs.

"Mr. Dunne returns."

"Hello Lambertus."

"Do you have the report about the sugar plantation in order for Mr. Grayson?"

Taken back by his tone James purposefully ignored the question and entered the space moving straight over to his desk by the window. It had been completely rearranged.

"Lambertus, are these your things all over my desk? Get if off of here at once. I have a lot of work to do."

"James," purposely using his front name as a clear sign of disrespect, "I think you should read this before you start reprimanding me." He handed him an envelope on outstretched palms as if he were presenting a hari-kari knife to a defeated samurai. He smiled waiting for a reaction.

James snatched up the paper and read the letter inside which had been written diagonally over one of his own like an angry rainstorm:

> *You are effectively—TERMINATED—from your position as general manager of Grayson & Company. You will remove all personal belongings from the building and take that brother of yours with you. You have disappointed me to no end. The notion that you could give away half a warehouse of goods without my permission—to a load of foreigners no less—is absolutely criminal. The $3763.23 you have on account at the Company and Peter Dunne's $236.59 have been confiscated and won't make a dent in my losses. You should be happy I don't get the municipal police to arrest you on the spot.*
>
> *In other matters, I would NEVER, EVER give a conniving backstabbing Irishman like you permission to marry my daughter—May she rest in peace.*
>
> *I hope to never lay eyes on you again.*
>
> Elias P. Grayson

Looking up from the letter he saw Lambertus with arms folded wearing a snide grin. The only consideration that prevented James from dropping him to the floor was the three burly warehouse men in attendance.

Everything he had accumulated while working at Grayson's fit into a burlap sack.

Returning to a crowded Grumwalt's, James and Peter dined with the employed commission merchants taking in their suppers. News of the Dunne brother's dismissal had already spilled throughout the coffeehouse before their arrival. Peter could feel compassion, contempt, jealousy and pity steaming up from every corner. A faintly familiar face approached their table and asked if he could join them.

"Who are you?" said a disinterested James.

"My name is Captain J.M. McDonald, you might remember me. I've been running riverboats up and down here for a while now."

"I've seen you," James said, glancing in McDonald's general direction. He didn't seem like the other river rats that scurried along the levee's docks. Smartly dressed in a dark navy suit with gold epaulets, a narrow black necktie and flip-flap fringe poking out from under his cap he looked believable but too young to be a seasoned riverboat captain.

"I know you too, Mr. Dunne, your grand reputation proceeds you."

"Yes, well that's all shot to hell."

"I've just heard. You, um, left Grayson's company."

"Los chismes vuelan," James momentarily reverted to Spanish.

"Pardon me?" said a confused Captain McDonald.

"Nevermind. Say, what is it that I can do for you. If you're looking for a shipping contract you're a little too late."

"No sir, I'm looking for a partner," McDonald said abruptly in a brisk fashion that proved he was distinctly American.

"Continue," said a now fully engaged James.

McDonald talked in rapid fire with his eyes sparkling and his mouth flapping, flicking off saliva like his riverboat's paddle. "It's a ways off still but we are going to win this war with Mexico and President Polk's vision of this country stretching from sea to sea is going to happen. America wants that 3,000 miles of coastline in California."

"I've never heard that," said Peter.

"Brother, you can't get all your news from the bartender. In Cuba that's all they wanted to talk about," said James.

"Precisely. We could dominate trade with China or Japan, with Latin America, hell with the whole ocean! Now, when it's all said and done I aim to be ready to set up shop on that big, beautiful Pacific Ocean. There is a bay by a town called San Francisco in upper California that can accommodate big ships from around the world. They say it's the most natural harbor in the world. Seems farther away than the moon but that's where all the opportunity's going to be and that's where I'm headed."

"A shipping company?"

"No, a mercantile company like Grayson's. This port can become a supply depot for that whole part of the world and accommodate fleets of ships. Import for now and export when the West starts to grow the kind of crops I'm hearing it can."

"That could take forever." James said in his dark mood pointing to the dark side.

"That's fine. Just import for now. I can handle the shipping and you can handle the merchandise."

"You're a man filled with push and go aren't you?" James said sharply.

"There are fortunes to be made."

"Possibly, but that will require capital and both of ours have just been forfeited. We are quite literally penniless," said Peter.

"And hopeless," added James.

"I can procure all the ships we need and you can get credit from any bank in New Orleans for the goods. We all know what you did for those starving folks in Ireland. It was in the newspapers. Grayson got more happy publicity out of that move than money could've ever brought him."

"We got clippings from our people in Ireland too, made all the papers there," said Peter.

"Well, who is going out West? Not me, New Orleans is all I know," said James.

"No, no, no. That's the point. I am going no matter what. I heard tell from a navy admiral that they got big plans to pour lots of money into the West Coast. They want it to be a port for all the trade they can do with the Far East. President wants it. Congress wants it. Can you imagine? We've never had a western seaboard before. China. Japan. All them countries."

"Pretty ambitious."

"They'll need people like us that know how to get things done. We can put our shingle out tomorrow and start to plannin'. When the time is right I will go out there and be the California half and you two stay here and be the New Orleans half. McDonald and Dunne!"

"I know the warehouse below our flat has been vacant for months. I can talk to the landlord," said James lightening up his outlook. McDonald's all-knowing attitude was starting to take an inspirational effect.

Peter had been lost at the name of the whole enterprise, it simply would not do. "James has the reputation and there are two Dunnes here. If it's going to be a grand as you predict it has to sound big, impressive. It would be more suitable to call it Dunne, McDonald...and Company!"

"I think that is a fine idea. Grumwalt! Bring whiskey!" Captain McDonald ordered. As the night worn on and the bottle wore down the men became giddy with excitement toasting to this and toasting to that. James felt sufficiently hopeful to raise his glass high and give his favorite Irish blessing to his new partners:

"May those who love us, love us;
And for those who don't love us,
May God turn their hearts;
And if He doesn't turn their hearts,
May He turn their ankles,
So we will know them by their limping!"

The new company was up and running by week's end. James had secured funding from the City Bank fronting him up to $10,000 on his good name alone. McDonald set sail for San Francisco and reached that glorified encampment through the Isthmus of Panama in three months' time. News of the United States' victory over Mexico met him at the makeshift docks and he figured it wouldn't take long for the town of 1,000 inhabitants to double or maybe triple along with its needs.

Trading mostly in red and white beans at first, Captain McDonald glad-handed every ship captain and first mate he could find to ply them for information. Kentucky bourbon was his favorite lubricant to learn about how the game was played along the western coast of the Americas. Valparaiso, Chile was the designated hub where all commodities and manufactured goods seemed to flow into San Francisco. He knew someone who knew someone but it wasn't the same as actually knowing someone. He wrote to the Dunne brothers with all his findings, hoping they could do more than just send beans.

James buried himself with work back in New Orleans. Regular life in the city had become unbearable for him. As an exile from Ireland he had mostly nourished himself on hope but now it, along with his wife, had vanished. Everything inside him had dried up. He rarely went out. He found it impossible to sleep in the flat he'd shared with Kitty. At night the space closed in on him, making it seem so tiny, so dark, so haunting. Valerian could not help. He abandoned the entire floor to Peter, preferring to sleep on a cot in the warehouse below. After reviewing McDonald's dossier on San Francisco he contrived a plan of reformation for himself.

Two blocks up from the river sat a little shop bursting with maps and supplies for sailors. The proprietor was a white-bearded, buck-toothed slip of a man named Hugo who had sailed a few times around the horn in his youth then talked about it ever since. James purchased several maps and peppered Mr. Hugo with questions. He was more than happy to answer in exacting detail but when the stories veered off to include native customs, wild monkeys and edible insects James, politely at first then rudely, steered the conversation back on course.

He finally procured enough information to formulate an itinerary that would allow him to set up his own South American contracts, locate the best stockpiles and finally deposit him on the sandy shores of San Francisco in six months where he would start over, again. He would use his Spanish to communicate, his American to bargain and his Irish to charm. He was finally excited about something. Coordinating with Captain McDonald's extensive list and his new maps, James researched ports-of-call and hoped to source:

From Venezuela: asphaltum
From Brazil: coffee and sugar
From Buenos Aires: cow hides, salted meats and Spanish almonds
From Chile: bricks, potatoes, flour and European goods
From Ecuador: bananas, nuts, cacao and straw hats
From Peru: lumber and lamp oil
From Mexico: beans, corn, eggs and quicksilver

Peter, being the older brother but the junior partner, had no power to restrain James from taking the voyage, which seemed to him purely reactionary and far too dangerous. Peter knew Kitty's memory lurked behind every street corner and coffeehouse, every whiff of a blooming magnolia and every whistle of a steamboat.

James Dunne left.

CHAPTER 22

Letter from Captain McDonald to James and Peter Dunne

March 18, 1848
San Francisco, California

Dear James & Peter:

Disregard my first three letters I wrote to you about the need for more goods. Business has taken a dramatic downturn & the San Francisco settlement is now deserted. Some damn fool got up in the town square here & hollered about a big gold discovery near 100 miles away. Everyone is pulling up stakes & heading off to the Sierra Mountains in search of gold. This place is now a ghost town. I'm rethinking our whole scheme now.

Tomorrow, I might head off to Sacramento (which is a town closer to the digs) & see if we should conduct business from there instead of S.F.

For the time being DO NOT purchase any more goods to ship here & sell everything you purchased to ship here on the open market. I am praying to God I caught James in time before he left on his buying trip to South America. If he has left—try & get word to him to go back to New Orleans—this is a bust here in S.F.

Sincerely yours,
J.M. McDonald

Peter Dunne, for all of his pomposity and braggadocio, was not used to being at the reins of anything more than perhaps a two-wheeled hack. But now he was the de facto head of Dunne, McDonald and Company's New Orleans warehouse and unlike James, he didn't much care for the responsibility. Or that humiliating deal-making mumbo jumbo. In fact, Peter was different from his brother in many ways. Whereas James was naturally rugged, ruddy and rustic, Peter worked at being erudite, sophisticated and courtly. His accent had been chiseled into a strange Anglo-American hybrid that purposely belied his Irish heritage. He knew the pleasures of a good tailor. His dark looks favored more that of his cousin, banker Jeremiah Dunne, who had just been elected Lord

Mayor of Dublin. Peter was adept at working that fact into almost every conversation and exchange.

But the brother's fundamental difference was rooted in how they each viewed the world. James preferred to see things in terms of black or white, it made decisions easier. Peter thought black and white was the perspective of simpletons. Peter preferred shades of gray. He reasoned all true philosophers appreciated the nuances of gray. Subtle distinctions, slight variances, minuscule details only visible to those of the highest intellectual order. He had it all sorted out.

True, he was concerned about the recent upheaval in San Francisco, however, the resulting lull in business left time to pursue his passion for lawyering and make further inroads into Southern society.

He began visiting all the leading law firms in New Orleans, still tinkering with the idea of somehow becoming an American attorney since the California experiment looked bleak. Besides, he was not much enamored with the notion of being a common merchant anyhow. He got himself invited to lazy, leisurely lunches and a few dinners. Peter dazzled the men with his knowledge of English law, much impressing the former colonists. In the space of a few weeks, they welcomed him into their inner circles and sponsored his membership into that formidable institution, Perfect Union Lodge #1, the seat of Freemasonry in Louisiana.

Of course, secret societies were forbidden to Catholics but like many Irish immigrants, Peter had relaxed his faith as soon as he touched the free soil of America. The church of the Old Country was replaced by new republican and capitalist institutions that promised heaven on earth. He would attend mass at St. Patrick's on Camp Street once in a while and no one would be the wiser. Tried and true axioms about business or religion were not so obvious to one who sees the world in shades of gray.

He belonged to a few benevolent associations, dined in French restaurants and attended the Opera, giving him cause to don his cape and top hat. As for women, at sunset he would promenade on the levee with the rest of the leisure class where he would flirt and be fussed over but he had come to believe no one quite measured up. In secret, he had been introduced to a New Orleans custom that fulfilled his current needs at a Quadroon Ball.

Mixed-race ladies of tainted but otherwise splendid patrilineage attended these social events in the old part of town, flaunting their exotic beauty to wealthy white men. Some of these men were long-term European visitors, some were married and some were, like Peter, single men not ready to marry. James knew his brother was partaking in these cotillions long before he left but had turned a blind eye. Peter was encouraged by his fellow Masons to retain a placée and set a girl up in a low rent apartment behind Congo Square. Plaçage had been a hold-over institution from the French where mulatto woman, forbidden to marry white men by law or black men deemed their inferiors by choice instead turned into concubines. Peter declined.

A letter had serendipitously reached Peter at the Company's offices from Mr. Pierre Calou, former overseer of the Fairview Plantation. Practically illegible and unintelligible, Peter understood it to say he was looking for a lawyer to sue Mr. Grayson over the sale of the plantation. Calou requested a meeting at a cafe in Baton Rouge. Peter was intrigued. Squishing Grayson like the insect he was in an open courtroom brimming with onlookers was tantalizing. Did Calou even have a case? Could Peter actually represent him on his paper thin qualifications as a lawyer? He decided to meet the old man and find out.

Baton Rouge did not suit Peter. Although it was Louisiana's state capitol it had none of the polish of the Crescent City. If you were banished from New Orleans, Baton Rouge seemed to him like suitable punishment. No joy, no culture, no style. He found the people to be almost foreign. He could barely understand an old Cajun woman's mutterings when she gave him directions to Mungery's Place, his meeting spot.

"Hey there, are you Dunne?" came a voice from a corner table by the window.

Peter scowled at the old man, unappreciative of his manner straight away.

"It is I, Peter Dunne, Esquire. Are you Pierre Calou?"

"That's me. Take a seat," Calou motioned like one would summon a hound dog. "From what I hear you hate Grayson 'bout as much as I do."

"Hating people is a waste of time, sir. If you have a legal case, hate is an even worse companion. Facts. Facts, Mr. Calou. What are the grounds of your lawsuit?"

"I have grievances a mile long."

"And they are?"

"That snake promised me I'd have a job for life. I stayed on when he bought the place and that's what he said. I'd always be there. Then he just up and sold the place out from under me last week. I gots the boot!"

"Did you have a contract with Mr. Grayson?"

"He made a fortune on that place I he'ped him—"

"A contract Mr. Calou, did either of you sign anything?"

"Well, not exactly."

"Then I can't help you."

"Are yous a real lawyer or just playing one? I hears you kinda a junior lawyer, that right? I bet a real lawyer could he'p me."

Peter tugged at his earlobe and realized this charade was just a wasted day of travel. Quickly tiring of Calou he gazed out at the busy street and the scruffy pedestrians walking by the window.

"Mr. Calou I have enough experience with the law to know that you are out of luck."

"The way I sees it, you can find a loophole, that kinda thing. Doesn't a handshake mean anything? What they call it, a Gentleman's Agreement?"

"No such thing as a Gentleman's Agreement, even between so-called gentlemen."

Calou, who wouldn't know a sophisticated insult if it kicked him in the shins, continued his diatribe about how he might be able to sue for this or for that. On and on.

Not able to get a word in edgewise, Peter slowly twisted his head towards the window in amazement. Without warning he pushed his chair away so hard it ricocheted off the wall and he dashed out of the café. Not so much as a farewell to the old windbag.

Such bad manners for a gentleman, a lawyer.

CHAPTER 23

Announcement from Fintan Lalor in *The Nation* Newspaper

April 19th, 1847
Tenakill, Queen's County

TO THE LANDOWNERS OF IRELAND
 The constitution of society that has prevailed in this island can no longer maintain itself, or be maintained. It has been tried for generations; it has now, at least, been fully and finally tested; and the test has proved fatal. In Ireland men are bound to live on for ever, slaves to a dominion that dooms them to toil, and cold, and hunger—to hardship and suffering in every shape; they have no right even to life except at another's license, they are bound to submit in patience to perish of famine and famine-fever—it cannot continue.

 When society fails to perform its duty and fulfill its office of providing for its people, it must take another and more effective form or it must cease to exist.

Ж

It's been said that those who die by famine die by inches. And those that survive only live by that same measure.

"Feeling better this morning?" Patrick asked Bridget as he scanned Fintan's article in the newspaper.

"Aye," she said roughly kneading dough on the kitchen table, her face momentarily obscured by a cloud of flour dust.

"I am glad."

Then it came, that elongated and tortured silence that would stretch between their sparse talk. Each imagined horrible thoughts were harboured against the other. Patrick waited for any given moment when his wife would blurt out, "You incompetent fool, you've lost half our land." And she wondered if each time he looked at her with adoring eyes he was actually thinking, "You wretched woman, you've lost half of our children." But the love was still there. A bond made stronger by strife yet buried under imaginary malice.

Bridget was uncomfortable. She worried about the luxuries they could not afford, like children. She was on the cusp of giving birth to a new baby, the third one, or the fifth one, as the captious ones would have it. Into a brash new light, wee John Lawler came on a cold January morning, followed by his Irish twin brother Peter in November. By all counts the lost children were found. Patrick hoped the new additions to his family would double his joy and divide his misery but worried too about new luxuries.

The famine crisis was entering its fourth year and he was exhausted from its effects and the talk of its effects. So badly did he want to just get on with it, transcend the frustration and cynicism. Patrick had become accustomed to worry. Every morning his pillow would be covered in hair that had been securely fastened to his scalp the night before. His wife's answer was to join her brothers in America where they could live the life they deserved. She talked about it every day, at every opportune moment. Patrick recoiled at such talk. He was Irish. He boasted of never having left the island and he planned on telling his grandchildren the very same thing one day.

Ireland's proud son had kept his farm just profitable enough to avoid eviction himself and amass some local admiration at the feat. There were sparkles of hope peeking through the cloud cover. He'd been invited into Dublin where he would speak in front of a Parliamentary committee on the agricultural state of the Midlands. His speech was a rousing little screed that echoed his cousin Fintan's beliefs and motifs:

> "It was an outrage against the bounty of the Most High, and a blasphemy against the mercy and justice of the Omnipotent, for any man to say that the right over the soil was unreservedly his, or that he could do what he liked to with the land."

Beautiful babies, full bellies and polite applause would not be enough for Patrick. An implacable return to the farm's tedium week after week exhausted him. His dreams were being eradicated by forces beyond his control, his plans fettered. Tomorrow frustrated him.

Irish landlords that had the wherewithal for Continental travel or had a residence in England fled the island during the great famine. It was just too distressing to witness the misery at such close range. Francis Plunkett Dunne all but abandoned Brittas, preferring that his land agent Anton Oster run things according to a plan that kept the bailiffs at bay. He would look after loftier issues from his sanitary new seat in Parliament, a safe distance away from any unpleasantries that might occur as the estate's new scheme moved forward.

Frank took a modest room at the Cavendish Hotel in St. James's and walked through the park to the House of Commons for his first session. Turned away at the chamber's door, he was forced to dash back to the Cavendish and change out of his army uniform before being admitted. Not necessarily against House rules, it just wasn't done, except perhaps in war times. He was completely unaware of that stipulation in the dress code and subsequently became known as the Honourable Member for the Army.

He would sit on every committee, support any legislation and debate any opponent in defence of the institution. On behalf of Ireland, he gallantly fought off new relief taxes the House tried over and over to impose on him and his fellow landowners. The Right Honourable Francis Plunkett Dunne was born into a feudal system and fervently believed in its ideas of hierarchy and obligation yet he made no real stand in Parliament on behalf of his serfs. There were the Dunnes of Brittas and then there were the Dunnes of dark corners and wretched hovels. Those Dunnes of distant bloodlines and lowly circumstances were slowly wasting away throughout the Midlands or escaping to America, for MPs had far more in common with each other than with their constituents.

Wholesale clearances and evictions were systematically carried out in the new chieftain's absence. Landscape that had once been silhouetted with cabins, pigs and people was flattened. Tumbled stones and broken fences were the only remnants left of that life.

The theoretical map Oster had envisioned for a Brittas with vast grazing lands and bountiful crops was slowly taking shape. Sympathy was handed out in the form of one gold sovereign per family if they chose to leave freely and peaceably before the wrecking crew arrived. Alternatively, if Anton Oster's offer was refused, his orders would be enforced with Roman severity.

It took a certain breed of man to throw a starving family out into that brutal winter of 1847. One who saw duty over humanity, mission over means and victory at any cost. It required a military man. The forfeiture of his soul over these deeds did not concern Oster for he felt he had lost it years ago on Europe's bloodiest battlefields.

One of the last families to be ejected was that of Duarte Miquel. He once had a wife, five children and an aged mother living under his roof in a townland ironically named Bellair. Growing up as a Spanish war bastard in Catholic Ireland had indeed been difficult but he endured, even thrived. Miquel had been esteemed a valuable, improving tenant by Mr. Dunne and the General. A faithful rent payer for twenty years, he eventually succumbed to the turmoil of the times. Duarte Miquel had been an itinerant labourer in England for a year, served on public works for a time but now found himself at a complete loss. One-by-one his family had been consumed by fever, disease and hunger. Only he and his aged mother remained, cloistered in the two-room cottage awaiting their fate.

Oster, a bachelor, had no sentimentality for family and no special recognition for Duarte's mother who had been General Dunne's cook before being terminated after his death. Although Mrs. Miquel had legitimate ties to the Old Family she refused to trade on her associations and insisted her son not approach them on her behalf. The Miquel eviction was particularly disturbing as Mrs. Miquel was manhandled and thrown to the ground into a deep puddle of mud. A 12-man eviction party mocked her difficulty escaping from the pit as they clamped her son in a chokehold. Oster's parting words: "Don't ever come back. You don't belong here anymore."

Many of the evicted from Brittas entered the Mountmellick work-house as a matter of course but for the Miquels it was not to be. Packed to the gills. They were turned away at the door after a nine-mile walk. A local Anglican church was offering free soup at the parsonage. Mrs. Miquel forbade such charity fearing she would be exchanging her faith for food. She'd heard rumours of children being forced to renounce Catholicism in order to eat and be schooled in Protestant ways. She told her son she would rather just die than be a "souper."

Mother and son shifted from pillar to post in search of food and shelter growing weaker with each move. Like a couple of snails they carried their home with them. After a fortnight of drifting and foraging, in a damp culvert under the low road from town, Mrs. Miquel died in her son's arms. In her satchel he discovered a letter addressed to *Señor James Dunne/Nueva Orleans/America*. It pleaded for help. It included everything that had transpired since his departure and lacked only the stamp it took to reach him in time.

Duarte Miquel, weak from hunger, carried his mother to the pauper's burial pit where an experienced undertaking crew was standing by. Their techniques had evolved from those frantic early months of the famine when carcasses were unceremoniously heaped like sacks of grain into holes. Mrs. Miquel's spindly body was wrapped in linen before she was placed in a wooden box, a donation from the local gentry. The entire process took less than 10 minutes. Other burials would continue throughout the day with all the precision and repetition of a canning factory.

Duarte made his way back to Bellair.

Anton Oster was acutely aware of the enemies forged in his remodeling of Brittas. He always traveled through the county with at least three lackeys; burly, soft-headed tenants willing to ride or walk alongside the agent's horse.

There were reports of a burglary at the eastern gatehouse of Brittas. Upon arrival Oster and his emergencymen discovered a window had been smashed and the gunroom was emptied. Fearing a revolt he sent his men back towards the mansion house to rescue the General's widow and daughter Fanny, who were the last of the Dunnes still residing at Brittas. They needed to be collected and evacuated quickly to a safe haven.

Oster whipped his horse until it was nearly airborne, careening towards the Clonaslee police barrack. He slowed long enough around a corner for Duarte Miquel to take aim at the back of his head from behind a hedge on his old Bellair plot. As the shot rang out Miquel hollered, "It's you what don't belong here you evil son-of-a-bitch!" A direct hit sent the agent thrusting forward. His mount, spooked from the noise, reared up and threw Oster backwards to the ground where his neck snapped before the horse stepped directly on his face, turning it to jelly.

When the time came for an execution in England, the gallows were erected then quickly disassembled, letting the citizenry go about their days without the morbid reminder plunked in the middle of their town square. However, it was felt a disobedient Ireland needed the public spectacle along with a permanent reminder. Unique to Irish architecture is the infamous iron balcony with a trap door, perched above the entrance to village constabularies throughout the island. Duarte Miquel swung from the one in Maryborough three weeks after Anton Oster's ambush.

Sheep dogs barked wildly as the chaise rolled up to the Lawler farm. Inside, school lessons were interrupted by the yapping and Bridget's mother went to the window to see if the commotion was a threat.

"What is it, mother?" Bridget called out.

"It's a dapper auld man being driven by some slovenly boy. Ahm, wait he's getting' out. It couldn't be."

"Couldn't be who?"

"I believe it's Mr. Sneed. Oh, he looks ancient. Help him down boy, honestly. He has on the full Brittas livery. He's swimming in it. Poor soul."

An aged Mr. Sneed, butler to the Dunnes of Brittas for more than fifty years was making a house call on his old friends. He was warmly welcomed, feted with tea and muffins then they got down to the gossip of the moment, the evisceration of the Miquel family.

"I had seen her only once since she left service," said Sneed with his proper English accent very much intact. "She was terribly missed as were all of you."

"Well, we've landed on our feet and Patrick has taken very good care of all of us. He could not have been kinder to me. I consider it a blessing," said Mrs. Dunne.

Bridget mused, "The whole thing is terribly upsetting. If we had only known we would have helped. I grew up with her, Mrs. Miquel was like an auntie to me."

"God bless her soul," said Mrs. Dunne as she made the sign of the cross.

"It's like the world has gone stark raving mad! And I am sure the ladies of the house will never come back from Dublin now. How could they feel safe up there? What, they're going to live in fear that some disgruntled tenant will burn the whole place down next? What would the General think of all this? It honestly feels like the end times."

"You are right, Miss Bridget. No one feels safe. They haven't for years," said Sneed.

"Patrick likes it better when we don't leave the house. We are prisoners here."

"We've a skeleton staff at Brittas and the auld place feels like one of those ruined castles you see out in the fields. It's falling down, leaking like a sieve. All the children are gone. The laughter. Only the rats remain." Mr. Sneed brushed a crumb from his sleeve. "And who would have thought Mrs. Miquel would starve under the streets of Mountmellick? With her talent you'd imagine she could've made something exquisite from a batch of nettles." The stoic gentleman started to get teary eyed.

"Come now Mr. Sneed, don't upset yourself." Bridget patted his arm and noticed a ripped seam on his dilapidated uniform. "Let's talk of happier things. What have you heard from Mrs. Kavanaugh? She's always a ray of sunshine on a dark day."

"This is her plot you're living on here isn't it?" asked Sneed.

"It is. She has been a better landlord than any man in this Godforsaken country," observed Bridget.

"That she has. All her tenants on Gracefield speak of her generosity. Not one of them was turfed-out. She got them working clearing trees, building roads even got jobs for some of them in her colliery. Nobody is starving at Gracefield. Ahm, remarkable woman," added Mrs. Dunne.

"She's got all the gold in the world to be generous, hasn't she?" Sneed countered.

Mrs. Dunne immediately sensed she had offended the loyal servant of Brittas who was as proud of the old family as one of its own members.

"But may I say, while my Lord is doing what he can in the halls of Parliament to keep this country going, Mrs. Kavanaugh is safely ensconced at some sumptuous villa on the Riviera."

"Well, who could blame her really? I would if I could," said Bridget.

"Before I forget, I have something for your Patrick." Sneed reached into his breast pocket and produced an envelope. "Please deliver this to Mr. Lawler." Bridget promised she would.

Pine coffins were neatly stacked high outside Mr. Drady's workshop on the edge of Brittas Lake. One of the only men in a decimated county who had found steady work was waiting for his latest boxes to be hauled away to the workhouse. Deaths had slowed enough to dispatch with the rude trap door coffins. Patrick Lawler trotted by on horseback, tipping his hat in the estate carpenter's direction without a word. A mystifying bond developed instantly between survivors.

Memories of Bridget and their courtship danced around in his imagination as he rode up through the trees. Two men in uniform stopped him before reaching the house. He produced Sneed's letter from Francis Plunkett Dunne and was escorted to the tower entrance.

Mr. Sneed greeted him warmly, opening up both doors to the guest; a gesture of great respect reserved for important visitors but completely lost on this one. Lawler followed as he was brought past the grand staircase through the long corridor to the ornate door of the General's old library. The elderly butler turned and gave Patrick the once-over then plucked a tiny leaf from his lapel and dusted off his shoulders with a tiny silver-handled whisk broom before opening the door. Unused to such fussy protocol Patrick stifled a giggle when he was announced as:

"Mr. Patrick Lawler of Mountmellick for you, sir."

The Lord of the Manor rose from his desk and said, "Do come through Mr. Lawler, please have a seat. May I offer you a brandy?"

Patrick had only seen the man once at General Dunne's funeral but never had the opportunity to size him up. "No thank you, that is quite all right."

Frank had about ten years on him but they were of equal height and similar build. They both had military, nearly athletic postures. Their beards were trimmed in the exact same style, identical colour. Right away he appreciated the parallels until they shook hands. It startled him. Although firm and hardy it was clear Francis Plunkett Dunne did not work with his hands. Even the women in his life did not possess hands so tender and moist. Patrick pulled back and resisted the temptation to wipe his palm on his trousers. He took a seat on a frayed Louis Quinze chair.

"How shall I address you then? Your honour? Colonel Dunne? Mister Dunne? I admit I am ignorant of these things."

"To my face my tenants call me Your Honour but I get no such respect in Parliament. Colonel is fine."

"Colonel."

"I've summoned you here in person, 'tho your reputation precedes you Mr. Lawler. I've heard tell you are a master of the land. An expert farmer, orchardist and cattleman."

"I try my best."

"Indeed, I've heard it from all classes of men. And resourceful! That shipment of food you engineered from America saved a lot of people from the abyss. Quite admirable. All the gentry noticed such gumption.

Your tenants respect you and you made quite an impression on the agricultural committee when you spoke in Dublin."

"Thank you Colonel," he said, wondering where exactly this was leading.

"Using some of that spunk you Lawlers are famous for—"

"I'm not political like the Tenakill family. I just work the land and leave the talk to others."

"Just the same, the Lawler name still holds formidable sway with the common folk of Queen's County." Patrick admired the politician's obvious gift for flattery and was enjoying the accolades.

"Good of you to say Colonel."

"No doubt you know all about the troubles we've had up here."

"Hard not to—"

"Yes. I lost a valuable man in Oster. But he was not of this country and his ways had no finesse, no, no gentility."

"I see."

"Lutheran. Needed more understanding of the Papists to really be effective."

"Do you think that was it?" Patrick said, wanting to draw out more information from the Colonel without seeming to care.

"One never knows. Situations look far worse when we fear we'll be blamed for the poor outcome, aye?"

"Aye."

"He did start to right the estate from its dire condition. In some ways things are better than they have ever been. In other aspects we are quite, shall we say, lacking. Ultimately he paid with his life trying to secure this place for the next generation."

"Are you planning on getting married, sir?" asked Patrick.

"No, at first I was married to the army and now I am married to the government. Who has time for a real wife and family?"

"Aye sir, quite demanding."

"My brothers have large families. Eddie is next in line after me so I imagine it will travel down his line. Did you know he is now the agent for father's old nemesis Sir Charles Coote over at Ballyfin?"

"You don't say?"

"These times are forcing us to heal auld wounds. Fathers' auld battles."

"He's the one that is named Edward Meadows Dunne?"

"That's him. Making a good go of it from all accounts. However, I am still chief of the clan for now and I will fight until my last breath to save this place."

"Aye, it's a strapping responsibility to be sure."

"Now, Mr. Lawler I think this is something you can help me with."

"Sir?"

"The legacy." Frank spread his arms widely as if to say Behold!

"I don't quite understand sir." He understood perfectly well.

"Mr. Patrick Lawler, I am formally offering you the agency of Brittas. You can move your family into the lodge and pick up where your father-in-law left off. I am sure Bridget would be most fond of the idea."

She most certainly would not.

Anticipating this moment from the start Patrick clarified, "I am honoured of course Colonel."

"Very good—"

"What are the holdings?"

"All tolled, nearly 10,000 acres."

"Do you know I have only managed about 100?"

"I have every confidence. You'll just do what you did with the 100 and scale-up."

"I am a good farmer, an adequate landlord but I am no barrister. I know little about the law aside from the basics." Patrick thought he should acknowledge his inadequacies so they couldn't be used as a leverage against him.

"Trust me, I can hire all the barristers we'd need to assist you. Sad to say these tenants can't read anyhow and will sign anything put before them if they are told to do so. I need a man who knows how to work the land. Oster remodelled the place enough to where we really only have about 75 tenants left. It's mostly a cattle and farming business."

"And what'll happen to my farm?" Patrick scratched at his temples, thinking out in the open.

"Keep it, lease it out or turn it back to Mrs. Kavanaugh. Whatever you decide."

Their discussions continued for nearly an hour covering large issues of land management, theoretical discourse on the treatment of tenants and then they got down to the brass tacks of compensation. Patrick was most pleased on every detail and was promised more than he could have ever imagined.

It was the opportunity of a lifetime. His mind had clicked over and he was going to accept despite the fact that Bridget would be mortified at the notion of resurrecting her life at Brittas. She let her feelings be known in the contentious argument they had before he left for his meeting. She wanted to go to California and leave the whole of Ireland to the nostalgic and beaten down.

But she didn't know what was best for his family. *He was the man.* He would make the decision. He had relinquished too much power to the woman in the past. His reasoning was sound and he would convince her somehow.

Colonel Dunne produced a burgundy portfolio of Morocco leather emblazoned with the gold crowned portcullis of Parliament. He elegantly rotated it on the desk in Patrick's direction then pinched at the gold-filigreed metalwork in the corner to open it up. Inside, a stack of contracts waited for signatures. They were collated in order, starting with the ones to Patrick's advantage.

"These have been drawn by my brother, remember he's Coote's agent, made sure you are adequately covered. No need to have any one else review. They are quite liberal in your favour. This first one is about your fees and your immediate payment of £50 upon acceptance."

£50? That sum alone could fix most any problem. Patrick looked over the document carefully, nothing seemed devious or an effort to hornswoggle him in its four sentences.

The colonel dipped his stylish pen into the pot and told his new agent, "Sign here."

Patrick signed.

They went through the other documents one-by-one, each wordier and more complicated than the last. The Colonel made small talk, keeping Patrick from concentrating too intently.

"There has been quite a lot of union between our two families lately. Two grand auld tribes of Queen's County coming together."

Patrick acknowledged with a nod.

"Those Lalor boys of Tenakill have all married well, three Dunne sisters in a row from Mountrath," Frank said trying hard to cinch up those family ties.

"Ah huh."

"And now you have been welcomed to the fold. First a marriage to my dear cousin and now a position with the family firm so to speak—"

"Right. If I may just reread this one again if you don't mind," Patrick interrupted.

"Certainly, take all the time you need." His questions were answered directly as they went through the next three contracts.

Colonel Dunne continued, "My fellow landlords think I've gone all wishy-washy hiring a Catholic for this position. Quite unusual. Quite unusual. I don't suppose I could convince you could to switch religions at this point?" he asked sheepishly.

"The Church of Ireland?"

"Yes. Why not?"

"Colonel, the Catholic Church is the church of Ireland. Don't let the name fool you," Patrick said with a grin.

"Ha! Come now, there's not much difference between the two."

"Afraid not. Bridget would have my head." Patrick looked down and reread the same phrase of the agreement again trying to understand the implications.

"Very well." Frank let him read on for a bit then continued, "I must say though, this will elevate your status tremendously. You will become part of the history of Brittas. Part of the Dunne legacy. Moving up dear boy."

Patrick paused for a moment adding, "And if it pleases the pixies, the Dunne family will benefit from the Lawler association."

"To an extent that is possible I suppose," Frank said with hesitation.

Patrick ceremoniously set the fancy pen down and collected his thoughts. "Sir, with all due respect," meaning he owed him none, "I need our partnership to be built on a clear understanding."

"Very direct aren't you?"

"It saves time."

"I agree—"

"But dare I say, I do not see the Lawler name as being any less important than that of your own."

"Well, I would not put it that way my good man. But as we all know, the Dunnes have been the overlords in this territory for centuries."

"To be quite frank, Colonel, the Lawlers have been here just as long, have just as much standing as the Dunnes and we didn't compromise with invaders to do it either," Patrick stated in a blithe disregard for manners.

"You speak in a high tone Lawler."

"I am simply stating facts. I would not be trading on your name if I took this position I am quite happy with my own."

"Be that as it may, no need for an ancient history lesson. I would like to deal with the here and now. Now, I am offering you a lucrative post of a legendary estate. Let us just proceed from there."

"I do not think we shall proceed at all. I do not cringe to any man and will not work for one who sees me as his inferior. It's doomed from the very start."

"You've just doomed yourself."

Lawler grabbed the stack of signed papers and carefully ripped them in half. He neatly re-arranged them back into their elegant portfolio, closed the cover and rotated it mockingly on the desk's polished surface in the Colonel's direction.

"We shall see, Frank."

And with that he removed himself from the room making sure to slam the door for a final exclamation point to their negotiations. The decrepit wood paneling shook with a jolt sending Squire Dunne's famous rapier mounted above the door spiraling downward, puncturing the floor below. The Colonel watched, puzzled and perturbed, as the sword slowly vibrated to stillness.

CHAPTER 24

Fragment of letter from Lucy Rogers to Henrietta Welch

[September 1, 1930]

Before he came to San Francisco my Uncle James sailed around The Horn from New Orleans. He spoke fluent Spanish and visited many foreign countries throughout Latin America. I remember as a child being fascinated with a tray he brought from Brazil—made of butterfly wings. San Francisco was in a wild and untamed state when he finally arrived in 1849.

The ship's crew excitedly repeated the Captain's call of "Land Ho" but James could not see anything remotely resembling land. San Francisco Bay was hiding in the night under a fluffy bed of heavy fog like she did periodically for thousands of years before. Spanish and English explorers that had found her once could not find her again on return voyages. Hills and mist were so intricately woven together that morning the coastline itself would only be navigated blindly by marine instruments.

After its years of elusion, seclusion and tranquility San Francisco could not hide from the world any longer.

James Dunne had been hiding from the world as well. He left New Orleans on a pilgrimage to South America in search of commodities and purpose. With his young wife dead, he had agreed to leave the eastern side of the business to his brother while he created a western outpost with their new business partner. Gold had just been discovered in California shortly after his departure. While sipping coffee in a Buenos Aires café he read a short snippet about the event in a Spanish language newspaper. Although he thought it interesting, he did not fully comprehend the magnitude of mania that would follow. He felt no need to rush his odyssey. He continued his meanderings, sailing around the tip of South America under unusually calm seas.

Chile contained the most enterprising men of all the former South American Spanish republics and they had an eye for talent in others as well. James made such an impression on a local industrialist that he was offered a tidy sum to stay in Valparaiso for a time and help construct a flourmill. Dunne & McDonald, commission merchants from San Francisco, became the mill's primary customer and James would eventually accompany the first shipment on its high sea voyage up the Pacific coast.

Salty sea air commingled with the rank odors of unwashed humanity. After weeks of ripening above and below deck, the passengers were nearing their destination. Who among those assembled would be the first to spot the shimmering land holding so much promise? James Dunne caught a glimpse of cypress trees through the mist and his heart began to leap. As the clipper ship sliced through the bay waters it approached the straits of the Golden Gate where murky land became visible to all on the port and starboard sides. The men did not erupt in hoots or hollers. They were oddly silent as if they were somehow witnessing their own sacred rite of passage.

James had one last Cuban cigar he was saving for himself when he set eyes on California. Eager to light it up on deck, he bit the end off and spat it into the bay. He moistened the other tip and stuck it in his mouth. He combed through the front pockets of his pea coat searching for a match. James reached into an inner pocket and found a slip of paper. What's this? The wind almost blew it from his fingertips before he could unfolded it. He took a deep sigh. It was a doodle of a little yellow cat, with a green collar balancing a bright pink heart on its tail. A hidden love note from Kitty. He put the cigar away.

A significant amount of confusion followed as they sailed deeper into the bay without so much as a hint of civilization with the exception of a few whaling ships docked in the distance to the north. James had studied his maps and knew the port of San Francisco faced the bay not the ocean so he was not worried, everything's just where the map said it would be. Alcatraz Island appeared in the middle of the bay, an outcropping of rock made glistening white by countless generations of seabirds. A faint pink glow rose behind the torn paper shapes of the hills to the east, far beyond which lay the reason for the invasion, the goldfields.

When they sailed leeward, through an armada of ship masts and flapping flags the encampment of San Francisco revealed itself. An amphitheater of sorts had been scooped out of the treeless sand hills forming a crescent-shaped beachhead. Above the waterline was a mishmash of wood frame buildings, their shadowy outlines revealing haphazard design and construction. The landscape was dotted with burning campfires and hundreds of canvas tents stitched together from sails of those 600 abandoned ships in the cove. One by one they began to glow with light as their inhabitants awakened. James became visibly moved at the serene beauty of a thousand giant lanterns on the hillside welcoming him into the harbor.

Small boats containing wheeler-dealers rowed up to the arriving ship asking for permission to board. They would attempt to reach the captain and buy his entire ship's contents before it had a chance to dock. Inexperienced captains jumped at the generous offers. Not today. They were waved off as the vessel inched toward the rude pier that jetted out from Clarke's Point. From nowhere a blistering boom shook James to his core. He instinctively ducked.

"On your feet man. It was a gunshot from that warship. They just announced our arrival," said a bemused German crewman as he helped James up. "You're safe…for now," he added with a wink.

Men scurried on board or raced below to gather their belongings, each wanting to be first to set out for the mines as soon as they walked on land. The ship had anchored and men on the dock helped with the gang-plank. Throngs of Chileans in their broad sombreros and stinky ponchos jostled for position at the railing. Four rugged crew members with clubs kept the exodus orderly. James let the others pass. It took him eight months to get to San Francisco and he was going to step onto her shore under his own terms. After all, he was in no need of accommodation nor employment, he only needed to find the corner of Kearny and Pacific Streets.

Swarms of Jack Tars, longshoreman, flop-house agents and teamsters crowded the wooden sidewalks already strewn with piles of lumber, cargo, luggage. Goods were stacked so high against the storefronts it appeared as though the establishments themselves were constructed of crates. Crude signs shouted out from makeshift tin buildings, posted haphazardly like letterforms strewn into the wind. Languages of a half-dozen tongues jabbered away competing with the sounds of snapping canvas awnings, horse whinnies, sawing and that incessant hammering. James tucked his pant legs into his boots and squeezed through the chaos moving into the gutter to make better time, his paraphernalia balancing about him. A bedraggled mule strained to move an over-loaded cart through the muddy thoroughfare. Suddenly James felt sand fleas nipping at his neck and dropped his luggage to swat at them. His case cracked wide opened and the spilled clothes were quickly trampled over by oblivious roustabouts too busy shouting and scouting to care. He left them right where they fell.

People were swirling around him, this way and that. He stood in a doorway to get his bearings for precisely one minute and exactly 70 men swished past him. He imagined he was a hummingbird trapped in a cyclone. Not a friendly face could be found to provide directions. Not that Celestial with his long tail and robes or the identical miners in their red-flannel shirts. Wait, maybe that Spanish girl sauntering by with a mantilla and fandango shoes? Each passer-by as different as night is to day. It didn't seem to matter, they were all just people in search of the same thing, gold and opportunity: El Dorado.

By now, after leaving Ireland, exploring New Orleans, trekking through the Caribbean and more than a half-dozen South American countries James considered himself a sophisticated traveler but nothing prepared him for this. He was completely bewildered. A spectacle so bizarre, so otherworldly that it just might be a different planet altogether.

Gentle fanning sea breezes so prevalent in his other ports-of-call were replaced by forceful bursts that kicked up whirling clouds of dust and sand from the San Francisco streets. He walked aimlessly through the mayhem until he looked around to see Pacific St. crudely painted in green on a fence post. Two stray mutts sniffed at his boots before wandering off. Just a few blocks up from the water, across from Graham's Hotel, he found a new wooden building on the corner with crisp white letters spelling out: Dunne, McDonald & Co. Commission Merchants on its corniced false-front. It was a handsome structure. Standing next to the office door lighting a cigar was his partner, J.M. McDonald, looking smooth and spruce.

"Are you ready to make some money?" he said casually blowing smoke into the morning air.

"So, is that what's happening here?" James asked incredulously.

"Oh, my friend, you have no idea."

They robustly shook hands. McDonald brought James up to the second story office that also served as living quarters, the smell of progress emanating up and down the fresh pine staircase. Bathed in light from large casement windows facing Pacific Street the room had a long table where men were inspecting ledgers or fiddling with beam scales and gold dust. Sample pouches of grain and beans were scattered around. A kettle whistled on the pot belly stove next to the vault.

"Well now, this is quite an impressive operation you have going here, McDonald."

"We have going Dunne, we. All the contracts you made on your travels have been honored and we are the most reliable trading house in town. You are seeing this for the first time but it's thanks to you we have product to sell and a spanking new warehouse to store it in!"

"That is splendid," said James as he proudly looked around at his new company.

"We have stables in the rear for 30 horses and run a drayage business back there."

"An empire—"

"Yes! And we already have the flour sold that sailed in with you on that ship. We'll have to get our warehouse boys to go fetch it and deliver it to the buyer today. It's absolute arbitrage, we won't even take delivery."

"All day long I feel like I've been dreaming. Please tell me I not."

McDonald smiled and they walked down a short hallway covered with maps and shipping lists then opened the door to a smaller office. "Was your brother in your dream?" Sitting at an ornate oak desk was a man looking quite *famillionaire* in a black pinstripe suit with a diamond stickpin popping out of his purple silk cravat. It was Peter.

"What the, wha, what are you doing here?" James asked in complete confusion. "But who's in New Orleans? How'd you get here? What the hell's going on?"

Peter sat up momentarily catching his gold watch chain on the desk. Brothers hugged.

"I came over on a bloody oxen team and only beat you by a couple weeks!"

"But did you shut down New Orleans?"

"No, our sister Mary's son, Bryan, showed up from Ireland and now he's running it. I just had to come here."

"Peter you old scalawag! This is something. Unbelievable. We have lots to discuss, the inventory, what about…never mind. I guess we aren't going back anytime soon?'

"No James, not ever. This place is our destiny."

"And we're destined to be millionaires!" yelled out McDonald.

All three men exploded in thundering laughter like pirates digging up hidden treasure. When the laughter died down a child-like cry could be heard from an adjoining room.

Puzzled, James lowered his booming voice to a whisper. "McDonald you're the scalawag! Have you made a family out here already?"

Shuffling in from the adjoining bedroom came a small woman holding a golden haired toddler, grumpy and scowling.

It couldn't be.

She looked James directly in the face.

It couldn't be.

As magical and mysterious as any day James had ever lived now become completely surreal. Those eyes!

His lips began to quiver. His organs seemed to be twisting around inside of him until he felt completely paralyzed.

"Kitty? Is that you?"

It just couldn't be.

Kitty Dunne, with a babe in one arm, reached for her husband with the other. All three of them huddled in a family embrace that lasted until all three dissolved into tears of one kind or another. James was completely, utterly and simply overwhelmed with joy.

"It's true. It's really her! I spotted her on a trip to Baton Rouge. She walked by my window with little Caroline in her arms," explained Peter in a whirlwind of frenzied story-telling. "I'd know her anywhere!"

"Baton Rouge?" James said as he rediscovered the contours of Kitty's face with the back of his fingers.

"Yes. Grayson kicked her out. Disinherited her when he found out you two were married."

"Kitty, I don't, I, I am so sorry." James delicately lifted up her smooth chin as if he were inspecting a porcelain angel.

"Threw her right out he did. Said she had to leave town and was never to return."

"Jaysus."

"He's heartless."

"Oh Kitty, say something. Your aunt told me you died of the fever." James longed to hear her voice. What did it sound like again?

She began to speak, "I was there when you came that day. I saw you in the courtyard from the upstairs window," she looked up at him with her giant twinkling eyes, the ones he remembered every day since their separation.

"How could you let her tell me that?"

"My father was there too and pulled me away. James, he, he was so cruel."

"I know the whole story." Peter excitedly took over the conversation.

"Grayson beat her, took her for a curettage in the French Quarter and she ran. Her Aunt Amelia set her up in a flat and said she had to stay in Baton Rouge. Then the baby came—locked away in that God-forsaken city like a prisoner. The aunt's an angel and Grayson's the devil incarnate. I hope he rots in hell," said Peter.

"But, but you were just living on your own? Couldn't you send word to me somehow? I was so broken without you." James continued to be absolutely incredulous.

"James, I was scared and confused. I don't know. Father made so many threats. His eyes went black with rage. I thought he would kill me and Amelia too! He went crazy. He promised me to some British aristocrat from one of his deals. He said I made him look foolish." Kitty pleaded for mercy.

"He was going to trade her off like he trades everything," Peter said shaking his head. "You can see why I couldn't stay in New Orleans. I had no idea what country you were in so I pulled up stakes and brought us all here. That's what you would want, right?"

James lifted up Kitty's chin again and gazed into her face. "Peter, this is the best and finest thing you have ever done." He took his little daughter from his wife's arms and breathed in the sweet smell of his baby's head.

McDonald ushered Peter out and they closed the door behind them.

While young men caroused in the boomtown below gambling and drinking, cussing and fighting, upstairs at the warehouse on the corner of Kearny and Pacific three reunited people started a family.

SAN FRANCISCO

A. *St. Patrick's Church*
B. *St. Patrick's Orphan Asylum*
C. *Patrick Lawler's Dairy*
D. *Pacific Club Rooms*
E. *Poodle Dog Restaurant*
F. *Bella Union*
G. *Alphabet House*
H. *St. Francis Church*
I. *Dunne, McDonald & Co.*
J. *Dunne House*
K. *Dunne & Co. Offices*
L. *Phelan Brothers' Store*
M. *Pacific Warehouse*
N. *Flour Mill*

BURNT DISTRICT OF MAY 1851

CHAPTER 25

Advertisement in the *Daily Alta California*, San Francisco, July 30, 1850

*HAY, CORN, OATS, BARLEY, BRAN and flour—Dunne, McDonald & Co.
corner of Kearny and Pacific Streets, offer for sale: 600 bales Californian
and New York North River Hay, 1500 sacks red and mixed corn, 1000
sacks Australian and Oregon oats, 1200 sacks Chilean barley, 500 sacks fresh
Chilean bran, 500 sacks fresh Chilean flour, ashore & afloat.*

Buildings seemed to sprout up overnight like mushrooms in San
Francisco. Others just floated up. Ships of every size that had carried
fortune seekers from around the world were abandoned right in the
harbor. Their passengers and crew headed straight to the goldfields. A
few ships became floating buildings or made their way onto the streets
and became ship-stores or ship-hotels. Others sunk into the ground,
mixed with sand and debris to become building foundations at the
shoreline, the heart of the business section.

Restaurants could charge three dollars for a single egg, rooming houses
gouged patrons and scant provisions were sold at exorbitant prices. Dunne
& McDonald had a hand in almost every big deal in town from hay to
bricks to real estate. Odd-ball items like used bottles salvaged from the
Sandwich Islands could be imported for a handsome profit to the needy
frontier. Commission merchants were at the highest echelon of the young
city's commercial kingdom. They controlled the waterfront and could
get piers built out within days. Power came from the cargo they were
capable of importing from around the world, consumable goods more
precious than gold. The trader's warehouse would be filled and emptied
every week keeping a steady stream of gold dust, bank notes, Spanish
doubloons or coin from private mints flowing to the upstairs vault. James
learned his craft in New Orleans, the city credited with inventing modern
mercantilism, so this was his golden moment in time.

At times, competing ships arrived exactly at the same hour with
the exact same cargo causing prices to plummet. Only commission

merchants with large warehouses could afford to store the goods until the glut passed and prices bounced back even higher than before.

Plans were in the works for a flourmill with drawings James lifted from the Chilean enterprise. Peter Dunne would improve the occasion of the low bar set for professional men and open up a makeshift law office. Fellow Irishman and pioneer land baron Martin Murphy became his first client.

The three partners had more bold notions than available employees. They were like little boys on their hands and knees building a toy village. Able-bodied entrepreneurs with good business schemes could turn to the swashbuckling merchants Dunne, McDonald & Company for backing. They might also store commodities like coal or grain at the Dunnes' warehouse and use it as collateral for cash loans from the brothers at sky-high interest rates.

Very few would get rich in the mines. The real money was to be made by those who could mine the miners.

Along with the ambitious who came to town were the outlaws and the miscreants. Assorted hoodlums, vagrant veterans from the Mexican-American war and a gang of Australian criminals known as the Sydney Ducks stalked the rat-infested, lamp-less streets at night posing a danger in every darkened corner. During the day, The Ducks would shake down the Company for protection money. Suspicious fires consumed the warehouses of those that didn't pay up. McDonald was tasked to deal with crimps, bandits or politicians who made business difficult. He had seen it all during his tenure as a riverboat captain in the South and although he admired honesty he wasn't averse to dealing with wickedness. He would kick the extortionists a few coins now and then. Unknown to his partners, McDonald also used the gang to shake down a few of their own customers who reneged on payment.

James hated anything unseemly and bristled at being blackmailed. He spent a good deal of time worrying about his young family's safety, likening it to his boyhood days looking after the Brittas sheep. Disgusted, he joked with Peter that there were no wolves in Ireland anymore because they had all sailed to San Francisco.

Kitty got pregnant again within days of her husband's arrival. James kept watch over her and made one of his men escort his wife around town when she did her errands, much to her annoyance. A fetching girl like her would attract attention walking around any city in the world but one in which men out numbered women 50-1, she was viewed as an absolute goddess.

Kitty Dunne was ostracized and alone in Baton Rouge. She rode the rough wagon train out West through uncharted territory, a tiny girl in tow, and never once complained or displayed any bitterness. Serenity was her natural state-of-being. She didn't even mind being pregnant, she liked the condition, said it suited her creative nature. Not a cross word was uttered about her cramped San Francisco quarters or the fact that she was living with three men. James was more madly in love with her than ever.

Kitty was having difficulty delivering her baby who had refused to pass through the birth canal. A surgeon was fetched to perform a dangersome caesarean delivery. With the first cut into her belly the doctor broke out into a fit of laughter immediately followed by a cry from the healthy infant.

After his new daughter and Kitty were out of harm's way James pulled the doctor aside in private to ask what had been so funny. The surgeon replied, "When I got in there her little rump appeared in the incision and she crapped on me." Although the exceptionally beautiful little baby was formally named after her mother she would be called Poopsy by her amused and adoring father.

On their first Christmas Eve together as a family of four, fire broke out a few blocks away in the town's center known as Portsmouth Plaza. It raged all night long and into Christmas morning. Many people perished and 300 buildings were lost. Whether the Australian gang set the fire or not was unclear but they were certainly Johnny-on-the-spot to plunder all the stores and warehouses in the district.

It was difficult enough raising a family in the rough-and-tumble world of San Francisco but living above a raucous, flammable warehouse, whose very existence was under constant threat, proved unbearable. James heard about a substantial new three-story brick building for sale on Sansome Street next door to the Phelan brothers, his distant cousins from Queen's County. Among the fireproof features was a tar-covered flat roof with a short wall around the perimeter that corralled a foot of standing water. Exterior doors and window shutters were forged of iron. He suggested the company buy it.

Peter understood his brother's concerns and readily agreed to the purchase but J.M. McDonald put up a fuss. He saw no need to buy such an expensive building, especially one that sat in the middle of a northerly street. All the easterly streets in the district ended in piers so goods could be hauled right off ships and up the road to a warehouse. Property on those streets were wise investments for commission merchants. James argued they could still keep the Pacific Street location as a warehouse but the office and store should be on Sansome where his family would be safe and sound on the top two floors.

McDonald steadfastly refused to consider such an expenditure whereupon Peter drew up lawyerly looking papers he titled "Dissolution of Partnership." In conjoined hardship and glory the Dunne brothers had forged an impenetrable family bond. They shared almost every thought, every action. When they were in conversation no one else existed or could make a point. Their time spent together in New Orleans mourning Kitty had bonded them together forever. A club of sorts existed between them with room for only two members. McDonald's rascalism was tolerated when it grew the business but there would be no defiance of the Dunnes. He had to go.

Upstairs at the warehouse, a legal showdown was about to begin. The long counting table had been cleared, accountants and brokers given the afternoon off. Kitty and the girls were escorted over to the empty building that sat at 164 Sansome Street, the title having already been purchased by the brothers.

Peter, looking every inch the cultured man of the law, represented himself and his brother. J.M. McDonald hired a brash young attorney in town by the name of Hall McAllister who appeared more like a baby-faced pugilist stuffed into an ill-fitting suit than an attorney. After formal introductions McAllister fired the opening salvo.

"Here we sit gentlemen, a couple of spurious Mc's on this side and a couple of genuine Micks on that one."

What temerity! Peter and James twisted their heads to look at each other and snapped them back staring blankly at the opposition. In its infancy San Francisco was a harmonious melting pot. Newcomers joined together from all parts of the globe in a common struggle, without malice or prejudice, to build a community. But as time wore on the familiar ugliness of bigotry bubbled up like scum upon the surface of water.

"Let us not start the insults already if you please," Peter said in a strange forced accent that muffled his Irish roots.

"Yes. Business is business so let's just stick to the facts and spare the sarcasm," added James in his sing-songy brogue that he ratcheted-up just for effect.

"My apologies I meant nothing by it, just trying to be light-hearted," McAllister pleaded in his quaint Southern drawl.

"Sounds like we are all from someplace else so let us continue in a spirit of camaraderie," Peter acquiesced with the elegance and grace of a capable barrister impressing his new legal rival.

"Perfectly said dear sir. Where may I ask did you get your obviously brilliant schooling in the law?"

"In London at Gray's Inn, not that I expect you would be familiar with that supreme English institution," Peter said as his body slightly wiggled with the kick James served under the table.

"How very impressive," replied McAllister.

"And you Mr. McAllister, what venerable law establishment did you attend?"

"Some podunk one in Georgia you never heard of in your life."

"I only say this as a point of reference but back in Europe I had the chance to meet King George, assorted Earls and the like but now I am fully acclimated to the American way of life," crowed Peter who just couldn't help himself.

"Yes, and the American law. I saw from the papers you served to my client for his signature. Very thorough."

When James sifted through the papers he could not make heads-nor-tails of them. Barely hiding his disgust for Peter's pomp and half-truths he added, "I wanted him to be fair and square to Mr. McDonald. He's the one that had the notion to come out here from New Orleans before this gold fever even started. I want him to be fully compensated."

"James, I am the attorney and I think it's best that I should be the chief talker if you don't mind."

"I don't want this to be acrimonious, I just want to be thankful," concluded James.

"Mr. Dunne that is completely understandable and appreciated by Mr. McDonald. I just took the liberty to revise a couple of things in these new documents, just a few fixes. Americanized if you will from my friend's impeccable English, the Queen's English. It's all in order now," he said in his folksy way.

Peter carefully reviewed the agreement and after sufficient perusal he signed with minor notations written and initialed in the margins. James signed and it was done.

Later when the accountants began to divvy out the company's sizable holdings they were first puzzled then alarmed. Seamlessly concealed into the final papers behind flourishes and double talk was an arrangement that left McDonald with half the real estate assets of the company where Peter thought he was only agreeing to give away a third. The Irisher could throw about all the nobility titles he liked but nothing in San Francisco was held in more respect and awe than that of the land title. The backwoods Kentucky lawyer had played the Dunne brothers like a fiddle.

CHAPTER 26

Advertisement in the Daily Alta California, San Francisco, February 24, 1851

COPARTNERSHIP—The undersigned, late of the firm of Dunne, McDonald & Co. of this city, have formed a copartnership under the new name and style of DUNNE & CO. from this day, 12th February, 1851, and will continue at the old stand, corner of Kearny and Pacific Streets

JAMES DUNNE
PETER DUNNE

"Poopsy, come here to me," said a beguiled and besotted James Dunne as he got up from his velvet chaise in the family's plush front parlor.

"I do wish you wouldn't call her that!" Kitty scolded as she handed the little bundle over to her father.

"Aye, but she'll always be my little Poopsy, aye Poopsy?" James had missed the delicate infancy of his first daughter Caroline when she was sequestered in Louisiana and was fully enjoying this phase with his second one. Caroline had clung so tightly to her mother that her father felt a slight rejection and his fawning over the newborn widened the distance between them.

But from the domesticated setting of their new home only bliss and contentment could be detected throughout the elegantly furnished rooms and hallways lined with Oriental carpets and bric-a-brac. As James was starting to acquire wealth from his efforts he was starting to acquire something else from his family he hadn't ever fully experienced in his life, purpose.

Kitty was preparing a Saturday evening meal of jambalaya as a treat for the hard working new partners. Peter waltzed out of his room wearing his flashy red-lined cape and holding his silk top hat reeking of Bay Rum.

"Peter, are you leaving us?" asked Kitty in a sad voice.

"Afraid so dear lady, the tables are calling. James why not come fight the tiger with us tonight?"

"Why don't you leave that gambling for those nincompoop prospector and tenderfeet?" James asked. "Isn't there enough thrill for you already with all the betting we do on commodities?"

"Yes I know, but there is also the music and that Pisco Punch! You're more fun when you pour a couple of those down your gullet."

"Not tonight, Kitty is making my supper and she wants me to hang up some new pictures she bought."

"Do that tomorrow. The Senator is in town."

"Peter I want to stay home. It's my favorite place to be. You go, have fun and don't lose!"

"I never lose."

"Leave your jewelry here just the same," said Kitty with a familiar giggle, a smile on her pretty face.

For Peter Dunne, it was his routine on Saturday evenings to mix business with pleasure. He had been admitted into the rarefied atmosphere of the Pacific Club rooms located above Steve Whipple's mangy saloon. Men of distinction deserved a place where they could fraternize with their equals, smoke cigars, drink and scheme in the same way their counterparts did in New York's Union Club or Boodle's of London. It was a primitive attempt at a lofty snobatorium but it was all the city had to offer a social mountaineer such as Peter.

What constituted as Society in early San Francisco was broken-up into two groups, The Chivalry (an elite group of Southern gentlemen who were wealthy, well-bred and pro-slavery) and the opposing Shovelry (mostly working class Northerners who felt the only real threat to America came from slavery).

Peter was initially torn between the two rival factions. He was drawn to the aristocratic pretensions and clout of the "Chivs" but knew his Irishness would prevent him from genuine acceptance. He found a respectable compromise in his friendship with a club member who was a fellow Irishman and a fallen Catholic like himself. David C. Broderick, curly-haired and charismatic, was a leader among the Shovelry and earned his political spurs back in New York City. He modeled his tactics on the Tammany Hall example of intimidation and bribery. No civic contract or important position could be decided upon without Broderick's blessing. Son of an Irish immigrant, he seemed to emerge like a modern day chieftain amongst his Hibernian tribesmen. As he jumped, so precisely did they all jump. He was San Francisco's first Big Boss. The state was one gigantic oyster from which he would pluck the pearls. Initially brought out to search for gold he was now a member of the state senate, incredibly rich and a good man to know.

Smooth whiskey in the gentrified surroundings of the club coaxed business rivals into laughing together and political enemies into finding common ground. Conversations would heat up then cool down after each member had his say. When glad-handing and bogus sincerity reached sufficient levels Broderick and Dunne escaped, holding on to the brims of their top hats while making their way across the windy plaza to their next stop. Peter's ostentatious cape fluttered in the air.

If money poured into San Francisco from its shoreline, Portsmouth Plaza was the place where one could watch it all disappear. Ringing the park situated at the center was every sort of device known to man that could separate him from his riches. The old adobe Custom House, a Mexican-era holdover, collected tolls, duties and tariffs for the Federal Government. Bordellos offered an evening of passion at unconscionable prices and assorted gambling halls would take what's left over. In the morning, resourceful scavengers trolled the plank walkways and exchange doorways to scrounge for any spilled gold dust or dropped coins from careless carousers.

The Bella Union Gambling Hall was Broderick and Dunne's preferred place to wager. Patrons admired the exquisite French paintings of nude ladies that lined the walls and the lascivious painted ladies waiting upstairs.

Entering off the Plaza, the place was in full-swing and waiting for Senator Broderick to mingle with his constituents. Always planning his next political move, he kept his behavior in check. Crystal chandeliers flooded the pleasure palace with dazzling light. Hoochie-coochie dancers kicked their legs up high on the gilded stage, ogled by the loafers waiting for a glimpse of their privates or a free drink given away by a lucky winner. Occidentals and Orientals alike who gambled at the mines now took their chances at the Bella Union. Music of Stephen Foster and Franz Liszt competed with whirling roulette wheels and the occasional gunshot from an skittish faro dealer. Green felt tables staked with thousands of dollars in gold could bring out the worst in losers.

Passing by the crowded monte table, Peter deferentially asked, "Care for a game Senator?"

"Are you insane, man? Monte was born without a conscience. He'll swindle you out of every last cent!"

A couple of players at the Vingt-et-Un table were brusquely tapped by the croupier indicating that Senator Broderick required their seats. Peter smirked, made himself comfortable and condescendingly called for chips. Slap! Slap! Slap! Went the cards on the table followed by a quick scoop of the ivory chips into the house coffers. An exquisite lacquered black box lay at the center of the table into which loser's gold dust would be deposited. Dealers wasted no time in between hands for time was money.

Fawners tried to pay their respects to the Senator but Peter chased them away, Broderick was concentrating. Dunne was wondering how many other men of influence wished they were sitting in his spot as he looked around the room. He noticed a congregation at the doorway and guessed a good fistfight was happening outside, then came the familiar cry feared by all San Franciscans, "F I R E!"

Quickly came a command to the card dealers from the casino captain, "Close tables!" as he brought a barrel around collecting the house's bankroll. Gamblers complained about their impending win but pried their wagers back from the tables and headed out. Peter and the Senator pushed through the door to see flames leaping into the air directly across the Plaza. Excited men fled out to help extinguish the fire while annoyed ones went back for another whiskey.

Peter stepped into the park to get a closer look at the blaze and shouted over the fire bell, "It doesn't seem terribly bad Senator, just needs to be nipped in the bud right now." Broderick looked at the trees bending with the wind and disappeared. He had duties at the nearby Empire Engine Company.

An explosion rang out, shooting a fireball 50 feet into the air knocking Peter to the ground. In front of a blazing structure the wooden plank sidewalk caught fire and rambled on to the next building, and the next, and the next. The vertical inferno mutated into a horizontal wild beast, and it was hungry. Veils of flames danced on the rooftops until the glowing trusses all crumbled beneath. An entire side of Portsmouth Plaza was now brightly illuminated with consuming flames as men scurried like ants on a hot summer's day to contain the fire or rescue their possessions.

"I can help." Peter wedged his way into a bucket brigade that passed well water from hand to hand to save a storefront. His top hat was lost in the ruckus.

"Grab 'hold," said a man in a green flannel shirt.

"Keep going, faster, faster!" said Peter as he recruited another two volunteers.

The line switched over to the next building forsaking the first to flames of fate.

When the wind changed direction the flames blew across Kearny Street and towards Dunne & Company's warehouse. Peter abandoned the bucket chain. He ran as fast he could out of the Plaza just as the fire engine approached from the other side. Water from its miserly fire hoses vaporized on contact. It was complete chaos as stores succumbed one after another, their canvas awnings shriveling away like dried leaves beneath the heat. Burning chaparral tumbled behind him. Chinese gongs and bells and trumpets warned of the flames that now spread in a broad sheet towards the east.

Peter ran at top speed and when he reached the warehouse his men were already positioned around the building with rifles. He yelled out as he ran: "Fire is waiting only two blocks away! Keep alert!" Peter wanted them to take aim at any looter that thought to take advantage of the commotion. After the Dunne brothers had paid their ex-partner off in cash they had to borrow money to restock the warehouse, which at the moment was filled to the rafters with top quality flour from Chile. Their business would be in collapse if they lost the warehouse and Pacific Street would be devastated if the fire reached the gigantic building packed with flour, a substance as explosive as dynamite.

"Rumson, go up there and see where it's headed!" Peter sent one of his men up to the roof while he cleared the office of ledgers and outstanding invoices, stuffing them into a flour sack. There was no cash to worry about.

Outside, flames twirled up into the darkness. Despite the powerful sight of his city burning it would be the sounds that sent Peter into a panic: crackling and popping of blazing wood, collapsing roofs with the occasional explosion. The screams ringing out in the night competed with others shouting incoherently at the top of their lungs.

Word came fire was headed down Sansome Street. James! Kitty! The babies! Peter ran with his sack down a smoke-filled Broadway to the Sansome corner where he saw nothing but a wall of flames. Breathless, he stood silent absorbing the horror. The Dunne brothers' handsome house was right in the middle of the catastrophe and there was absolutely nothing to be done. He wondered if the family been lucky enough to escape or at least die painlessly in their beds. Peter kept running around the area trying to make sense of what was happening. Checking on the house, checking on the warehouse and back again.

Morning soon broke over a decimated San Francisco. In ten hours fire had incinerated eighteen blocks and reduced the heart of the city to a heap of charred rubble. Brick buildings and chimneys poked through the ruins. Dunne's warehouse had been spared and Peter kept men stationed at all four corners, forbidding them to leave their posts.

Sansome Street was still in the middle of a smoldering disaster zone but Peter could not be kept out any longer. It was light enough to see. He walked down a narrow trail with glowing embers emitting smoke that was drifting leeward. Small puddles of molten glass in assorted colors at his feet. The smell of destruction and death hung in the air like a slaughterhouse on a sweltering afternoon. But through the soupy atmosphere Peter could make out the blackened brick edifice of 164 Sansome standing tall in the aftermath. Iron shutters had been closed around the windows and doors from the inside.

Peter approached, cautious but hopeful. He instinctively grabbed the entry door handle fully expecting to walk right in. "DAMN!" Peter singed his palm. With the pain he screamed out an ungodly, mournful wail.

Besides him a bucket of water soon appeared and a soot-covered old man said, "Put your hand in here, you fool."

"Thank you. I think my brother and his family are still in here."

"Well, they's gone now. People think they so smart with all them iron fittings and all but the metal gets all swoll in fire. We just saw the same thing happen over on Jackson Street. They's couldn't get out if they wanted to. Baked like bread. Sorry. Really am. I's got work to do." And the man drifted off into the grayness.

James Phelan, liquor merchant and a distant Queen's County relative, was sifting through his ruined business next door with a pry bar. The spirits stored in his building burned hotter than kerosene. He noticed Peter and called out, "Did your warehouse burn down?"

"No. The fire stopped just before. Looks like you're ruined."

"I'm trying to find my safe."

"I can't get in here. I'm worried James and his family are dead inside."

"They're OK. I was with them last night. We all went down to the wharf and hopped on my little sloop. Saw the city burn all night long from the bay. It was the worst thing I've ever seen. James and I left Kitty and the girls on board. We told them to stay put."

"I figured James would find a way." Peter sensed deep down James and Kitty were safe but he was still relieved at the confirmation.

"He's around here somewhere."

"Peter!" A haggard and soot covered James called out from the other side of what used to be Sansome Street. He hopped over the debris to greet his partner.

"You're a sight! How's Kitty? The girls?" Peter nervously asked.

"Good, good. They're fine. I saw the warehouse is still there. What a disaster."

"I don't think I've ever been as scared in my life," Peter began to say.

"It's completely ridiculous." James kicked away a charred wooden balustrade that impeded his step. "This damned city is inept! Can't they get a grip on the fires? How many times does this have to happen? My God!"

"This looks to be the worst of them all. Now what?" said Peter.

"Now what? What do you mean, you fool? Let's find some shovels to sell."

CHAPTER 27

What follows is James Dunne's letter to Bridget Lawler. It would be the longest letter he would ever write:

November 5, 1852
San Francisco, California
United States of America

My Dear Sister:

 Your recent letter has only added to my sadness. I have been horrible about writing back to you since I arrived in San Francisco. I am a heel. To learn now of our mother's return to God made me cry, something I have been doing much of lately. I will have a mass offered for her. She was so very lucky to have you & Patrick to take care of her these past few years. I am grateful & indebted to you both.

 I have met with much success in this place. Like I did in New Orleans, I am a commission merchant. Peter & I have created something here that has made for us a handsome profit. We have property all over town now & want for nothing. It has not always been easy. Over the past three years we have suffered a series of terrible conflagrations that has left the city in ruins & each time it has come back stronger than before—gets reduced to a few feet high & within no time there are three-story buildings everywhere— destruction & construction—like a Phoenix it rises from the ashes.

 The fire we had last year in May was the one worst yet—it scorched our city to the ground. Afterward there were mountains of burnt debris that encumbered any attempts to rebuild. The city fathers brought in these beastly machines they claimed could do the work of 20 Irishmen. Called them "Steam Paddys" of all things! These giant mechanical shovels moved the charred remains of San Francisco right into the bay waters & created more land upon which to build. Lots of fancy buildings & graded roads & fine streets now—a far cry from the crude settlement that met me when I first set shore here.

 Last June there was another smaller fire. We lost our warehouse in that one & it was chock-full of goods. Peter had insisted the place be fully bonded & insured by a New Orleans outfit so we were far luckier than other merchants in the area. At considerable expense a new building on Broadway is being erected that will be called the Pacific Warehouse. It will be two stories high with amble amounts of floor space. It is located only a few blocks from the wharf & will be the finest in the city. Each disaster only improves the place & this warehouse will be a fine start.

My family escaped every fire that has plagued us but death has come regardless. In February we were finally blessed with a handsome son we named Peter. Not-so-much named after father but after our brother. He is a strapping young lad. Two weeks after he was born my youngest daughter I called Poopsy, somehow got into rat poison, which is everywhere in this vermin-infested place. She languished in agony for 2 days & died a horrible death in my arms. Not three months later my older daughter Caroline—who was born in the Louisiana —died from an outbreak of cholera. It has absolutely divided my life in two. They say foreign ships are to blame for bringing the dreaded disease to our shores now & then. I wanted to strangle every Chinaman & Greaser I saw on the street but have only recently come to my senses.

Kitty has taken everything in stride. She lives in her own fairy tale world where nothing seems to make her blue. It is quite remarkable. She is the strongest person I have ever known although to look at her you would think she could be blown over by a feather. I have grown much older in the last year & my beard is already turning gray. Peter is fine & looks younger than I do. His law pursuits seem to elude him but he makes a fine businessman. Kitty tells him he needs to find a wife before he loses his looks but he seems intent on being the single man-about-town.

Although I have failed to answer your letters in the past I have read them with much interest. The years of famine have only made you all stronger Christians. It warms my heart to know that the people of Queen's County still remember the shipment of food we sent from New Orleans but it was surely Patrick who twisted my arm into such actions. He is a fine fellow. You don't know this story, but if your husband had not asked me to ship that corn I would never have been forced to leave the South & come here.

I know too that you have also lost your two daughters & only now do I recognize my callousness in not writing to comfort you earlier. I am so sorry. Death leaves a parent with an indescribable emptiness. But there is something about this country that gives me hope. America is more than just a country—it is a brand new idea. I tell you I feel more American than I ever felt Irish. We could never, ever do in Ireland what we have done in just a few short years here in America. It is a glorious place.

Bridget, now that Mother has died there is no reason for you to pine away in a miserable country that will never recover from the devastation that has befallen it. California possesses some of the richest land & one of the finest climates anywhere in the world. A man of Patrick's skill & industry could make his fortune here. You could be happy here. Come to San Francisco! Peter & I have just opened a flourmill & Patrick could help by running it. You could live with us until you find a place of your own. Our children could grow up together. Wouldn't it be wonderful to have us all together again like the olden days? While you are at it, convince Mary & her family to come with you. We could be the Dunnes of San Francisco.

Please write & tell me when to expect you.

Your loving & faithful brother,

James Dunne

Ӿ

Bridget woke up to see a candle burning in the front room and the comforting sound of her husband's snore missing. She wrapped herself in a blanket and got out of bed.

"What are you doing up in the middle of the night?"

"Just reading."

"Reading what?"

"Oh, a wee adventure novel."

"Let me see." Bridget tilted up the little blue book to reveal the title. She put her calloused hands over her mouth and glared at him. Her head started to buzz and she felt a tingling sensation in her body. Shaking her head she whispered, "O my eye! Are you teasing with me, husband?"

"Just researching. Don't go all thuzzy-muzzy."

He was reading The Irish Emigrant's Guide to the United States.

"After all my nagging, have you come around? Truly Patrick? Truly?" Bridget asked over and over.

Patrick continued, "Now it says right here, 'The Utopia of the imagination, is not the United States of our experience. By substituting fancy for judgement, romantic hopes are first formed to be afterward destroyed.' Goes on to say a thousand difficulties stare you in the face when you land on the wharf of some sea-board city…a stranger in a strange land."

"Please, Patrick! We've gone over it a hundred times. I want to go and you don't. You've never been off the island and you have no intention of ever doing so. Why are we even discussing it?"

"No, I just want to make you happy Biddy. That's the top and bottom of it."

"I will be happy in America."

"Then we shall go."

"What? When? Patrick!"

"Soon, before your brother rescinds his offer."

What may have seemed to Bridget that night to be an impulsive decision was actually an exhaustively planned exit from Ireland by her husband. No matter how many he ways he calculated, there was no getting away from the fact that his prospects were dismal in his homeland. Efforts at land grabbing had been a spectacular failure. His tenure as a sub-landlord managing tenants left him frustrated and owing rent to his own landlord. An offer from the Lord of Brittas felt like a trap. Livestock prices were down and the wet spring had left his wheat crop in sorry shape. If he were lucky he could sell every last thing he owned and come away with £300.

Patrick grumbled to anyone that would listen, all he had to show for 40 years of toil were six hungry children.

Much had to be sorted out before the Lawler family could be shoveled out to America. Mary Donnelly, Bridget's sister, had been systematically sending her children over to the States in batches for the last five years. She still remained with the two smallest boys and her aged, alcoholic husband Hugh. They had survived the famine from their Maryborough hotel and tavern hiding behind whiskey bottles. Mary was determined to bring her boys to San Francisco with or without a husband.

An exceptionally beautiful Irish summer had Bridget in a tizzy. She had begged her Patrick to quit the country for so long and now that it was about to happen she wavered. Bringing her innocent country children to live in some foreign city conjured up frightening scenarios. Her father's family had been so vital to the history and progress of Queen's County. How could they ever duplicate that success and heritage in America? Maybe they should just stay and carry on. Patrick held her hand, calmed her down, speaking in the low soothing tones he reserved for his horse.

He had relinquished his land to the agent so they had to leave after the harvest regardless of any second-guessing. The die had been cast.

Patrick's final Irish harvest was delivered and the livestock auctioned. All the farm equipment, every scrap of furniture and every kitchen utensil had been sold, leaving only a few barrels and crates of belongings heaped in the front room. After paying off creditors and Mrs. Kavanaugh's agent he purchased the family's passage from a broker in Dublin. He also picked up the tab for Mary Donnelly's fare and that of Edward and Andrew, her two boys. She left Hugh in a drunken stupor.

The £300 Patrick had hoped to net by selling his worldly goods was now reduced to a meagre £200 equaling about $875 in gold coins, a monetary unit accepted in all parts of the New World. Canada was the cheapest place to sail to and San Francisco was twice as much, a place far out-of-reach for the average family fleeing famine.

On a mild October evening a scant number of folks gathered in the Lawler farmhouse for a final farewell, an American Wake. These festivities had become commonplace as more and more refugees left Ireland. It was treated as a death but celebrated nonetheless. A green bottle of nasty poitín was passed around but no one felt like drinking. A disappointing turnout of friends and neighbours made the sad occasion even sadder. Bridget and Patrick looked into each other's crestfallen faces as if to say, "So it's come to this?" To fill the emptiness they made small talk.

"Who ended up buying all the chickens?"

"Is it the afternoon now in California?"

"I should have trimmed the baby's fingernails."

Hours ticked slowly waiting for the sun to come up. Patrick decided it was time to load the wagon for their walk to town where they would all board a mail coach headed for the Dublin docks.

Eleven sons and daughters of Éire rambled out of the house for the last time. Bridget crossed herself and kissed the front door before ceremoniously pulling a gray shawl over her head. Her husband had all their possessions secured in a wagon and with the mule gone, pulled it himself. Babies were carried and the rest of the children walked behind the adults in a forlorn procession, the squish, squish of gravel the only sound. The sky was a deep, dark purple bruise. Through the thicket of trees before the gate Denny, the oldest, saw a glow up the road.

"What is that? Is it the sheriff?"

Lining the pathway were throngs of townspeople, farmers, friends and children with torches to light their way. They cheered and hooted when they spotted Patrick and Bridget.

Then they started to sing.

When the travelers stepped into their midst the assembly held high above their heads single ears of fresh corn as beacons. No one had forgotten them, their charity or the American shipment of corn and seed the Lawlers had procured for their ravaged country town. Famine still pervaded their thoughts but gratitude was now in order.

Memories flooded back as long-lost faces appeared from the crowd. The Lawler's children were offered purple asters; warm cinnamon bread was handed to Mary and Mrs. Phelan from the workhouse gave Bridget her amethyst rosary for safe passage. A man stepped out to greet Patrick, it was his old nemesis and former tenant from Kildare, Bruce Duffy.

"Lawler, came out to see you off."

"Very kind of you, Bruce."

"You know I thought you a perfect ass?"

"Aye, no one is perfect, Bruce."

"I hated you…but I don't anymore. You taught me how to be a proper farmer. You saved my family from starving. I could never thank you enough. Never."

Patrick looked him square in the face, "No you're the one that saved your family. It was you lad." Duffy fell back into line and held up his corn high in tribute, his eyes glossy and wet. Bridget witnessed their exchange with reverence. She almost began to weep but suddenly held back. She had not cried in sorrow in all the years of the famine and she wasn't about to start now. Blubbering with sentimentality. No. Even if it was the most touching thing she had ever witnessed.

A peppy pink streak shimmered at the horizon line and Patrick wasted no time in pulling his wagon forward through the people. His family followed and the torch-bearing crowd of well-wishers accompanied the party all the way to town. Blessings and stories continued long after the coach had whisked them away.

Patrick's herding skills were required to corral the women and eight children, ages 1 to 12, along with all their cargo onto the steamer crossing the Irish Sea destined for Liverpool. The family patriarch acted like a seasoned sailor in front of his wife and children although he had never been on anything larger than a canal boat. Bridget and Mary sat on their barrels with the babies. A thick hive of humanity met the travelers as they stepped onto the long Liverpool dock in search of the ship that would bring them to America.

Patrick's patience was wearing thin.

Everyone made it safely aboard but only two crates of their belongings were allowed on the ship to cross the Atlantic. An exhausted and fully-dressed Bridget and Patrick collapsed into bed with their infant daughter in the second-class bunkroom. Each thought the other had aged a year already.

"I think little John is coming down with a cold," said Bridget.

"Hmm," Patrick huffed out a response.

"Does Mary have the rest of our things?"

"No, I meant to tell you I had to leave some on the dock."

"Why?"

"I told you we packed too much. They wouldn't even let me bring my father's scythe on board. That's gone through every lucky harvest we've ever had."

"Honestly. That was a ridiculous thing to carry all the way over here. They say you can buy everything cheaper in America."

"English vultures grabbed it as soon as I laid it down. Did the same thing with the barrels."

"Patrick! What barrels did you leave?"

"You wrote on them auld clothes."

"NO! Those weren't auld clothes!"

"You wrote that in red chalk on the tops, I made sure."

"That was written on there to fool thieves. That had all my jewelry at the bottom."

"Hah, fooled me too."

"For God's sake! The Viking brooch James gave me was in there. I wore that on our wedding day."

"In California I'll get you a proper gold one."

"It won't be the same."

"That's true Biddy, nothing will ever be the same."

PART II

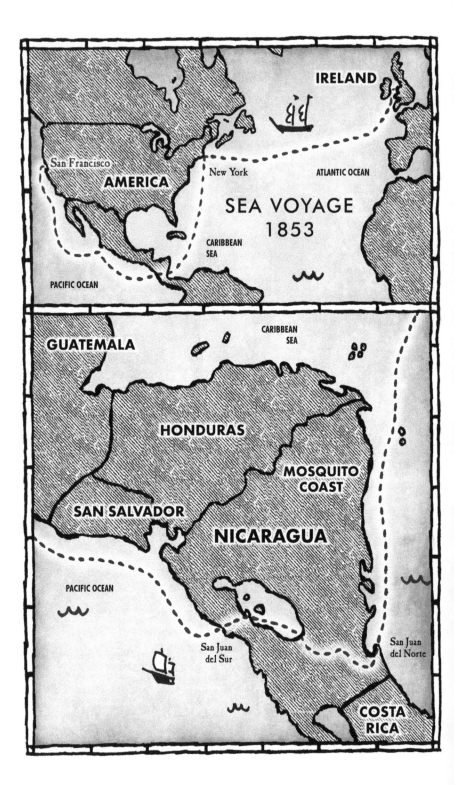

CHAPTER 28

Letter written to Michael Dunne of Ballintlea House from his sister Bridget Lawler while aboard the clipper ship Underwriter

November 30, 1853

Dear Michael:

We have just sailed by the Sandy Hook lightship off the coast of America— Denny saw it from our own porthole! The purser has come round to our cabin and said all letters are due to him this evening so I will get this off to you and it will be mailed from New York. Mary is writing to you as well and I will include hers with mine.

Our voyage has lasted 31 days so far and much to my surprise has been quite enjoyable. The seas have been calm and the weather mild. It is a good time to travel. Patrick's been researching this operation for years and nothing has been left to chance (he says). Some New York millionaire bankrolled a shortcut through Nicaragua to the Pacific Ocean that's faster than the old one via the Isthmus of Panama. Our ship is American through and through and only a couple of years old. It has three decks. We're in second-class with our own cabin and our own wee table. We have 6 beds amongst the 12 of us but the children never complain. They are excited and only rarely quarrel. There's been two weddings aboard the ship and two new babies. It's like a floating village with many interesting characters and all the attending gossip.

Tomorrow we will land in New York and switch over to a steamer that will take us down the Caribbean Sea. We will walk ashore on the frightfully named "Mosquito Coast" and somehow get to the other side. I am afraid I am so comfortable on this ship that I dread the next part of the journey. All day I pray like one of those babbling nuns from the Stradbally convent. This is the longest stretch in my life I haven't been in a church—they do have a priest on board and he says daily Mass but it's not the same as our little chapel back home. He's from Cork with that funny accent of his.

For the Atlantic passage there is much live poultry on board. Last week the crew provided us with a delightful meal of fresh goose in celebration of a Yankee holiday called Thanksgiving. It was a welcome treat. I fuss to Patrick that all we have in the world is in this tiny compartment and he says that is all we need. I am indeed thankful.

We should be in San Francisco before the end of the year and my next letter will have to wait until then. Please give my regards to friends who ask about us.

    With love and affection,

    Biddy

P.S. Mary has not finished with her letter yet so I am sending mine now to the purser. Just know that she is fine and is complaining in her usual fashion. Patrick says she had best adjust her sail and go with the wind. You and I both know this will not happen.

    – B.

Among the adventurers, Argonauts and exiles making their way inland from the lawless Mosquito Coast, a young Irish family stood mesmerized by the jungle that lay before their riverboat. Leaves in sizes and shapes only imagined in dreams stretched out over the water in graceful festoons, reflecting on the smooth emerald surface. Towers of greenery banked the river's edge. Dank and delightful smells reached her nose. Wild, bizarre cries came from the palm trees poking out behind the undulating plant life, a grass shack was faintly visible obscured by a vine-wrapped banana tree. As green as Ireland was on her sunniest day, it could not compare to the variety and intensity of that color in the wilds of Nicaragua.

Standing next to the Lawler family at the second deck's railing was a fellow passenger who had been at their side since they boarded together in Liverpool. He styled himself as Mr. Caspian and was regaling young Denny with stories of his long life on the Seven Seas as a merchant mariner over the din of a rotating paddlewheel. No one really believed his fanciful tales but they were in the mood to be entertained. At more than three-score years he was going back to California to try his hand at prospecting, admittedly a young man's game.

Competing with the sounds of chattering monkeys and screeching parrots Mr. Caspian pointed out a toucan bird perched on a branch and said, "Look there!"

"I don't see it!" said a frustrated Denny.

"See that bit of orange there?"

"Aye."

"That's the tip of his beak."

"Oh blimey, now I see him."

"He's masquerading as a papaya fruit so he can sneak up and devour it later."

"Are fruits able to move down here in the tropics?"

"Oh lad, a gullible mind is a weak one. Use your head or you won't last a minute on the streets of San Francisco."

"Sorry sir."

"No, it's all a big masquerade, that bird's hiding from somethin' what wants to eat him and the papaya is hiding from somethin' what wants to eat it. See?"

"I see, just like San Francisco?"

"Right." Denny made Mr. Caspian laugh and that made him smile.

Five full days on the riverboat were followed by an anchoring and overnight stay at El Castillo, an old Spanish fortress town hovering above the San Juan River rapids. The passengers were crammed into dirt floor hostels or homes of accommodating villagers where they were presented with a wooden platter overflowing with tropical fruits and roasted monkey. The later appearing like a charred infant and roundly rejected.

The next morning the émigrés walked around the portage, avoiding the rapids below. Breaking up into smaller groups they were put into bungoes for a ten-mile row to the next bit of rough water, the Toro Rapids. Although it was the start of dry season everyone got sufficiently drenched as the boats splashed around the torrents. At least no one was lost overboard. Bridget and Patrick clung tightly to their two babies while the four older ones found it to be the most exhilarating event in their young lives. Edward and Andrew Donnelly did their best to sooth and comfort their mother who was flailing about the canoe like an unhinged cockatiel. Heat from the blazing sun dried them off completely in a matter of minutes followed by another dousing, this time from sweat of their own making. Mr. Caspian had warned the Dunne sisters to leave the frilly under layers of clothing in their carpetbags but Bridget ignored his advice and was now sweltering. She'd had about as much of the jungle as a proper Irishwoman could stomach.

Early the following day another transfer was made to an older steamer for the route through the windswept open waters of Lake Nicaragua. Tousled passengers braved the murky, treacherous lake filled with more white caps than they had seen on the entire Caribbean. Ample railing circulating around the ship provided support for heaving hordes of the seasick. Healthy ones clamored for suitable sleeping arrangements as night fell. Women made do with benches and men found the smoothest planks on which they would catch a few winks. Discontent spread over the travelers like the mist from the lake.

A rough night settled into a smooth morning.

By noon, twin volcanoes protruding from Ometepe Island appeared as sentinels on the starboard side of the steamer. On the port side was the sleepy village of La Virgen where they would finally disembark for their overland expedition. Word reached the party that the ship SS Sierra Nevada that was to take them to California on the other side was delayed. It was decided they would spend the night in La Virgen and head out over the Nicaraguan isthmus at daybreak.

A company representative assigned everyone a hammock swinging from outdoor verandas of the rancheros and haciendas that edged the town. The Lawlers, Donnellys and their new friend Mr. Caspian boarded at the Castro house. Mrs. Castro kindly offered indoor accommodations to the ladies and smaller children for an additional fee, which Patrick readily paid. For dinner, beans and rice were plentiful; despite herds of noisy cattle, meat was not served. Outside, the group commiserated together over guava juice and some hooch that Mr. Caspian supplied. He reflected on the journey, his red-rimmed eye sockets drooping with sincerity, "Things 'ave been quite satisfactory up 'til that blasted lake crossing!"

"Just one more leg and we are on our way through," a chipper Patrick replied.

"Satisfactory? It's been a damned-i-ble nightmare and tomorrow will be even that much more horrendous," came Mary's observations as she took an uncouth swig from the bottle, wiping her mouth with her sleeve.

Caspian took the bottle back, fearful that his share was getting depleted.

Bridget sat silent in a weathered old rattan chair watching one-year old Frances sleeping comfortably in her arms. She gently squeezed at the baby's chubby wrists and felt her cheeks, which she had been doing incessantly to all her children searching for any elevated body temperature. Worry about sickness and circumstances was getting to her. She had experience with such things.

Distant shrieks and chirps infiltrated the night air and caused her fertile imagination to conjure up elaborate ways in which they were all to be devoured. This was madness. She willed herself to stop. With that she summoned her thoughts back to the scene on the veranda and noticed Mary was decidedly flirting with Mr. Caspian. Did the liquor bring on this behavior or was she just reverting to the old habits of a lady tavern keeper? Look at the way she's tilting her head though. Acting so interested in his hogwash. Really? She's slipping the bottle out of his hand again. Enough! Bridget tugged on Mary's skirt and they went inside, leaving the men and boys to the hooch, the hammocks and the hum of mosquitoes.

Mules and modern American carriages were assembling in the dirt streets when the morning sun brought out the vibrancy trapped for the night in the brightly painted buildings. Fees were negotiated for the coaches with additional money being extracted from Patrick by the native Indians for the pack animals to haul the luggage. He grumbled to himself as he situated his family inside the coach. He would ride on the outside with a few other men.

The caravan wobbled along muddy roads in a light rain until it reached the edge of the jungle where it quietly slipped through a clearing and into the forest. The pace was slow, the carriage rocked up and down with every contour of the jungle floor. Branches scraped at the roof and tangled with the passengers who held on for their life to the outside rails. Rain intensified and the tweeting sounds were interrupted by an occasional thunderclap. Every few minutes the horses' hooves would be mired in mud. Stop and start. Stop and start. Finally the wheels succumbed and they were completely stuck. The party would have to make the rest of the journey on foot.

Tap, tap, came a light knock from Patrick on the coach door. "Out you go. I can take the babies. They are offering mules at another $5 each but it's not that far to walk. "

"How far?" came a voice from inside.

"Not far, let's go," Patrick said making a frustrated swishing motion with his hand.

"Mr. Caspian, tell me honestly, how many miles," pleaded Bridget who could tell when her husband was beclouding an answer.

Patrick glared at Caspian through the water dripping off the brim of his hat.

"Dear lady, I've been this route before. Three miles. Maybe seven at the most."

"Seven miles!"

"I'm not trying to be some kind of skin flint. I'd get the bloody mules but they are so slow. We can make better time on foot." Patrick was losing his patience. "We'll get less wet the less time we spend out here. The walk's not hard. Let's get going!"

"We're staying in here until the rain stops!" said a defiant Mary Donnelly.

"You'll be in there 'till Christmas then," shot back Patrick.

Bridget stepped out on to the ground with a soggy squish followed by her daughter Mary, her sister Mary and a few ladies they had met along the way. Rain immediately pelted them through the mesh of treetops. They all assembled for a short lecture by a representative of the Accessory Transit Company who was in charge. Behind him were several dark-skinned, shirtless Indians, who donned nothing more than breech cloths, strings of beads and machetes. The children blatantly stared. Patrick gently swatted his daughter Mary about the head and smirked.

Mr. Caspian offered his new friends some advice with a theatrical flair. "Now just be careful when you're walking not to trip over the creeping vines. They're everywhere. Also don't go touching any trees or push on them willy-nilly. You'll shake loose vicious red ants that'll get in your hair or down your neck." Bridget stood silently repulsed, pulling at the button on her high collar.

After the pack mules caught up, the party continued infiltrating the jungle. Natives lead the way, continuously hacking at the new growth of less than three weeks. The Irishers walked closely together and noticed that everything around them was rustling in some way. Raindrops bounced off plants causing each one to flinch in a different direction. Everything else was moving of its own accord.

Throbbing piles of Mr. Caspian's red ants covered tree bases, gigantic centipedes crawled at their feet, butterflies floated above their heads and iridescent frogs were leaping in front of them. Wild poinsettia trees lined the footpath with the occasional flamboyant orchid being recognized by Bridget. She smelled sweetness for a moment, wondering what tropical flower could emit such an odor but as she walked on the familiar stench of death wafted her way. She held her handkerchief over her nose and mouth as the group passed one dead burro after another. Victims of some previous death march covered in hordes of creeping opportunists that would eventually help to reincarnate the animals into some new jungle life form.

Mr. Caspian took the occasion to point out various unusual species of plants and insects. When he spotted a gigantic poisonous snake known as a fer-de-lance lurking within a tangle of roots he quietly stopped in front of it and waved the group past. Not to pile on additional fear he mentioned nothing about the snake nor any of his assorted tales involving snakes of which he had a treasure trove. He said nothing about the black jaguar high in the canopy that watched their every move. He hadn't noticed.

Out of danger, Caspian went on to tell about the millions of dollars' worth of California gold that had come through the passage. His stories were filled with sparkling details and high drama. He warned Denny to be on watch for pirates and hidden banditos then casually winked as if that would somehow put the lad at ease. Denny would have preferred a good snake-bite story.

Caspian was enjoying his worldly status among the novice travelers. He kept up his ramblings until they reached a flowing water and mud crossing, worsening by the moment from heavy rain. It was the only transit road through the gap to the seaside town of San Juan del Sur where they would meet the ship to San Francisco. Everyone stopped to reconfigure the route.

"Men, it's come time where I think we must hoist the ladies on our backs and carry them through this part. It's mucky as all hell and steep. There's no other way," yelled out the guide to the crowd.

Caspian was certainly in no shape to take on anyone except maybe a baby. Bridget suggested Denny carry his little brother James and Patrick should take their daughter Mary. The Dunne sisters of Brittas determined they would not be carried, they could very well walk through themselves. It couldn't be worse than the sludge they faced in the fields back home. Another downpour ensued and the guide came 'round with two of his brawny Indians.

"Here these two are complimentary for the women. Hop on ladies, they won't bite."

Bridget looked at the dark servant with her mouth ajar. She had read about wild savages in literature but never dreamed she would be standing next to one. Or touch one. But have one touch her? Desperate, she glowered at her husband for reassurance, permission or something. He impatiently twitched his head and yelled out between the raindrops, "Get on with it!"

Mary Donnelly had been situated first on her Indian boy and looked rather amused as her sister was trying to mount hers.

Bridget began to straddle the young man, pulling herself up by his shoulders with some assistance from the guide. Strange and unladylike, she reassured herself it was just an innocent piggyback ride like the ones from her childhood She reasoned decorum had no place in the jungle. She must endure the embarrassment.

The Indian threw a lightweight cloth around Bridget's bottom and tied it at his chest, securing her to him. He held her legs and she was pressed to his naked flesh. They set off in the rain. Her pride and nerves fought for control yet she was mightily impressed with the skill and speed her Indian showed while darting through the rocky stream. His black shiny hair swished to and fro, Bridget could see taut muscles oscillating underneath his smooth brown skin as he hiked. Not sure what to feel next she looked back towards her husband.

Patrick trudged along trying to keep pace finding it difficult with a nine-year old daughter fastened to his normally agile farmer's frame. He was still hampered by the weeks of boat travel that left him with wobbly sea legs. His soggy boots could not gain the same traction as the bare-footed youthful Indians dashing ahead. Frustrated and irritable he lost his balance and tumbled down, plunging little Mary headlong into the muddy water, narrowly avoiding a craggy outcropping.

Bridget gasped in terror.

The worry was worse than the heat and the exhaustion was worse than the rain but the constricting corset was the worst of everything. It was not designed for this sort of travel and neither was Bridget. Her head tingled and her body went limp. She fainted. Her ruddy cheeks squished up against the smooth back of her carrier. She rode along for several blissful minutes, passed out cold and oblivious to the perilous journey while safely nestled in the sling her clairvoyant, dark-skinned handler had provided.

Not a word of the episode was spoken of when the troop reached the village port, she'd hoped it had gone unnoticed. After the family settled into their lodgings Bridget left her babies with Patrick and bounded to the little colonial church she had spotted in the center of town.

She sat alone in the rustic building, raw wooden walls were pierced every so often with misshapen, unglazed gothic windows. The open beamed ceiling had all the religious majesty of a horse barn with the simple altar looming in a darkened alcove. A few primitive statues of familiar saints stood on crooked pedestals of fallen tree trunks. There, in that Nicaraguan hovel, on a sweltering evening, she had a formal talk with God. She would ask for a legion of favors.

Dear Lord. Please keep us safe. I'm not asking for riches now. I'm asking that you bring the blessings of happiness to our family. Only happiness. Safety and happiness.

Plunging headfirst into a mysterious new world she needed divine intervention. She found some peace in prayer.

The backwater pueblo of San Juan del Sur had been left isolated and undisturbed for generations until it was destined to became the Pacific port of choice for Cornelius Vanderbilt's new Nicaraguan venture, the Accessory Transit Company. Stalls and shops had sprouted up selling food and supplies to international voyagers. American flags were draped from every building. The West was open for business. It was as if a giant gypsy carnival had come into town with new tents and dazzling colors prepared to fleece every traveler and drive out every native inhabitant. When all the money was extracted the apparatus of opportunity would move onto another unsuspecting part of the world.

After a lingering delay of six days they waid anchor and left the shores of Nicaragua aboard a wooden side-wheeled steamer. They reached Acapulco easily without incident and the ship took on more coal.

Off the coast of Mexico passengers were at the mercy of the waves and endured rough seas for several nights, the ship often pitched as steep as a roof. Bridget was certain someone must have been tossed overboard. Mr. Caspian became a great comfort to the families when the Placid Pacific heaved, hissed, rebelled and belied its soothing nickname. After the bad weather subsided he cooked on the open deck a concoction he called flatfish chowder seasoned with spices he had purchased on their trip down the river. It was a welcome treat from the bland food provided on board ship and he shared it with everyone. Then he took to his bed.

"Are you feeling any better?" asked Patrick from bended knee.

"Worse," replied a resigned Mr. Caspian looking every minute his age. "The ship's doctor's been 'round but he's a quacking drunkard."

"Did he give you any diagnosis?"

"Aye, he may be a lush but he knows jungle fever when he spots it. Me too."

"It'll be alright, you'll see."

"No, it won't. Already got the colds, now I got the hots. I'm burning up."

"Here, have some water."

"Patrick, you've been blessed with a wonderful family."

"Praise be to God."

"I feel lucky to be with them on this journey. I was an orphan, never got married and got no family of me own. Your children made me feel part of theirs."

"I am glad they gave you joy."

"An' you, an honest man. I be needin' an honest man to help me. I 'aven't been one in my life."

"What are you saying?"

"I've been a swine. Despicable. A pirate, a highway man, a swind'lr. I'm going to die and go straight to hell."

"No, you won't."

"Oh yes, I will."

"Tell me what you need."

"My soul is going to hell but I want my body buried in England. I saw them rolling in casks of rum down below when we were docked in Acapulco. I want you to fetch one and put me in it."

"Caspian!"

"Name's not Caspian, that's a sea ya Goddamn fool. My real name is Carl Crabill and I am wanted in four countries and seven states."

"I see. You're on the run." Patrick was beginning to feel stupid for allowing such a desperado to infiltrate his family.

"Pickle me in rum and send me to England and have 'em bury me somewhere in Devonshire. It's lovely there."

"I'm not sure I can keep a promise like that Cas—eh, Carl," removing his hand from the bed.

"I've got $100 in gold, a leather pouch under me bed. Use it to fulfill my last wish for God's sake. I'm counting on you Lawler." Caspian pulled out his shaking hand and struggled to point at Patrick.

"Why not just don't die and I won't have to concern myself with it?"

Patrick sat at his bedside throughout the night and in the morning Caspian expired as predicted, the fate of his soul undetermined. A meeting was called with Captain Tanner and the ship's doctor.

"You prepared to buy 40 gallons of my quality rum to float him in Lawler?" asked the Captain.

"How much would that be?" asked Patrick

"I'd have to get what it's selling for in San Francisco, $2 a gallon. It'd be $80. You got that?"

"Aye."

"Doctor, can we put old Caspian here in a cask of rum without him exploding all over the ship?"

"Technically yes, although I'd have to remove all his vitals so he didn't."

"Cut him to pieces?" asked Patrick.

"Well, yes and that's not part of my ship duties so I'd be charging for that too."

"I see. Let me go talk with the family. I won't be long."

Bridget gathered her sister and all the children on deck to discuss Caspian's dilemma with her husband. The young ones displayed sound reasoning as they discussed all disgusting options. Master Denny had grown to love Caspian as a grand storyteller and a grandfather so he objected to the man being buried without his heart. It just didn't sit right with the boy. After lamentations and considerations were exhausted a vote was taken. It was decided that Caspian should be cast out into the open sea rather than be mutilated. Patrick claimed to be impartial and abstained from a vote but he was not sure he was willing to dip into the family coffers for the folly of a self-described criminal.

And so the dead pirate was stuffed into a canvas bag with his wanted face exposed long enough for a quick tribute among the gathered passengers who cared.

"Let me say the prayer father, please?" asked Denny.

"Go ahead," said Patrick.

"We here are dumping this—"

"No! We are gathered here to commit this body to the deep…." Bridget said as she allowed her son to continue with a gentle wave of her hand.

"Sorry, course, Mr. Caspian here is committed to the deep. We pray that he will be resurrected again one day unto eternal life through our Lord Jesus Christ, amen."

"Amen, well done my boy." Patrick rested his hand on his son's shoulder as a crewman sewed up the canvas and slipped their friend off a plank into the cold Pacific waters. A porpoise breeched up as soon as Caspian disappeared beneath the surface causing a superstitious Patrick to declare it a good omen.

For days after the family mourned. They had lost its newest and oldest member all at once. Thoughts of Caspian would ebb and flow through their minds as the vast ocean with its noise and rhythm propelled them forward. Christmas came and went with little fanfare. Somehow they had all silently agreed to postpone any type of celebration until they safely reached their destination.

CHAPTER 29

Fragment of letter from Lucy Rogers to her niece Henrietta Welch

[January 25, 1936]

They had six children, my aunt, my mother's sister and her two boys, making eight children and two women that my dear father had to take care of. They came through either the Isthmus of Panama or Nicaragua, I've heard mother say both. They rode in rowboats part of the way and on donkeys part of the way. In order to get on the ship waiting in the Pacific, the natives carried them. Poor mother fainted when she saw them at first. Father liked to tease her about that for years after. In crowds he would say—oh, look Biddy, a native—and then hold his hand up to his forehead and pretend to faint. She would get so cross with him but we children always laughed, which made it worse.

She was about 39 years old then. She missed all the friends she left behind. They sailed into San Francisco Bay on New Year's Day 1854 and my father had $600 in gold coins when they landed.

Early on that crystal-clear Sunday morning the immigrants were not met at the dock by James or Peter but by their friendly coolie, Sam Goo. It was a mystery to Bridget how he knew them or found them, but he did. He packed them into a magnificent coach with his quiet greeting in broken English. He patiently inched the rig away from the wharf onto the newly planked streets of San Francisco.

The children's eyes widened and absorbed every detail. Air was crisp. Streets were dirty. Women looked fancy. Why did all the men wear those strange beards? Little did the youngsters know but the rough pioneer encampment their uncles had first encountered was swallowed up in change through a succession of devastating fires and it had grown-up, matured into a stylish American city complete with its share of elegant buildings and refined citizens.

Dunne & Company's various businesses and buildings had grown as well, now encompassing several intersections throughout the wharf and warehouse district that splayed out from Broadway. In the middle of it all, the partners built for themselves a fine new three-story brick residence on a steep stretch of Kearny Street with twin balconies reminiscent of those found in New Orleans. Not every transplanted American idea was going to adapt to San Francisco and a sun-kissed balcony was one of them. The chilly winds that blew through town rendered such features more decorative than practical for most of the year.

A tiny figure was bundled up in a heavy woolen blanket on the top balcony when Sam Goo trudged the horses up Kearny. It spastically waved about then disappeared, reappearing at the carriage house in back as the visitors were disembarking.

"For land's sake, you must be Bridget," an excited Kitty said guessing her identity by the puff of red hair protruding from a sullied, old-fashioned bonnet.

"That I am."

Kitty quickly wrapped her arms around Bridget with an exuberance that left the genteel Irishwoman a little stiffened. Bridling at such familiarity she wondered if this was a servant girl? *They are very bold in this country.*

"Oh, I've waited so long to meet you. Finally a sister of my own!" Seeing Mary Donnelly still in the back of the carriage she revised her thought, "Two. Two sisters! How lucky am I?"

Bridget caught on but was thrown by the notion that James had married a mere child. Why, she still looked like a teenaged girl. Acted like one too.

"I take it you are James' Kitty," she said with all the warmth of a schoolmarm.

"Yes, so sorry, yes, yes. Welcome to America!"

Mrs. Lawler then formally introduced her husband, children and the Donnellys to their new American hostess. She wondered if the whole of the city acted with such forwardness. In Ireland, chummy greetings like Kitty's were common among flower girls trying to hawk tired lilies about to wilt.

Inside, Kitty introduced them to her baby, little Peter Dunne, patted her belly for the one yet to come, then brought all to the third floor where two good-sized rooms had been cleared out for them. The household staff boarded up there as well, echoing living arrangements the Dunne family had in the servants' wing at Brittas. Full-circle.

"If we leave right now we can go to mass around the corner. Everything's close. Would you like that, Bridget?" Kitty asked trying in earnest to please her pious new houseguest.

"That would be fine but I look a wreck and am sure I smell like fish."

"Nonsense, you look divine and everyone in this town smells like something or other. Come now, gather your kin and let's go. James and Peter are working like usual so they won't be home 'till supper."

Bridget got the feeling America had relaxed any notion of decorum or the traditions she had grown up with in the hallowed hills of Hibernia. Everyone attends mass on Sunday back home.

There they were, on New Year's Day, thankful to be in their new country sitting safely in the pews of St. Francis of Assisi Catholic Church. Bridget was surrounded by her loving family awaiting an inspirational sermon. God had delivered them.

A young priest brought over by the Bishop from China's Hunan Province delivered the sermon. His original mission was to proselytize to his fellow countrymen but he only spoke Mandarin while most of the city's Chinese spoke Cantonese. In turn, he was transferred to a parish of Irish immigrants where poor Bridget couldn't understand a word of his Latin or his English.

"No, no, you're doing it all wrong! Watch." The finicky chef grabbed the spoon from Mrs. Farnham's pudgy hand and instructed her on how to properly stir a simmering pot of bordelaise sauce. It was all in the wrist. Counterclockwise. Normally she was the nanny and cook at the Dunne residence but tonight she had been demoted in favor of a visiting culinarian from The Poodle Dog, Peter's favorite restaurant. The prosperous merchant wanted to impress his sisters with something special for their first family meal together in America. Curiously, only French food would do. Mrs. Farnham muttered sarcastically under her breath, something to the effect that Irish people only put gravy on meat that was about to go off.

James and Peter greeted the new families with a subdued level of vim. Bridget went over and embraced them both.

"James you look so, so manly! How are you?" she asked.

"Fine, fine. Busy, very busy."

"Peter! You are just as handsome. How are you this evening?"

"Fine. I'm very busy as well."

Bridget preferred a longer explanation but she quickly surmised that to be busy in America meant that everything was as right as rain, a man could be in no better state.

And with that, they all sat down to a resplendent table in the larger dining room lined with flocked wallpaper in a popular shade of velvety red that looked somewhat faded, intending to give the certitude of wealth and power. The abundance of food spread out before them in feast-like dimensions. Bridget was talking with unusual speed sensing she had to condense years of her life down into tidy little snippets to keep her brothers' interest. She was three sentences into a poignant story about the famine, "The boy had been eating grass, his mouth was stained green. What a sight I tell you…" when James butted in, "Peter, we must remember that Clark's shipment's going to be at our warehouse tomorrow, 6am sharp. Are you going to meet him or am I?"

"I'll go. I have a meeting there at eight anyhow."

Bridget continued, "It wasn't so much the grass but I will never forget those eyes—"

"You know, why don't I go? Clark needs to pay up front and I don't want him weaseling out again," James decided.

It was difficult for Bridget Lawler to summon up any story about the famine, she had purposely buried those heart-wrenching memories deep inside her. She stupidly thought her brothers might want to know what had happened to her, to her family in the last 15 years. Their rudeness cut her to the quick. Patrick observed the whole interchange like he was an eagle perched on the fancy gas-lit, brass chandelier dangling above the scene.

Bridget felt a warm hand on her thigh, it was Kitty. Their eyes met in a clear and silent understanding. Kitty's were glossy and wet. Bridget's were wroth. "Oh, you poor, dear thing. To think you had to face all that. It must seem like a terrible nightmare. Thank God you made it through such an ordeal and you are sitting here right next to me, right now." Kitty went in again for one of those invasive embraces but this time Bridget wrapped her arms around her too and squeezed just as tightly.

"So, Pat," James turned the conversation abruptly to his brother-in-law, "they say the greatest gift a newcomer to San Francisco could be given is time to explore the city. Why don't you take a few days to walk around town and start at the mill on Wednesday?"

"That'd be grand," said Patrick.

James and Peter excused themselves and went into the parlor for cigars and business talk leaving Patrick with the women and children. Their private cocoon was only built for two. It would be left to Kitty and the staff to see the guests off to bed.

The next morning Patrick and Bridget would spend the day walking about town with Sam Goo as their guide.

"Now dear Kitty," Bridget had a plan and pulled her aside, "before we set off I'd like to know if there is a nearby orphanage of any kind?"

"Well, let me think. Oh yes, I know just the one. Have Sam take you all the way down Kearny to the corner of Market Street. There is a Catholic orphan asylum right there next to the church. Can't miss it."

"Thank you."

Bridget gave Kitty an enthusiastic hug that was fast becoming their private ritual.

Walking down the street for several blocks Sam pointed out certain buildings the Dunne brothers owned and spoke of interesting spots and restaurants along the way. He stopped in front of a haberdashery, "Mr. Patrick, tomorrow you go in here. Need new clothes. Pants too short. Only schoolboy wear that here. No fashion. Me, I no got robe no more, chop my pigtail. Don't I look American now?" He put his hands on his hips and preened. "You look American too if you buy clothes here tomorrow. It be good for you."

"Thanks for the advice, Sam," said Patrick not offended in the very least.

They continued their amble. "Madame Bridget, that place for orphans," Sam motioned over to an old brown house.

"Thank you Sam."

Bridget locked arms with Patrick and crossed Market Street dodging people and horses and carts loaded with freight.

"What are you doing?" Patrick asked.

"We are going in here," they ascended the steps and immediately encountered a kind-looking nun about Bridget's age in a wide white cornette.

"May I help you?" the Sister asked in a soft, pious voice.

"We'd like to make a donation."

This was news to Patrick.

"How very kind of you. My name is Sister Frances," a trace of a County Wexford accent immediately put the Lawlers at ease.

"Why of course you are. How do you do, Sister Frances?" Bridget pulled out the gold coins Mr. Caspian had given to Patrick on board ship for his burial. Patrick glared at this wife, angered yet not the least bit surprised. "This is in honor of Mr. Caspian, a very good friend of ours who was himself an orphan. He died on board ship coming to America," she said handing the offering over to the woman.

"How very generous. We shall remember Mr. Caspian in our daily prayers."

"His actual name was Carl Crabill. Pray for Mr. Carl Crabill. Caspian is a sea," grunted Patrick.

"We shall pray for Mr. Carl Crabill. This comes to us at a very auspicious time. We have big plans here. Things are changing by the minute. May I show you around?" she asked, casually slipping the gold coins into a pouch under her black habit.

"Why not? We are new to San Francisco and won't be eating anytime soon," said Patrick as he stared daggers at his chuffed and grinning wife.

Sister Frances took the group through the orphanage room by room. It was tidy and small. They met many of the children who were tidy and small. Each one thought they were being sought out by new parents. They walked the expansive grounds and complex of buildings: a barn, a corral, a little dairy, a work shed, the rectory and a modest clapboard church with mock columns fronting Market Street.

"And here we have St. Patrick's Church," exclaimed Sister Frances.

"A fitting name," said Patrick in that prideful, juvenile tone of his.

"So in a few weeks' time we are going to start building a brand-new Catholic orphanage right here next to the church. It will be made of brick and three stories high. The needy children of this depraved city keep coming and we are here to serve them all."

"What a blessing you are to San Francisco, Sister," said Bridget.

"Mr. and Mrs. Lawler I cannot thank you enough for your generous donation. It will be put to good use I can assure you. Now, shall we all go inside and say a prayer for the soul of Mr. Carl Crabill?"

"Let's do," Bridget agreed.

"He could use it," reckoned Patrick.

Dunne & Company's flourmill wasn't a big operation but it did fill a void in the brothers' supply chain. As the city's most enterprising commission merchants, money had to be made at every corner of a deal. Gristmills of the time were usually built along rivers and run by waterwheels but this one fit into a tiny 50 vara lot. Its millstone was turned by oxen, horses or whatever animal power was available. When the price of flour was high the place ran at maximum capacity, day and night, but when prices fell it was shuttered until flour rose again.

James oversaw the mill from behind a desk several blocks away but was on site that first morning showing his new recruit and brother-in-law the inner workings of the place. To him, Patrick was just another hired hand and he did his level best not to show a smidgen of partiality to him in front of the other workers. If anything, he was going to be much harder on the man. There was enough of that family nepotism back in Ireland. Bridget's husband needed to be schooled in the ways of America and earn his place on merit alone.

Patrick had sold plenty of his own grain to the mills of Queen's County and had a rudimentary knowledge of the process. However, the flourmill where he envisioned working in highfalutin San Francisco would be as expansive and impressive as America itself. He was quite underwhelmed when he actually set foot in the grubby little mill that was nothing more than a barn with bits of antiquated machinery. It would look backward even in the poorest parts of rural Ireland. Making matters worse, he was given the lowliest of tasks. Patrick Lawler would be employed for three days.

"First you're going to unload those sacks out back and stack them neatly here," James shouted above the milling gears pointing to an empty corner of the dirt floor with a cigar wedged between his two fingers. "And be quick about it too, we plan to grind all that today!" Patrick waited for further instructions as James barked out orders to the head miller then turned back around and snapped, "Lawler, what are you waiting for?" followed by the rudest way to tell an Irish peasant to hurry-up, "*Déan deifir!*"

"Oh, I thought there might be more—"

"Let's see if you can handle that before we give you anything more complicated," he said through the haze of cigar smoke and assorted grit spewing from the grinder.

Patrick brought in the first few sacks and positioned them perfectly in the corner as a foundation for the rest. "Christ, you are only bringing in one bag at a time? The boys I hire bring in at least two. I have a big Mexican that can handle three," James badgered Patrick as he went outside and struggled with two heavy sacks of grain. He continued stacking them like building blocks in a neat and orderly fashion trying hard to survive the scrutiny of his new boss. He even pinched the corners of the bags to make it easier for the miller to grab.

"Hey now, you don't need to be spending any time doin' what you're doin' with those corners, just stack it so it doesn't fall down." James ordered. "You still have two more wagons out there."

"Aye-aye captain!" Patrick said in a playful, slightly sardonic tone.

"Hey, I'm not captain. My men call me Mr. Dunne and that's what you're going to call me. Got it?"

"Yes sir, Mr. Dunne. Oh, and do you get that you're not supposed to be smoking in a flourmill? This whole place is a tinderbox and one spark could blow it all to smithereens." Shots fired.

"Who the hell do you think you're talking to? I was just leaving but wanted to make sure you had proper G'damn instructions. And I be needin' no instruction whatever from the likes of you." Fuming, James stormed out nervously stroking his beard, which was indeed white with flour dust. He wondered how this arrangement could ever work.

Later that afternoon a handwritten message on engraved company letterhead was delivered from James' office requesting Patrick to assist the miller until late in the evening. He would need to miss eating with the family. When Patrick finally got into bed he whispered to his wife that everything was fine.

The second day he worked until 2 o'clock in the morning and even ran the millstone with aplomb. James had stayed away at the warehouse on Broadway but reports of his brother-in-law's progress pleased him.

On the third day, Patrick arrived early at the mill after four hours sleep. The night crew was relieved to see him take over from Toby the miller who had worked for 20 hours straight. It was just before noon that James arrived to find Patrick adjusting an ox harness to the millstone.

"Are you alone in here?"

"The others will be back soon, they're just getting a couple winks in."

"Who told them they could do that?"

"I said I'd be all right by myself for a couple hours. We made good time last night."

"So, after two days you think you can run the place, Pat?"

"Oh, I could run it after a couple of hours, it's not complicated."

"Toby is in charge. He runs the show, for God's sake you just got off the boat."

"Beg your pardon, James—"

"Mister Dunne."

"Before I got on that boat I was knee deep working every part of the land whilst you were just a wee lad hanging on to your mother's apron strings."

"I couldn't give a fiddler's fart about any of that. You work for me now. The Dunnes are in charge and you need to know your place and wait your turn."

"Just trying to make you some flour here, Mr. Dunne. Just trying to get the bloody work done."

"You're not going to get away with this kind of insolence though, Patrick. I can't have it."

"Must be some family trait that makes you Dunnes think you're somehow superior to the rest of us mortals. Same thing back home...the illustrious Dunnes of Brittas. Get off your high horse, James, you're no better than me."

"And like all the other Lawlers you are running around with some chip on your shoulder. I bring you out here to work for me and you pay me no gratitude whatsoever! That's the thanks I get."

"First of all you didn't bring me out here. I brought me out here. And I was under the impression that you needed me to run some big flourmill in the great metropolis of San Francisco...America...with all your fancy talk... but this, this thing you got here, it's nothin'."

"I didn't say it was some grand job, ever. I promised you nothing. Nothing but some work."

"Why you fool, that's exactly what I'm trying to do so why not just leave me to it?"

"If it weren't for my sister I'd toss you out on your ear right here and now."

"I'd like to see you try that."

"Don't tempt me."

"That's it, here you go Mr. Dunne, take over, get your hands dirty. I quit."

"So be it."

Patrick picked up his old coat and said out loud to himself, "Them's the first three days I've ever worked for any man and they'll be my last." He turned back around at the doorway and told James, "We'll be out of your house by nightfall," and they were.

CHAPTER 30

Herald Office, 6 P.M.
Extra! *Daily Alta California*, San Francisco

EXPLOSION OF THE STEAMER JENNY LIND!!! --- Awful Destruction of Life! We have just received the following bulletin and hasten to lay it before the public:

> *The steamer Jenny Lind blew up at 2 o'clock this afternoon opposite the Red Wood Embarcadero. After the explosion she drifted over to the other side of the Bay. The schooner Milwaukie assisted the sufferers.*

> *We learn that Mr. Bernard Murphy of San Jose was on board and has perished at the home of Messrs. Dunne.*

> *Immediate assistance from this city is urgently asked for.*

Although his business empire in San Francisco had expanded beyond his wildest dreams there was only one tick of time during the month when James Dunne found himself completely and utterly content, when all the payables had been paid and all the receivables had been received. When his bank account surged and he owed nothing to no one, except perhaps an apology to his brother-in-law that would never come.

Bridget wondered what James thought of them quitting his house so abruptly. She would be saddened to know he hadn't given it much thought at all. Business vexed the Dunne brothers from within like an invasive ivy plant overtaking their minds. Convincing Bridget and her family to come out West was checked off his list and he was just on to the next line item.

Peter had been consumed at his desk with the estate of Bernard Murphy, son of his client Martin Murphy, patriarch of one of California's leading families and owner of a sizable chunk of Santa Clara County to the south. As a courtesy to the senior Murphy, the Dunne brothers had taken in his badly burned son after the explosion of the Jenny Lind. He died in their front parlor while Kitty attended to his gruesome wounds. Bernard Murphy left an infant son, a grieving widow and a large estate beleaguered with a last will and testament poorly drawn up by one Peter Dunne, Esq.

The implications of such an inadequately prepared document had finally proven to Peter that his fascination with the law might just be an elaborate joke he played upon himself. As a boy, he believed becoming a barrister would be the best way to showcase his towering intellect and elevate his status from the son of a dirt farmer to a worthy heir of a dynastic noble family; right tree, wrong branch. This one-man, frontier law practice required absolutely no credentials. Peter merely dashed-off mediocre legal ephemera for an ignorant clientele that happened to stumble on the dumb luck of the mines or the easy money of a boomtown.

To boot, his billings added practically nothing to the profits of Dunne & Company. The whole enterprise had always struck James as pure folly and his brother was about to confess.

"I am running into difficulty with the probate court on the Murphy matter," blurted out Peter.

"What does that mean?" asked a half-interested James.

"It means there are a few omissions in the will."

"The will you set up?"

"It's very complicated James, you wouldn't know."

"Sounds like you don't know either."

"Well, now I have this Murphy and that Murphy asking questions of me."

"They didn't build an empire by letting life wash right over them now, did they?"

"James, they might think I bungled the whole thing up and come after us for a malpractice of the law."

"Peter, I've let you muck about with this law foolishness just so you can advertise yourself as some kind of barrister to those pompous friends of yours. But when it starts to eat into my lunch we have problems."

"We have problems."

"Right, why don't you hire that attorney McDonald had when he raked us over the coals at the dissolution of our partnership. He seemed pretty sharp. Mack something too…McAllister."

"Hall McAllister."

"That's him."

"I tried already. He's the best in town. Isn't taking any new clients."

"Damn. He made quick work of us."

"He offered to send over his student law clerk. I guess the kid is studying law down at the Santa Clara College."

"I think we've had enough of amateurs and pretenders."

"I'm going to pretend I didn't hear that. This kid is supposed to be brilliant and now that you say that I think I'll take McAllister up on his offer," Peter said knowing more of his brother's abuse would rain down upon him with the next misstep.

He looked all of his sixteen years. Lanky and intense, his wispy beard crawled around his chiseled jawline in an effort to age and dignify. He was respectful, he asked probing questions that revealed his understanding of the law. But as he poured over the solicitor's work Peter began to squirm. He was intimidated not just because the lad was endorsed by Hall McAllister but because he saw shades of himself. The cock sureness, the way he moved his young fingers over the law books, why even the squint in his youthful eye brought Peter back to a time when he himself was filled with dreams and delusions.

It took only a few hours for young student Thomas Bergin to define a legal way to protect the Murphy estate as well as the Dunne brother's liability. Upon doing so, he promptly suggested all the remaining work be turned over to a law firm Old Man Murphy used in San Jose with the excuse that a local attorney would save the client time and money. All pertinent documents were shipped south and the Dunne Law Office precipitously shut its doors for good. Peter felt like a complete failure.

The loss of his so-called attorney's badge wasn't the only thing weighing him down. At 41, he had spent the whole of his youth pursuing a career that would constantly elude him, in two cities and three different countries. All he had to show for it were the riches he'd made as a common merchant, a peddler! His man-about-town-status would undoubtedly be affected. Would they boot him out of the Pacific Club? Would the gewgaws of society reject him? And would he need to lower his expectations of taking some golden noble heiress for a wife? He felt old all of a sudden. Alternative plans were being set into motion.

After their short time working together looking for loopholes and conjuring up codicils, Peter and Thomas Bergin formed an unlikely friendship. Bergin continued his studies in Santa Clara but would often stop by Dunne & Company offices. Adding to their camaraderie, the Bergins hailed from Queen's County and had fled their famine-ravaged village to eventually run the bustling soap and candleworks on Green

Street around the corner from the Dunnes. Thomas enjoyed gossiping about the San Francisco law scene with Peter and thought perhaps the distinguished businessman wore long enough coat tails he could ride along into the city's high society after graduation. He also had a little ingénue in mind for his older bachelor friend.

Bridget Lawler had suffered through a week of life with her family crammed into two rooms of the bawdy boarding house Patrick had procured after rushing out of her brothers' home. The boarders were no nastier than any of the other single men adrift in the city by the bay but they had exposed Bridget's children to filthy language mixed with boozy and lecherous behavior. It was bad enough to witness it on the city streets but not where one sleeps. Seeking refuge she brought the children into St. Francis Church to pray and be redeemed. They weren't having it and began to fuss. She was absorbed deeply in prayer when she felt a gentle tap on her shoulder. It was the young Chinese priest who had delivered that undecipherable sermon on New Year's morning. He introduced himself.

"I am Father Thomas Cian. Who might you be?"

When she could look him face-to-face and watch his lips move he was no more difficult to understand than a mumbling Irish villager would be trying to speak English. "My name is Mrs. Lawler. These are my children."

"Do they not have a father?"

"Oh yes, he is looking for work around town at the moment."

"What does he do?"

"He was a farmer back home. In Ireland."

"I see. Not many farms down here by the wharfs."

"No, I suppose not but he can do most anything."

"He should do what he knows best."

Patrick often accused his wife of worrying herself into an early grave but she countered with the notion that although it might appear like worry to him, she was only thinking of solutions. And as she was worrying, or thinking rather, she noticed the beautiful stained-glass window behind Father Thomas' left shoulder. It was an illuminated nativity scene and over the Virgin Mary's right shoulder was a big, fat, beautiful cow.

"Aye Father, you are absolutely correct, he should do what he knows best. You have been a tremendous help and I mustn't trouble you any longer. Come along, children. Thank you Father, much obliged. See you again on Sunday."

Bridget whisked the children around the corner and dropped them with Kitty while the Dunne brothers were busy at work.

"Kitty, I won't be long. I have some business to attend to," Bridget said while rushing her children through the elaborate front door of her brothers' house.

"No bother. I'm just happy to see you again. I apologize for all the ugliness my husband has caused."

"We are both married to a couple of stubborn Irishmen with more pride than sense."

"I'll try talking to James again. I would love to have you come back and live here. We have plenty of room."

"You are too kind."

"My husband can start at the top o' the stairs happy as a bluebird and by the time he gets to the bottom he's madder than a bulldog!"

"He's always been like that."

"I can fix it. I'll catch him at the top of the stairs one of these mornings—"

"Kitty you are a dear but Patrick won't change his mind or his ways. I'll be back lickety-split," a term Bridget overheard at the boarding house and now adopted. Kitty gave her a hug and sent her on her way.

With purpose, Bridget stomped down Kearny Street and traipsed up the steps of St. Patrick's Orphan Asylum presenting herself again to Sister Frances.

"Mrs. Lawler! How good to see you! Please have a seat," said the nun hoping that she was about to be presented with another sizable donation. "How are you? And how is Mr. Lawler?"

In her mind, Bridget had been structuring her proposal to sound as mutually beneficial as possible.

"He is fine, although we are finding ourselves at loose ends."

"Oh, my."

"He is drastically in need of employment."

"Do you need your money back?"

"Nothing like that Sister. He wasn't too keen on me giving away $100 I can tell you but we were happy to help," she casually reminded.

"Bless you."

"When you gave us a tour of the property here you brought us 'round to that little dairy in the back. It didn't seem to be in use."

"That's true. It's kind of alone in its little corner back there and it's just easier for us to buy all of our milk and butter."

"You have enough to do taking care of the children without tending to cows I imagine."

"Precisely."

"What would you say to my husband if he were to buy that little corner and run the dairy himself?"

"The Bishop would never consent to some nun selling diocese land!" Sister Francis laughed out loud. "But I might be able to arrange a long lease." She folded her hands in her lap.

"Well if you could, my husband might buy his own herd and get that dairy up and running again."

"Interesting thought."

"Back home, not to be immodest, I was known for making the finest butter in Queen's County and people would line up outside my door to buy it."

"San Franciscans would pay good money to get their hands on some rich butter!"

"There you go, and I could whip up enough butter so that we would make a donation to the asylum every week."

"We go through heaps and heaps of butter—"

"And you could use your ready cash for other things."

"We go through gallons and gallons of milk too," Sister Frances added hoping the deal could be further sweetened.

"I'm sure that can be arranged, Sister. Of course, I would never ask you to break a commandment but can I send my husband to you telling him of your scathingly brilliant idea?"

"My idea?"

"Yes, the one where you propose that he lease the dairy from you and become your milk and butter supplier."

"Yes, my idea. Or better yet, how about you summon him here and I can make it look like it was all his idea?"

"Aye Sister, if you weren't married to God you'd make the perfect wife."

CHAPTER 31

A letter from Edward Meadows Dunne, Esq. to Bridget Lawler

March 3, 1854

Hold for Mrs. Bridget Lawler c/o Dunne & Company
*   164 Sansome Street*
*   San Francisco, California*
*   United States of America*

Dear Mrs. Lawler,
*   With profound regret I must inform you that Mrs. Alicia Grace*
Kavanaugh has passed away. She died among friends at her villa in Nice,
Italy. She has been buried back here at the Grace family vault in Arles.
*   She was eighty-five years of age.*
*   I am writing to you from her study at Gracefield where I have been*
put in charge of her estate. In her Will the deceased bequeathed unto you a
measure of inheritance in the amount of £150. You may retrieve your legacy
at Wells, Fargo & Company in San Francisco, California.
*   May this lawfully bestowed inheritance prove as a reminder of the*
generosity of your Irish family and of a woman who did not forget about
those she admired.
*   Very Sincerely Yours,*
*   Edward Meadows Dunne, Esq.*

Patrick Lawler was a superstitious Irishman who washed up on the shores of America believing in good luck and bad luck, fairies and phantoms, curses and spells. His wife believed in God, God and her husband. But when an inheritance appeared at just the right moment to set up the family in the dairy business, it was hard to decipher divine providence from luck.

A decent sized mixed herd of Holsteins and Guernsey cows, purchased with Mrs. Kavanaugh's gift, were corralled in a public square right up from the renovated St. Patrick's Dairy leased from the Diocese for a whopping 25 years at Patrick Lawler's insistence. He plunked out money for a real lawyer to draw up the papers.

Bridget discovered a handsome little cottage for rent on the grounds of a Van Ness Avenue mansion. The mansion's owner, Mr. Ephraim W. Burr, a stranded whaler turned gold miner turned merchant turned banker, was impressed with the hard-working couple and introduced them to his many clients and friends. A network of alliances also formed from the sizable number of Queen's County expatriates in San Francisco where they all patronized each other's endeavors. Within minutes of an introduction the Lawlers would find some familial connection to just about anyone from the Midlands, if they weren't related to Patrick then surely they were related to Bridget.

By late summer the couple had accounts crisscrossing the city. Bridget made her butter behind the orphanage. It didn't taste exactly the same without the Irish Sea salt. She'd have to work on that. But for now, she couldn't churn it out fast enough. It was the most requested product from the dairy. Bridget was more accustomed to country lanes rather than city streets but she adapted quite well to her new life in America.

She was pregnant again.

Bridget and Kitty had both confided in the Chinese priest, Father Cian, about their husbands' ridiculous feud. On a beautiful September morning Father Cian was on the church steps greeting his parishioners after Sunday mass. He asked Patrick how things were with Sister Francis and the dairy hoping the answer would be long enough for James to make his exit from the church.

"Mr. James Dunne!" Father called him over to chat holding onto Patrick's arm at the same time. "I would like a moment with you gentlemen."

"G'morning Patrick," said James. Patrick only nodded his head.

"Did you know we have camels back in China?" the priest asked seemingly out of nowhere.

"I thought they were only for A-rabs," Patrick played along knowing he was being led somewhere he wasn't sure he wanted to go.

"Yes, yes. They in the Gobi Desert very far North China."

"Interesting, you learn something new every day," said James.

"Strange looking animals. Two humps!"

"OK." Patrick said hoping he could be excused.

"But the stranger thing is, the camel never sees his own humps but the ones of his brother's never leave his eyes." Silence prevailed as James and Patrick realized they had been ambushed. "I urge you now to patch up your differences. In this tough place we need the family. Family. Worth more than all the gold in hills. Please now, brothers, shake hands and be done with your fight."

The Irishmen shook hands and the Chinese priest put his hands upon theirs and recited: "Dear Lord, may these brothers find the humility they need to stay not only in your good graces but also the good graces of their wives." Eastern wisdom was no match for Irish pride.

Peter did not attend mass that Sunday. He had a whole day planned at the Pacific Club Rooms.

After the great fire of 1851 the club had relocated to a suitably spiffy building at the corner of Montgomery and Jackson. Lush landscape paintings in gilded frames hung from the walls, celebrating the forests, oceans, mountains, deserts and fields of the Golden State. Members browsed through the library's impressive collection of newspapers in the morning and drifted into Pisco Punch and poker by the afternoon. Peter held several losing hands in a row and was trying to make his way back when the fast-paced conversation among the city's influencers turned from horrible theater productions in Portsmouth Square to the Chinese inhabiting Little Canton a few blocks away.

"They'll work for practically nothing. I use 'em to load and unload. Ain't nothing wrong with that," said a sleepy-eyed parvenu from Savannah who'd just made a fortune importing wagons of Sierra Mountain ice.

"But you see the difficulty with that is able-bodied men around here are idle while they see these Chinese men working away. Everyone is just trying to earn a living—the situation is hotter than a whistling tea kettle," said a disgusted Peter Dunne as he threw his cards into the center of the table.

"Go ahead and pay your warehousemen as much as you want. Any idiot can do that work and I want the cheapest idiot I can find," said the Iceman.

"Well, the Devil finds work for idle hands," warned the former State Senator David Broderick as he laid down three aces and swept another pile of chips to his side. "Crime is running rampant again, I'm hearing it from all sides."

"I don't think this lull in the economy is gonna last any longer than a whore's moan," said the Iceman with a wink.

"Might be time to organize another vigilance committee," added a well-dressed player fondling a brandy snifter.

"Vigilantes have no place in America. The last thing we need is a bunch of hot-tempered merchants taking the law into their own hands again. The Chivs don't like the way the wind is blowing at the moment. And let's all remember these folks don't like Irish either. They'd be happy to bring their scandalous slave trade out here and send all us Irish back to that abandoned little island," added Broderick trying to head off any troubles that might encumber his ambitions to be a United States Senator from California.

"I'm no Southern sycophant but we all like a safe city Senator, it's good for business," said Peter.

"We have ways to deal with this overpopulation of Celestials through legislation. They are working on several bills in Sacramento right now. They think the yellow ones can be controlled—"

Causing Peter to add, "…or maybe it's just the wishful thinking of bigots," risking the wrath of powerful hypocrites.

Topics switched with the flip of a card. "What do you hear about any other legislation in the works? Anything we should know about?" asked another newcomer to the club, Billy Ralston, at the moment an agent of Cornelius Vanderbilt's Nicaragua Steamship Company.

"Come on David, give us a little morsel," begged Peter. Access to prominent people was a perk of Pacific Club membership but being privy to wandering conversations could change fortunes.

"I suppose the biggest debate on the horizon is about the huge rancheros still left in the Californios' hands."

"What's to debate?"

"Do they really own all that or should it revert to the State?"

"I thought they settled that with a treaty when California was admitted to the Union?"

"Things change. Even signed treaties are negotiable. If I were one of those fat Mexican Dons I'd start selling now and if I had a stash of cash I might want to take some of that land off their hands," advised the Senator.

"Not me, leave that ranching to the lunkheads. Speaking of which, Dunne are you really going to have some candlestick maker's daughter as your wife?" said the Iceman changing subjects back to the mundane.

"Yes, it's true, I am finally taking the deep," admitted Peter anteing up for the next hand.

"I had you marked for some Brahmin's daughter, the daughter of a hundred Earls or some girl like that." The senator teased.

"Well, she's no Irish washwoman. On the contrary, haughty as hell. I like it. I worked everything out with the father," he said casually as if negotiating another business deal.

"Large dowry?"

"Sufficient. I have a feeling she will be quite an acquisitive wife."

"You're getting married as a Catholic then? Do they know that you belong to every secret society in town and haven't set foot into church since you've been here?" asked Broderick as he called for three cards.

"That was part of the bargain. Staunch."

"Where will they let you do that?"

"The monsignor is away at St. Francis so we're doing it there while he's out of town. No questions asked."

"That's where they have that chink priest. You gonna get married by a chink priest?" asked the Iceman. "I'll let 'em move around frozen water but that's about it. They're all born heathens."

"Be hard enough for me to go into a Catholic church let alone sit and listen to some Chinaman mangle the bible," said Ralston.

"So you'll marry in The Church, get some money from Bergin and that's all fine but what's his daughter look like anyhow?" wondered the Iceman in his wheeler-dealer drawl.

"She's pretty, milky skin, gold hair, petite. Must not like her teeth though, she doesn't show them when she smiles. She is very, very young."

"Ew, I likes 'em young. I'd spin her around like a windmill over and over and then grind that cherry down to a little nub!" suggested the Iceman.

"Why is it you Southerners are so crude? Butter wouldn't melt in your mouth and then you go into some foul-mouthed tirade like that! You're disgusting. Be gone." Broderick motioned for Henry the bartender to remove the Iceman at once. He ruled the Pacific Club with the same iron fist he used to control the city.

After the scuffle, the table resumed to the game and talk at hand. "As we were saying, what's her name Peter?" continued Broderick.

"Margaret."

"Is Margaret educated? Can she read and all that?"

"I imagine she can. She speaks well. Witty. We've really only met twice through her brother Thomas."

"Does someone have a gun to your head or are you afraid you're getting too long in the tooth?"

"Time to get married, David. It's time."

"So you say."

"I require a wife that I can mold into my perfect partner. I need children, a legacy. Time and tide wait for no man."

The Dunnes of Brittas had carved out a storied place for the clan through hundreds of years of Irish history-making but the five or six years Peter and James spent in Alta California qualified them as pioneers, 49ers, native sons of the golden West. As such, if an early merchant of the city married the daughter of a fellow settler, savvy enough to sell soap and candles to prospectors, they would be known in the right circles as a pioneering couple. That moniker was the future and completely acceptable to him.

The wedding eventually took place at the Church of St. Francis officiated by Father Thomas Cian surrounded by Dunnes, Donnellys, Lawlers, and Bergins. A reception followed at the Poodle Dog.

Kevin Lee Akers

CHAPTER 32

Fragment of letter from Lucy Rogers to her niece Lucy Drees

[July 6, 1938]

By the time my mother was pregnant with me she was 46 years old—I was her ninth child! As I told you, Esther and Catherine died in the famine but all the rest of us lived in that brown house on Polk Street. My parents kept their horses and wagons on a little street now called Maiden Lane and the corral was in front of the St. Francis hotel, which after the Civil War was named Union Square. It only took a few years until they made enough money in the butter and eggs business to consider buying land, which of course is every Irishman's dream.

Mother worried terribly and thought living in the city was becoming far too dangerous. You must also remember they were always at heart country people.

San Francisco went from a tiny encampment to a city with 40,000 inhabitants practically overnight. It did not have the luxury of developing like a normal city in incremental stages over many generations. She was always scrambling to keep up with her own ambitions.

Fashionable parts of town seemed to change with the weather. Monstrous mansions with mansard roofs, two-story columns and wrought iron gates populated the elegant, sunny enclave of Rincon Hill. Montgomery Street held steady as the epicenter of business where all the important banks safeguarded the wealth of the west.

One of those bankers, Billy Ralston, a former shipping agent and consummate capitalist studied the city maps with an eye for opportunity. Where the elite residential area met the business district would make the perfect crossroads for his next big idea: a world-class travelers' hotel. Much had to be accomplished to transform an entire section of the city into his vision. Streets had to be moved, palms had to be greased, influence had to be exerted and land had to be either purchased or condemned. Defiant property owners hired lawyers to stop the steamrolling. It was a messy business but Ralston had what every visionary needed for success, endurance.

A perfect parcel large enough to accommodate such a dream surfaced on Market Street but unfortunately it was already occupied by a new building, St. Patrick's Orphan Asylum. Ralston and his league of accomplices went toe-to-toe with the Catholic Church trying to concoct some sort of deal but every negotiation ended in stalemate. Exasperated, Ralston finally went above the bishop's head and directly to the institution's Board of Directors. He knew one of the directors, Mr. Peter Dunne, from the Pacific Club and thought him a reasonable gent. Surely he understood that sleepy little villages of the world could go unchanged for hundreds of years but great cities needed constant modification and growth.

States too.

The illustrious Mexican Dons who still presided over large swaths of California where feeling those forceful winds of change as well. They were systematically selling their rancheros faster than a bucket of peaches beginning to rot in the summer sun. They feared hold-over land grants from Mexican rule would be lost to squatters, lawsuits or U.S. government reprisals if they didn't liquidate soon.

James Dunne had been a commission merchant for almost twenty years and accumulated his fortune quietly. Showy displays just attracted jealousy and avarice. But, in reality, he was one of the wealthiest merchants of the city. He held vast gold reserves in numerous banks, common stock and as an alternative to his San Francisco real estate he had slowly been purchasing rich farm and grazing lands in Santa Clara and San Benito Counties from a Californio Don named Francisco Pacheco. Don Pacheco sold him both El Rancho Ausaymas y San Felipe and Bolsa San Felipe for a cool $20,000 in lawful U.S. money.

Six square leagues of land sounds quaint, almost tiny. Put another way, it was in excess of 25,000 acres. James preferred to think of it like this; it was three times bigger than the Brittas estate his father managed and more than half the size of Queen's County itself. Never one to pat himself on the back, this time a celebration was in order.

In celebratory dress, James, Kitty, Peter and his new bride Margaret piled into the coach for a short ride down to the elegant Poodle Dog Restaurant. In the driver's seat of the coach Sam Goo seemed a little tense compared to his normally affable self. The streets below were teaming with promenading couples, cackling children and it was difficult to maneuver the rig. There were more than a few shady characters strewn about. Depositing the group at the restaurant, Sam sniffed at the air then made a sour expression. "What time shall I be back to pick you up Mr. James?"

"Give us three hours," said James.

Kitty tugged on his arm and said, "Darlin', it's so balmy out tonight, let's walk back on our own."

"No, no, Miss Kitty, I think I come back to get you, it's better. I think mo' better."

"You heard the lady, Sam."

Sam shook his head but dutifully bowed and took his leave.

At their corner table soft candlelight illuminated the ladies' faces and James took a moment to study the contours of his wife's beautiful features. He couldn't take his eyes off her. She caught him staring. He was only just comparing her loveliness to that of his new sister-in-law. Although Margaret was considerably younger than Kitty, James felt he was blessed with the prettier of the two wives. Competition ran deep among the Dunnes.

Peter raised a brimming champagne glass, "To the Rancho San Felipe, may she fulfill every dream my brother has for her!"

"I was born to be a vaquero, don't you think? Walk bow-legged? I'll get me some Indians to tend to the fields and make every acre of those ranchos profitable, you'll see." A prediction aimed squarely at his doubting brother. "Someday the gold mines are gonna dry up, you know there's only so much of it. What California needs now is beef, beef and wheat. Stuff we can keep making. We're importing less and less food. Who wants to depend on grain from South America forever? We have the best damned land in the world to grow our own!" he smoothed his mustache and puffed out his chest.

"Yes James, so you keep saying," said Peter.

"But what about all of your businesses here?" asked an obviously uninformed Margaret.

"I'll come up once a month. Peter can be the man-in-charge the rest of the time. He looks like the boss there with his gold watch and diamonds."

"Speaking of such, Kitty what a dazzling pin you're wearing! I've never seen it before," said Margaret with just the slightest smattering of jealousy.

"Why thank you. I hardly wear it. James got it for me when I gave him his third son." Kitty caressed the diamond and sapphire clusters with her elegant fingertips and the ladies began to talk amongst themselves. James and Peter drifted into their predictable cliquish cocoon.

"Ralston came at me in the Club again yesterday," whispered Peter.

"About the orphanage?" asked James.

"He and his investors finally got the bishop to agree on a price but then Patrick up and says no, he has a 25-lease on that dairy of his and is making a colossal fuss. Scared the poor priest right out of his collar."

"Can't they just pay him off?" James asked.

"He's gone all wild like he does. Says he's worked too hard to give it up. He's staying put. Oh, says he'll get the best Jew lawyer in town to fight the church if he has to—"

"Sounds like your unstoppable forces have met an immovable object. Did you talk to him?"

"Hell no, I don't want Patrick to know I have any involvement whatever."

"Peter, you're on the board. You're involved."

"He's too thick to penetrate. That clodhopper has an iron grip on his plot."

"Get Bridget to do it."

"I know him well enough that he's not going to budge. Stubborn like all those Lawlers."

"Then that's that. Why do you care anyhow? Just trying to look big in front of those fat cat friends of yours again?" James had no dog in the hunt.

"No. I care because it's a good plan. Can you imagine a gleaming new caravansary for San Francisco? Ralston says it's going to be grander than anything in Paris or London."

"And in the meantime you can look like the sophisticated power broker, I know. How many more boards do you want to be on? Oh, maybe the bank's? Clever."

"Brother, how could you utter such nonsense?" Peter asked wryly.

"The only way you're going to maneuver Patrick out of there is if he wants to go himself. Has to be his idea. He doesn't like to be pushed around, I can tell you that."

"Do you have an extra little rancho down south he can afford? Just to get him out of town?"

"We can't even stand to be in the same room with each other, I don't want him to be my neighbor."

"This is true," admitted Peter.

"But I heard up north General Vallejo is dumping his land at good prices."

"Sonoma?"

"Yes. I read it in the newspaper. The big one is Rancho Petaluma. Something like 60,000 acres he's selling."

"Selling out before it's stolen out from under him?"

"Patrick could go back to farming instead of hauling milk around town."

"Maybe. I'd actually be doing the dolt a favor. I'll put a bug in Bridget's ear."

At the end of their seven-course meal the gentlemen were enjoying cigars when the ladies suggested they head out and enjoy the warm evening stroll back home. Peter and James got caught up chatting to a table of business associates, not bothering to introduce the wives. Moving on, the Dunne woman made it past the crowd of elegant diners to the plank sidewalk outside. Kitty was still able to turn a few gentlemen's heads in the process.

"Hang on Kitty, they're still blabbing," said a frustrated Margaret not quite accustomed to being frozen out by the brothers' private camaraderie.

Outside the door they waited. "We could be out here all night, Megs. But it's wonderful isn't it? Just lovely." She welcomed the night air into her lungs with gusto and let the bliss softly waft over her.

On that sticky, almost tropical evening, the sea air was especially noticeable. Groups of pedestrians intermittently filled the walkways, dashing this way and that. Uncomfortable, the ladies stood aside to make room when people careened through and then moved back to continue their chat. Kitty was beginning to sweat. After a while they both became annoyed at their husbands' brush off.

"What are they doing in there? Are they going to walk us home or not?" asked an irritated Margaret.

"Taking their sweet time as usual. Sometimes I think those two should have just married each other!" They laughed and waited.

The traffic had died down on the sidewalk leaving the ladies very much alone in front of the Poodle Dog. Margaret turned her back to peer inside the restaurant looking for the men. Enough was enough, she wanted to go home. From out of the darkness a grimy young man materialized before them. He reached out and snatched Kitty's diamond brooch, tearing her light blue dress as it was pulled loose. With a mighty thrust he shoved the dainty lady backward against the café building. She looked like a rag doll thrown onto a playroom wall by a child in the midst of a temper tantrum. Her head struck a gilded plaster corbel with an ominous thud. Kitty's petite body slowly trickled down to the wooden slats of the walkway into a puddle of lace and ruffles. Margaret screamed. The thief sliced through a darkened alleyway and disappeared into the night.

"Kitty! Kitty! Are you alright?" Margaret begged for an answer on bended knee. Blood was starting to saturate Kitty's blonde hair under her floppy hat.

The Dunne brothers came rushing to the scene. James knelt down and saw a lifeless face that sent his own body into tremors. Margaret could faintly be heard babbling an incoherent story in the background. He cradled Kitty's head in his hands, the oozing blood warmed his skin. Someone fired a pistol. Yelling. Confusion.

Patrons poured out from the Poodle Dog and surrounded James and Kitty. A balding gentleman claiming to be a doctor pushed through and knelt down next to the couple. He felt the lady's dainty wrist for a pulse. Turning to James he said, "Sorry friend, she's gone I'm afraid." James violently reacted by pushing the man away sending him straight into the gutter. "You don't know what you're talking about, she'll be all fine. Right, Kitty? Right?"

"James," Peter put his hand on his brother's shoulder. It was furiously flicked away. Seething with anger and hate, James Dunne would suffer through the death of Kitty a second and final time.

The sweet smell of gardenias wafted throughout the Dunne family's handsome parlor. Flowers of kaleidoscopic colors filled the space around a 28-year old Kitty, laid out in a white enameled coffin, looking radiant and unbelievably still. James stood by stoically in his everyday black suit greeting the mourners with his sons, five-year old Peter and tiny three-year Jimmie, clinging to his pant legs. Beside them, Bridget held her newborn daughter Lucy as well as Kitty's eight-month old baby boy, Joey. All three were crying.

Patrick coaxed the babies from her arms with the kindness of an adoring husband. She moved through the throng of people in black armbands and sat herself down at the dining room table to collect herself. Bridget hadn't shed a tear since she was a girl and now she couldn't stop. She loved Kitty as something more than family, as a best friend. Along came Peter and sat down beside her.

"It's a terrible thing," said Peter.

Bridget nodded, her red nose buried in a lilac-colored hanky.

"The city is a savage place."

"To, to be sure, I tell Patrick the same thing," she said as she sniffed.

"James has the right idea, out to the country," said Peter.

"You'd think now that he has to raise those boys by himself, he'd change his mind and stay in town. I'd help him," said Bridget giving a glancing eye towards James in the next room. Her heart ached for her little brother but he was so angry. He grimaced every time someone tried to comfort him. Best to leave him be.

"Oh no, he's dead set on going. He's quitting city life altogether. Mary's going with him."

"Well, that's news to me. Our sister'll be no help to him at all. I'm surprised."

"James can hire all the help he needs." Peter became shrill. "Killers coming out of dark alleys, that he doesn't need."

"No and the vigilantes are just as bad. It's like some lawless region of Babylon. My son John saw them hang Cora and Casey right there in public! He is still having nightmares."

"Have you ever thought of moving house?" asked Peter as he handed his sister a fresh handkerchief.

"More than once but Patrick says we have business to attend to here."

"I found this in the paper for a friend but let me give it to you instead." Peter reached into his breast pocket where he just happened to have an advertisement, Parcels for Sale on the Petaluma Rancho.

"What is it?"

"There is a land sale going on about 40 miles north. Premium farm and cattle land at cheap prices." Bridget read through the scant details. "Patrick could get more acreage than he ever dreamed of back home. Beef and wheat, that's what James says. Farmers up there just send everything they grow down the river into the bay and sell it here for premium prices. It's a natural highway," Concurrent events depended upon the Lawler's decision.

"Makes things easy." Bridget stopped and gave the idea some serious thought.

"Have a word with Patrick. Don't tell him I alerted you. We know he's terribly fond of his own ideas."

"I do know that Peter and I appreciate it. You're a dear." Bridget gave her brother an enthusiastic embrace with all the passion taught to her by Kitty.

It was long and cathartic.

Patrick Lawler's dairy herd was so large that it was getting difficult to find a suitable place to pasture them downtown. Arrangements were being made to take them way out to the old Presidio fields north of town. He was grumbling about business at the supper table not three days after Kitty's funeral.

"But Pat these are wonderful problems to have. Don't you agree?" said his sympathetic wife.

"Aye. An embarrassment of riches."

"I must say that even the dairy is too small to handle everything we have going on now."

"It's tight."

"What about getting a big milk ranch of your own like James did?"

"I don't be needin' to follow your brother's example. People think he's mad to leave the city. Tempting though—"

"So you've thought about it?" asked Bridget.

"Of course I've thought about it. And yes, I know where you stand on that issue."

"Let's look in the paper and see what there is to see, shall we?" She handed him the Daily Alta that still contained Vallejo's advertisements. Patrick put on his spectacles to peruse.

"Lots of land up for auction."

"Oh, auctions can get quite tricky," cautioned Bridget.

"Three acres of land for sale outright in Oakland."

"That's barely enough for an orchard."

"Hang on. Here's a big notice from General Vallejo himself. He is selling off the Petaluma Rancho up north."

"How big?"

"This ad is for a 2,000 acre parcel."

"Hold your horses, Patrick! How on God's green earth could we afford that much land? You know what happened before when we took on too much, things went terribly wrong. Let's not get carried away."

"I like this line, To capitalists the Rancho offers great inducements."

"No, no. I was thinking something on the scale we had in Mountmellick, 30, maybe 40 acres."

"This is America now Biddy, we must think big." Patrick said with an American accent.

"Oh, dear."

Don Mariano Guadalupe Vallejo was born a Californio in 1808 as a Spanish subject in Monterey. He would reside in three different countries despite never living anywhere else but California.

He found favor with the Spanish and Mexican provisional bureaucrats who were impressed with his intellect and his heritage. Vallejo's father had accompanied the early missionary Father Junípero Serra on his quest to Christianize the Pacific coast. Eventually Don Marino was awarded the military title of comandante-general and granted expansive territories above San Francisco, almost 300 square miles of it.

After the United States defeated Mexico in the war, Vallejo's obliging demeanor helped to keep him alive after being seized at his fort in Sonoma during an uprising known as the Bear Flag Revolt. Statehood and the Gold Rush brought about even more upheaval into the General's private paradise but he was clever enough to survive with his family and land intact. Like his fellows Dons of the late 1850s, he was getting tired of trying to juggle the multitude of problems associated with owning unmanageable tracts of land that used to take an entire army to defend.

La Casa Grande was General Vallejo's adobe hacienda at the foot of Sonoma Mountain, six miles outside the fledgling town of Petaluma. The rancho had once been a thriving enterprise where Californios and native Indians worked side-by-side in his New World fiefdom reaping the bounty of the land and it's animals. Today, Vallejo was at his desk signing away deeds to his former holdings. It was March when the landscape was at its most beautiful. The estate agent was introducing a new buyer to the General, a Mr. Patrick Lawler out of San Francisco.

"Do take a seat Mr. Lawler," invited a warm and gracious Vallejo. Coffee with sweet cream and sugar was brought into the workroom by an Indian servant.

"We have all the documents ready to sign. Did you bring payment?" asked the bald little annoying moneyman sitting to Patrick's left.

"Aye, but I haven't even seen the land I'm buying," said Patrick.

"It's all here in the deed. You can see the breakdown, grazing land acreage here, meadow here, this part is suitable for farming, these are the mountains, streams and pond, etcetera, etcetera."

"I can see the little dots on that map but I be needin' to see the land for myself. That's why I've come all the way up here," Patrick said to the agent (who he suspected of being a vegetable-diet sort of fellow.) He looked directly at General Vallejo.

"Yes, yes, that's a reasonable request," said the General. "When is our next appointment?"

"This afternoon," the agent replied.

"Mr. Lawler I would be more than happy to ride out with you and show you the holdings myself. I know it well. Been cooped up in this place for two days."

"That'd be grand," Patrick said as he slapped his knees. The rays of sun coming through the unglazed windows illuminated the plume of road dirt floating up from his dungarees.

Out in the courtyard, the Irish dairyman couldn't believe his eyes when Vallejo's men brought out his prized ebony stallion. The horse's head was festooned with enough silver on the bit and bridle to strain his mighty neck. On his back sat a saddle adorned with ornate silver plates from the horn to the seat collar. Black richly-tooled leather was carpeted with an array of dazzling sterling silver conchos. The tapadero stirrups looked like they were sculpted out of a block of solid silver. It was the most flamboyant display Lawler had ever witnessed thrust upon any unsuspecting beast of burden. He wondered to himself if the portly Don could even ride the damn thing.

In contrast, a very sad-looking brown mare with a beaten-up saddle awaited Patrick in the yard. The two men mounted and left the hacienda grounds through a secure perimeter of prickly-pear cactus then out onto the property for a survey of the new Lawler Ranch.

A smattering of Vallejo's cattle roamed the grassy hills as they ascended along up a muddy trail. Oak trees dotted the idyllic terrain. Patrick looked back to the sprawling Hacienda that got smaller as they traversed the hills. They rode to a place where it flattened out into a lush meadow the General noted would be perfect for crops. He pointed out landmark maple trees as boundaries to the parcel that continued on and on, up and up. They then turned their horses and followed a creek through a thick section of trees. Nearing the top of the knoll Vallejo turned back and shouted, "Mr. Lawler we're coming up to the spot where I think you should build your house. This way."

Through the shady wildwoods and into a clearing Patrick could see for himself what the General meant; a good ten acres of flat land, like a mesa, just ready for settlement. Through the center a silvery stream flowed, filled with speckled trout. Looking westward from the knoll was a wide enchanting valley with the rooftops and buildings of the Petaluma settlement visible below. Not far past the opposite range of mountains was the Pacific Ocean.

Immediately the rolling hills and dales reminded Patrick of his homeland, lush and green and smelling like clover. He could not believe another Ireland existed so close to San Francisco.

He was absolutely mesmerized.

He dismounted and walked to the edge of the mesa, put his hands on his hips and gazed out. Before him he could see his past, present and future all at once. Behind him walked the General and asked, "Is this not the perfect spot to build your home?"

"Aye, it is more perfect than perfect." Patrick had tears in his eyes. He turned and walked away from Vallejo for a moment to dry up, embarrassed at such raw sentimentality.

"I never get emotional over land," said the observant General, "but then again I'm not Irish."

"Well I am and we do."

"I understand. Out here we have very few towns, no remarkable buildings or centers of culture, nothing like Europe. But we do have land. Masses upon masses of beautiful land. But in the end, it isn't ours. We are merely squatters on God's country."

Immediately Patrick launched into his building plans. Barn there. Dairy there. Orchard there on the downslope for the best irrigation.

Wheat fields that direction. And the house? Right, right about here where he stood. He held his arms straight out bringing them up and down in a chopping motion.

"I have the name of a good builder here in town. He could build you a nice hacienda here in the old Spanish style."

"No offense General but I want a good American-looking house here."

"What would that be?"

"I don't know. Something an old patriot from Virginia would live in…someone like Patrick Henry. I admire that man. Give me liberty or give me death! Those are words to live by."

"Very well. Put in an order for one Colonial-style, two-story clapboard house suitable for a hero of the revolution!" said the learned and knowledgeable General, himself a champion of the new American spirit that swept him out of power and bled him of his land.

"Ten rooms. I always wanted a house with ten rooms. Nice even number."

CHAPTER 33

Letter from James Dunne to his brother, Peter Dunne

July 18, 1859
Dunne Ranch
San Felipe, California

Dear Peter:

I am writing to you formally so my intentions are clear. You will soon receive a Dissolution of Co-partnership notice from my San Jose attorney. I have contacted auctioneer to liquidate our San Francisco business and real estate holdings.

As you know it has become impossible for me to inhabit the house on Kearny since Kitty's murder. I have been planning on quitting the city entirely for a long while. It's a wicked place and conducting business there has only gotten more difficult over the years. The San Felipe ranch suits me just fine and the boys like the country life.

This should not come as a surprise but after the treatment I received from you and Senator Broderick at your snooty club last week my decision has been cemented. I want out. Let me once again clarify for you and him, my time in New Orleans did not make me a Chiv or a Rebel or a Confederate or whatever other slur you thrust against me that night. I do not approve of slavery. I do not. However, I understand how the economy of the South needs the slaves to survive and they'll start a war to preserve their way of life. It's pretty clear cut. I am not prepared to lay down my life for a darkie.

That is all I was trying to say before the two of you jumped down my throat and made me look like a blithering idiot in front of all your Republican cronies. HOW DARE YOU—brother! That is not how business partners, let alone family, should treat one another. You've belittled the wrong hombre.

Since I own 60% of the company it is a mere formality that I send you this letter. I hope we can remain civil to each other during this process and then we can part ways.

Very Truly Yours,
J. Dunne

Maybe America itself was just too big to keep an Irish family close. For the Dunnes of California, having a happy and close-knit family meant they would all have to live several counties away from each other.

Saturday, September 17, 1859 was the date set for the auction of Dunne & Company. Rumors of a rift between the brothers had the vultures circling above Broadway, hoping to feast upon the remains of an empire. The announcement of the real estate inventory alone went to two columns in the Daily Alta.

A calendar had to reach September before San Francisco would finally acknowledge summer and reward its citizens with radiant sunshine and warm temperatures. The second anniversary of Kitty's death loomed large over James. Inside the Sansome Street offices, he and Peter toiled silently in chilly conditions with an communication limited to truncated business-speak. Their political differences hung in the air like the stale cigar smoke emanating from James' side of the room.

Peter acknowledged that it was his loathsome behavior that caused their relationship to fracture but he did not regret it in the least. He had been deprecating and arrogant towards his younger brother for most of their lives and only when James became successful did he act somewhat obsequious. Now Peter was almost as wealthy, had strong Republican convictions about slavery and easily reverted to his natural tendencies to squash intellectual inferiors.

In his mind it was not a question of morality or race, legally the institution of slavery was incompatible with American democracy pure and simple. It could not be justified. He considered James an intellectual midget incapable of objective thought. Politics divided families all across America as it marched towards an inevitable civil war. The fracas among the Dunne brothers foreshadowed the destruction awaiting the entire country.

"I sold the contents of the Pacific Warehouse and the money is already in the bank," James said not looking up from his paperwork.

"Fine," Peter said sharply.

"Did the announcement come out in the paper for the auction?"

"Don't know, Sam just put the paper on your desk right there in front of you."

"Let's see." James unfolded the paper and scanned it. There it was, printed in every conceivable font the typesetter had at his disposal. The ebbing commission merchant scrutinized it for errors and became numb at the site of his life's work up on the auction block.

"Everything's correct."

"May I see it?" asked Peter.

James folded the paper up and slapped it back on the corner of his desk not willing to walk it over. He dipped his pen back into the inkwell and continued without looking up. Peter scooted over in his revolving office chair, the brass wheels made pathetic little squeaks as they rotated across the parquet floor. He snatched up the newspaper and rolled back to his desk searching for the death notice of their company but found something even more disturbing.

"They went through with it! Broderick's been shot," Peter read the article to James with alarm in his voice.

Proxy civil wars had started amongst San Francisco society.

David Broderick, an abolitionist who had been elected to the U.S. Senate, was challenged to a duel by David Terry, a leading Chiv who claimed Broderick had besmirched his good name. The irascible six-and-a-half foot Terry was a Southern zealot hell-bent on bringing slavery to the Golden State. He saw the Senator as the first important politician to stand up to the growing power of the Chivs. Conspiracy theories would blaze through the city with the speed of its frequent fires when it was revealed that Terry owned the pistols used for the duel.

"Is he dead?" James interrupted the reading in a hopeful tone.

"No. Doesn't say. Oh. He's languishing. I must go to him."

"Leave it be, Peter, he's probably surrounded with capable doctors who can actually help him." Peter had his hat on his head and slipped out the door before the sentence was finished.

James was worried. Broderick could die. The implications would be huge. If he died the city would be lost in a sea of tears and a lone bidder could buy up the all Dunne real estate holdings while no one was watching. The auction must be canceled.

The United States Congress declared an official thirty-day mourning period after the death of Senator David C. Broderick and as James predicted, San Francisco came to a complete standstill. His body lay in state at the Union Hotel in Portsmouth Square where citizens filed past in utter disbelief. Almost every building in the district was draped in black crepe including all those still owned by Dunne & Company. More than thirty-thousand people filled the square for his funeral.

A couple of years later, Peter would boast that the murder of David Broderick was the first fatality of the Civil War. James would claim his death cost Dunne & Company a fortune when the real estate market plunged right before their auction. It also widened the personal and political chasm between the two brothers.

The cozy cocoon the two brothers lived in together as partners had withered and they were released from their bond to fly away.

After the final accounting of the company's assets, Peter would build Margaret an ostentatious mansion dangling with gingerbread decoration on Franklin and Broadway. His wealth allowed him to while away the hours at the Pacific Club, sit on several company boards and commandeer leadership positions at prestigious charitable organizations.

James Dunne retreated southward with his three boys to the San Felipe rancho. After the loss of his wife and the sale of his San Francisco concerns, he found it to be a healing place, taking refuge in fiefdom amongst his growing herds of cattle.

Earthly concerns and the responsibilities of running a ranch the size of an Irish duchy filled his days, leaving him on the brink of exhaustion by nightfall. He had no energy left to agonize about any of his losses, until the next one.

Peter would have two sons in quick succession. He named them Joseph and Peter, blatantly ignoring the fact that James already had two boys named Joseph and Peter. With all the space and spite between the brothers, there wouldn't be any family gatherings that would cause confusion anyhow. Busy young families tend to forget about the old ones even in the best circumstances.

Acrimony made separation easier to condone.

Death can play cruel games with its survivors. Some of them predictable, understandable. Others are irrational and demented. James lost two of his three young sons to a sickness that broke out at the San Felipe. With both of their burials he arrived early to the cemetery so he could gaze upon Kitty's casket when the grave was opened up for his sons. A steady stream of death had primed him for the torment and agony. Hate began to show up on his face. His misery was expressed through savage and cruel resentment of innocent parties. In calmer moments he knew it was wrong but it did not stop him from fixating on the fact that his nephews Joseph and Peter Dunne survived and his own sons of the same names did not.

It was as if the laws of gravity itself had been upended. If James hoped to survive he had to completely retool his equilibrium. He ruminated on his hardships as he rode through his vast acreage searching for answers and solace. Somehow he needed to cleanse the hatred from his soul.

By 1861 America was engulfed in a war with itself. Hate was tearing the country to shreds. Buffered by the thousands of miles of prairies and mountains that separated them from the battlefields, Californians eagerly read about the catastrophe in their newspapers then quietly went about their business.

Bridget Lawler, dressed in purple finery, had driven the wagon down before dawn from their Sonoma Mountain ranch into Petaluma where she would eventually meet Patrick at the steamer landing. He'd accompanied a large shipment of wheat to San Francisco and then signed papers to forfeit his lease on the dairy that he had been managing from his northern outpost. Billy Ralston had finally triumphed in his bid to procure an entire city block for his grand hotel on Market Street. Peter Dunne had used all his influence on the board of the orphan's asylum to get the Catholic Church to sellout but it was the heartfelt pleadings of Sister Francis that finally convinced the holdout Patrick Lawler to give up his dairy's lease and leave the land free for redevelopment. The unwitting nun played her part well in the land speculation deal.

Bridget brought along her 4-year-old little daughter Lucy to attend morning mass with her at St. Vincent's, an American facsimile of a Gothic chapel roughly rendered in redwood near downtown. She did a bit of socializing with her fellow parishioners who all fussed over the adorable toddler. A few Irish women but mostly Swiss, Italian and Portuguese immigrants, wives of dairy farmers. In the spirit of noblesse oblige that came with her status as the wife of one of Petaluma's Big Ranchers she would bow and smile and listen to their gossip but made no attempt to befriend them. She preferred the colorful and sophisticated people from San Francisco. These country people were not as congenial or worldly as a San Franciscan, not her people. Yet, she realized they were better company than the cows and chickens up on the mountain. She was disappointed in herself for seeming so snobbish.

After church the two got provisions and Bridget reluctantly purchased a wedding gift her son for Denny's new bride. On her ride to the landing she calculated how she would tell the story of their whirlwind romance to her husband.

"What happened to your head?" Bridget asked as Patrick tapped her feet to scoot over on the buckhorn.

"Fell through the damn hatchway. Some kind soul bandaged me up. I'll be fine."

"Do you think we should see the doctor?"

"For God's sake no." Patrick took the reins. He was anxious to get back up to his plow.

A ruffled deckhand called out, "Hope you're feeling better, Mr. Lawler!"

"Aye, I already feel better," he shouted back.

"Good-day Mrs. Lawler. You have a beautiful little daughter there with you."

"Pst, you should have seen the one she left at home!" cracked Patrick. Little Lucy figured out what her father had just said and started to cry.

"Did everything go well in the City?" asked Bridget as she pulled her whimpering daughter closer and gently rubbed her back.

"Made some good coin on the wheat and signed my lease back to the Church. Sister Francis sends her regards."

"That little dairy has been good to us."

"Sister was like a mad dog with a bone. She wouldn't stop until I signed over the blasted thing," Patrick said, for the moment, oblivious to any hint of her deception.

"You could have said no like you did to the others." Lucy's head was buried in her mother's lap. Bridget smoothed her hair.

"It's funny, she made it seem like the Lord Himself was on her side. I just folded like a house of cards."

"They don't call her Mother Superior for nothing."

"Ha!"

"No matter, there's near enough going on up here, easier to be done with it," Bridget said in a comforting matter before she dealt the next blow.

"I suppose," Patrick shrugged as they rolled away.

"Denny got married on Tuesday in Santa Rosa," Bridget just blurted it out after spending a day fretting about how best to break the news to her husband.

"Whoa!" Patrick pulled back on the reins almost causing Bridget to catapult over the wagon's front end. "What did you just say?"

"It's true. Got the letter yesterday."

"What? Who did he marry?"

"Some woman named Eugenia."

"I've never heard him mention a word of her. Damn fool. What's the matter with him? Is he afraid of getting drafted into the war?"

"You know a lot of boys are doing that."

"He looks like a coward."

"Oh, and he wrote that she is pregnant."

"A lustful coward then."

They rode back up to their ranch discussing the war, the current state of San Francisco and Denny's chances for happiness.

Having children spread so far apart in age, Bridget had been raising them in this phase and that for almost 25 years now but she was not at all sure she was ready to be a grandmother. The cruel calendar does not lie and indeed she was approaching 50. Her children, one-by-one, would be out leading independent lives and make hers seem less and less meaningful by comparison. Bridget, as was her habit, worried. Patrick was more hopeful about Denny, grandchildren, the Union winning the war, everything.

If he wasn't an optimist he wouldn't be a farmer.

CHAPTER 34

Letter written to Michael Dunne of Ballintlea House from his sister Bridget

April 19, 1865
Vallejo Township, Petaluma, California

Dear Michael:
    War is over and the President has been assassinated! I have never felt so low or more American.
    Out little town is in mourning. All of the private residences and business houses have been hung in black festoons giving a ghostly specter to every street. Today—all the townsfolk gathered at our plaza in front of the Baptist Church where the procession included a rider-less horse, a hearse, the Petaluma Guards and a brass band that puffed out a sad mournful dirge. The choir was much better. That Baptist preacher breathed down fire and brimstone like I have never heard…none of the majesty of a Catholic service. I must admit he did give a respectful eulogy of our fallen President. Very many of those who listened had been bitter, implacable enemies of Mr. Lincoln just a few short days before but managed to shed tears on his behalf this morning. Cannons have been firing at the half hour all day long and I can still hear them in the distance from where I sit writing to you at the kitchen table. That's 6 miles away. Patrick says it will go on till sunset.
    In time, I hope we can go back to the peaceful county it once was. Thank the Lord we have been spared any real bloodshed in the Western States as all the fighting has taken place mostly in the South. Many of our young men, single or married, would have been drafted if the war went on much longer. As a mother with five sons I am truly thankful. Surely the Confederate States will have a tough road to hoe and some say they will never return to their former glory.
    My intention is not to weigh you down with America's woes; you asked about the family in your last letter and I want to tell you everyone is well.
    At 55 years of age I am a grandmother! Denny—24—had a baby boy (J.P.) with his wife. They live with us for the time being with plans to get back down to San Francisco. He has dreams of being a constable. Daughter Mary, who has red hair brighter than mine, is 21 and engaged to be married.

Son John is 17 and a better help to his father on the ranch than any of the hired hands. Peter is 16. James is 14—the brains of the bunch. He has informed us he would like to move out from the country and study law when he grows up. Frances is 13. Little Patrick Henry is already 9 and very shy. Not like the Dunnes at all. My baby Lucy is all of 7 now and attends St. Vincent's Catholic Academy in town.

I'm so busy I don't know what side of me is up. Patrick continues to be the hardest working man I have ever known. He has accumulated more land so that now the ranch is quite large. Many fields for wheat, a sizable orchard, some woodlands for timber but most of the ranch is hilly grazing land for sheep, cattle, horses. We had a very wet winter and he kept a bunkhouse full of men that hardly worked. You'd never know they were so idle by the way they ate! I begged Patrick to turn them loose but now that Spring is here they are busy again. It is our favorite time of year because all of Sonoma County has turned the brightest of greens—just like dear Queen's County. By June the hills will be brown again and remind us that indeed we are far away from home.

Our brother Peter is living in what I can only describe as a mansion in San Francisco. Since our brothers sold the business Peter and his wife Margaret have busied themselves socially. They hired an English nanny to help rear their children besides the cook and the chambermaid.

You mention you got the news about James in his letter. Sad to say I haven't laid eyes on him for more than five years. I write periodically but don't receive any letters back. Once in a while Patrick will read about him and the San Felipe Ranch from the San Jose newspaper. He is one of the biggest landowners in County Santa Clara now. I do worry about him down there on that big ranch without the guiding hand of a good woman. He gets so lost in his work I'm fearful that is all he does. He still has one son left to raise. They call him little Jimmie and he came up here last summer and spent a month with his cousins. I found him delightful. Patrick thought him undersized, kept referring to him as a little runt. I think the boy heard him too. My husband's hogs are better bred than he is!

I do miss all of you terribly and often feel lonely and isolated up here on this mountain but the children give me little time to ruminate on such things. Please write to me again when you can, your letters bring me great joy Michael!

Your Ever Loving Sister,
Biddy

P.S. Another cannon fire! War has ended and yet it sounds like it's just beginning.

James Dunne's San Felipe Rancho lay in a fertile valley nestled between spurs of the Coast Range Mountains more than a hundred miles distance from the setting of his former city life. Stock raising took the most land and most of his time but yielded the highest profits with wheat coming in a close second. His efforts to grow cotton and tobacco failed. However, his orchards produced a dazzling year-round harvest of fruits and nuts. Grand oaks, graceful palms, stately eucalyptus and feathery pepper trees with bright red berries surrounded an expansive home garden where rows of golden marigolds were interspersed amongst a myriad of vegetables sprouting from the most arable soil California had to offer.

A few paces away stood his house. It was designed as a utilitarian building for supervising business operations and sheltering children but it lacked any architectural charisma or even the slightest evidence of a woman's touch. Army barracks had more luster. Large outdoor corridors were covered in creeping ivy, which made the structure seem more akin to a giant garden maze rather than the Spanish-style hacienda that inspired it. Bulky timber railing surrounded the second story veranda that served as a lookout point and living space in the sweltering summer months.

James Dunne could smell the pie even before he heard Sam shuffling in his silken slippers towards his office. "Another pie for you sir, is peach, this time from a Miss Farrelly. I send her on her way."

"Thank you Sam. You can eat it if you like or take it out to the men," said James as he took a moment to scratch his scalp through the thinning, rust-colored hair flecked with gray. It was much too long.

"Every young lady in county want to marry Mister James Dunne. Nobody want to marry Sam Goo." James laughed. He didn't want to marry anyone. He just wanted to raise little Jimmie, cattle and enough capital to buy even more land.

"Mister James, you look tired. You got no sleep again last night. Why you no go upstairs for lil' rest and I wake you in one hour?"

"I can't do that, too much to do, Sam. We have to leave for the Mission at four, maybe I can nap in the coach a bit."

"Yes sir. Will get everything ready to go."

The Valley's remaining Californios still hadn't taken kindly to their land being in the hands of the gringos and over the years flashpoints often erupted between the two factions. Bigger worries came from the interlopers and vagrants staking claim to isolated plots of land in an attempt to procure acreage through the murky laws of the Homestead Act.

Reliving his childhood with his father at Brittas, it had become James' practice to spend the night roaming six square leagues of his ranches in search of squatters, poachers and cattle rustlers. He had spent sleepless nights camped under oak trees with his posse of Spanish-speaking vaqueros, a brace of pistols at his side. Enduring the loss of his wife and children was one thing but the theft of his land must be prevented. He'd put his anger to good use. A meeting had been called at nearby Mission San Juan Bautista where the Valley's large landholders would confront the sheriff and county officials over enforcement of their property rights.

Catherine Murphy sat before her dressing mirror scrutinizing new tiny creases that had developed at the bridge of her nose; they looked like perfect "11"s on her 34-year-old face. She pinched her cheeks to liven them up and resorted to a little rouge for insurance. Black hair, dark eyes and olive skin pegged her for a typical Spaniard but she was Irish through and through. Black Irish. She'd come to Quebec on one of those coffin ships from County Wexford and ended up marrying into a well-heeled Western frontier family, the Murphys.

Born Catherine O'Toole she had wed Martin Murphy's savvy, shy and somewhat tubby son Bernard. Together they built a happy life on the 18,000-acre Rancho de la Polka, living in a tin house that Bernard had shipped around the Horn. The fertile Santa Clara Valley soon rewarded the young couple with its bounty of blessings including a handsome baby boy nicknamed Marty. A year later Bernard was dramatically killed aboard the side-wheel steamboat Jenny Lind when she exploded in the San Francisco Bay. A close friend and client of the Dunnes, he succumbed to his injuries in their front parlor on Kearny Street. Hailed as California's worst maritime disaster, it changed the trajectory of many lives.

The Murphy Clan encircled Catherine and Marty providing them with everything they would need to recover from the tragedy. A family with vast resources and a bevy of advisors including attorneys, bankers, clergymen, merchants and cowboys allowed the pair to concentrate on living without money worries. The Widow Murphy was a quick study, resilient and fearless. The bishop said it was her devout faith that sustained her; the astrologer said it was all in the stars. Catherine was a Leo.

Within three years of Bernard's death she had the de la Polka running smoothly with large profits. She replaced the tin house with a grand residence and became a force to be reckoned with in the rough and tumble world of California cattle ranching.

Catherine Murphy was the only woman called to the landowner meeting. The Murphys had casually mentioned the name James Dunne to her a month after Kitty's murder and practically every day since. Catherine and James hadn't seen each other for years. She wondered if he would be there as she put the finishing touches on her face, then called for the coach to bring her to San Juan Bautista.

Sheriff Kennedy called the meeting to order in a large spartan room once belonging to generations of Mission padres. It was loud. He had no gavel and was tempted to fire his pistol into the air to gain the attention of the unruly group of land barons. "Settle down men, take your seats, take your seats. Let's be civil. I call this meeting to order," the sheriff said not expecting order nor civility.

"Why don't you stop barking out orders and just do your job!" cried old man Breen in his Irish brogue.

"What do we pay our taxes for anyhow? To be ignored and unprotected?" taunted another.

"Sit down! We're not going to get anywhere with that kind of talk. I understand your predicament men, I really do. Your ranches and orchards are the financial backbone of this valley. You pay your taxes and you need representation—all the municipal protection that we can afford to give you."

"Here, here!" the crowd shouted in unison.

"But honestly we cannot patrol your places and prevent these squatters from setting up camp. We don't have the resources—"

"We don't either! It's hard enough managing the livestock and crops without having to spend all night looking for marauders!" complained James Dunne looking rested, trim and dapper.

"You can say that again Dunne! It's near impossible to watch over the ranch every night keeping track of squatters; 'course when they're caught they claim to be homesteaders. I've got more legal bills than Cornelius Vanderbilt himself!" complained the owner of 48,000 acres, Don Malarin, one of a handful of Californios who still retained ownership of the family's original Mexican land grant. "They're all lazy, terrible thieves expecting a handout."

"Why don't you just sell them a little land at a reasonable price?" A sweet feminine voice rang out from the back.

"Who said that? Oh, Mrs. Murphy," the sheriff said. Sensing a supportive beam he could lean on, "Please stand up ma'am, we'd like to hear your thought."

She rose and stood in a dignified pose, her silken black widow's weeds wrestled on the terra cotta floor.

"I face the same problems as you gentlemen and I've found a satisfactory way to deal with them. I've surveyed the ranch and set aside a strip at the South end of my tract. They are partitioned into 40-acre plots and I offer them to anyone found trying to squat on my land."

"They don't want to buy land they want to steal it!" said Don Malarin.

"Actually sir, I find that they're quiet and pacific men with families just wanting their chance at a good life. Of course they don't have enough money to buy it outright, so I have been carrying back the mortgages."

"They stand a good chance of carrying back their heads if they come sniffing around my place."

"Don Malarin, if we read the papers with any imagination we'll find you are on the wrong side of history. Most of America is made up of independent husbandmen who want to own the fields they plow, the trees they pick. Ask those poor landed gents down South in Georgia, in the Carolinas, about keeping their giant plantations running. Running without slave labor, I mean. Times are changing. We are not all greedy land sharks. Heartless. Violent.

I come from Ireland where the natural inclination of the people is to hate the gentry…with a passion they hate him. We must learn from the past, our past. We live in California! We were lucky to be in the right place at the right time and now we have more land, why, more than we ever dreamed of having. And our future success is guaranteed if we play our cards right."

The room slipped into an awkward silent. Catherine Murphy sat herself down completely satisfied with her performance.

Her pronouncement fell flatter than Santa Clara Valley itself.

After the landowners expelled their fury and the sheriff was through hemming and hawing, the meeting adjourned. James Dunne made his way over to the Widow Murphy.

"Mrs. Murphy you made your point loud and clear," offered James. "Eloquent. Passionate. Good."

"Thank you. It has worked well for me. Most pay on time. Only a few do not."

"I'm sure they'd rather owe you than cheat you out of it," he said in that wry tone he used for people he liked.

"Aye, Mr. Dunne, I have faith."

"And I have doubt. What would you say to going across the street to the saloon and we can work out our differences?'

She agreed. He was intrigued.

Although Catherine's husband died in the Dunne's front room, they were not well acquainted. For the first time in years James' broken heart skipped a beat as she addressed the landowners and at the same time, the beads of his mental abacus went clicking and clacking on their walk across the street.

"I apologize for not coming to visit you. I've become quite a solitary man," James confessed sitting upright in the tavern's sticky bentwood chair.

"It's me that should apologize. It was a terrible thing what happened to your wife and I should have been more considerate. And your boys, God bless them. This Valley loves the gossip."

"With that speech there, they're all gossipin' about you now!" Catherine giggled with all the composure of a giddy schoolgirl.

"Only a woman's perspective. You can take it or leave it." James winked and crossed over to the bar bringing himself back a whiskey and a dainty sherry for her. "What's this?" Catherine pointed to the miniature wine glass with her stubby finger poking out of from her black lace glovelette.

"Sherry."

"Mr. Dunne, if we are to toast to our new friendship we must start out on an equal footing."

"Pardon? A fine lady like you will slam back a whiskey with me?"

She smirked and her dark eyes twinkled.

"Maybe just the one."

James brought back a whiskey.

Conversation took on a bantering tone with each looking to uncover hidden meaning behind the other's quips. Tremendous volumes of information telegraphed betwixt and between them. It was clear to James that this woman looked the world straight in the eye. Smart. As a stockman he wondered about her breeding possibilities, his herd had dwindled down to unacceptable levels.

Catherine saw that James was not a middling sort of gentleman. He carried himself with a gravitas she found wildly attractive yet she could tell he was broken, which only added to his appeal.

The couple closed down the saloon and the barkeep locked the door behind them. Picking up their empty glasses he mumbled to himself under his bourbon-soaked breath, "Money, meet Money."

As American as he had become since his youth in New Orleans, his Irishness began to percolate back to the surface in middle age. James returned to the R.C. Church with a renewed faith and large cash donations. He constructed a thatched booley house on an impossibly high ridge of the San Felipe where he could look out onto 20 square miles of his ranch and contemplate his life. He ordered his cook to make Irish fare such as soda bread, boxty, barmbracks, corned beef and black pudding. He sang more. He drank more. But it was in his subconscious, where he dreamed about the next phase of his life, that he channeled the insidious maneuverings of the Irish landed gentry so repulsive to him growing up.

James Dunne was now richer than any Dunne who had ever ruled over the legendary lands of Brittas. With that achievement he felt a sovereign responsibility to ensure that wealth for future generations. As a romantic young merchant he married the boss's daughter, Kitty Grayson, for love not money. She was a docile, artistic waif that bore him five children of which only the frail and diminutive Jimmie survived. He could not gamble on his little runt building a dynasty. He needed more children. The Widow Murphy was a natural choice, a Marriage of State, so to speak, where both parties were of equal alliance, wealth and motive. Their combined land holdings totaled a staggering 40,000 acres.

Humans sorting themselves out into stratified herds like they do.

She was attractive enough, sturdy and smart but her headstrong ways might prove troublesome. Would she see things his way?

For her part Catherine was interested but had no intention of being moved around like a pawn in some man's game. The Murphys must have thought him worthy with their constant badgering over the years. She was too proud to throw herself at him and her outburst at the meeting was in no way meant as a lure. They did get on though didn't they? Those blue eyes. Handsome and svelte. Irish and Catholic. Their boys are almost the same age aren't they?

Her son needed a father and she wouldn't mind a daughter or two.

Prevailing winds of the Santa Clara Valley gently blew James and Catherine up to an altar in San Jose where inevitably, their vows were exchanged on a Tuesday. Patrick told Bridget it was too far to travel for a second wedding. Peter sent a handsome blue and white jardinière similar to ones from Brittas. It was antique, Ming dynasty and very expensive. James gave it to Sam for his room.

CHAPTER 35

Announcement on page 4 of The Daily Alta, San Francisco, Wednesday Morning, February 26, 1868

DIED

In this city, Feb. 24th, P E T E R D U N N E, (brother of James Dunne) a native of Ireland, aged 54 years. Friends and acquaintances are respectfully invited to attend the funeral this day (Wednesday), at 12 1/2 o'clock P. M., from St. Patrick's Church, Market Street, between Second and Third

Peter strolled around the park where thoughts ran in and out of his head like the scurrying squirrels before him. He appreciated the gleam from his glossy shoe against the rough gravel and marveled at the contrast of smooth versus rough. He looked up at the tall redwood trees and he was immediately taken back to the Brittas forest of his youth. What are all those Dunnes up to back there? Maybe he should visit Ireland on a grand tour of Europe? He could brag. He could show off. He could bring them a redwood sapling back as a gift to prove how colossal plants and people grow in America. Which of the General's sons was the lord now? What if his cousin Edward Meadows Dunne could see his mansion on Franklin Street? Barrister from Gray's Inn, who cares?

True, his own legal career had gone astray but he could hire the City's best lawyers on a whim if he needed. Real gentlemen don't need a career anyhow. He could afford to send his two brilliant young sons to Harvard Law School when they grew up if he wanted to. He could live out his unfulfilled dreams through them. Peter missed the intimacy once shared with James but his brother had been supplanted by Thomas Bergin, his brother-in-law. Bergin and law partner Hal McAllister had the premier firm in San Francisco and Peter was a moon pulled in their orbit. James was nothing but a narrow minded cowboy, who needs him? Ah, forget a Brittas homecoming, not worth the effort, next thought… stock investments…tomorrow's banquet at the Pacific Club…his new aubergine colored suit should be ready at Gustav's….

His mind was racing at a greater speed than usual. He puffed himself up with accolades yet there were regrets standing in the corners, typically ignored like the various aches and pains in his four and fifty body. Should he be worried about his unsettled stomach? Had his wealth made him too leisurely? Had he secured a suitable legacy in this town? Should he get a dog?

Observing the world in shades of gray was tiresome. So much to see, so many angles to examine. Peter thought too much.

He became tired with the traffic in his head and decided to walk home. He tipped his hat to a few highly-coiffed ladies who were trying to remain graceful on the slopping sidewalk before arriving back at his three-story, turreted, colonnaded, gabled and bric-à-braced mansion house, impeccably designed to his liking albeit one street off from Van Ness, the avenue of millionaires.

Inside he was met with the delightful aroma of his French chef's lamb cassoulet and the sweet sounds of his children running to greet him and for a few moments he was happy. He imbibed on a couple of gin and sugars before sitting down to supper with his family. Margaret and Peter retired up to their gilded bedroom at the usual time and after a few pages of a Jules Verne novel he drifted off to sleep before his wife snuffed out the lamp.

In the morning, unaware that his heart had been diseased for quite some time, she tried to frantically wake him but he had slid into the past by midnight.

Drawn back to the city that first welcomed them to America, Patrick and Bridget Lawler stood heartbroken on Market Street with a hundred others waiting for Peter's funeral cortège. They felt strange being back on that block.

So much was changing.

What should have been a solemn moment, when Peter Dunne's splendid casket arrived at his own funeral, was overshadowed by the chaotic, congested, noisy actions of a colossal building project next door. The procession into St. Patrick's Church was delayed while blundering workmen rolled away a long trolley of used bricks. They weren't quick about it either.

Upon finally entering the church Peter's casket was brought up to the front and the Lawlers took their seats next to Bridget's brother James and his wife Catherine. She was pregnant with their third child. 10 years had passed since the siblings had been together. They whispered cordial greetings to one another then sat back to listen to their brother be eulogized by a host of San Francisco luminaries. Peter was celebrated from behind the lectern as an intelligent, suave, erudite, capable man taken too soon from his young family. No one could disagree.

Bridget looked over to see tears streaming down James' face. She handed him her pink hanky.

"Thank you," he whispered.

"I know how hard this must be for you," she whispered back.

"For a time in my life he was my everything."

"He'll always be with you James."

"Yes, like a scar."

"Oh, hush now!"

The funeral was over quickly. No mass was said, no communion given. Bridget thought all the religiosity had been drained from the service. To her it seemed more like a civic ceremony.

It was the end of Peter and the end of St. Patrick's Church. His funeral would be the very last event held in the building before it was moved off the site.

Grander things were in store.

Gold had spurred the largest mass migration in history and put San Francisco on the map but it was silver, the less glamorous metal, that made the city shine. The various bonanzas discovered in Nevada far outweighed the capital brought in by the Gold Rush. Silver mining was an expensive operation, not the purview of the wandering lucky gold miner. It required investment by wealthy, capitalistic San Franciscans; vain and showy men who wanted their city to reflect its global status. A landmark was needed to prove its ascendancy.

After a lifetime of clamoring for recognition, of trying to be important, Peter had narrowly missed the moment in history that legitimately could not have ever happened without him. The Palace Hotel.

He helped procure the old St. Patrick's complex site when he sat on the board of the orphanage.

And he would have loved the place.

Rising seven stories above low frontier buildings, tin-roofed shanties and wooden eyesores leftover from bygone days, the gargantuan super-structure dominated the skyline of the Pacific metropolis. The massive American flag that flew from the roof could be seen from all parts of the city. A brutish display of all the power money could buy. Modern, impressive, exquisite yet foreboding from the outside, citizens renamed it the Bonanza Inn. Vertical banks of bay windows overlooking the street were designed to catch every ray of sun that cut through the fog. Unfortunately it gave off the appearance of a seven-layer prison cell-block.

Built from 24 million bricks, painted white and held together with bands of steel, it would be impervious to earthquake. 630,000 gallons of water in the basement tanks and 130,000 gallons on the rooftop were attached to automatic sprinklers in every room. The hotel would be advertised as fireproof. The Palace Hotel's harsh exterior was just a disguise, a ruse designed to intimidate from the outside while the tantalizing and beautiful lay inside.

An arched porte-cochère with a delicate fanlight honed into the giant edifice drew the guest's coach in from a frenzied New Montgomery Street into fourth dimension of splendor. Tiers of open floors with polished marble balustrades and a soaring roof of opaque glass surrounded the grand court where coaches circled in tune with the music pavilion's full orchestra.

Potted palms and exotic plants created the illusion of a tropical garden. In the magnificent lobby, behind a locomotive-sized walnut desk, stood an army of whisker-less young attachés waiting to attend to guests' every need or desire. A bank of five filigreed metal doors in the reception office painted in peach-blossom tones hid the most mesmerizing feature of the entire hotel, the rising rooms. Guests seated on a padded bench, admired themselves in mirrors while hydraulic lifts magically and silently transported them up to one of the 755 guestrooms.

The Palace's builder and mastermind Billy Ralston hired a New York City architect to visit leading American and European hotels, steal their best ideas and think up a few of new ones. No expense would be spared. At the time, California hostelries were staffed exclusively by Chinese or impudent whites, however at the Palace, American blacks would be transported from the east and trained to become the best chambermaids or porters in the business. Management believed this would help

Southerners feel at home and make the help easy to spot in a crowded hotel of light skinned people.

The bed chambers were double the size of ordinary hotels and featured fifteen-foot ceilings. Each had Carrara stone hearths handsomely carved by Italian craftsmen. Many people were introduced to in-suite water closets and basins for the very first time. Extravagant living at the Palace Hotel made it hard for the well-to-do to ever leave. Wealthy residents of the city shuttered up their Nob Hill mansions and leased suites on the top floor, preferring to be full-time guests. Other bankrupt or despondent visitors chose to go out in style, spending their last hopeless night on earth at the Palace, leaving their bodies and hotel bills unpaid in the morning.

It was a bustling city within a city and a great equalizer of men. Royal barriers required to enter Europe's palaces were abandoned and access granted to anyone who could afford the privilege. In the hotel lobby a successful shopkeeper could mingle with a senator or a German duke. A masterpiece of indulgence and the pride of San Francisco, the Palace had dwarfed every grand hotel in the world. It was San Francisco's coming-of-age gift.

As hotel guests scurried and staff fawned, neither gave a passing thought to the Herculean effort it took to actualize such a phenomenon. People often trample through life with little appreciation for the history beneath their feet. Peter Dunne knew every step of that history. Some of his methods could be questioned but it was all for the greater good of San Francisco, he would have reasoned.

But of course everything came at a price. By hook or by crook, the St. Patrick's complex had been demolished to make room for the hotel. Sadly, the eminent domain of death robbed both Peter Dunne and Billy Ralston from witnessing the fruits of their labor.

Ralston's mining and banking empires financed his dream project for years and often teetered on collapsed. Little more than a month before the hotel's grand opening, his business partner Senator William Sharon sold short his shares leaving Ralston bankrupt with all his assets transferring to Sharon. The next morning Billy Ralston waded out into the Bay waters for his daily swim and destroyed himself before he could see the impact his magnificent creation would have upon the world.

Old buildings made way for new ones and old Argonauts were vanishing into the obituary columns, leaving room for a new generation of restless San Franciscans eager to make a mark of their own.

CHAPTER 36

A letter from Lucy Rogers to Mrs. Henrietta Hardin Welch

507 Sycamore Avenue
Modesto, California

September 29, 1933

My Dear Niece,

 I forgot to include this in yesterday's letter so I will be brief.

 As you know the papers have been full of stories about Peter Francis Dunne, the famous San Francisco attorney. He was my first cousin. After Uncle Peter died, Aunt Margaret relied on her bachelor brother Thomas Bergin to help raise the three children. Mr. Bergin was quite a famous lawyer himself and had a lot to do with opening doors for Peter Francis. He spent a summer with us at the ranch but I didn't get to know him well. Too erudite for farm work! But I was great friends with his sister, Gladys. We attended boarding school together at St. Mary's in Gilroy (founded by my Uncle James and Aunt Catherine) and I was there when Gladys met her first husband at the MOST EXTRAVAGANT party in all of California's history and one I shall never forget.

 Your loving Aunt Lucy

James and Catherine Dunne enjoyed their status as co-regents of their massive cattle ranches. They made a good team and were blessed with three children of their own. Jimmie Dunne clashed with his stepmother and Marty Murphy was scared stiff of his stepfather. A blended family sounded better than it tasted. The two stepsons would be shipped off the San Felipe into a Jesuit prep school in Santa Clara.

 Uncomfortable in the classroom, Jimmie eventually went into business with Mary Donnelly's sons after her death on the San Felipe in 1877. Donnelly, Dunne & Co. would soon become one of California's predominant cattle baronies with business up and down the state. Beef came from the Valley's cattle ranches and was processed in the Donnelly &

Dunne stockyards and slaughterhouses located in Butchertown, south of their plush offices in downtown San Francisco—far away from James and Catherine but never far away from their connections or bank drafts. Jimmie Dunne was an altogether different breed from James. The father was rugged, gruff, practical. The son was slight, polished and extravagant as evidenced by his top floor suite at the Palace Hotel, his diamond jewelry and the Gainsborough in his art collection. Quick-witted and fast-talking, he inherited from Kitty his buzzing pixie energy, infectious to some, chaffing to others. Mocked as being too little to be a real cowboy he would need to settle for a being a stockman of colossal proportions.

Born to a princely estate of his own, Marty Murphy was sweet and obedient under his widowed mother's constant observation. He was beyond relieved when she diverted her focus from him to her new family with James Dunne.

Where his stepbrother was a gregarious chatterbox, always poking his nose in everyone's business, Marty preferred to put his squarely in a book. He kept to himself at school, belonged to no clubs and took no exercise. He graduated from Santa Clara College at the top of his class and received a scholarship to study law and logic in the East with the Jesuits of Georgetown.

Arriving in Washington, D.C. Marty came into his own and out of his shell. He threw himself into the scholarly vigor thrust upon him. He had an oriental fondness for oratory and wandering philosophy that left his audiences speechless. Their praise could not be too fulsome. His ethics professor put it best when he said, "Mr. Murphy was a rising young star, burning brightest right before his evaporation into darkness." Martin John Charles Murphy, one month shy of his twentieth birthday, died alone in his dormitory of a twisted bowel. He was embalmed at the college and his earthly remains, accompanied by a suitable escort, were put upon the transcontinental railroad for a journey across America. He was buried back at Gilroy in St. Mary's graveyard before his devastated mother and a crush of relatives.

Catherine Dunne's remaining link with the Murphy family was Marty and since his passing sorrow would overwhelm any chance meeting. Avoidance was better. But it would be impossible to avoid attending her former brother-in-law's 50th wedding anniversary party. The entire

Murphy clan would be there along with 5,000 or 10,000 others. Not wanting to slight anyone of an invitation, Old Man Murphy took out advertisements in Bay Area newspapers welcoming one and all to the celebration. Special trains were chartered to bring revelers to his Bay View Farm estate north of Santa Clara. Businesses closed, city governments shut down and courts adjourned all around the Bay in honor of the special day. It would be a spectacle the likes of which had never been seen in the Golden State.

Attendees came for different reasons, be it free food, free whiskey, business angling or even genuine reverence for an aging pioneer couple. James and Catherine brought their nieces Gladys Dunne and Lucy Lawler. Bridget had allowed Lucy to study at the convent school far away from Petaluma. This shindig would be a wonderfully opportune moment to introduce pretty girls to suitable bachelors from good families.

A large canvas pavilion topped with Bear Flags had been set up for special guests so the silk suited wouldn't need to rub against the bib-overalled. While the girls were in line for lemonade, the matchmakers began to talk.

"Maybe Lucy can be introduced to Willy Taaffe, his mother was a Murphy and he inherited a pretty penny," whispered Catherine into James' good ear.

"If he's that fancy he should have Gladys," shot back James.

"Oh, I don't know, she's awfully immature. Lucy is the charming one."

"Aye, but it's Gladys who's the Dunne."

"Don't be ridiculous James, Lucy's mother is your sister!"

"That Lawler blood though, I don't know. Not really the gentry class are they?"

"Thank God Bridget can't hear you."

"Dunnes are a notch above Lawlers, simple as that. None of these wealthy families in the Valley would choose a Lawler over a Dunne. All the Irish know, Dunne's the noble name."

"I see Willy over there. I'm going to introduce him to both girls and let him decide!"

James was momentarily alone to take in all the festivities. Outside of the pavilion was a gigantic raised wooden dancing platform the size of a paddock filled with a wild assortment of humanity bashing along together to Irish music. On the opposite side was an equally large pit of coals barbecuing prized beeves from the Murphy ranches. Men walked up and down the line with mops basting the meat using pitchforks to shuffle it around. Beyond that, set in a serene grove of ancient oaks, rows upon rows of tables where guest ate in shifts of 1,000.

A young mustachioed gent with slick hair parted severely down the middle approached James from behind. "Good morning Uncle!" James felt a firm hand on his shoulder and turned around to find his brother Peter's son, Peter Francis, beaming and laughing. The two vigorously shook hands.

"Your auntie is showing off your sister to prospective husbands over there," he said noticing Gladys seemed to have triumphed over Lucy for the attention of Mr. Taaffe.

"Poor fellow," Peter Francis winked.

"Did you come down from the City?" James asked.

"Came on the train. What a commotion, this is quite something."

"Can an up-and-coming attorney like you afford to take a day off?"

"Much better for my job to be here, Uncle."

"Better to know everyone than everything, eh?"

"Frankly, yes."

"Ah, your father is up in heaven smiling down on you right now. Of course you wouldn't know how close we were, would you? Like peas and carrots. For a time it seemed we shared the same brain."

"Mother said you got rich together."

"Aye, that we did, that we did. Got into some stupid fight over the war and it wasn't the same after that. Seems meaningless now."

"We learned in law school that you don't need to attend every argument you're invited to."

James laughed at his nephew's wisdom. "Your Da would like that one too. You're everything he dreamed of being."

"Thank you."

"Is Thomas Bergin here?"

"Yes, I came down on the train with him. There he is over there in that little cabal," Peter Francis said pointing to a group of distinguished-looking gentleman in the distance being served champagne from a silver tray.

"That one hombre in the middle is limping or something. Never trust a limping man would be my advice to you."

"Oh he's blind. They call him Blind Boss Buckley. He's the newest boss."

"Since I left that cesspool of a city I don't know any of the grandees anymore," griped James.

"Democrat. He runs the graft from his dank little saloon on Bush Street."

"Never heard of him. Always blind or did he go blind?"

"They say it was bad gin from his younger days."

"Blind Drunk."

"He gets a piece of every city contract. Knows what's going to be spent where and buys up land then resells it. Little certainties that he just happens to know about in advance."

"Same old story. Different crook."

"Correct! Buckley swooped in after the old boss died, now everyone has to kiss up, and pay up to him. His political machine is growing every day. To be known in San Francisco now means you have the Blind Boss' favor. You'll need that for any job or city contract. School teachers even!"

The group of men shuffled around to expose a tiny Jimmie Dunne delighting the men with some wild story and animated hand gestures.

"Jimmie!" cried James proudly. "My son in the midst of the ruling class, isn't that something?"

"Yes there's Jimmie, he's known. Then there's my other uncle, Thomas Bergin, you remember Mr. Phelan…mother said he had a liquor warehouse next to the Dunne & Company stand on Sansome. Is that true?"

"Yes of course. Come from Queen's County he did. Now he's a big banker."

"Next to Phelan is his son, James Phelan. I went to school with him. He's a chum."

"New generation coming up."

"Oh, see that handsome dandy in the blue suit? You know him surely…."

"Who's he?"

"Really Uncle?"

"Who is he?"

"Meticulous mind for the law. Worked in the best firms already. Ambitious?"

"No."

"Really? Take a good look. He's a chum too. He's on the ballot to be the new Police Court judge. He'll owe Buckley a lot of favors when he's elected. Still don't know him?"

"How would I know him?"

"He's your nephew too!"

"Your father have a son I don't know about?"

"Could be" Peter Francis chuckled, "but that man right there is Patrick and Bridget's son. For Christ's sake he was named after YOU!"

"James Lawler? I wouldn't have recognized him in a million years. Last time I saw him he was a finicky little ankle biter." The old rancher was filled with pride for the younger generation.

"Still finicky I'm afraid. Let's go over there, I'll reacquaint you."

They walked to the end of the pavilion where James winked and tipped his hat to the party's mascot, a taxidermy grizzly bear surrounded by golden poppies. He was in a playful mood, a mood that was becoming commonplace to him. Catherine had exorcised the hate from his soul. He showed his gratitude to God at daily morning mass then floated through the rest of his day like a playful banshee. Today he felt like taunting people for his own amusement. It was his prerogative.

Uncle James and Peter Francis made it over to the San Francisco contingent where lips were tightened immediately. The younger Dunne, as if presenting a friendly witness to the court, smoothly introduced his Uncle James to those who already knew him and those who didn't.

"Uncle James, you might not recognize me—"

"James Lawler of course, I'd recognize you anywhere!"

"In no time you'll be able to address him as Your Honor!" said the Blind Boss Buckley reaching out for the young counselor's shoulder.

"Your mouth to God's ear," said Uncle James feeling a bit usurped.

"This must be the famous Mr. James Dunne! Come from Ireland like my own father." Although blind he must have detected that unshakable Queen's County brogue.

"Why we're practically related," Uncle James' words dripped with sarcasm.

"I've heard you and your brother used to own half of Broadway. Just think of what all that property is worth now," said Buckley dressed in a glossy suit, shimmering like a tropical lizard.

"I'm glad I got out when I did. Not the same place anymore."

"San Francisco belongs to the people who believe in her. She may stammer and sway. She may burn down and need to be built back up but she will always endure. She will always thrive!" Buckley drew from the standard stump speech he taught his candidates. Jimmie felt a bit queasy. He knew the familiar look in his father's eyes right before he boiled over. It shook him to his core.

"Father," Jimmie said nervously, "Mr. Buckley is trying to help us with the city planners. They want to redevelop Butchertown and take out all our slaughterhouses and feed lots. I was just telling him how much Donnelly & Dunne, well, frankly, all the people of San Francisco depend upon those stockyards at the edge of town for food."

"I quite see their point. It does get rather noxious down there, wouldn't you say? The fuss is understandable. We will need considerable donations from all interested parties if we are to devise a successful campaign," Buckley warned.

Uncle James saw nothing good in the blind one. All the wickedness of the Big City personified, a downright blackmailer. "Better be cracking open that strongbox son," he quipped before turning his attention quickly to his nephew, James Lawler.

"Well, Yer 'onor, how are your parents up on Sonoma Mountain doing?"

"They seem to be all right. I was up there last month hunting. Mother has finally gotten accustomed to the isolation. She gets five newspapers delivered up to her there. Satisfies her curiosity about the world I suppose. Father still doesn't have much use for me. If I couldn't rope a steer to his liking or plow a field in an hour he'd call me his little soap bubble."

"He must be proud of you now, even graduated top of your class at St. Mary's!" Peter Francis added.

"In his own way but he keeps it to himself."

"Yeah, well, took a lot of roped steers to pay for that school now didn't it?" reminded Uncle James.

"True. My brother John has taken over most of the day-to-day operations of the ranch but Father is still the King."

"I've only known him to be King," said James in a sincere moment of sentimentality and guilt for his earlier bashing of the Lawler name.

"We've got much preparation to do if we are to land him on the bench," Boss Buckley said taking back the lead of the conversation, fumbling in his darkness until he found his young protégé's cheek to squeeze. "They say he is the handsomest man in San Francisco. I'll have to take their word for it," he chuckled. The mastermind always joked about his blindness when he felt the need to look harmless.

"Do you really feel qualified to stand in judgment of another man's life?" asked Uncle James.

"I am thirty years old already and—"

"He is more than qualified to dole out justice. Half the courtroom won't like his decisions either way," said Buckley, "I'm sure he'll always come down on the correct side."

"As long as he's not being thrown," added Uncle James.

"Sir, you have not been a citizen of San Francisco for quite some time. Back in your day I am sure it was full of corruption and inefficiency. But today every cog of city government runs smoothly and fairly," said Buckley.

"With a sufficient amount of grease," said Uncle James.

"You are most ill-mannered for a gentleman, Mr. Dunne."

"Ah, see, I am no gentleman."

"Your son and nephews standing here still have much invested in San Francisco and am certain would appreciate you showing a little courtesy to the man who could help them achieve their dreams."

"It's true, I haven't lived in that dung heap for a long time but nothing has changed. In my day the big boss was David Broderick. He thought he could part the Red Sea just as you do now. Y' know what happened to him, at dawn he was shot at ten paces."

"Uncle James, please," pleaded the nephews in unison.

"Take me away. Let us dispense with this Barbarian," instructed the Blind Boss as he reached out for an arm to guide him. His entire entourage left James Dunne alone chomping on a cigar. His son and nephews did not dare turn around or so much as wink in James' direction fearful Buckley would hear their necks squeak against their starched collars or their eyelashes flutter.

CHAPTER 37

A yellowing letter found wedged into a history book, addressed to Patrick Lawler from Sister Frances McEnnis, Superioress of the San Francisco Catholic Orphan Asylum

October 2, 1875
PLEASE DELIVER TO MR. PATRICK LAWLER, PETALUMA, VALLEJO TOWNSHIP, SONOMA COUNTY UPON MY DEATH.—S.F.M.

To My Dear Mr. Lawler—

I have just returned from a visit to the Palace Hotel & while I am awed at such a phenomenal accomplishment I am overwhelmed with guilt for my role in deceiving you. As an act of contrition, I wish to explain myself & leave it in God's hands if you shall ever receive this letter or not.

The 25-year lease you signed on the St. Patrick's dairy was solid & unbreakable. It was the one sticking point to selling the orphanage & church property to Mr. Ralston who developed the hotel. Mr. Peter Dunne was Chairman of the Orphanage Board at the time & said you had purchased your Sonoma County ranch. He told me you were only keeping the dairy open to supply milk & butter for the orphans & you were secretly hoping to be let out of your lease. He said you'd also put up a fuss but that I must be firm. He would donate $1000 to build a new orphanage elsewhere if I could convince you to give up your lease. I played along—fooling myself into thinking I was doing you a favor but I am an intelligent woman & knew better. I smelled a rat and kept quiet about it. You must have thought I was an ogre that day when you finally comported to my terms.

If this letter ever finds its way to you—I humbly beg your forgiveness —as St. Matthew professed— "If you forgive men their trespasses, your heavenly Father will also forgive you."

Most Sincerely,
Sister Frances

Weeks and months and years could go by at the Lawler Ranch without any break in the prosaic monotony of farm life. This day was different.

Bridget cherished her mornings before the ranch came to life. Dawn breaking over Sonoma Mountain always gave her a sense of peace and it was usually her favorite moment of the day. It was lambing season. Patrick, her son John and a few of the hired hands were sent out to the fields early with buttermilk biscuits while three granddaughters were fast asleep upstairs. She puttered a bit in the garden, as was her habit. Bothersome weeds had invaded the roses again. Her backbone was 70 years old and strong but rebelled when it came to tasks like weeding. Maybe she could get the granddaughters rousted later to help.

A profusion of daffodils were dancing unnoticed beneath the windows of her white clapboard farmhouse. Better to bring them inside where they'd get the attention they so wantonly craved. She pulled scissors from her apron and carefully snipped flowers that were not yet in full bloom. She chose more white ones than yellow. Approaching the back of the house with her bouquet she reached for the door's latch but it was ajar. She'd left through the front one. That's odd. Turning into the kitchen she laid her flowers on the gleaming copper countertop then heard a muffled scream from upstairs. She was beset with that cold, clammy feeling of fear.

She went to Patrick's desk drawer and pulled out his long six-shooter then bolted down the checkered floor and up the hall stairs. Not good. Not good. Not good, repeated in her head with each step of the stairs. The scissors in her apron pocket swung wildly to and fro. Silence. Which room? Susanne's room. Bridget twisted the knob and stepped in. Her thirteen-year-old granddaughter was at the foot of her bed with a knife thrust up against her throat.

"Augie, just what do you think you're doing?" Bridget asked, disguising her fright in a calm voice. But she was holding a pistol in her hand.

"Take one more step and I'll rip her," said Augie, one of the new young hired hands. Bridget noticed the neck of Susanne's nightshirt had been torn open, exposing her tender white shoulder.

"It's OK, it' OK. You best be careful with that knife Mr. Augie," Bridget said.

"Stay where you are!" Augie was shaking. "Move over to that corner now!" He pulled Susanne closer to him from behind.

"Now Mr. Augie, I know you don't want to hurt her. Just let her be and leave. Just go."

"Get out of my way, old lady!" Bridget stood aghast at the insult but moved further into the corner.

Augie started to shuffle away from the window towards the door.

"OK, I'm way over here now, see, you can let her go." He held Susanne even tighter. "I moved out of your way. Let her go." Her soothing plea was being ignored so Bridget raised the revolver, squeezed the trigger and blasted out the window beside him shooting a hole clean through the white lace curtain. Susanne screamed. Smoke filled the bedroom and glass crashed to the floor. Augie didn't flinch. He inched Susanne even closer to the door.

"I'm leavin' but you stay here."

"Fine Augie, let her go now."

"After I get outside." He and his captive shifted closer to the door frame.

Bridget backed up against the wall to give him access and her a little shooting distance. Her gun was now pointed directly at his head. Why wasn't he running? He has that knife still. I'm going to have to shoot him aren't I? Dear Lord. The idea made her snap!

Well-bred gentlelady, Bridget Lawler screamed at the top of her lungs, "You little scum bastard! Let her go right now or I'm gonna blow your God-dammed brains all over that fucking wall!" She fired off another round right next to Augie's head. He panicked and threw Susanne into Bridget, knocking both of them to the floor. The pistol fell under the bed.

Augie started for the stairs where he was met by Patrick who grabbed him by the shirt collar and belt loop then threw him down a flight of stairs with the ease he tossed a lamb into Cooper's dip. John took over at the bottom. Beating the molester about the face until he was unconscious.

John dragged him outside to continue the treatment.

That morning all the hired hands were rounded up, their belongings pulled from the bunkhouse and taken yonder to the Steamer Gold landing for the first boat out of Petaluma. Patrick and John waited with guns drawn to witness them leave. They were pretty sure Augie was still alive, but barely.

Bridget had been shaken badly by the episode and found it difficult to function for the rest of the day, ranch work was piling up but it would have to wait. The remainder of the day was spent tending to Susanne who assured her nothing had happened, she was rescued just in the nick of time.

Finally with a chance to rest, Bridget sat at the head of the dining room table in Patrick's chair, the one with the arms and the lion head finials. Her third cup of coffee had a wee whiskey additive. Her husband came into the room, she rose to her feet and he embraced her for the first time since the scuffle.

"Horrible, horrible, horrible," was all Bridget could muster.

"There, there my love, you prevented a tragedy. Suzanne still has the ringing in her ears but that's all. You saved her. You are a hero, my little bitty Biddy."

"I was pretty brave wasn't I?"

"Aye, a Celtic tigress you are!" said a bemused Patrick.

"I thought I was going to have to kill him."

"You did the right thing."

"I don't know."

"But I heard you."

"What do you mean?"

"Swearin' like a sailor."

"I don't remember that—"

"Oh yes, it was quite something."

"Don't remember."

"When we first met you wouldn't say shit if you had a mouthful, now look!"

"Living up here in this wilderness took all the lady out of me."

The two relived their eventful day and found humor in the darkest places. They laughed and were relaxed until the postman came up to the door right before sunset. He handed Patrick a stack of mail with a small letter containing an unexploded bomb folded neatly inside.

Sitting back at the table, Patrick shifted through invoices and bank notices but stopped when he came to the letter from old Sister Frances who he knew to be dead. Intrigued he chose to open it first. His eyes darted back and forth as he read the letter.

"Who is that from? Patrick. Who wrote that?" Bridget asked after seeing that furrowed brow her husband wore in times of distress. He dropped it on the table as if he'd handled something contaminated. He couldn't hear her. He couldn't hear anything except a strange sloshing sound, ocean waves in his head. And the words that splashed through his brain.

Stupidity! Betrayal! Dunnes! Fool! Serf! Vengeance!

Patrick slammed his fist onto the table causing a single white daffodil to fall from its vase. He pushed himself back from the table, stood up and started his rant:

"YOU! It, your, it was your brother! And his Pacific Club snakes! They played, manipulated me like a child. A toy. Argh!"

"What now?" Bridget said as she read through the letter, bristling at her brother's deceit.

"They were land speculators and they speculated that your husband was an idiot!"

"Calm down." She stuffed the letter in her apron.

"I will not calm down! I won't. I can't get that dairy back now can I? Built over by some golden palace."

"But Patrick you haven't thought about that dairy in years. You saw it demolished there that day of Peter's funeral. Look at you now, you're a leading citizen of this county. You're not just a milk and butter man anymore, you're a capitalist." She reached for his hand. "Why you're one of the biggest tax payers in Sonoma County! The townspeople love you. You give to the Church, you loan money to every Tom, Dick and Harry...you hire any derelict that comes wandering onto this ranch. You're much bigger than—"

"Don't you see woman?" He pulled away. "They thought me an imbecile. A clodhopper! Your brothers, both of them...they've always treated me like a dullard from Kildare. I know. Oh, I know. This kind of betrayal is out of the Bible! All of youse think the Lawlers are simpletons and I proved you right didn't I? They probably orchestrated our whole move out of the city. Don't you see it?"

Bridget flashed on a memory of Peter handing her the handbill about Vallejo's ranch at Kitty's wake. She stopped herself from remembering anything further. "Now listen here Patrick, you're working yourself up into a lather for nothing. That old woman had a guilty conscience towards the end of her life, she just wanted to release herself. That letter is almost ten years old. She should've gone to her grave with—"

"She wanted me to know, she wanted me to know what a ridiculous halfwit I am. A laughing stock."

"Patrick, you're as rich as Croesus! Who's laughing now? Let it go, you'll have a heart attack."

Seething, Patrick transformed into the backwoods Irish peasant they accused him of being, helpless in the face of an oppressive authority, equipped with the mystic's only weapon, a hex summoned from the netherworld.

He went into an eerie trance like an ancient pishogue mumbling sinister-sounding Gaelic, "*Loscadh is dó ort, Loscadh is dó ort, Loscadh is dó ort.*" He repeated the phrase louder and louder.

"Don't you do it, you will not, no, no, do not bring the devil into my house!" Bridget shouted.

"May that Palace of Sin, built on my milk ranch, on the backs of thirsty orphans and the Church of St. Patrick be damned! May it be destroyed by God himself…I curse it, I curse it, curse it!"

By this time the granddaughters were watching Patrick's hysterics from the hallway, snickering at his antics and funny words. He glanced over at them and quickly wriggled back into his body. Embarrassed by his behavior he settled down, went over and patted their heads then laughed, trying his hardest to put them at ease.

The old couple ended their eventful day by a glowing hearth in their warm, comfortable home where Bridget finished her needlepoint and Patrick finished the whiskey.

CHAPTER 38

Fragment of letter from Lucy Rogers to Henrietta Welch

[September 1, 1930]

After I married I stayed in Petaluma. My husband had various businesses around town. I kept an eye on my parents who were getting up in years but still ran the ranch with help from brother John. He'd purchased several other smaller ranches and a big parcel near downtown Petaluma where he was building houses to rent on Bassett Street. My father loved that the townspeople nicknamed the district "Lawlerville."

My other brothers—Denny and James—were down in San Francisco involved with the comings and goings of city life. Neither one of them much cared for ranching—too humdrum. As all of us Lawler children began to marry off and have our own families we sadly drifted apart—just like the Dunnes I suppose. It's funny, even though we all share the same blood it is truly astonishing how different we all became.

Denny Lawler was the oldest of Patrick's five sons. In looks he favored the Dunnes, ruddy complexion, red kinky hair and built like an ox. He wasn't the handsome one or the smart one or the ambitious one—he was the rebellious one. Loathing the dairy business, he married at 22 to avoid the Civil War draft and divorced a few years later after his young daughter died in a house fire. His drunken wife lay passed out in an adjoining alleyway. He couldn't stomach his overbearing father but left his young son, known to the family as J.P., at the Petaluma rancho while he shifted from pillar to post in search of steady employment finding only bar fights, thievery and whores. Finally landing in a profession, like many of his fellow Irishers, where he could be immersed in vice every day. Denny became a San Francisco cop.

Since he was in his freshly pressed Special Police Officer uniform he attempted to enter through the north portico of City Hall, reserved for elites only, but he was stopped by a fellow officer, "Gallant try, Lawler, go around."

Set on a triangular plot of land fronting the west end of Market Street, once home to a cemetery, San Francisco's new City Hall was an elaborate collection of civic institutions dressed up in the Second Empire, French style. The enormous structure rivaled the Palace Hotel for best-of-show. It was a never-ending building project and brokered by city officials on the take through Blind Boss Buckley. He divvied the work out to a jumble of independent contractors willing to make the necessary payoffs. A boondoggle of colossal proportions, no one bureaucrat was tasked with integrating all the work so floors didn't align between rooms, chimneys didn't draw, gas and sewer pipes were all misconnected giving the entire complex a sulfuric smell, the stench of corruption.

Denny waited on a bench outside Police Court Judge Lawler's office below a glossy black sign bearing His Honor's name and a gold painted manicule that pointed to his door. The policeman nervously adjusted his badge waiting for his younger brother to retrieve him. He wondered how hard the reprimand would sting this time.

"Come in, sorry to keep you," said the Judge before he took a quick peek down the hall to see who might have witnessed Denny waiting around. The Judge hung his robe on a bentwood hat tree in the corner of his finely appointed, dark and smoky chamber adjacent to his courtroom. Denny removed a stack of law books from a side chair. He wedging his large frame into the dainty seat and waited to hear what his brother had to say. "We've got trouble," the Judge continued, "more specifically, you've got trouble."

"I didn't do anything wrong," protested Denny.

"Fancy that, spoken like a true criminal," noted the caustic judge.

"I haven't!"

"You are being brought before the Police Commission yet again for malfeasance. I can't get you out of it this time. You're going to trial."

"Not that Annie Blane whore?"

"Denny. I shoe-horned you into a desirable Barbary Coast beat with your Captain. The most profitable route in town. I know you get protection money from saloons, the Chink gambling houses, the Tong whorehouses, the white brothels and that's not enough? Now you're fleecing the girls themselves?"

"No. Just gettin' my due and proper."

The Judge rifled through some papers, his elegant gold and ruby pinky ring twinkling in the light. Annoyed beyond belief by his brother's greed he put on his reading glasses and summed up the complaint. "One Annie Blane claims you extorted her for $1 a week and when she didn't pay you, let's see, you loitered around her door, blockading it, scaring off her customers."

"But that's—"

"Her claim is corroborated by one Katie Brown who says you do the same thing to her and several others on Waverly and Sacramento."

"Another whore—"

"Of course they're whores you pinhead, that's the point!"

"Now what?" Denny was getting a little worried.

"A public tribunal before the commission. Newspapers. Gossip. Bad. Bad. Bad. I'm coming up for election again and this hits me at the worst time."

"I apologize," said Denny.

"Quite useless to me, Officer. Do you understand how exasperating this is? I can only hope you get a little rap on the wrist from the fellas and it goes away. Even so, I'm going to have to call in favors I'd rather use for something more important."

"Maybe I should have just hauled those skanks in—"

"I answer not only to the people but a lot of other people you know nothing about. These men don't like this kind of publicity. One nod from them I'm out."

"Yes, I know."

"Don't be a money-grubbing fool. I can shut down your little racket toot sweet, have you put back to an honest beat tomorrow. Maybe that's the answer."

"No, no. I know, I'm sorry." As he was being berated he couldn't help but be jealous of his baby brother's position of power, his gravitas and his elegant mannerisms. Plus, he was just so damn good-looking. Flawless, like the man was carved out from a bar of soap. All around the City they were wondering why Judge Lawler wasn't married yet. Railroad barons, silver kings and politicians threw their willing daughters at his feet to no avail. He was wed to the law. Denny needed to change the subject.

"Let's worry about the commission later. Why don't you come out tonight and relax?"

"I have too much going on and a big case starting Monday," the Judge said as he rifled through some papers indicating the meeting was over.

"OK. Have some fun tonight and work through the weekend."

"I don't know."

"Meet me at Fong's, say 9 o'clock."

"I guess."

"Dress down, you always look like some Nob Hill millionaire. Be sly, no show."

"I'm taking advice from a sly constables who can't even shake down a prostitute properly."

Denny shook hands with the Judge and headed down to police headquarters in the basement. In the hallway he spotted his cousin Peter Francis Dunne walking briskly into court before removing his black bowler. Over the years Denny had been ignored so many times by the auspicious barrister that all his salutations ceased. Mister Dunne Esquire represented society matrons, banking heirs and San Francisco's biggest business concerns. The snob's north entrance was built for the likes of Peter Francis Dunne.

Since 1849 a steady stream of humanity from the Seven Seas had washed ashore in San Francisco. Some stayed for a long time, others only for a good time. The West's most famous city was everything eastern ones were never allowed to be. After mariners reached the docks they jumped ship and headed up Broadway, once home to warehouses and commission merchants, now a decadent playground for merrymakers and reprobates. Nicknamed the Barbary Coast by sailors after a notorious pirate's lair in North Africa, men could find whatever inebriant or entertainment suited their fancy. For more exotic fare a few blocks up, the siren's song of Chinatown called, offering whatever the Barbary Coast lacked.

At the appointed time, Officer Lawler, on his nightly patrols, met his brother at Fong's nondescript import-export shop fronting Pacific Street. The Judge had dressed modestly without his usual sheen. As soon as they entered, James was assaulted by the gamy, sour smells of Chinatown; a reminder that he was in another world, a faraway place where he could shatter the everyday norms of his life without consequence.

Mr. Fong was the head of an organization of entrepreneurial merchants known as The Six Companies. In addition to his bevy of businesses, he controlled all the Fan-Tan gambling joints. Nothing happened in Chinatown without his consent. It was a sign of much respect that he met with the Judge he knew only as Mr. Q personally, bowing deeply. Fong would be Mr. Q's escort.

While Mr. Q was adjusting to his surroundings the proprietor slipped Officer Lawler some silver before he stepped back out to his beat. Mr. Q did not acknowledge the policeman's departure but noticed the payoff. Fong passed significant sums to cops in protection money.

Fong and the client disappeared behind a drape festooned with golden dragons. In the darkness they passed through a narrow passage and up a 24-inch wide flight of flimsy steps. Stacks of wooden crates emblazoned with undecipherable Chinese chops filled the top floor creating a tight maze through which they wound around causing rats to scurry in all directions.

Fong waiting for Mr. Q to catch up then continued to the back where a large window was open to the outside. The two crossed through the window over a plank precariously perched above Bartlett Alley, a notorious home to brothels and opium dens. They flittered into a small factory building. Rows of tiny barefooted old women were noisily working sewing machines, smoking, coughing, spitting. Dust and lint filled the air as the two continued their journey down another flight of stairs, hopping over fabric and coils of ropes that blocked their path.

A menacing looking Tong gangster dressed in black and red, arms folded, stood in front of an iron door. The exposed dagger wedged in his sash emitted a silent warning. Fong spouted off some Chinese password and the door opened into a darkened pit. Hand gestures and facial expressions broke through the language barrier. Fong handed Mr. Q his own lantern motioning him to move onward. They slowly descended a rickety ladder. Somewhere below the helter-skelter streets of Chinatown was an oasis of calm and earthly pleasures known to only a few as Alphabet House.

A Moorish arch covered in green and blue mosaic tile had two flaming torches mounted outside. A petite Asian beauty with large almond eyes opened the elaborately carved teak door then looked down as the men passed by. The expansive room was bathed in a soft pinkish glow from paper lanterns hanging below lacquered red beams crisscrossing the low ceiling. Strains of a muffled Bach sonata sprang from the teeth of a large ivory inlaid music box on the floor. A mix of patchouli incense or sweet opium, Mr. Q couldn't decipher the difference anymore, made the air heavy and intoxicating. He hadn't visited in several weeks. He saw a few familiar faces but not the ones he was hoping to find.

Membership to Alphabet House was restricted to just 24 men from California's upper crust families or self-made individuals of wealth and privilege who had everything to lose if secrets from the club were ever divulged. These 24 formed a circular firing squad of sorts. One indiscretion or stray word would trigger mutual destruction for all.

Fong brought Mr. Q into one of the antechambers. He stuck his head through the thick beaded curtain and found a young man, slight of form with a military-style haircut on a rattan mat wedged between silk and satin pillows.

A moment passed. Mr. Q nodded and Fong left them to their night of bliss and buggery.

CHAPTER 39

Front page article in the *San Francisco Call*

RICH PLAN FOR LAWYER PETER DUNNE
Named as Chief Counsel of Southern Pacific.

Peter F. Dunne, the well-known attorney, has been appointed as chief counsel of the law department for the Southern Pacific Railroad, and will assume the duties of his important office next month.

Dunne is one of the most successful young attorneys on the Pacific Coast and one of the best-known professionals in the United States. He has been involved in some of California's thorniest cases, thenceforth his reputation and income grew apace. He was specifically chosen for his substantial settlements in damage suits brought against large institutions and he will now go on the defensive for the railroad.

A native son of San Francisco, his father Peter Dunne was one of the vigorous and admirable characters who made history in the early days of California. He was a merchant of considerable means, the owner of several spacious warehouses and an extensive landowner. Mr. Thomas I. Bergin, of the famous firm of McAllister & Bergin, is an uncle and was a guiding light for young Peter Francis.

Peter F. Dunne will devote his time to the duties of his new appointment but he will not entirely relinquish all private practice. He will attend to a few important cases outside of the railroad work when time will permit him to do so. Mr. Dunne remains in his beautifully appointed offices at No. 310 Pine Street, the walls of which are lined with accolades and proclamations from his exciting career.

Morning.

The Judge looked forward to reading the newspaper over strong coffee and searching for his name amongst court cases from the previous day. More public record than public adulation, Police Court No. 2 Judge James Lawler was set in type for everyone to see on a daily basis. Dear readers took perverted pleasure in seeing who got arrested, who was sentenced and who was granted divorces. Gossipy reports from Judge Lawler's courtroom provided serialized entertainment for those who couldn't attend the theater.

For his services he was paid $4,000 a year, a goodly sum, but nothing close to the payments he took on the side from cautious counselors insuring their clients received bail or not-guilty verdicts. Duly proud, he had been elected three times to the bench and all chicanery avoided detection.

He felt a proper success, this servant of the people. Today was his birthday. How irksome was it then to see this glowing article about his cousin? On the front page? With a line engraving of that smug mug to boot? "La-dee-dah, St. Peter," grumble, grumble, "most lawyers have clients, you have patrons!" the Judge mumbled to himself as he reread the article a third time. The Judge's ink was all matter-of-fact but Peter Francis Dunne was treated like a glamorous celebrity, a legal legend. Brooding and jealous, his morning had turned sour.

"Why don't you make yourself useful and get me another cup of coffee?" he called out to the shirtless young man who was sharing his suite of rooms at the American Exchange Hotel.

"Yes, yer 'oner, sir," said the bratty, sleepy-eyed youth as he got up and poured from the elegant silver pot.

"Why are you still here by the way? Shouldn't you be at work already?" asked the Judge, still perusing the paper.

"Nope, I quit yesterday. They don't know what they're doing. Plus, it stinks to high heaven in there." He slung his lanky body back onto the settee and dangled his legs off an arm.

"J.P. you can't just give a job a week and skedaddle. Bookbinding of all things. How hard could it be? I found you that one, you get the next one."

"Not sure about that one sir, working is for morons."

"Then you're not rooming here. I promised my brother you could stay if you had a job. No job, no room."

J.P. was Denny's son from his first marriage. Patrick and Bridget tried their best with the incorrigible lad up on the ranch but were just too old and too tired of his ways. No help at all on the ranch that called for a lot of it, he was sent back down to live with Denny' new family. Officer Lawler was on his beat all night while J.P. sat around all day upsetting the household. In a last-ditch effort he was shuffled off to his uncle for reformation. It wasn't working. A saloon habit was firmly fixed about him.

No one dupes the Judge.

"Going down to Abbott's saloon tonight. Maybe I'll pick up some work."

Judge Lawler removed himself from the table, neatly folded his napkin over the plate and finished putting on his cuff links. Glancing in the mirror he smoothed his broom moustache of stray toast crumbs. On his way out he invited J.P. to leave, "Sorry son, you knew the agreement. Pack up and be gone by the time I get back tonight. Good luck to you and your endeavors in the liquor industry." He dealt out the decree as bluntly as he sentenced criminals to jail.

J.P. wasn't upset, he had expected his eviction, accustomed as he was to the life of a tumbleweed. The Lawler family, as influential as it was, would be no influence on him. He felt no need to worry about the future. He liked being shiftless.

In no big hurry to vacate the premises, J.P. took his own sweet time. Eventually he packed-up his meagre belongings. On his way out he sat down to a scrumptious breakfast in the hotel's restaurant, signed the bill off to his uncle's room and blew out onto Sansome Street.

That evening the Tivoli Opera house was filled with San Francisco's foremost barristers, bureaucrats, one Blind Boss Buckley and some of his lambs. They had gathered to fete the celebrated jurist, James Lawler. After a performance of The Widow O'Brien a fellow judge called Hornblower began the toasts:

> "Judge Lawler, I am both glad and sorry to have been called upon to be the first to congratulate you. I am glad because of the honor I feel in carrying out their wishes but sorry that someone more able of the gentlemen sitting at this table was not chosen in my place. Your position as a Police Court judge is one of the highest importance; it is the portal of justice and is a position which taxes the logical ability, the integrity and temper of a man occupying such a position to the utmost. The dark side of human nature has its ugly side continually turned toward you, and when, on an occasion like this, you are able to meet your friends at the festive board, they trust that you will feel the pleasure of basking in the happier light of human nature and seeing those around who trust in and admire the

way in which you have conducted your office. We often hear of the ingratitude of republics, but you at least, can, after being three times elected to the position you now so honorably fill, say that to this rule, as to all others, there is an exception. Permit me now in the name of the men here present, to hand you this token of our esteem and confidence and, whilst presenting it, to wish that many happy years of life may find you ever surrounded by sincere friends."

Judge Lawler was then given a massive gold hunting-case stopwatch bearing the initials "J.L." in dazzling diamonds. The adulation brought a tear to his eye and he had forgotten all about the glowing tribute his cousin had received in the morning paper. A validation from his peers.

Several other capital speeches followed topped off with warm thanks from the Judge who pledged to continue meting out impartial justice and to free himself from outside influence. The roomful of influencers raised their glasses high in accord. Dinner was served.

A little before midnight the birthday party ended and the honorable judge became Mr. Q once again in the subterranean chambers of Alphabet House. However famous he was above ground, below the streets of Chinatown he was anonymous, incognito. A generous Mr. Fong paraded a number of prospects before him. He was pickier than normal. Tonight he deserved something special. He eventually chose a visiting young Latin lad who was a guest of Mr. S. To maintain secrecy very few words were ever exchanged at Alphabet House but Mr. Q noticed an anchor tattoo with the words *Vencer o Morir* on the chest of his conquest and believed him to be a mariner of some kind, perhaps from South America.

Afterward, they drifted off on a cloud of opium vapors.

Dawn was breaking over the City and Mr. Q made his way back to his hotel rooms, collapsing onto his bed after tossing his tailored suit on a side chair. Opium always made his dreams so romantic, so euphoric. Almost as if his condition could be normalized and he could be who he truly was.

But he did eventually wake up, albeit three o'clock in the afternoon. He laid in bed for a few minutes reliving his night of pleasure and the double life he was leading. It was surprising how he could push that part to the back. Compartmentalizing the crimes of his accused helped him survive to the next day in court. Ignoring his own truths helped him survive the next day of life.

Groggy and grumpy, he stumbled from his bed noticing the entry door was ajar. Did he even close it? Was he that affected? Panicked, Judge Lawler surveyed the room. His birthday watch was missing. His diamond stickpin gone. Gold and wallet gone. Check book nowhere to be found. Police were called in for a thorough examination to which the Judge withheld superfluous details.

The next morning his name appeared as usual in the newspapers but this time above the fold with a headline that read "Judge Lawler Looted. Robbed of $700-800 in Jewelry and Money."

Bigger difficulties would follow.

CHAPTER 40

Fragment of letter from Lucy Rogers to Henrietta Welch

[September 1, 1930]

I believe that I forgot to mention that my father's family played a part in British history. His first cousin, "Honest Patt" Lalor of Tenakill House— where my parents met for the first time—became a member of the British Parliament. "Honest" Patt Lalor had a son Peter who was educated and graduated from Trinity College.

This Peter Lawler went to Australia to make his fortune in the mines about the same time our family left Ireland. Peter led the miners in what came to be known as The Eureka Stockade Rebellion against the government that oppressed them. There was a bounty on his head. He became a hero of sorts then a politician. He filled every office of honor as follows— In 1855 was elected a member of the first Legislative Council of Victoria and on two occasions served the colony as Minister of the Crown. In 1880 he was finally elected Speaker of the House where he presided over four consecutive parliaments being regarded as the finest Speaker that ever held such office in Australia. He twice declined knighthood and when he resigned from office, the Government offered him £4,000. After his wife passed away (who was a Dunne and related to Mother) he retired and sailed to San Francisco hoping to restore his health.

I tell you all of this because I actually MET HIM when he made it up to the Petaluma Ranch for a visit. We were much impressed. He talked of Melbourne, Australia and how it was so like San Francisco. I remember him being a giant man of enormous presence despite his lack of an arm—which he gallantly lost in battle against the police.

The people of Australia idolized Peter Lalor. In the Parliament House today they have a statue of him, and also one in the Public Park. I have a book published there that tells all of these particulars and of his life in Australia. In England he is known as the First Commoner.

Bridget brought out a basket of freshly baked gingerbread cookies to a table under the back portico where her husband waited. It was Sunday. Carefully trained pink and yellow climbing roses battled for lattice space with the English honeysuckle and jasmine. The roses were winning. The stars and stripes shimmied on a pole. Gurgles and splashes from the stream were in perfect harmony with the birdsong. Patrick poured tea. Brilliant sunlight illuminated the Petaluma Valley beneath them. They had raised their children in this spacious country house that now felt a little too large and little too lonely without them. Bridget feared both she and the house had faded into drabness together. An unexpected letter from Patrick's long-lost Australian cousin announcing his visit had arrived, invigorating the couple's outlook.

"There's so much to do," said Bridget. "The entire place needs paint, the walkways are overgrown and this oak tree is ruining the view." She pointed and nagged. Patrick sipped his tea and chewed on a cookie.

"I've never tried impressing a soul and I'm not startin' now." He said between bites.

"Patrick! Your cousin is coming! He's an Australian patriot! He's famous. I've read about him in the London papers for years. You can't have him up here with the place looking like this. He's used to refinement. Luxury."

"Bridget, you've a lovely home. Everyone says so. It's fine. Don't fret. Peter Lalor was raised in a broken down old house with a caved-in roof and bricked up windows, for God's sake." Patrick removed his hat and slid his hand over the top of his head, now bald as a cucumber.

"I'm making a detailed list and if you won't do it for me I'll hire it out. We have a couple months still."

"Very well, I'll not argue. Why don't you come here, sit closer to me and rest awhile. Let's just be together for a few."

"You old fool, what are you after? Maybe just a minute, I'm going to go after those roses next." She sat beside Patrick and took some tea. She tasted a corner of her perfectly baked cookie and didn't think it was sweet enough. She took note of the rusty arm on an iron chair. As for Bridget herself, she had a bent back, her skin was weathered and her famous red hair had turned snow white. A gentle breeze brought a familiar unruly lock onto her creased forehead. Patrick reached over and tucked it back up in for her.

"I've decided this is the most beautiful place on earth and you, dear, are its most beautiful creature," Patrick proclaimed.

"Do you have whiskey stashed away in some tree trunk?"

"No, no, I mean it Biddy. I love you. Thank you for marrying me. My life has been everything I could have ever wanted and then some. I am content. Content with our overgrown roses, our shabby shack and our ungrateful children."

"Well, I suppose we've done well enough." Bridget had suddenly become quite compliant with Patrick's plea to relax and she laid back and loosened up under the warm California sun.

Until she heard a gunshot and spilled tea all down her front.

"James!" she yelled.

Across the stream they could see Judge Lawler outfitted in elegant English-style hunting tweeds emerging from the woods with a fistful of dead rabbits. He had taken a run up on the train to inhale some pure country air and expunge from his lungs the foul, dust-laden atmosphere of his court. He also had news to share with his parents.

Patrick beckoned him over. "Come have some tea but leave those dead varmints there."

"You look tired son, are you all right?" asked his mother.

"Do you have permission to hunt on his Lordship's estate?" Patrick asked in an English accent as James took a seat on the rusty chair.

"City life. Maybe I could just hang it all and come here to live again," James wondered aloud.

"A little soap bubble like you would pop if you had to do half the work I do, come to your senses now," said Patrick.

"What are you talking about, I did it all the years I lived here."

"Not very well."

James laughed a little. "Don't remind me."

"You have to use your mind, James. Just how you're made. Nothing wrong with that! This place is no good for anyone with a curious mind," Bridget said bouncing her head around for emphasis. Patrick gave her a scowl. "Well, it's true. Now, tell us the latest excitement in the City."

"Actually there is some."

"Do tell." Bridget wanted all the gossip like everyone else.

"It's ugly."

"Go on."

"J.P. has been arrested."

"Oh no, why, where, what happened?" asked a shaken Bridget.

"He was passing fictitious checks all around town."

"Why that little weasel," Patrick chimed in.

"And he forged my name to all of them."

"Oh James," Bridget held onto her son's hand.

"It's going to be in all the papers. Can't be stopped. I'm up for re-election and this comes out. Last time it was Denny's troubles. Those two—"

"Sorry son," Patrick and Bridget said in unison.

"Worse, he's the one who broke in and stole my watch and jewelry. Been slowly pawning the stuff off to live the high life."

"Ruining the family name just in time for Peter Lalor's visit. How could he? Shameful." Bridget seethed.

"I can't help him. I won't help him. In fact, I'd prosecute him myself if I could. He'll go to prison. He will. San Quentin most likely."

"He'll come out a career criminal then. Yep. What he doesn't know now he'll learn in there. Too bad…but he's no good. No good at all. We gave him plenty of chances. Even as a wee one he was trouble. You know he once told me I was a sap for working so hard at my age. He said that to me! That's when I booted him out. Quick-like," said Patrick abruptly getting up and disappearing.

"Father gets so agitated with people doesn't he?" James said.

"He's not mellowing as he gets older either."

"But I wasn't just joking that sometimes I feel like hanging it all up and living out here in a cabin. It wouldn't be all that bad."

"Believe me James you don't want that. It's an intellectual wasteland, this mountain, that town down there," Bridget said pointing her thumb down at Petaluma below.

"I realize those things but it's so blasted complicated in San Francisco. My life, my career. Trying to keep it all going is exhausting." Like any wounded soldier on the battlefield, James just wanted his mama.

Bridget lovingly glanced at her son, it was a knowing glance. She leaned over and gave him warm embrace.

They chatted a little longer before it was time to leave. John took his brother down in the buggy for the 4 o'clock train back to the metropolis.

Early Monday morning Patrick got to work on his wife's long list of repairs. By Thursday evening he had transformed the gardens to Bridget's liking though he resigned himself to hire out the painting to a team of younger men. After four days of relentless chores he didn't quite feel right. Perhaps he had too much coffee, his stomach was unsettled. He had retched on the side of the house and kicked gravel over the remnants to hide it from his wife as she checked on his progress.

Pleased and grateful, Bridget prepared thick lamb chops with apple-sauce as a special reward for her husband's supper. He ate like a ravenous farmhand. Afterward they retired to their fireside where she took up her needlepoint and Patrick resumed reading his farming journal.

"I'm going up. Lots to do tomorrow," Patrick said as he set off to bed.

"I just want to finish this one last patch of bright pink and I'll join you." Bridget pulled her needle through the linen with an away knot to start the last section of her rose pattern. Seconds later she heard a thump coming from the staircase. She rushed to investigate and found her husband had collapsed mid-flight.

"What's the matter. What? Did you trip?"

Patrick gripped the railing and gradually pulled himself to his feet. "For God's sake I don't know what the hell just happened. I'm fine. I'm fine. Don't worry. Just exhausted I guess…."

As she tried to help him up the steps he reassured her again that he felt OK. Waving off any more fussing he readied himself for bed. Bridget sat at her glass brushing her hair wondering if she should worry. Patrick came up from behind and kissed her cheek.

"You gave me a fright on those steps."

"Just a clumsy old clodhopper."

They both tucked into bed and Patrick drifted off. Still, she felt uneasy. Maybe he was just a clumsy old clodhopper she told herself, yet she nervously watched him breathe in and out. He did seem fine. Eventually she fell asleep too.

In the morning she was the first to wake. Bridget always started her mornings with a list of the day's worries. She got right up close to Patrick's face. She was happy to find him quite comfortable and soundly sleeping. Maybe she would let him be a while longer. She crept downstairs to make a hardy breakfast. John always helped out on Fridays and he would be over any minute. She cut some roses and collected eggs from the hen house. The cock was crowing when she returned to the kitchen but Patrick wasn't at his usual spot at the table. Not like the man to burn daylight like this. See, I knew something wasn't right about that fall! She headed up to roust him.

"Pat, time to get up." She jiggled his shoulder but he was immobile, unconscious. His chest heaving slowly. "Patrick!" Bridget's heart began to race. Oh no, oh no, oh no.

John appeared at the foot of the bed where his frantic mother yelled out, "I can't wake him up!" Bridget proceeded to tell her son in rapid fire the seemingly inconsequential events that brought them to this morning. "But he said he was fine, he said, told me three times!" Bridget appealed to her son. Patrick would never lie to his wife but, then again, he had never died before. How would he know?

John fetched the doctor from town.

Family was summoned.

Rosaries prayed.

Father Cleary came.

It all came to an end on that warm Friday afternoon. The family patriarch was dead at 75 years of age.

On Saturday the doctor pulled aside the Judge, assuming he was provisional head, and told him that it was most likely a ruptured aorta. Bridget kept her sangfroid throughout the entire ordeal, stoic, managing family, making food. She asked John to take care of the funeral arrangements and to send his father off with an Irish wake.

In shifts, the children and grandchildren sat beside Patrick Lawler's coffin splayed in the front parlor. Flowers had been delivered. Food mounded up on the sideboard. John procured plenty of whiskey and ale. A few visitors came for a spell then left quietly. Hour after hour ticked by in solemn silence.

Where were the stories? The drunken toasts? Laughter? Dancing? But American puritans would never dream of drinking in front of the dead or appear to revel in front of a new widow. Dignified reverence was not what Bridget wanted. The quiet was excruciating. When she heard the grandfather clock chime again in the front hall she tersely asked why someone hadn't stopped that bloody thing. It should be set to 4:36, the minute he died! A frightened little granddaughter, Grace, ran to reset the contraption.

Lucy got up from her chair and pulled back the green brocade drapery to see if any people were outside. No. No horses. No carriages. No more mourners.

Bridget just could not hide her heartbreak, for the moment, it was the low turnout rather than the death itself that was eating her up. Worse yet, not a single one of her Dunne relatives bothered to show their faces. It was in all the papers. Where were the nieces and nephews? She was anticipating at least her brother's arrival. James Dunne would know how to conjure up a proper Irish wake.

But no.

Reality slapped Bridget squarely in the face. Over the years, incident-by-incident, family ties had been slowly frayed and now they appeared completely severed. Stone cold disrespect.

Without her husband she would be isolated up on this monastic mountain now for the rest of her life. Alone. Her Patrick was dead. An Irish wake would have helped her forestall that devastating conclusion. And for the first time in their collective memory the children witnessed their mother cry, inconsolably cry. They could never have imagined their father surviving without their mother, she was the rock. But how would she survive? John Lawler had the look of discovery about him and darted out into the fields with an empty wagon.

Hours dragged on until Monday morning when it was time for the funeral. The undertaker's glistening lacquered hearse with its team of four black horses appeared outside the Lawler ranch house. Bridget, the new widow, watched on as six pallbearers brought Patrick's remains out the front door and ceremoniously placed the casket in the hearse for the long, six-mile trek down to town.

As the mourners made their way into the incense-filled interior of St. Vincent's Church the bell tolled from the modest belfry. Bridget was gladdened to see the pews filled to capacity with friends and acquaintances lining the walls. More people than at midnight mass on Christmas Eve she reckoned. She spotted not a single Dunne though. Father Cleary did his best to eulogize one of the oldest pioneers left to die in Sonoma County. Patrick would have agreed with all the accolades he was given and would have added a few forgotten ones. In an attempt to escape, Bridget became fixated on the heralding angels crudely painted above the altar. She was missing vast swathes of the traditions and rituals of a

Roman Catholic high requiem mass. She was going back in her mind now to Ireland and the start of their life together. How did she survive the famine and end up in America again? In California? Was this really her life? She tenderly drifted off into the past during the service to avoid the present.

However, it was happening.

Her husband's coffin was getting sprinkled with Holy Water. He would be buried in the Lawler family plot next to an infant granddaughter. And her only consolation was that she had fulfilled her wedding vows to the best of her abilities.

Final hymns were sung and closing prayers were chanted. Bridget came back to the here and now, pootling out of the church with her family behind the priest and Patrick's casket. Intense sunlight silhouetted the pallbearers in the doorway.

On the sidewalk outside St. Vincent's, lining the way to the family carriage, townsfolk held high in their hands ears of golden corn forming a virtual pergola for Bridget to promenade through on her way to the coach. How glorious! She was completely taken aback but knew immediately what they were doing. As she walked she lovingly grabbed John's collar and pulled him close to her black veil, "You did this?"

"Yes mother, like our exodus from Mountmellick father always remembered. I had to tell everyone the story when I handed out the corn."

"Oh yes, he loved that….thank you dear."

Bridget acknowledging their kindness like a queen would acknowledge her subjects with dignified head bobs and nobs. She choked back tears. John helped her up inside the coach. At the undertaker's direction the caravan, some 50 conveyances strong, set off for Cavalry Cemetery at the edge of town with Patrick's hearse leading the way. The rough cobblestoned streets of Petaluma were empty in anticipation of the mile-long procession. When the cortege turned on to the main boulevard all of the iron-front shops and businesses were closed, lighting snuffed and black crepe paper draping the windows.

The sidewalks however were brimming with people, crowded together like a parade day, all silently waving their corn cob symbols high above their heads in final tribute to a resting city father. From the sanctuary of her coach Bridget wept quietly, pathetically poking away at the glass when she recognized the myriad of townspeople from the corner drunk to the grocery store clerk to the mayor. It was Patrick Lawler's proudest moment.

CHAPTER 41

Notice in the *Petaluma Weekly Argus*, Petaluma, October 29, 1889

SETTLEMENT—The controversy among the heirs over the will of the late capitalist Patrick Lawler of Sonoma Mountain has been amicably settled. By the will each child will receive $500 but by compromise the sum is increased to $1500. The estate is valued at $80,000.

𝕏

The estate was far from settled. It was easier the Irish way when the oldest son just got everything.

Patrick Lawler was barely in his grave a month before his children started squabbling over their inheritance. The deceased hadn't helped things with his codicils of bias, grievances and favoritism. Decreed threats to his children if they contested the will were ignored. John claimed his father was not of sound mind and had his mother deed him portions of the rancho outside the auspices of the probate court. Daughter Frances deceived Bridget through a sneaky back-end deal with a real estate agent. Bridget sold land to the water company that Patrick had forbidden and she was beset with a variety of lawsuits from plaintiffs crawling out of the woodwork. Bridget revoked John's power of attorney. James sued John. John counter-sued. In the meantime Denny died and his six children moved into the maelstrom. After years of wrangling, the whole mess would finally end up in the California Supreme Court where the rulings made everyone equally unhappy.

Bridget felt that the Dunnes had already deserted her and now her own Lawler clan was breaking apart at the seams. The family had walked together through one of hell's three gates: greed.

Since the death of her husband and before the inheritance squabbles began in earnest she had only one true moment of happiness, the day the Australian came.

Peter Lalor had arrived in San Francisco aboard the Oceanic Company's Royal Mail steamship Alameda two months after Patrick died. His doctors had prescribed a long bout of sea air to lessen the effects of diabetes. Lalor was dubious but played along. San Francisco might be interesting. He knew several family members had settled there. From his suite at the Palace Hotel he gave interviews to local journalists about his adventurous life, Australian history and political events of the day.

"Mother, everything's ready. Mr. Lalor should arrive soon," said Lucy, Bridget's youngest.

"Can you help me with my eye black?" Lucy delicately brushed on some lash potion to her mother's eyes.

"How about that?" she held up the silver mirror to her aged mother's face.

"Oh, it looks ridiculous."

"No mother, it's pretty," encouraged Lucy.

"I look like an old, white-haired granny, some desperate widow trying too hard to look pretty. I used to be pretty like you are now."

"Nonsense, you are pretty! Let's go downstairs. Bridget's steps were as elastic as a schoolgirl's. Just as the two women descended the stairs Peter Lalor's hulking figure appeared in the front doorway.

John, who had chauffeured him from the train, made the introductions. Lalor was polite, perfectly groomed with an almost military bearing. He immediately put the family at ease about his missing left arm. His joke, "still waiting for it to grow back," drew hearty laughs. They retired to the parlor where Lucy had prepared a little tea reception and asked "Shall I be mother?" as she poured from a delicate Belleek teapot. Small talk was made about this and that, about how Melbourne and San Francisco could be sister cities, the rain and lack thereof. Then Lucy and John left the two old Irishers alone to reminisce.

"Your son took me around the ranch a little on the way up. What a spread! The views! And the loads of fine-looking sheep you've got here… near and dear to an Australian's heart," Peter said in his colonial accent with only a trace of his Irish brogue remaining.

"Well, it might all go to rack and ruin now without Patrick. I do wish he could be with us today. He was so excited to have you visit," Bridget said with her Irish lilt undefiled.

"I received word. Condolences to you. He'll be missed to be sure."

"We're so happy you decided to come up to Petaluma anyhow, it's very kind."

"I had a long time to think out there on the big ocean. About Ireland, life. My life."

"I suppose it's that part of the novel where we survey such things," Bridget said being both ancient and an avid reader.

"I often wonder how this little tyke that ran around Tenakill could rise to be Speaker of the Victorian Legislative Assembly in such a far off land as Australia?"

"Oh I don't know, your father was an MP. And your brother Richard is an MP. Not that far-fetched."

"I suppose. All-in-all pretty impressive for the Lalor clan of Queen's County."

"Ha!"

"But you must admit, for years it was always the Dunne clan that ran the county." Peter gave Bridget a sideways glance.

"Grand families, both. I couldn't be prouder. Although you'd never know it. Me. Sitting here. Cooking, cleaning, working sun up to sun down. No servants. Still! To this day. At my age even. And without Patrick who knows how long I can go on."

"Come now Mrs. Lawler. You, living up here. This is paradise. So, it'll last as long as it'll last. Your enormous brood will help you I am sure. They're all prosperous. Healthy. All here with you in golden California. Amerikay!"

"Pst. I feel like my life has been a little like an oak leaf blowing in the wind. Never thought I had any control of it whatsoever." A blunt assessment.

"It looked mighty bleak. We did it though. We endured, we even thrived while others just wilted. San Francisco's own patron, St. Francis said it best: Start by doing what's necessary, then do what's possible and suddenly you're doing the impossible".

"How lovely. I've never heard that quote."

"No? But you've lived it. All you have here," Peter made a grand gesture waving his lone arm about like he used to do before Parliament, "it could've never happened in Ireland. Never! We'd just be prisoners of the past there—"

"Patrick used to talk of those that left the island as traitors. It took him a long time to become an American in his mind, in his soul. Did your brother Fintan reckon that as well, bless his soul. He tried to change the country from within."

"Aye, but the little agitator paid with his life didn't he? Ireland her own, and all therein, from the sod to the sky. The soil of Ireland for the people of Ireland…and all of that."

"Did he die in Newgate prison, I can't remember?"

"No, they let him out because he was going to die anyway. He was always sickly, as you know, but that cell finished him off. The government didn't want him to be too much the martyr."

"From what I read in the Freeman's Journal he is most certainly a martyr and a true Irish patriot for the cause."

"Now Mrs. Lawler how do you know what's printed in the Dublin newspapers?"

"I get copies delivered to me here, a few months behind, but I keep up on the world, Mr. Lalor."

"Good on you! But what you won't read in any of those papers was how lovelorn Fintan was…over you." He eyeballed her as if to catch some kind of romantic reaction he could posthumously attribute to his brother.

"Oh come now. I do have fond memories of Fintan, we were just friendly."

"He only spoke of you until his last breath." He nudged further.

"Please, you'll make me cry." Bridget was both saddened and proud that she could have such an effect on any man, let alone an Irish patriot.

"No, no, you were right-thinking in the end. He wasn't the marrying type. Not robust. Besides, you'd always be sharing him with Lady Ireland. Everything that's supposed to happen usually does."

"Imagine me, Bridget Dunne, caught up in a Fenian Uprising! Rebel warrior! I think not."

"I'd say we both got out in the nick of time."

For a while they compared stories about the departed and remaining characters of Queen's County, their foibles and fate. While Bridget enjoyed talking about old friends and old times, her favorite part of the visit was discussing the present state of the world with one of its leaders. It wasn't just a lecture. She had opinions too and he spoke to her as an intellectual equal. It was exhilarating. Culture came sailing around the world and docked itself right inside her hilltop farmhouse.

Their time together whizzed by leaving Mrs. Lawler crestfallen when the hour came for Mr. Lalor to catch his train back. She waved goodbye and closed the door to face her new life without a man.

He returned to Australia aboard the Alameda having made the trip purely for a sea voyage.

Even in their adulthood, Bridget continued to worry about her children in varying degrees. As she told Peter Lalor, for all his fame and glory, it was indeed James who concerned her most. It seemed counterintuitive. He appeared to be the most successful of the children. She wasn't sure if it was just an Irish mother's penchant for anxiety, a fear of sudden prosperity or an actual premonition. She was well aware of the dangers facing a big city judge. It took a special breed of man to wade through those shark-infested waters after all.

On any given day James Lawler could chastise truant boys about the necessity to attend school, grant divorces to battered wives, listen to the pathetic pleadings of a pick pocket then minutes later sentence an attempted murderer to hard time in prison. His own summons to appear before Blind Boss Buckley had him nervous.

He arrived on a sunlit afternoon to Buckley's new tavern, The Manhattan Club at the corner of Bush and Stockton. A crowd of hard-looking, hard-drinking highbinders, looking for loans or favors from the Boss, loitered at the entrance forcing respectable citizens to cross the street. The Judge himself was glared at by a few of the desperados who had been before his bench once or a dozen times. A well-dressed Negro with a friendly face spotted Lawler and welcomed him inside. The Boss wanted a word in the backroom.

Chris Buckley, affable and at the zenith of his power, had compensated for his blindness with a heightening of all his other senses. He could recognize a man by his footsteps, his cologne or his handshake. As the queue got shorter it was the Judge's turn for a diagnostic salutation. Now James Lawler might have been a handsome man, a dandy, even a confirmed bachelor but he carried himself with the cocksure confidence of a pugilist. He put his hand directly into the Boss' and gave it the squeeze of Sampson.

"I see we have here Judge Lawler," the Boss said.

"Hello Chris," said the Judge.

"Feels like your grip's gettin' to be a little sissified, don't ya think?"

"I think not!" said the Judge with his heart up around his throat.

"Be that as it may, I'm in a bit of a jam."

"Your arrest?"

"Yes, yes, totally unfounded of course. A bunch of soreheads are claiming I tried to fix a case in the State Supreme Court."

"I read the Attorney General's claims."

"Balderdash!" exclaimed the Boss.

"It has me worried Chris, perhaps—"

"Your Honor, an intelligent jurist such as yourself can surely determine a way to unleash me from this conundrum?"

"That's a tall order, the thing is—"

"It needs to go away."

"I really have no power to—"

"You know I have eyes all over Chinatown. Albeit little slanty ones, but still, they're mine. They see ev'rything that goes on in that putrid, heathen hellhole. One of my lambs goes by the name of Little Pete. Know him?"

Judge Lawler's heart was back up around his throat. Little Pete was the reigning Tong hatchet man and surely knew all about Mr. Fong's various business concerns.

"Chris, stop toying with me, of course I know him. I've set that individual free every time you've asked me to." Obfuscating the obvious he continued, "Now let me look into your predicament. I'm sure there is some maneuver in case law I can find."

"I had a feeling you'd see it my way."

Times were trying for the Judge. He was mired in lawsuits surrounding his father's estate in Sonoma County, the political winds of San Francisco were shifting and his own re-election was in serious doubt. Boss Buckley's veiled threats and demands to be rescued from trial put life as he knew it in jeopardy. Lawler had a scheme to free Buckley but it would only annoy his Democratic rivals and incite his Republican enemies in their claims of vast citywide corruption.

A growing brigade of good government reformers, nicknamed Goo-Goos, were on the march but James Lawler saw no other way out. He had grown comfortable on the bench, up there where power protects. To fall from that exalted perch into the abyss below, into the jaws of the predators who inhabited such dark places, could mean certain annihilation.

Wresting control from the higher court intent on prosecuting, the Judge was able to sneak proceedings into his lowly Police Court against Buckley, charging him with obtaining money by false pretenses. The Boss had indeed taken a $500 payment from an attorney to secure a fix in a client's lawsuit, however, if that accusation could be eradicated then the more serious charge of corruption connected to the State's case would evaporate.

After many postponements and continuances the Boss finally had his day in court. He liked the feel of his new blue suit. He could tell it was checked by the subtle shift in the weave's nap. Twin torchiere globes on either side of the bench flickered unevenly and the room, like most of City Hall, faintly smelled of the sewer. Judge Lawler looked out over the gallery of Police Court No. 2. being much pleased at the sparse attendance. The time was at hand. After nervously shuffling a few papers around he called the gathering to order using his standard provisos.

Attorney-General Edward Marshall and his mighty beard opened the proceedings.

"Your Honor, I have made a thorough investigation of this case and have arrived at the conclusion that the present examination has no bearing upon future actions of the matter. I have no intention of prosecuting this claim of
obtaining money by false pretenses. The defendant's own attorneys have admitted such. The real charge is corruption and that shall be heard within the hallowed halls of a proper tribunal, not this shabby little Police Court, no disrespect intended."

"None taken sir," responded Judge Lawler.

"If the Attorney-General in his eternal wisdom does not wish to prosecute then I shall also refuse to proceed on the same grounds," said prosecuting attorney T.P. Ryan.

"And what say you, Mr. Preston?"

Buckley's attorney addressed the court in thunderous language, "The defendant is owed a trial. I say we proceed! It is the sworn duty of the officers of the law to thoroughly examine every charge of this alleged crime. The vital question before this court is, is there a reasonable probability that a crime has even been committed?' My defendant's only desire is to clear his good name."

Chris Buckley sat expressionless listening to things others could not hear. His attorney had played his part well.

Judge Lawler interrupted, "As much as I would welcome the challenge, I cannot constitute myself as both a Magistrate and a prosecutor. The prosecuting attorneys have declined to act in this matter. Therefore, with the defendant now exonerated from the underlying accusation, the concurrent charge of attempting corruption cannot be justified. Mr. Buckley you are freed of this entanglement. Case dismissed." He delicately tapped the gavel down and bellowed, "Next case?"

When the revolting news seeped out of the courtroom, outraged journalists encouraged citizens to rise up against such a travesty of justice. A new firebrand publisher by the name of William Randolph Hearst had been gifted The San Francisco Examiner from his father, a staunch Buckley ally. With one punch at the graft and perhaps another intended as a rebellion against his father, Hearst took after Buckley with a vengeance. He claimed San Francisco was a nefarious pigsty, corrupted beyond redemption under management of the Boodle Millionaire. Bad press combined with a backlash from his farcical legal con games set into motion a series of devastating blows and reprisals. Buckley's old friends were complaining about his lack of interest in their success. Access to the Manhattan Club was restricted. His political instincts dulled and his famous sixth sense abandoned him. His political machine was starting to break down.

All the ward heelers and ballot-box-stuffers couldn't stop his inevitable downfall. The election of 1890 sealed the fate of Buckley as well as his candidates who were trounced at the polls.

For his part in the calamity, Police Court Judge Lawler lost his seat despite pouring a significant amount of his grappled inheritance into the re-election campaign. The worm had turned and with his downfall complete, Christopher Buckley was rode out of town on a rail and ended up touring the European continent for an extended holiday. He would never regain his control over the City.

Ex-Judge Lawler was made the recipient of glowing testimonials from a grateful police force at his farewell banquet held at highfalutin Delmonico's. He was presented with an engraved silver plaque extolling him for the honest and upright manner in which he had acted as Police

Judge over four terms. Before a rapt audience he expressed his gratitude for the flattering reception and said:

"I have always endeavored to perform the duties of Police Judge honestly. I have tried to give justice to the poor as well as the rich. For eight years I have performed my duties and I dare any man to point the finger of scorn. How well I have succeeded my friends and the public will testify. For the kindly expressions of my friends at this board and the public officials who have aided me in my duties I have no words to express to you my gratitude."

Easily spinning through the revolving door of the legal system, he was wined and dined all around town by opportunistic attorneys begging him to join their law practices. He had lost his gavel but was set to cash in on the lucrative offers laid before him as a result. Surely City Hall would dole out defense cases in its criminal courts to the former judge. Who knew how to play the game better? It seemed he had also been able to keep his deepest, darkest secrets buried in the catacombs of Chinatown where they belonged. Emboldened, he visited Alphabet House with renewed frequency.

CHAPTER 42

Fragment of letter from Lucy Rogers to Sarafrances Welch

[December 1938]

I am sure your mother has filled you in on all the difficulties the family had after my father passed. Everyone acted horribly. Mother ended up moving into town. Seems all of us took turns living up at the ranch. My mother tried her best to mend things with all of us siblings and we were at least cordial to each other.

You asked about any family secrets I may know about James Lawler. He's taken the brunt of the blame from all corners. Whether it was justified or not—the family deserted him—leaving San Francisco to eat him alive. It was as if he had never even been part of our tribe. Toward the end I was the only one of us talking with him—& that was quite infrequent. The rumors that got passed around about your Great Uncle James were dreadful and I've heard all of them. But I for one will not sully his name by addressing any of those outrageous tales. I am sorry, I know you asked, but I will have to leave that be.

Distasteful things should soon be forgotten. They will not make us happy.

꙾

The United States had taken refugees from a starving, downtrodden island and conscripted them into becoming industrious Americans. Britain was glad to be rid of what she saw as contemptuous, lazy leaches. But the laws of unintended consequences being what they are, in less than a generation, those of Irish ancestry helped propel America to the pinnacle of nations. They consciously put their unhappiness behind them and decided to build a brighter future in a new country. Some became laborers, farmers or cops and some became captains of industry, cattle barons and cunning politicians. By the 1880s, rich or poor, they were ready to make their power known.

San Francisco, now a booming cosmopolitan city, had a large Italian population, a contingent of French and Germans, clusters of Chinese and Mexicans but it was a city governed by the Irish vote. With old Boss

Buckley out of sight, a newer, more genteel leader emerged to take his place as chieftain.

His detractors called James D. Phelan just an Irishman dressed up as a peacock but he was not just for show. A San Francisco born native with familial roots going back to Queen's County, he had spent a year of his childhood traveling in first-class style throughout Europe. Returning to the City with an inherent appreciation for culture and civics. He was a top student in the Golden State's Catholic schools before completing his law degree at University of California, Berkeley. He learned about big business from the ground up at his father's bank, moving up to be its president. Finally, in his mid 30s, he turned his attention to politics. His town had matured enough for a real government and yearned for an honest mayor not beholden to racketeers or bullies.

Phelan modeled his campaign strategy on that of another son of Queen's County, William Russell Grace, a relative of the late Mrs. Kavanaugh of Gracefield. Grace was independently wealthy as was Phelan and had the resources to buck the oppressive Tammany Hall system to become the first Irish Catholic mayor of New York City.

3,000 miles away in California, James Phelan became the 25th mayor of San Francisco and vowed to fight corruption with every tool at his disposal.

Soldiers of the Old Guard, like ex-police court judge James Lawler, had fallen out of favor. Lawler held high hopes that his career after the bench would be as dazzling as cousin Peter Francis Dunne's. Yes, there were a few celebrated cases where he successfully defended murder suspects but the Goo-Goos were in control. Over a short period of time, Lawler went from his high-society clientele to defending penniless prostitutes, low life forgers and a litany of lawbreakers from Chinatown. Criminals he once passed sentence upon were now the clients he was trying to please. He had acquired a persistent stench of shyster-ism about him.

The ex-judge sunk from his suite of rooms at a luxury hotel to a small flat and finally to a dingy room of a run-down boarding house in the Tenderloin. Expensive lawsuits against his Petaluma kin severed family ties and strained resources. James would have welcomed a reconciliatory visit from any one of his relatives, except the one that came.

Around 4pm on a Sunday the Cantonese landlord led a scruffy stranger up to the ex-judge's room and rapped on the door with all the gentleness of an angry gorilla. "You got visitor Mr. Judge," he yelled out. Opening the door the Judge was aghast to see what was lurking over the Celestial's shoulder.

"Good afternoon Uncle, how are you?" It was the recalcitrant nephew, J.P. Lawler, previously known as Prisoner Number 15840.

"OK, OK," said the landlord as he trudged noisily back downstairs, his long queue slithering down his spine.

Freshly discharged from San Quentin, the once lanky youth had mutated into a creature that more closely resembled a bloated seal. His translucent gray skin was shiny and pulled tightly over his skull. The familiar heavily lidded eyes now ran cold and empty. He seemed taller beneath his ill-fitting, prison-issued pea coat. Startled and disgusted the Judge instinctively blocked the doorway.

"They let you out already? You've got a lot of nerve showing up here."

"There, there Uncle Judge."

"Go away or I'll have you arrested all over again!" When the Judge tried to shut the door, J.P. stuck his filthy boot inside the jam and said, "Not so fast Uncle, we have a few things to discuss." He pushed the door in and the Judge stumbled backward.

"From the looks of this flophouse you've fallen on hard times, eh? The mighty do that sometimes don't they?" said J.P.

"Disappointed you can't spot anything to pilfer?"

"I didn't steal from you."

"J.P. you are a thief as well as a liar. That's been proven quite handily. We have no business together. He elegantly motioned towards the exit trying to remain calm while simultaneously planning to retrieve his derringer from the top dresser drawer.

"Come now Uncle, who is the bigger degenerate here?" J.P. smiled a devious smile.

"Have you forgotten who you're talking to? I think you'd better leave before I lose my temper."

"I thought you could give me a little money until I get back on my feet."

"You thought wrong. Out." His patience had run its course.

Then his nephew sweetly hummed a soft lullaby to the tune of *Twinkle, Twinkle Little Star.*

Puzzled the Judge responded, "Lovely, you learned that in the clink did you? Now go!"

"Don't know that song, Uncle?"

"Shall I call for the police now?"

J.P. went in for the kill. "Oh come on, you recognize it. A-B-C-D-E-F-G—"

"What?"

"Now, do you know you're A-B-Cs Uncle?"

Oh dear God, he's talking about Alphabet House. How does he know about that? Some inmate chatter from San Quentin? Impossible. All the color drained from the Judge's face. He was speechless.

"Cat got your tongue?"

"What do you want?" The judge said moving J.P. hastily to the point.

"$1,000."

"A thousand dollars? Are you joking? Look at me, I'm clean busted, dammit!"

"$1,000 and I'll go away, you'll never see me again."

"If had a $1,000 do you think I would be living in this squalor?"

"$1,000."

"And if I refuse?"

"Then you'll see me at the newspaper offices, and City Hall, and the Police Station. Lots of places would like to know how you learned your A-B-Cs…." J.P. was so pleased with himself.

"Thief, liar, extortionist. Finally got your education in treachery at prison."

"$1,000."

"I don't have that much money with me. Meet me at Wells Fargo tomorrow at noon."

"I need cash now."

Draining his pockets he gave J.P. a $20 gold piece and a few coins.

"That's all I have."

"Good. I have some celebrating to do."

"Now go."

"At the bank tomorrow at noon or I'm at the Examiner office at 12:10."

Opening the door for J.P. the Judge glared as his nephew who grinned and tipped his hat on the way out.

Weak kneed, he trembled and sat on the corner of his bed, the springs squeaked from his weight. How did that idiot know anything about

Alphabet House? Who else knew? He quickly flipped threw a dozen scenarios in his head. He had exactly $439 to his name. He wouldn't be paid on his latest case until the end of October, two months away. And that would be if he won which seemed unlikely. He could be ruined. His first thought was to run up to Petaluma and extract some money from his brother John who by all counts was now the richest Lawler. But that would be too humiliating, plus he might get shot on sight.

If he groveled to his mother she might acquiesce. But could James actually dare to look her in the face after suing her in an open court? She was so hurt by the whole ordeal. That would be soul crushing. James put his fingers to his temples. Soul? What soul?

His mind was stretched in so many directions it actually throbbed with pain.

After exhaustive deliberations with himself he devised a plan so intricate, so ingenious, so outrageous that it just might work.

It was time to go see Mr. Fong.

CHAPTER 43

Advertisement in the *The San Francisco Call*, August 25, 1897

LATEST SHIPPING INTELLIGENCE
—Movements of Trans-Atlantic Steamers. NEW YORK – Aug. May 24 –
Stmr. Mohawk from London: stmr Westernland from Antwerp.
— Foreign Arrival. Lrg. Portuguese-flagged junk allowed del. cargo dried
shrimp Broadway Wharf. Loaded redwood lumbr Mendocino Cty. Sails
Monday for Macau. Stmr McKaskle, from Honolulu, del. sugar cane at
Harrison St. Wharf. Loaded cattle. Sails bk Monday.
— Foreign Ports. MARSEILLES – Sailed Aug. 21 – Stmr Neustader, for
New York, ISLE OF WIGHT –Passed May 20 – Stmr Patris, from New York
for Hamburg.

Abbott's saloon wasn't such a bad place. There was a gospel hall in the basement and a free dance hall upstairs but recently it had become a resort for petty larcenists and gunslingers. Just the place new parolee J.P. Lawler should avoid and just the place that magnetically drew him in.

Tonight he would carouse, tomorrow morning he'd grab his claim from former Judge Lawler and set off to the Klondike where a new gold stampede was underway. It was all planned out from within the walls of San Quentin. The other inmates talked endlessly about their hare-brained Alaskan schemes. Even the guards were considering making their way North. Family legend spoke of how rich the Dunne brothers became in the Gold Rush and J.P. was going to do just the same. But for now, after a year-and-a-half of lock-up, he required the soft touch of a woman.

Perched at the bar, he was pontificating to a dance hall pretty girl with all the confidence of a man who had been free to ruminate on the workings of the world while incarcerated by it. A fresh-from-prison-know-it-all.

"I'll be gone without a trace, no checking in with nobody. Be up there for a couple years, make a cool fortune and then who knows? Sure won't have to work again. Maybe I'll buy me a tropical island somewhere. Bathe myself in rum."

"Sounds dreamy, can I come along?" asked the dance hall girl.

"See, I don't plan on actually doing any mining. That's for suckers. I'm going to be a supplier to the suckers. I'm going to sell picks for $100! Could probably get $20 for a gold pan. Like I said, you gotta be smart about these things."

"You really have it all figured out, haven't you?" she asked as she took the last sip of her beer.

"Matter of fact, I do. My father's uncles did that same thing here in '49. They owned half this area by the time everything was said and done." He made a clumsy waving motion around his head. "This kind of intelligence can't be learned, it's in my blood, you know?" He slapped his wrist.

The pretty girl listened intently. She knew a con man when she saw one but they were usually much better looking. J.P. blabbered non-stop, not seeming to falter until he began to slur his words. She told him to pay the bartender for her next drink.

"Sure, why not." J.P. ordered another for himself. What price for his companion's company tonight? She was probably already in love with him and would do it for free.

J.P. started to feel the exhaustion of his busy day. He had better work fast.

"Sorry, I've been going on and on with my spiel. That's quite enough about me, what do you think of my plan?" J.P. decided it was time to pour on the ample charm he assumed was his.

"That's all right, sounds like a Grade-A adventure," she said.

"Is dancing all you do?" he asked.

"Oh no, I'm actually a world famous opera singer on the side," giving him a grandiose dose of his own medicine.

"How much for a private recital?"

Without hesitation she blurted out, "$15."

"Too rich for my blood, Honey. Haven't made my fortune yet."

"Hey Yukon, your blood is going to be richer than rich soon, remember? You gotta start acting like a big shot!"

"Not that you're not worth every penny darlin' but—"

"Here we go—"

"I've got $5."

"$7."

"Deal. Where's your place then?"

"Next block. Shall we?"

"I'm coming," J.P. drained his glass and got up from the stool a little wobbly. He almost slipped to the floor. Not used to real booze like this in prison he thought through his haze. Whoa.

"Need some help there, Yukon?" She let him lean on her as they shuffled across the sawdust floor. The convict felt quite snockered. Kind-heartedly the pretty girl pulled his arm around her and practically dragged him outside through the alley.

J.P. looked out at her from his trademark sleepy eyes and mumbled, "You're awfully nice for a famous opera singer."

"Come along," she said.

Into the darkened alley they went when two crimps came up from behind the pair and thumped J.P. over the head with a blackjack.

He was leveled to the ground.

The men brutishly threw him into a hack waiting at the other end of the corridor. It disappeared down Kearny Street. The pretty girl smoothed her dress, straightened her hat and returned to Abbott's.

When J.P. Lawler regained consciousness early Monday morning he was out at sea approaching the Farallon Islands. Still groggy he could see the Chinese crew shaking out the ship's sails. They knew just enough English to tell the felon he was now a sailor and brandished just enough weaponry to encourage him to get to work. He was gone without a trace.

James Lawler's fascination about the nature of good and evil began with his law studies on the foggy campus of St. Mary's College in San Francisco's outer lands by the ocean. He wanted to be among the righteous. Back then he idealized the intrinsic properties of good vs. evil, believing that, although they would intertwine throughout his career, they would always be immediately recognizable.

In his fiftieth year he was couldn't tell the difference anymore.

Clouding his judgement further were the proclivities he hid in the chambers of Alphabet House. He didn't blink twice at the notion of having his nephew Shanghaied to protect his secret. A citywide crackdown on vice compelled Fong to shut down the establishment just in time. No word of its existence was ever written about in personal journals, diaries or newspapers. No records of its membership would ever be known. Families denied ever hearing of the place. The magnitude of such a salacious discovery would forever elude historians and it faded into the many forgotten mysteries of Chinatown.

Without it, people like Mr. Q had to resort to the tawdry tactics of less well-heeled Uranians. He knew all the dives on the Barbary Coast where wayward seamen sought entertainment in the bawdy reviews and peep shows. Tainted names of these establishments were noted crime scenes in many of his Police Court cases. Usually there would be one or two blokes in the rear who seemed disinterested. Mr. Q was still handsome but at his age money was required in exchange.

Money. He grew up never wanting for a thing. His career as a jurist provided a handsome salary and then some. He inherited thousands of dollars' worth of real estate that he slowly sold off piece by piece until there wasn't a single acre left. Meagre legal fees trickled in from his roster of insolvent clients. Grasping at straws, he risked his last reserves on a failed stock speculation. The velocity of his downward spiral was increased by his growing dependence on the opium he imagined would absolve him from sin. But there was no absolution, only rapidly deteriorating health.

It was with regret and sadness that John Lawler read of his brother's predicament for the first time in the San Francisco paper:

FORMER POLICE JUDGE SLOWLY DYING

Ex-Police Judge Lawler is dying. About a week ago the once popular jurist was taken seriously ill, and as he was without a home he was provided a room in the New Western Hotel by a genial boniface, an ex-supervisor who preferred his name not be mentioned. Most of the attorneys who were once glad to clasp his hand when he was in the heyday of his success refused to assist him, even to the extent of providing him with the proper medical attention. As his condition grew worse, a former Police Court prosecutor befriended him during his darkest hour and yesterday sent Lawler to the City & County Hospital. He is walking in the shadow of death, according to physicians at the sanatorium.

James Lawler's sister, Lucy Rogers, rushed down on the train to comfort him but she did not recognize the shell of a man in the pauper's ward. He did not recognize her either. The astonishing amounts of laudanum the nurses needed to administer to an opium addict for any type of pain relief rendered him incoherent.

His remains were met Friday morning on the 9:30 train by a couple of reluctant nephews and were taken to a Petaluma undertaking parlor. The honor of lying in repose at any of the Lawler homes was made unavailable to him. Lawsuits over Patrick's estate left a lasting welt. The constant rumors that swirled around the ex-judge had also gained a foothold in the small farming town and embarrassed the family.

James Lawler couldn't be buried fast enough.

Like his father before him, James had a full requiem mass at the Catholic church with all of the ceremony and none of the sincerity.

Peter Francis Dunne was quite aware of his cousin's plight but had long ago put plenty of distance between himself and James Lawler. Few in his circle even knew the two were related. But then again Peter Francis had put himself at a distance from all the Lawlers and most of the Dunnes.

The Old Family would try to hold him to old standards.

After all he was a big man, very busy with not enough time for anything except being big. In addition, he had adopted the habits of the Brahmin class and maintained strict standards for those allowed into his inner sanctum. Membership to the Pacific-Union Club as well as the Bohemian Club helped filter out the unqualified. Ability to travel abroad was a plus. Donations to the proper charities—check. Discretion and loyalty, yes. And of course, money—the more the better. Peter Francis Dunne never received a lucrative case from a poor prospect.

But he had strayed a bit from the habits of San Francisco's Blue Book society by building his new home outside the customary neighborhoods of the City. Far out on Clay Street he had erected a four-story redwood-shingled mansion designed in the new Arts & Crafts style. Thoroughly modern in conception it abandoned all the Victorian gingerbread that adorned his father's Franklin Street pile. It was hailed as an architectural triumph with spectacular views of downtown from the top floor.

In his dark paneled dining room he and his young family were hosting a debonair little gentleman that was certified enough to consume a bit of his evening. They were comparing construction costs of their new buildings.

"It's difficult to get the kind of expertise, you know, the Old World craftsmanship I need down at the San Felipe," Jimmie Dunne confessed. He was starting to build a grand new residence of his own on his father's ranch. The City Dunnes invited the Country Dunnes to see their new creation and give some much needed advice on dealing with architects and contractors.

A second bottle of claret was opened and hit its mark.

"Will you be living there during the construction?" Peter Francis asked.

"Heavens no, we always winter here at The Palace and plan on staying until the house is complete. My father looks in on the builders once in a while but he thinks the whole ordeal a bit too showy for his taste."

"You just need a good bunkhouse son!" said Peter Francis.

"Exactly."

"How is dear Uncle James doing otherwise?"

"Besides being irascible? Fine. Actually, quite well. Still rides every day. Not as hard as he rides the ranch manager but very much the cowboy at heart."

"More than four-score and still rides? That is remarkable."

"Yes. I bet he would love to see you."

"I would love to see him too."

"How about Auntie Bridget, she's even older!"

"Good Grief, I haven't seen her in years." Closer to 29 years, five months and seven days. "Is she even still alive?" asked Peter Francis.

"She most certainly is. I do a lot of business with her son John. He has several ranches up there. Cattleman. Sheepman. I think Bridget moved down from the Sonoma Mountain into town with one of the daughters," said Jimmie.

"Say, do you remember that summer after my father died? They sent us both to live up there for a couple of weeks?" Peter Francis lifted his elbow to allow his servant access to an empty dinner plate.

"I most certainly do. Farm life, not for you."

"Ugh, I absolutely loathed it. Uncle Patrick was tougher than a bull moose. Woke me up at the crack of dawn with a tin horn blasting in my ear."

"Get your ass up, you're burning daylight!"

"Yep."

"Auntie Bridget was always kind though," said Jimmie.

"When was the last time Uncle James saw her?"

"I couldn't tell you. Years." 38 years, one month and eighteen days. "I think he was only ever up to the Sonoma Mountain once."

"I imagine when they were children they thought they'd always live in some little Irish village together for the rest of their lives," said Peter Francis, draining his glass.

"Fate had a different idea. They must have felt so far away from home."

"Shear bravery to leave everything you had ever known to come here. And it was dangerous, this town, back then. I couldn't do it."

"Do you think I could get everyone down to San Felipe for a family reunion when the new place is all done up?"

"How long do you think two old codgers can wait for a party?"

"Good point, let's do it sooner rather than later. Maybe we could do it here?" Jimmie bluntly asked.

Peter Francis considered it for a moment and thought the Lawlers might be, let's say, uncomfortable, in such sumptuous surroundings. "I don't know, the place isn't really designed for older folks. All the stairs and whatnot."

Jimmie was able to easily toggle between country folk and city folk so he knew exactly what his imperial-minded cousin was implying. "Yes, yes, quite right. Let me handle everything. I will get on it tomorrow. This will be such fun."

CHAPTER 44

5:03 PM

Lucy taps on the door then quickly turns and surveys her mother's carefully rendered coiffure. Bridget had been unusually fussy about how her hair was arranged as if the once fiery red curls, now snow white, was a form of surrender or some jibber jabber like that. She wants to look as youthful as possible so her younger brother wouldn't feel so old.

An exquisite young footman in black tie and tails answers the door. Immediately the women become dizzy with anticipation. "Welcome ladies, please do come in." He invites them into Jimmie Dunne's spacious suite on the seventh floor of the Palace Hotel facing Market Street.

"Auntie Bridget! You're a sight for sore eyes!" Jimmie delicately embraces her hoping not to damage her fragile frame.

"Dear, thank you for arranging this, it's been a long time coming." She holds on to his arm and keeps him at a distance taking a good long look. She decides he looks nothing like her side of the family.

"I hope your room is comfortable."

"It's grand."

"I worked around Mister Peter Esquire's schedule," Jimmie said followed by a comical eye roll. "He has a big case for the Southern Pacific in New York and must leave on the 11:45 train tomorrow morning."

"Lucy was kind enough to come down and manage me. Do you two remember each other?" Bridget asks.

Lucy, dressed in a fashionable green silk voile gown with layers of ruffles, is deferential. Jimmie uses his common touch that works equally well on society matrons and his vaqueros. He introduces his wife Viola who outsizes him by 5 inches and 50 pounds. Those same society matrons refer to her as his little Brunhilda behind his back.

"Father should be out in a minute."

"I've never been in this hotel after all these years," says Bridget. "You know our little milk ranch was on this site ages ago. Would have been over there." She points.

"I know, father was just telling me the exact same thing."

Lucy chimes in, "Was it in that far corner?" She wants to know exactly.

"Yes. You wouldn't believe the loads of butter I churned out from here. Those poor cows." Bridget chuckles.

"Oh, I want to show you something," says James.

They move over to a large wall with a small painting in a delicate gilded frame. It has its own private electric light hovering above.

"I bring this with me wherever I go. It's titled *Landscape with Cattle Returning Home* by Thomas Gainsborough."

"Apt title," says Bridget insufficiently impressed, "it looks like that's what they're doing alright."

"Isn't it wonderful?" asks Viola.

"Auntie, I wonder if it reminds you at all of Ireland?"

"A bit."

"I thought it so charming with cattle being my line of work and all. The various hues of green. See how the sunset hits their hides here? Early eighteenth century…gouache…a bit loose, just a sketch really. If I didn't know any better I'd say it was a Turner rather than a Gainsborough. Acquired it on a trip to London." He is lost in the details but suddenly worries the Lawlers might mistake his love of art for braggadocio.

Bridget wants to see her brother not some silly painting but she puts on her spectacles and examines it further without saying a word. Lucy declares it lovely.

5:17 PM

The bedroom door opens slowly and Catherine Dunne emerges first, waiting for her husband James to slowly shuffle in. Bent and bow-legged, Bridget hardly recognizes him. Her baby brother? Really? As she gets closer she is gladdened to see his eyes have remained the same. Through wrinkles and time the twinkle is the same. She holds out her hands and he draws them up to his face. They gaze upon each other while everyone in the room gazes upon them. Jimmie had designed the entire evening for a moment such as this.

"Sister, look here, the gods have been good to you," James says with all the cracks and gurgles of an old man's voice.

"Do you remember this?" Bridget turns around to reveal the Viking brooch James had found in the woods of Brittas when they were children. Lucy had drawn her snowy hair back into a chignon with the ancient silver brooch set amongst the curls and ribbons.

"Blimey!" he whispers a word he hadn't used in years. "I do remember. I dug it out from the dirt."

"Yes. I thought we had lost it on the trip out to America but it survived somehow at the bottom of a barrel. Divine intervention. I wore it on my wedding day. It is very dear to me, James."

"That makes me happy. I don't have one thing from home. Left with just my clothes and my dreams."

"Please, please have a seat," Jimmie pats the plush velvet cushions of a settee and motions for the butler to help. Champagne and hors d'oeuvres are promptly delivered.

"Biddy, you look the picture of health," James says with wispy fervor, his days of yelling out orders from horseback long gone.

"Yes, I saw Jimmie's picture."

The brother can barely talk and the sister can barely hear.

"NO! YOU LOOK HEALTHY."

"I am, except I have trouble hearing."

"It's come to this has it?" he says, once again inaudible.

Throwing vanity to the wind Bridget reaches into her beaded purse and brings out her little ear trumpet that she was hoping not to have to use. Holding it up she asks her brother to repeat himself.

"I said, so it's come to this?" The two break out into hysterics then exchange the gadget and agree on its usefulness.

"Are you in town for a few days then?" she asks.

"Yes. It's so damn expensive to come up this way on the train. I suppose it's why I never got up to see you very often."

"Oh, come off it James. You're rich enough to hire a French hot air balloon to drop you directly on my front stoop."

"OK. It was, I suppose just finding the right time."

"It's not like I was listed in the Registry with visiting hours on a first and third Wednesday of the month." Lucy is eavesdropping on the entire conversation and concerned her mother is starting off on the wrong foot. That lecturing tone was quite familiar and quite annoying.

"Right—" says James.

"I myself had all the time in the world stuck up there in the wilderness. Your time, it seemed to me, was always a bit more valuable with everything you're involved with—"

"I am sorry sister. Really I am. I apologize for all of that. Selfish, haughty, ungrateful, whatever it was I lost my time with you and I regret it. But we are here now, the very last of us, let's not waste a moment arguing."

Bridget's heart is unlocked by his sincerity and she softens her tone. "It's just that I've missed you so terribly much James, truly."

"Me as well."

"You know the real me. You know the child I once was and the one I always see in my mind's eye, the one God sees."

James expands his chest and holds his head up. "I feel the same way, Biddy. When I left home I was just a scared, well, a scared, stupid boy really. When I reached New Orleans I wondered what you would say to lift me up and it always did. It was your voice in my head that kept me going."

"Oh, James!" The old woman shakes her head. "We all worried so!"

"I'm sorry"

"But then it was you that told us to come out here. Patrick would never have left Ireland if it hadn't been for your letter. Thank you. Thank you. A thousand times thank you. You made all the difference."

"But I think of you as the wise one, the kind one—"

"You were the visionary—"

"And you dear sister, you, will always, always…be older."

"Aye, s'pose the meeting of The Mutual Admiration Society is adjourned."

"Let's drink to that!"

6:30 PM

Dinner is delivered up from the Grill Room and served in the suite's dining salon to the assembled members of the Dunne family. The menu includes an exceptional Beef Wellington. James and Bridget are seated next to each other but the barrage of competing conversation is challenging for the oldsters. James borrows the ear horn several times.

"Tell me Aunt Bridget," Peter Francis says loudly, "did father really study law at Lincoln's Inn in London?"

"He was there all right but I think mostly just as an errand boy for our cousin who became a barrister." Bridget says not knowing about her brother's misrepresentation of events.

"Mother, wasn't it actually Gray's Inn?" Lucy says gently as to not embarrass her mother and expose her forgetfulness.

"Yes, yes. You're absolutely correct. Gray's Inn."

"And my father studied at Trinity College in Dublin, right?"

"NO." Bridget and Lucy both say loudly in unison.

Peter Francis had always wondered about that claim. "Lucy, you are quite the family historian. Quite a head for remembering places."

"Oh, I just retain certain details. Sometimes it crowds out what I should know about the present, I must confess."

"Well, I wish all of the witnesses I present in court could be as observant. Or lucid for that matter."

"My, my. That's very kind." Lucy says sheepishly as she so rarely receives a compliment of any kind.

"Yes. But, actually eyewitness testimony in court is often unreliable. Everyone perceives facts so differently." He continues, "I'd wager you'd be the exception though, Cousin Lucy." Peter Francis says, displaying his father's intelligence and something else his father so painfully lacked, tact.

Bridget chimes in, "I thought all my babbling went in one ear and out the other."

"No, no mother, I remember everything," Lucy said.

8:15 PM

Dessert is served. Viola drops her fork; a footman immediately replaces it.

9:07 PM

Before he retires to work in his room, Peter Francis invites everyone for breakfast as his treat the following morning. "Meet at the Garden Court at 9am sharp." He has a train to catch. The rest of the clan withdraws to the living room for coffee. In keeping with the spirit of the evening, Jimmie sits down with a rather large glass of Irish whiskey. His father takes a few shallow puffs on a cigar. Viola and Lucy start an old fashioned game of whist with Catherine and Bridget.

10:52 PM

The Lawlers bid their adieus having enjoyed themselves to the hilt and promise to meet downstairs for breakfast in the morning.

11:33 PM

Back in their room, Lucy pulls the heavy chintz drapes closed, blocking any light from being a nuisance in the morning. She helps her mother to bed. Two hot water bottles have been placed under the sheets by the staff. Bridget is impressed.

1:47 AM

Jimmie, unable to sleep, swallows a digestive pill to help with his frequent heartburn.

5:12 AM

Bridget suddenly awakes and is about to get cross with her daughter for shaking the bed so violently.

5:13 AM

Half asleep and half a minute later she quickly realizes it's not the bed, the entire room is now rumbling. The iron bed frame slams up against the opposing wall.

C R A S H!

Unseen objects hurl themselves to the floor. In complete darkness Bridget hears the furniture shuffling and shifting around the room.

"What's happening?" Lucy asks reaching for her mother like a frightened child. Plaster plummets from the ceiling onto their heads. Coughing, they breathe in dust. Groans and creaks rapidly grow into a crescendo of deafening booms followed by a staccato of shattered glass. As the tremors continue, Bridget fears the worst. She patiently waits for the bed to fall completely through the floorboards. They feel doomed.

Should they get up or just wait until it stops?

They spring out of bed, but are immediately knocked to the ground. Dear God, the shaking will not stop. It must be the wardrobe closet that toppled over. Did that chandelier just fall? And after an eternity the earth calms and the building vibrates to stillness. Pipelines and ductwork continue squeaking from within the walls.

Mother and daughter look into each other's paralyzed faces.

They wonder what to do next.

Lucy gets up and feels her way to the door. She hits the pushbutton to turn on the lights. Nothing. Electricity out. A candle? No, better not, might be a gas leak. She feels her way over to the bay windows and cuts her foot on something. She yells out, "Mother stay put! There is glass everywhere."

Throwing back the curtains of their third floor hotel room the wind rushes in through the broken windows. Lucy is aghast at what she witnesses beneath her. Out of the dust and darkness could be heard the chaos from the streets below. Buildings are in the process of tumbling to the ground, others look like they have been whacked in half by a cleaver. Plumes of particulates spew out in all directions. Small flashpoints of fire erupt in the dense atmosphere. Muffled voices, screams and shrieks drown-out the sound of horse whinnies.

Lucy looks back into the room where she could make out the shadowy figure of her mother on the floor. "Stay still Mother, let me get your shoes."

"Get my dress and coat too, we need to get out of here," Bridget says as calmly as she can.

5:32 AM

Jimmie and Violet have been bounced from their beds onto the floor from the earthquake. He would later liken it to a bucking bronco. Disoriented, they wrap themselves in robes then collect the aged James and Catherine for the arduous task of descending seven flights of stairs. The famous rising rooms are stuck in their tracks. A mad rush of silhouettes can be seen dashing and darting around the floors surrounding the courtyard, now open to the sky. Crumbled amber colored glass of the once opulent dome has rained down into the Garden Court where an old Chinese janitor is trying in vain to sweep it up.

5:58 AM

Jimmie reaches the pandemonium of the hostelry office, swarming with guests. The unruly crowd, in various states of dishabille, shout out a barrage of questions in multiple languages to a lone frazzled attendant behind the counter: Was it an explosion? Where should we go? Why aren't the telephones working? I need help with my luggage! Are the restaurants open? Will I get a refund? My friend is dead in Room 303. Where are the carriage houses?

It is impossible to get any information.

By sheer luck near the grand staircase Lawlers and Dunnes find each other amongst the madness. The family is complete. Another trembler hits. Catherine is knocked back against the railing.

6:23 AM

Dawn is beginning to break outside and the group decides they must flee the Palace "before we are crushed into powder," Catherine's great fear.

6:26 AM

Lucy looks up at the colossal hotel from outside, it appears unfazed compared to the remnants of buildings surrounding it, although hardly a single pane of glass remain in its window banks.

Most of the excitement has calmed down and taut nerve endings fire more rationally. One plan after another is discussed by the Dunne family reunion party with special consideration given towards the elderly ones. A little nook outside the hotel on New Montgomery is chosen to perch James, Catherine and Bridget. Violet is still in her dressing gown clutching the Gainsborough. She and Lucy watch over them while Jimmie and Peter Francis spread out to investigate.

7:00 AM

Mayor issues shoot-to-kill orders for looters.

7:07 AM

San Francisco is backlit in an eerie glow between shattered and thrown-down buildings. Market Street is in an uproar of vehicles, debris and citizens are tangled up in fallen wires covering the wide boulevard. Running down the center, rails of the trolley cars are twisted like slashing bullwhips frozen in time. Water gushes from broken mains through the fissures in the pavement. Hills and dales of buckled sidewalk are strewn with fallen chimney bricks. An entire iron-front façade has peeled off in one piece, blocking passage down a side street. Dead horses line both sides of the street while the dying ones cry out for mercy, trapped in their harnesses.

7:37 AM

Although the morning is sunny the air is crisp and cold. Jimmie and Peter Francis, having surveyed the damage, decide to check on their respective offices off Montgomery Street. Jimmie's little legs carry him faster than his cousin's directly to the open door of his pal's saloon. Peter Francis catches up. Jimmie suggest they dip in to take the chill off. The bartender plunks down a full bottle of bourbon and two glasses. Jimmie reaches for his billfold his friend waves him off, "No charge today for you Mr. Dunne. I'll keep it flowing 'till the last drop." Peter Francis wants to keep moving. Jimmie leaves a $100 bill on the bar top and makes off with the bottle.

7:52 AM

Bridget has struck up a conversation with a young army soldier sent to guard the Palace against looters. He is rousting the group out. "Move along people. Don't linger here. Three blocks up is Union Square. It's open. You'll be safe there, away from these collapsing buildings."

No sooner did the command leave his throat than another aftershock hits with great velocity. One of the few decorative features of the hotel, a stone cornice, has been shaken from the roof line and plunges down violently from above striking the young man squarely on his head. He drops to his knees then slumps right onto Bridget's black boots, dead.

"No, no, no!" she reaches for him then quickly retracts her arms. Mortified. She fears the grim reaper's next swipe will slay her. She is prepared for the end, she believes she will not survive the catastrophe. This will be the thing that does me in.

Everyone looks up anticipating the next piece to fall. It is decided they need to get away from these murderous buildings. To Union Square. Viola is chosen to stay at the Palace to wait for her husband and Peter Francis. She is becoming concerned over their prolonged absence. She nervously clutches onto her painting.

The rest of the group head off. James leads the way. He was a survivor of San Francisco's many conflagrations since the Dunne & Company days and knows exactly what to do now. He will just do it a little slower this time.

9:36 AM

Dunne party safely reaches Union Square.

10:10 AM

Peter Francis runs by the Palace and connects with Viola. "Are you alright?" he says in between the huffs and the puffs.

"Yes, yes. Where were you two?"

"Checking on our offices, both gone. Piles of rubble."

"Oh, lord."

"Jimmie went to look for the carriage house. We need our cars. I'm going to help. If we can get out of here my house should be a safe place. Just stay put."

"Please hurry."

11:57 AM
Hearst building catches fire.

12:34 PM
After exhausting detective work, Jimmie finally locates the unattended Palace Carriage House, several blocks south of the hotel. He climbs over piles of rubble and wood blocking the entrance. An abrupt tremor hits! The carriages roll around back and forth. Horses rear up and kick frantically in their stalls.

Jimmies decides the automobiles must be in a corner garage covered over in debris.

12:41 PM
At the waterfront, refugees crowd the Ferry Building and try desperately to get on any sea faring vessel that will whisk them away from the destruction and turmoil. Destinations trivial.

1:03 PM
Chinatown erupts in flames.

1:21 PM
Peter Francis locates the Palace Carriage house after several failed attempts. He spots Jimmie trying to move the mounds of wreckage that is blocking the garage.

"Our cars in there?" Peter Francis yells out.

"Finally! Yes. We have to get this crap out of the way." Jimmie says.

"It's going to take forever."

Peter Francis digs in. Relieved he has some help at last, Jimmie takes another swig of bourbon.

1:27 PM
Inside the disheveled board room of the Palace Hotel a tense meeting is taking place. The quake had damaged the water supply lines that run

underneath the City making it impossible to fight the growing inferno. Ralston and his architects designed the Palace to withstand both earthquake and fire. People were already marveling at how the behemoth could twist and turn with the tremors yet snap back without any significant damage.

But as fires raged closer, management decides how to best use the half-million gallons of water in the huge tanks that sit above and below the building.

There might be enough reserves to ward off flames from devouring the hotel but other factors need to be considered. The Grand Dame of San Francisco is nearly 30-years-old and beginning to show her age. There are plans in the works to remodel, even add more stories but its sheer size rendered it a bit of an albatross since the very beginning. The existing 700-room hotel was only twice filled to capacity. Besides, it would never be brand new like the new Fairmont Hotel reaching completion on Nob Hill.

A cost accountant enters the room with the final death sentence. He holds in his hands the insurance policy that had been scrutinized by all concerned. His recommendation: As a public service, the hotel must release its water reserves for the benefit of the citizenry of San Francisco and allow the municipal fire department to decide how best to use the precious resource. Clause 7.07 in the policy allows for such benevolent actions. It's best to let the Palace burn.

1:49 PM
The Wells Fargo building is burning.

2:18 PM
Viola finally spots the big touring car of Peter Francis' rumbling down New Montgomery with her husband's dusty Buick following closely behind. They stop for her. She loads the Gainsborough into the back seat. Jimmie apologizes for the delay and attempts to incoherently describe how they had to dig out the cars from the rubble, smash windows, blah, blah, blah.

She could see he was inebriated.

"James Francis Dunne, you're drunker than a lord! At a time like this? Move over, I'm taking the wheel. Honestly. You are something else."

They snake their way up and down, over and around to Union Square where they rendezvous with the others near the St. Francis Hotel. Everyone piles in. A Marine on horseback directs them out. He heard upper Market Street was open but it would be almost impossible to reach.

3:12 PM

Dynamite blasts could be heard throughout the city. Fire is closing in from every direction. Bridget worries. What the earthquake hasn't ruined will surely be devoured in flames.

The Dunne family automobiles eventually turn onto Market Street heading west. They pass Sixth Street, Seventh Street, the pedestrians along the way bring Bridget some much needed amusement. A stuffy-looking woman is carrying a birdcage with her parrot safely inside unaware the bottom is missing. Where was that lady going with that ironing board? A well-dressed gentleman totes his pot of blooming Easter lilies with religious reverence.

At Eight Street another shock comes.

City Hall's dome hovers like a crown in search of a monarch, held up by a few stray iron beams above skeletal remains of the politically-built complex. Its notoriously shabby construction proves deadly to prisoners, police and hospital workers alike.

Before their eyes, it falls in on itself like a house made of cards. A vivid reminder of the insidious graft San Francisco had hoped to keep secret for generations. Peter Francis wonders, who would expect the earth itself to expose such corruption?

3:53 PM

The group arrives safely at the Dunne family home on Clay Street high above and far away from the inferno engulfing the city center. House servants attend to them.

4:12 PM

Since 1875 the Palace Hotel had played host to presidents and potentates, prima donnas and millionaires but now it is about to confront a most unwanted guest. Its many grand parlors, guestrooms and corridors are now abandoned in anticipation of fire's inevitable arrival. Jets of water stream from the rooftop. Firemen tap its basement tanks. Water runs dry.

It comes from the east and enters through the same portico that had welcomed travelers the world over. Inside a glorious feast awaits its insatiable appetite. The seven-story courtyard, the one that made the hotel so famous, so airy, so memorable, proves to be just as inviting to a firestorm. Within minutes pillars of flames bring the curse to every corner of the building. Scrambling San Franciscans in the vicinity take a pause in their individual troubles to witness the glow from the Palace Hotel's trademark window banks. Sounds of the crackling, consuming beast bring renewed terror to the spectators. Fire starts to flare up through the roof.

People keep their eyes on the flagpole; the whipping colors of Old Glory had flown over the city for 30 years. It disappears and reappears between the flames and smoke. Finally, a twirling orange spike consumes the red, white and blue in seconds. An audible sigh is heard from the crowd and just as quickly they resume their scurrying.

5:08 PM

All city morgues full. More than fifty bodies are quickly buried in Portsmouth Square.

6:48 PM

Stars begin to blink on above it all as night falls over the inferno. Peter Francis is relieved the family is safe and insists everyone spend the night at his house before they figure out how to get back to theirs. His new mansion is left untouched by the tremors. For the first time that day they don't smell smoke and take a moment to appreciate the salty sea air floating in from the Pacific Ocean.

A fourth floor terrace becomes the family gathering spot. An unflustered butler serves drinks and sandwiches from a silver tray. James and Bridget are seated up front with panoramic views of the apocalypse. They observe new fires breaking out in all parts of San Francisco. Lost in her thoughts, Bridget wonders if a long forgotten, feckless hex cast on the hotel by a certain superstitious Irishman could have caused such devastation.

"Please take something to eat," Peter Francis says "it's been a trying day and we never got our breakfast in the Garden Court. We might as well watch everything from up here. Nothing else to do."

"Nothing but everything." Catherine quips.

Jimmie has sobered up from his earlier bender and is fast on his way to the second when he offers up his thoughts for consideration:

"This has to be the fastest destruction of a city in all of human history. So much work to build this amazing place...all that toil and strife. Now up in smoke. Is God telling us something? Like Icarus, maybe we just flew too close to the sun for His liking?"

"I'm having a hard time believing what I am seeing," says Catherine. "I just can't look any longer."

Peter Francis says, "I can't stop looking. I shall stay up here all night and keep watch. Such devastation. How could...I mean...what...it's all gone," his famous courtroom eloquence eludes him, "it's all just so, so horrible."

Bridget, not believing she would live to even see sunset, puts her hand up to her mouth, her wedding band has black yarn twisted around the inside to fit her bony, aged finger. She leans over to her brother and says, "I'm sorry James dear, your city has been ruined."

James puts his hand on his sister's knee to try and comfort her then asks "My lord, how will we ever get it back again?"

Bridget thought for a moment and in a soft, matriarchal voice replies, "We'll start by doing what's necessary, then we'll do what's possible and before you know it, we'll do the impossible."

THE END

EPILOGUE

Final letter from Lucy Rogers to Sarafrances Welch

May 7, 1941
538 Balboa Street
San Francisco, Calif.

My Dear Niece,

I just received your letter and it is very complimentary, thank you, but I feel that I do not deserve it.

My life has been spent rearing my children and caring for my home—and never very much out of it. Someone said we are all actors on the stage of life. We must play our part as it is given us and make the final bow.

It pleases me to know that you enjoyed reading the history of our family. My birthday was yesterday. 84! My son Edward—the realtor—promised to take me to Ireland one day to see all the places my mother and father spoke of. Could never make the journey now—not that he's asked either—but I do wonder what it would've been like. I'd love to have seen all the villages my mother spoke of.

Most of all, I so longed to see Brittas and if it even still remains. You do know during those troubled years of the Irish Civil War a number of big houses were burnt down by the rebels. Terrible. I read all the newspaper accounts.

Some woman I recently met at the grocery store was from Queen's County—they call it something Irish now, Leash (sp?) County or something —she told me the last of the Dunnes of Brittas were a couple of sisters that sold up and moved to England. For all she knows, the house itself was still standing.

I do hope Brittas is still there. I can picture the place in my mind although I must admit, I have no idea what it actually looks like.

So very excited to hear you are coming to San Francisco, now you must look me up when you come. I can show you all the sites if I am still able.

Finally dear, you asked me about where all the Dunnes and Lawlers are buried, let's see—

My Uncle Peter Dunne is buried at Cypress Lawn in Colma. They moved all the old graveyards out of the City after the big earthquake. He's in a plot with Auntie Margaret and others—I may think of who later.

All the Big Wigs from Olde San Francisco are buried in that cemetery: Hearst, Phelan, Broderick, Ralston, Spreckels. Lots of history, worth a visit if you can get past the nature of the place.

Down in Gilroy is where my Uncle James rests. He is in a little graveyard behind St. Mary's Church under a colossal headstone—must be 14-15 feet high. Sad though, all his lost little children are inscribed on that thing too.

He is buried with his first wife, Kitty.

Next to them rests his other wife, Catherine O'Toole Murphy Dunne. She lived to be 96 years old! You won't believe this but she was once the richest woman property owner in ALL of California. She was very kind to me.

Most of the Lawlers are resting in Petaluma.

My brother John upset my parents to no end when he switched religions to Episcopalian. (After all the generations our Irish family did to maintain The Faith—honestly!) Essentially, John wanted to become a Freemason and felt his religion was holding him back. I think he wanted to cavort with the town's rich folk until the money rubbed off on him.

As a matter of course he got his own family plot on the Protestant side they call Cypress Hill. I'm glad my parents aren't alive to see that disgraceful Mason's symbol on his tombstone instead of the Crucifix.

Now—on the other side is the Catholic Calvary Cemetery.

My father bought our family plot from Fr. Cleary. My husband and two of our infant sons are buried there along with my sister Frances and three of my brothers. In the middle stands the Lawler obelisk. Patrick Lawler's name is chiseled into the front of it and my mother, Bridget Lawler's name is inscribed on the back—facing a giant oak tree.

Sara dear, if you do get a chance to set foot on my parents grave, please look up to the East onto Sonoma Mountain. In a stand of oak trees, near the top, you can see the Lawler Ranch.

Father would want you to appreciate his planning.

Always Your Loving Aunt, Lucy

THE CHARACTERS

Baldwin, Rev. John. Curate of Clonaslee.

Bergin, Thomas I. Attorney-at-law, uncle of Peter Francis Dunne.

Broderick, David C. San Francisco political boss, U.S. Senator from California.

Buckley, Christopher. (Blind Boss). San Francisco political boss.

Butler, Eleanor. Irish aristocrat, fled to Llangollen, Wales.

Cian, Father Thomas. Hunan-born Chinese priest of St. Francis Church.

Craybill, Carl (Caspian). Jungle guide for Lawler family.

Coote, Sir Charles. Political opponent of General Dunne.

Donnelly, Hugh. Owner of Maryborough hotel and public house.

Donnelly, Mary Dunne. Sister of Bridget Dunne.

Drady, Mr. Brittas estate carpenter.

Dunne, Catherine O'Toole Murphy. Second wife of James Dunne.

Dunne, Edward Meadows. Second son of General Dunne, barrister.

Dunne, Francis Plunkett. First-born son of General Dunne, heir to Brittas.

Dunne, Frances (France) White. Wife of General Dunne, sister to Earl of Bantry.

Dunne, Fanny. Only daughter of General Dunne.

Dunne, James. Youngest son of Mr. (Peter) Dunne.

Dunne, James Francis. First son of James Dunne, cattle king.

Dunne, Jeremiah. Cousin to General Dunne, banker, Lord Mayor of Dublin.

Dunne, Kitty Grayson. First wife of James Dunne.

Dunne, Margaret Bergin. Wife of Peter Dunne, sister of Thomas Bergin.

Dunne, Margaret Plunkett. Mother of General Dunne.

Dunne, Michael. Oldest son of Mr. (Peter) Dunne, heir to Ballintlea House.

Dunne, Molly McDowell. of Mantua House, high-born mother of
   Bridget Dunne.

Dunne, Mr. (Peter). Second cousin of General Dunne, land agent of
   Brittas Estate.

Dunne, Peter. Second son of Mr. (Peter) Dunne, father of Peter Francis Dunne.

Dunne, Peter Francis. San Francisco attorney-at-law.

Dunne, Squire Francis. Father of General Dunne, saved Brittas from seizure.

Goo, Sam. Chinese servant to James Dunne.

Grayson, Elias P. New Orleans commission merchant.

Kavanaugh, Alicia Grace. of Gracefield, cousin of Molly McDowell Dunne
   and General Dunne.

Kennedy, Jim. Clonaslee publican.

Lalor, James Fintan. First son of Honest Patt Lalor of Tenakill, Irish revolutionary.

Lalor, (Honest) Patt. of Tenakill, Queen's County politician, cousin to Patrick Lawler.

Lalor, Peter. Ninth son of Honest Patt Lalor of Tenakill, Australian politician.

Lawler, Bridget Dunne. Second daughter of Mr. (Peter) Dunne.

Lawler, Denny. First son of Patrick Lawler, San Francisco beat cop.

Lawler, J.P. First son of Denny Lawler.

Lawler, Judge James. Fourth son of Patrick Lawler, San Francisco Police Court Judge.

Lawler, John. Second son of Patrick Lawler, Petaluma stockman.

Lawler, Patrick. Born County Kildare, husband of Bridget Dunne.

McAllister, Hall. San Francisco law partner of Thomas I. Bergin.

McDonald, J.M. Partner in Dunne, McDonald & Company.

McEnnis, Sister Frances. Superiorese of the St. Patrick's Orphan Asylum.

Miquel, Delores. Spanish cook of Brittas.

Miquel, Duarte. Son of Delores Miquel.

Murphy, Bernard. First husband of Catherine Dunne.

Murphy, Marty. Step-son of James Dunne.

Phelan, James. Queen,s County born liquor dealer and banker.

Phelan, James D. Son of James Phelan, mayor of San Francisco, U.S. Senator from California.

Phelan, Mrs. Classmate of Bridget Dunne, matron of Mountmellick Workhouse.

Ponsonby, Sarah. Friend of Eleanor Butler.

Ralston, William. Banker and founder of the Palace Hotel.

Rogers, Lucinda (Lucy) Lawler. Youngest daughter of Patrick Lawler.

Sneed, Mr. Butler of Brittas.

White, Richard. Earl of Bantry, helped repel French invasion at Bantry Bay.

Vallejo, General Marino. Californio general, granted Rancho Petaluma by Mexican Governor.

ACKNOWLEDGMENTS

Creating a work as vast in scope as *The Dunnes of Brittas* started out innocently enough with travel to Ireland, England, New Orleans and my native California searching for inspiration and clues to the past. As research into the Dunne and Lawler families grew I commented to my wife, Judee, that their story would make a great novel. She agreed and said I was the one who needed to write it. Special thanks to my cousin Joan MacLennan Mahon who curated and published Aunt Lucy's letters on-line. Jim Kennedy of Clonaslee was my expert guide when I visited Brittas. Kevin Lalor-Fitzpatrick showed me around Tenakill. Betsy Wolf was my perfect beta reader. Thanks to Maur and Richard Tavernetti for their care and preservation. Ancestry.com, newspapers.com, genealogybank.com were helpful resources.

I am grateful to all the authors, researchers and novelists whose work helped shape the book:

Asbury, Herbert. *The Barbary Coast: An Informal History of the San Francisco Underworld.* Alfred A. Knopf, New York: 1933

——————— . *The French Quarter: An Informal History of the New Orleans Underworld.* Alfred A. Knopf, New York: 1936

Bailey, Catherine. *Black Diamonds.* Penguin Books, New York: 2007

Bartoletti, Susan Campbell. *Black Potatoes: The Story of the Great Irish Famine, 1845-1850.* Houghton Mifflin Company, New York: 2001

Basso, Etolia S. (Ed.) *The World from Jackson Square: A New Orleans Reader.* Farrar, Straus and Company, New York: 1948

Bean, Walton. *Boss Ruef's San Francisco: The Story of the Union Labor Party, Big Business, and the Graft Prosecution.* University of California Press, Berkeley, CA: 1968

Bence-Jones, Mark. *Burke's Guide to Country Houses.* Burke's Peerage Ltd., London: 1978

——————. *Twilight of the Ascendancy*. Constable, London: 1987

Buckley, David. *James Fintan Lalor: Radical*. Cork University, Cork, Ireland: 1990

Bullough, William A. *The Blind Boss and His City: Christopher Augustine Buckley & Nineteenth-Century San Francisco*. University of California Press, Berkeley, CA: 1979

Bunbury, Turtle. *1847: A Chronicle of Genius, Generosity & Savagery*. Gill Books, Dublin: 2016

——————. *Ireland's Forgotten Past: A History of the Overlooked & Disremembered*. Thames & Hudson, London: 2020

Burchell, R.A. *The San Francisco Irish 1848-1880*. University of California Press, Berkeley, CA: 1980

Chambers, Anne. *The Great Leviathan: The Life of Howe Peter Browne, Marquess of Sligo 1788-1845*. New Island Books, Dublin: 2017

Coogan, Tim Pat. *The Famine Plot: England's Role in Ireland's Greatest Tragedy*. St. Martin's Press, New York: 2012

Curtis, L. Perry. *The Depiction of Eviction in Ireland 1845-1910*. University College Dublin Press, Dublin: 2011

Cusack, M.F. (The Nun of Kenmare). *The Present Case of Ireland: Plainly Stated; A Plea for My People and My Race*. P.J. Kenedy, Excelsior Catholic Publishing House, New York: 1883

David, Saul. *Prince of Pleasure*. Grove Press, New York: 1998

Delany, Mary Murray. *Of Irish Ways*. Dillon Press, Minneapolis, MN: 1973

Delgado, James P. *Gold Rush Port: The Maritime Archaeology of San Francisco's Waterfront*. University of California Press, Berkeley, CA: 2009

Donnelly, James S. *Captain Rock: The Irish Agrarian Rebellion of 1821-1824.* The University of Wisconsin Press, Madison WI: 2009

Douglas-Fairhurst, Robert. *Becoming Dickens: The Invention of a Novelist.* The Belknap Press of Harvard University Press, Cambridge, MA: 2011

Douthwaite, William Ralph. *Gray's Inn: Notes Illustrative of Its History and Antiquities* (Classic Reprint). BiblioBazaar, Charleston, SC: 2016

Dunne, Joe. *Dunne People and Places.* Gill & Macmillan Ltd., Ireland: 1996

Dunne, Tom. *Rebellions: Memoir, Memory, and 1798.* Lilliput Press, Dublin: 2010

Edgeworth, Maria. *Castle Rackrent: An Hibernian Tale.* Printed for J. Johnson, St. Paul's Churchyard, London: 1800

——————— . *Ormond.* Printed for R. Hunter and Baldwin, Cradock, and Joy, London: 1817

Eliot, George. *Middlemarch.* William Blackwood and Sons, Edinburgh & London: 1871

Emmons, David M. *Beyond the American Pale, The Irish in the West, 1845-1910.* University of Oklahoma Press, Norman, OK: 2010

Fardon, George Robinson. *San Francisco Album: Photographs of the Most Beautiful Views and Public Buildings.* Chronicle Books, San Francisco, CA: 1999

Flanagan, Thomas. *The Tenants of Time.* Dutton, New York: 1988

——————— . *The Year of the French.* Holt Rinehart Winston/Dutton, New York: 1979

Gallagher, Thomas. *Paddy's Lament: Ireland 1846-1847. Prelude to Hate.* Harcourt Brace Jovanovich, New York: 1982

Guinness, Desmond. *Irish Houses and Castles.* Viking Press, New York: 1973

Horner, Arnold. *Mapping Laois.* Wordwell, Dublin: 2018

Jackson, Henry Joseph. *The Western Gate: A San Francisco Reader.* Parker, Strauss & Young, New York: 1952

Jordan, D. &. O'Keefe, T. (Eds.) *The Irish in the San Francisco Bay Area: Essays on Good Fortune.* The Executive Council of the Irish Literary and Historical Society, San Francisco, CA: 2005

Jordan, Eddie. *If a Towerhouse Could Talk.* Original Writing, Dublin: 2010

Lavender, David. Nothing Seemed Impossible: William C. Ralston and Early San Francisco. American West Publishing Company, Palo Alto CA: 1975

Lewis, O. & Hall, C.D. *Bonanza Inn: America's First Luxury Hotel.* Alfred A. Knopf, New York: 1939

Longford, Elizabeth. *Wellington: The Years of the Sword.* Harper & Row, New York: 1969

Marler, Scott P. *The Merchant's Capital: New Orleans and the Political Economy of the Nineteenth-Century South.* Cambridge University Press, Cambridge, UK: 2013

Marryat, Frank. *Mountains and Molehills.* Longman, Brown, Green, and Longmans, London: 1855

Mavor, Elizabeth. *The Ladies of Llangollen: A Study in Romantic Friendship.* Moonrise Press Ltd., Ludlow, UK: 1971

Nicholls, K.W. (Ed.) *The O'Doyne (Ó Duinn) Manuscript: Documents relating to the family of O Doyne (Ó Duinn) from Archbishop Marsh's Library, Dublin.* Stationery Office for the Irish Manuscripts Commission, Dublin: 1983

Niehaus, Earl F. *The Irish in New Orleans 1800-1860.* Louisiana State University Press, Baton Rouge, LA: 1965

O'Donnell, Edward T. *1001 Things Everyone Should Know about Irish-American History*. Gramercy, New York: 2002

O'Flaherty, Liam. *Famine*. Random House, New York: 1937

O'Hanlon, John. *History of the Queen's County, Volume 1*. Sealy, Bryers and Walker, Dublin: 1907

Phillips, Catherine Coffin. *Portsmouth Plaza: The Cradle of San Francisco*. John Henry Nash, San Francisco, CA: 1932

Phillips, Nicola. *The Profligate Son, or, a True Story of Family Conflict, Fashionable Vice, and Financial Ruin in Regency England*. Oxford University Press, Oxford, UK: 2013

Pierce, Marjorie. *East of the Gabilans*. Western Tanager Press, Santa Cruz, CA: 1976

————— . *The Martin Murphy Family Saga*. The California History Center & Foundation, Cupertino, CA: 2000

Rogers, Lucinda Marie *Lawler. Family Letters*. San Francisco: 1934-1938

Rosenus, Alan. *General Vallejo and the Advent of the Americans*. Heyday Books, Berkeley, CA: 1995

Sheehan, W. & Cronin, M. (Eds.) *Riotous Assemblies: Rebels, Riots & Revolts in Ireland*. Mercier Press, Cork, Ireland: 2011

Stellman, Louis J. *Port O' Gold: A History Romance of the San Francisco Argonauts*. Richard G. Badger, Boston: 1922

Trobits, Monika. *Antebellum and Civil War San Francisco: A Western Theater for Northern & Southern Politics*. The History Press, Charleston, SC: 2014

Trollope, Anthony. *Castle Richmond*. Chapman & Hall, London: 1860

————— . *The Eustace Diamonds.* Chapman & Hall, London: 1871

————— . *The Way We Live Now.* Chapman & Hall, London: 1875

Uris, Leon. *Trinity,* Doubleday, New York: 1937

Ware, J. Redding. *Passing English of the Victorian Era, a Dictionary of Heterodox English, Slang and Phrase.* Routledge, London: 1909

Wilson, Simone. *Images of America: Petaluma, California.* Arcadia Publishing, Mount Pleasant, SC: 2001

ABOUT THE AUTHOR

Kevin Lee Akers is an award-winning designer, illustrator and author of *All Wrapped Up! Groovy Gift Wrap of the 1960s*. His interest in Ireland, San Francisco and the nature of family culminates in the authorship of his first novel, *The Dunnes of Brittas*.

If you'd like the good faeries of Brittas to smile upon you, please leave a review for *The Dunnes of Brittas* on its Amazon and GoodReads pages:

https://www.amazon.com/Dunnes-Brittas-Irish-Familys-Endurance-ebook/dp/B08PW26FRD

https://www.goodreads.com/book/show/56349412-the-dunnes-of-brittas

I'm an indie author and appreciate every reader who takes the time to give my work a lovely rating. More information is available in the Facebook group, so be sure to like:

https://www.facebook.com/The-Dunnes-of-Brittas-111980943919385

Lightning Source UK Ltd.
Milton Keynes UK
UKHW011118161121
394065UK00002B/251